PRAISE

THE *Virgin Queen's Daughter*

"If Elizabeth I had a daughter, Nell is surely what she must have been like—brilliant and daring, risking everything for the right to fully exercise mind, heart, and spirit."
   —DONNA WOOLFOLK CROSS, international bestselling author of *Pope Joan*

"Beautifully written fiction with a fascinating hook."
   —KAREN HARPER, *New York Times* bestselling author of *The Last Boleyn*

"An absolutely wonderful read."
                    —MICHELLE MORAN, national bestselling author of *Nefertiti*

"The Virgin Queen's Daughter is both gritty and glittering, revealing the sharp blades beneath a silken court. I finished it in a day—well, two, if you count the five minutes past midnight!—and enjoyed it immensely."
                    —INDIA EDGHILL, author of *Wisdom's Daughter*

"A fresh and fascinating new glimpse of the infamous Tudor clan. An unforgettable story full of rich characterization, palace intrigue, and the perilous, often heartbreaking reality for those who lives depend on the whims of queens and kings."
                    —SUSAN HOLLOWAY SCOTT, author of *The King's Favorite*

"A feast for all of those fascinated with the life and loves of Queen Elizabeth I."   —JUDITH MERKLE RILEY, author of *The Serpent Garden*

"The Virgin Queen's Daughter is a beautifully written book with vividly drawn characters and a fabulous plot. I didn't want to put it down."
                    —DIANE HAEGER, author of *The Perfect Royal Mistress*

"Ella March Chase spins a rich tapestry of history and fiction, weaving all the vibrancy of the Tudor court and the quest of a strong, unforgettable woman into a mesmerizing tale."
                    —SUSAN CARROLL, author of *The Dark Queen*

THE

Virgin Queen's Daughter

a novel

ELLA MARCH CHASE

THREE RIVERS PRESS
NEW YORK

Copyright © 2008 by Kim Ostrom
Reading Group Guide copyright © 2009 by Kim Ostrom

Published in the United States by Three Rivers Press, an imprint of the
Crown Publishing Group, a division of Random House, Inc., New York.
www.crownpublishing.com

THREE RIVERS PRESS and the Tugboat design are registered trademarks of
Random House, Inc.

Library of Congress Cataloging-in-Publication Data

Chase, Ella March.
   The Virgin Queen's daughter / Ella March Chase.
   1. Elizabeth I, Queen of England, 1533–1603—Fiction. 2. Mothers and
daughters—Fiction. 3. Illegitimate children—Fiction. I. Title.
   PS3553.A845V57 2008
   813'.54—dc22   2008012202

ISBN 978-0-307-45112-5

Printed in the United States of America

Design by Lauren Dong

5 7 9 10 8 6 4

First Paperback Edition

In loving memory of Reverend Richard A. Swanson,

Augustana College's "Swanie,"

Who reassured me that God is strong enough to handle my questions.

AUTHOR'S NOTE

GAZING THROUGH THE MISTS OF HISTORY FROM OUR MODERN vantage point, it seems inevitable that Elizabeth Tudor would be crowned queen, her destiny to become, arguably, the finest monarch England would ever know. Yet after her mother's death Elizabeth was dismissed as so unimportant that her governess had to beg the king to allow her to get clothes to fit the child. As daughter of the notorious Anne Boleyn, the King's Great Whore, Elizabeth was declared a bastard by Henry VIII himself; even Elizabeth's older sister, Mary, often said the girl must be the daughter of Mark Smeaton, one of the men condemned of adultery with Anne Boleyn. Left largely without friends after her mother was beheaded, Elizabeth languished on the fringes of the powerful world she was born into. Once Henry died, Edward, Henry's son by Jane Seymour, ascended the throne and was expected to marry and have children. Failing that, the eldest of Henry's children, Mary, would inherit, wed, and breed heirs for England.

Elizabeth's happiest years were those when she was under the care of the last of Henry's six wives, the learned and motherly Lady Katherine Parr. When Katherine Parr married Sir Thomas Seymour after the king's death it seemed as if both women would finally know peace. But written historical accounts from Elizabeth's own servants have come to us through the centuries, revealing Thomas Seymour's attempted seduction of the fourteen-year-old Elizabeth. These include the fact that Katherine Parr found Elizabeth in Seymour's arms. The question remains: Did Seymour actually deflower Elizabeth or not? We will never know for sure. But rumors sprang up after Katherine Parr's death that Elizabeth had borne Seymour a child. A midwife was heard to claim she had delivered a babe to "a very fair lady," thought to be Elizabeth Tudor herself. I have faithfully threaded what remains of this account through my story, taking what seems possible, embellishing for the sake of the story.

This tale begins in a time when Elizabeth's fate balanced on the blade of a headsman's axe. King Edward had died a fanatical Protestant who would not name either of his sisters heir. In their stead he declared their cousin, the ill-fated Lady Jane Grey, queen. Jane ruled for nine days, before the country rose up, loyal to Mary in spite of her faith. But when Mary stubbornly insisted on wedding the Spanish King Philip and putting a foreigner on the throne, England seethed with rebellion. Jane Grey was executed as a condition to Philip setting sail for England. But other conspiracies followed. Their object: to place Protestant Elizabeth upon the throne. It is a fate Mary fears so deeply that she seems willing to execute her own sister to prevent it. As Mary and her advisers search for evidence that Elizabeth has committed treason with Sir Thomas Wyatt and his rebels, there are few in England who foresee Elizabeth's future glory. No one knows if she will survive, let alone live to become England's greatest queen.

THE
Virgin Queen's Daughter

December 1565

TOWER OF LONDON

RAMBLINGS OF A MADWOMAN MIGHT BE DEADLY. THE same words, spoken in sanity: treason. This truth I have discovered to my woe. Yet, imprisoned within my cell, I find it hard to discern the difference. What is truth? What is lie? God alone knows, for by my soul, I do not. Still, death silences all. And death waits for me beyond this vaulted chamber, its walls etched with the words of prisoners who came before me. Their names haunt me; their pleas for mercy mock me, letters chipped into stone during endless hours.

I spend my days following ghostly footsteps: around the stone pillar, past the tiny nook where the garderobe is tucked. I loop the bed with its clean linen and the table laden with comforts my mother's coin has bought me—a fresh loaf of manchet bread and thick wedges of Lincolnshire cheese, a bottle of wine from Calverley Manor's cellar. I stare at the iron-fitted door in the hope one of my guards forgot to lock it, but I dare not touch the oaken panel. I fear that if I find it still barred against me something inside me might shatter and I will pound on it until my hands are raw.

Wet splotches, like blood, darken the walls and trickle to the floor, reminding me that my own test of courage is yet to come. I shudder under the appraisal of rats' eyes that glitter in the shadows.

Part of me is glad I will not waste away long years until I am too weak to fight them off. I am too dangerous to languish here, forgotten. Wood clattering in the courtyard outside my window jars me from dark musings and I am grateful for the distraction. It is noisy work, building a scaffold. Sweating joiners hammer boards together with pegs, testing the platform to make certain it is strong enough to support the heavy block, the axe, witnesses for the Crown. And the condemned. How much does a lifetime's worth of dreams weigh when the axe falls? I am sure of little these days. Even whether or not they build that scaffold for me. The precious burden I carry has earned me a brief reprieve, but soon it will slip away from me.

Who am I? I am Mistress Elinor de Lacey, who was to be Baroness Calverley one day. What I would not give to be simply Nell again, safe on my father's estate tucked in the Lincolnshire weald. I have heard the Princess Elizabeth scratched a windowpane in one of her many prisons, proclaiming her innocence when her half sister, Queen Mary, held her under lock and key, just waiting for enough proof to destroy her. *Much suspected by me/Nothing proved can be, Quoth Elizabeth, prisoner.*

Solid evidence can be elusive, as Mary Tudor learned to her frustration. But Elizabeth is nothing like her tragic half sister. Elizabeth knows when a ship is becalmed the wise sailor merely takes another tack. Our good Queen Bess survives by being changeable as wind. In the end, any crime whose penalty is death will do to destroy me.

Fear is poison. It gnaws with rats' teeth, first at your spirit, then at your mind, until your body breaks beneath the strain. I understand that now, as I measure my own days through this hooded window. The world within the Tower is different when you fear it is your neck the axe is sharpened for. I have a slender neck like Elizabeth's mother, the Witch Queen Anne Boleyn. And I have forgotten how it feels to be safe. Or was I ever secure at all? Perhaps had I never set foot beyond the confines of my father's beloved Calverley Manor. Without knowing, I had already committed the transgression which will condemn me: My greatest crime the fact I was ever born.

Chapter One

Spring 1554

To London

THE GALLOWS WERE HEAVY WITH REBELS THAT SPRING. So many still dangled at the crossroads that even my beloved nurse, Hepzibah Jones, could not distract me from them all. In the days after our entourage set out for London, leaving our redbrick manor tucked behind its moat in Lincolnshire's hills, I saw much but understood little about the uprising that had gripped the south of England. Sir Thomas Wyatt had attempted to topple Queen Mary from her throne.

Jem, the towheaded stable lad in charge of my pony, told me that Father's boyhood friend, the Lieutenant at the Tower, had chopped off Wyatt's head and there still might be a few mad rebels running loose ready to snatch up red-haired girls. But it would take a desperate rebel indeed to attack a party large as Father's. For ten days as we traveled along the Great North Road the grand procession filled the muddy track ahead of me and behind.

Banners of red rippled from the staffs in the herald's hand, the Calverley lions warning simple people to clear the way for persons of rank. William Crane, our Master of the Horse, with his deeply lined face and gentle eyes, directed all from astride his sturdy dapple gelding. I wanted to position my pony beside him. Crane never ran out of animal stories to tell. But my nurse, riding pillion behind

Jem, would not hear of it, afraid one of the two wheeled carts jolting along the road might crush me despite Crane's efforts at order.

Eight wood-and-iron carts rumbled at various stages along the rutted road, carrying traveling chests and furniture, bedding and clothes. Their most precious cargo: Father's instruments for looking at the stars. Mother's maid, Arabella, with her face bonny as a gillyflower, had packed them all in linen and locked them in coffers. That was why we were going to London—to fill up chests with books and scientific equipment for Father to take back to Lincolnshire, where we could experiment to our delight. We were bound to stay with the Lieutenant of London's Tower while mother refilled her medicine chest and chatted with the Lieutenant's wife, whom she knew of old. Most exciting of all, Father would spend three weeks studying with the most brilliant man we would ever know, Dr. John Dee, whom father had studied with at Cambridge.

"I think I spy a brigand there!" Jem teased, pointing to a shadow in the trees, but I had been on the road too long now to be fooled by his tricks. What brigand would attack such a procession? Yeomen guards marched at the beginning and end of our caravan. Their halberds bristled, ready to repel any highwaymen who might hope to steal rich clothes and jewels. I was glad the guards were near, since Father rode far ahead of me in the procession, much preoccupied with my mother, who rode in a chariot pulled by four horses. She had felt poorly a good part of the journey, the incessant jostling turning her olive complexion gray, her sharp tongue clamped behind pinched white lips.

On the ninth day we left our horses at the town of Reading where hostlers from the inn we stayed at promised to bring the beasts into the city. The rest of us finished the last leg of our journey by barge. I collected ever more questions to ask Father about the curiosities I spied upon the bustling river-highway filled with those wise or prosperous enough to avoid the crowded city streets.

Boats skated like water bugs across the Thames's sour-smelling water: Great oceangoing vessels bristled with masts. Richly appointed barges carried important personages to and fro. Wherries ferried simple people about their daily tasks.

Even those rare breaks in the crush of humanity on the river-banks overwhelmed me, where high stone walls held the city back from the elegant grounds of houses grander than any I had ever seen. Sprawling palaces glittered with windows, and whimsical tow-ers soared up so high that if you climbed to their tops I imagined you could see all the way to the ocean.

Yet the barge we had boarded in Reading could not take us all the way to our destination, Father had warned me. Even the queen her-self could not pass London Bridge without disembarking from the royal barge. Travelers had to cross the road leading to London Bridge on foot, then board another vessel to take them farther downriver, switching boats the only safe way to escape the rapids rushing through the great stone arches that held the bridge aloft.

Three of the Calverley barges docked and a trumpet blared, Fa-ther's servants clearing a path through the fat pool of merchants' wives, flocks of sheep, and farmers trying to squeeze their way onto the much narrower bridge.

I could not wait to reach shore. "Do not fall in the river and drown, child!" My nurse, Eppie, nearly crushed my bones in her grip as we scrambled out of our first boat. I lingered, fascinated by the rac-ing water. "Hold on tight lest you get lost in this thieving crowd." For once I did as I was bid. People churned through the narrow streets, horses and carts and figures small as dolls pressed against the half-timbered houses. An apprentice darted past us, knocking Eppie's headdress askew. She made a sound like a cat when its tail has been trod on. "I shall be glad when we are on a barge again, safe from the villains that crowd the city streets."

"Do you think there are Gypsies somewhere in that crowd?" I asked, eager.

Eppie made a sign to ward off the evil eye. "May those wild demons go back to the hell that spawned them!"

I did not want the wild demons to go anywhere at all. I was fascinated by those exotic rogues so lately come to England, selling horses they enchanted with a breath. Eppie said the Romany wanderers were dangerous, low creatures. Yet, I had seen them do magic with my own eyes when a dark-skinned Gypsy boy charmed my pony. She never shied away from water again. But thoughts of Gypsies vanished as Eppie and I neared London Bridge. My eyes almost popped, I was so stunned by the structure. Houses marched across the Thames from one shore to the other as if it were another street. How had they built them in the middle of the river? I was certain Father would know. But my parents had got so far ahead of us they disappeared from view.

I tugged Eppie faster until I spied my parents already settled in a fine tilt-boat. A canvas canopy painted with stars shaded passengers from sun and rain, while piles of red cushions mounded the seats. Delighted, I wrenched free of Eppie and scrambled down the slippery stone jetty that thrust into the Thames. My Father laughed as I clambered into the boat. "So you have decided to join us, Mistress Curiosity?"

"Mistress Rat's Nest, I would say." Mother tucked back a lock of my tumbled hair. "You look as if you crawled through a hedgerow."

"Did you ever see such a bridge? If you stood on top of the house in the middle, I wager you could take a bite out of a cloud."

"What do you think a cloud tastes like?" Father asked. I peered up at the bridge, to puzzle that out. But my gaze fixed on something far different, pikes bristling with traitors' heads mounted above London Bridge's gatehouse.

"Father, look!" I pointed at the birds who circled, diving to pick the flesh. "How can there still be people in the streets when so many have lost their heads?"

But my mother answered. "Do not forget that sight, Nell. *That* is what happens to people foolhardy enough to anger a queen."

"Foolhardy or brave," Father muttered.

"John!" Mother shot a frightened look at the steersman who

manned the oaken rudder. Luckily, he was arguing with the man drumming out the rhythm for the sweaty oarsmen rowing us along.

"What do you mean, Father?" I asked, intrigued. Mother's world was simple as brown bread. Father's was delicious with imagination, like cake. "A traitor is bad," I said, absolutely certain. "Like Hobgoblin Puck who sleeps under my bed." I rubbed the old scar on my hand from habit. "People whose heads got stuck up there did something wicked." His expression left me uncertain. "Did they not?"

"Are you able to keep a secret, little Nell?" Father's eyes turned solemn beneath the brim of his brown velvet hat.

"You know that I can."

"By God's soul, John!" Mother gasped. "She is five years old! And the things that come out of her mouth! You will have us all taken up for treason!"

Father switched to Greek, the language we spoke when he taught me my lessons. "Is your mother right? Are you too young to understand you must say nothing of this to anyone once we reach the Tower? Especially my friend Sir John Bridges?"

"They could stretch me on the rack until my bones break and I would never say a word. Wat Smith says that is what jailers do down in the dungeons."

"We will hope very fervently it will not come to that then, won't we, Little Bird?" Warmth spread through my middle whenever Father called me by this pet name. "You know who our queen is, Nell?"

"Queen Mary."

"That is right. She is old King Henry VIII's eldest daughter. Do you know who Queen Mary intends to wed?"

"King Philip of Spain. I heard you talking to Father Richard about that before he had to go away." Father Richard had been our priest at Calverley. He had answered all my questions about God and Martin Luther, the monk from Germany who had nailed a letter to a church door telling all the things the Pope was doing wrong. Trying to figure it all out made my head ache, but Father Richard never got cross with me for pestering him. Mother warned me not to expect God to be as patient as Father Richard. Even her eyes got red when he had to flee to France so no one could take his wife and sweet baby away.

My father cleared his throat. I knew he missed Father Richard, too. "Sir Thomas Wyatt and the other men who rebelled against Queen Mary last winter were very afraid of King Philip." Father ignored mother's reproving glare. "Do you know why?"

That was easy for a girl who had been raised in the reformed religion to answer. "Because he is Catholic." I hesitated, and then asked in a hushed voice, "When he is king will he burn us up like they did my godfather?" Father had locked himself in his library for three days after the messenger brought that grim news from Smithfield.

Sadness took over Father's eyes again and I knew I had put it there. I hugged my belly, the whalebone busks that kept my bodice stiff digging into my hips. "Wat says Protestants burned up Catholics, so they are just making it even. I did not believe him."

"What Wat said is true. I wish it was not. Would God we could allow each other to come to faith in our own way. There is only one Christ. He cannot be happy His followers are trying to murder each other in His name."

"You would allow Rome to rule us?" Mother demanded. It was a shock to hear her speak Greek as well. She had learned much while serving as one of Queen Katherine Parr's ladies before King Henry died, but mother rarely bothered speaking anything but English. "You would have us be vassals to Spain?"

Father patted Mother's hand. "Your mother has cut to the practical root of the problem as always, Nell. Spain is much bigger and much stronger than England."

"But not braver!" There could be no doubt of that. I had been raised on tales of Agincourt and Crécy, where my ancestors had fought.

"No. Not braver," Father said. "Still, think of the conflict this way. You know your friend, Wat?"

"Wat is not my friend! He pushes me because I am littler than he is."

"What would happen if you had some marchpane and he did not? Would he try to take yours?"

"He might *try*." I scowled. "I would stick him with a pin."

"I am sure you would fight bravely," Father said, "but chances are Wat would succeed in taking your sweet, because he is twice as big as you are. That is what people fear Spain will do with England. Take all that is sweet from our country and force us to fight their wars, follow their religion. We would become more Spanish than English."

"But I do not want to be Spanish!"

"That is what the rebels thought. They hoped to sweep the Spaniards out of England."

"And Queen Mary off of the throne," Mother added.

"But then who would be Queen?" I asked.

"Sir Thomas Wyatt hoped to put the crown back on Lady Jane Grey's head."

I remembered the story of Lady Jane. King Henry's sickly boy, King Edward, made her queen of England after he died. She only ruled for nine days before Mary took the throne away from her. They had chopped off Jane Grey's head at the very fortress we were going to visit. "If Jane cannot be queen, then who else could be?"

Father cuddled me close. "Princess Elizabeth."

"Wat says she is a bastard and her mother was a witch."

"People who say Elizabeth is not King Henry's daughter are fools." Father stroked my red curls. "Anyone with eyes can see she is Tudor to her bones. The Protestants will rally around Princess Elizabeth in earnest now. May God save her."

"Why does God need to do that?" I asked.

"Because the princess's head is loose on her shoulders, that is why!" Mother said. "Mark my words, Queen Mary will treat Elizabeth just as she did Lady Jane!" Mother's voice caught the way it did whenever light hurt her eyes. It almost sounded like crying.

I shivered. Now that I had seen the traitors up on pikes it was easy to imagine someone's head coming loose and rolling away. "Where is the princess now?" I asked. "Is she hiding from the Spaniards?"

"I wish that she were somewhere hiding," Father said. "No, the princess is locked up in the Tower while Queen Mary decides what to do with her."

"Someone should let her out." I was amazed no grown-up had thought of it.

"Indeed, Little Bird. I wish someone could." Father gathered me in his arms; I loved the smell of him: ink and leather and books.

The barge cut through the water until a cool shadow fell over us, the curtain wall surrounding the mighty fortress. As we drew abreast of the Tower wharf to land, I could see the White Tower peeping over the top of the walls, its turrets gleaming in the sun. Thoughts of the princess fled as Father told me how William the Conqueror had brought those golden stones all the way from France to build a castle so the Saxons knew he was here to stay. Never had I imagined a structure so big. My head filled with the treats Father promised: booksellers and trips to the king's menagerie, with strange creatures from lands far away. I was in London at last, where we would visit the mysterious conjurer who had once been imprisoned for making a wooden beetle fly. It was science that had wrought Dr. Dee's famous feat, Father insisted. And yet, magic was far more enthralling to my mind.

A guard whose face was ruddy as his livery glanced at the de Lacey lions baring their teeth on the banners rippling above us. He hastened toward us, saying that the Lieutenant bade him watch for visitors from Calverley. We were to be escorted to Sir John at once. The two men visited each other every five years to talk of pranks and theories and people I had yet to meet. Father had told me Sir John was forever laughing and could solve more riddles than any man he'd ever known. Yet when we entered the house close to the fortress's thick wall, the man who embraced my father looked as if he had never smiled at all.

"My dear friend, have you been ill?" Father's shock was evident in his voice. Mother grasped my hand and pulled me away from them. She was fearful of contagion where I was concerned, and had been wary of bringing me to London. Everyone knew the crowded city was a breeding ground for fevers of every kind.

"You need not fear for your child's safety, Lady Calverley," Sir John soothed, as if he sensed her fears. "My sickness is of a most singular kind. I am only sore at heart."

"I am sorry for it." My mother relaxed her grip on my hand.

"Your visit will cheer me. My wife is depending upon it. We will reminisce about happier times while I become acquainted with this remarkable daughter my friend has written about so often."

Father chuckled and laid a hand on my shoulder. "I think you will find I have been modest in my estimations. She could best many scholars twice her age." Pride made my chest feel tight. I dreaded the possibility of failing him. "Make your curtsey to the Lieutenant, Nell."

I executed my curtsey passably enough. "Good morrow, Sir John."

"Good morrow, Mistress Nell. You are most welcome after your long journey. What do you most wish to see here in the city? We have shops full of pretty trinkets."

"It is books I want. Father says there are more in London than I could ever read."

I saw the Lieutenant flinch, and I feared I had offended him. But he looked into my eyes with a mournful gaze. "I knew a girl who loved books above all things."

"May we find that book-loving girl?" I asked. "I should like her very much."

"The Lieutenant is an important man," my mother chided. "He cannot be chasing after children."

"But he said there is a girl—"

"*Was* a girl," Mother quelled me. "*Was*, Nell."

"It is all right, my lady," the Lieutenant told her. He hunkered down the way Father sometimes did so he could look into my eyes. "The girl I knew gave me something precious." He reached inside his doublet and withdrew a small volume. I opened it.

"It is a prayer book," I said, unable to hide my disappointment.

Sir John ran his thumb over the velvet binding. "Can you read the name written within?" It was squeezed at the bottom of the page, the words penned in by hand.

"Lady Jane Dudley."

"Most still remember her as Lady Jane Grey."

I sobered. Lady Jane—no matter what surname one called her—was quite dead. "No wonder you are sad," I said.

"You would have liked her. She was very brave and good. However, she was not as fortunate in her parents as you are, Mistress Nell."

On impulse, I kissed him on the cheek to chase the sadness away. Sir John's eyes brimmed over with tears. Appalled, I shrank back against Father's legs, expecting a reprimand for being so forward. But both Father and Mother smiled at me as Sir John swiped at his eyes with the back of his hand.

"Enough gloom, little Nell," Sir John said. "You did not travel all this way to listen to my grim musings. Perhaps while the servants help your parents settle into their lodgings you and I could walk over to the menagerie?"

"I would like that, sir. Very much. If my lady mother does not mind."

He turned to my mother. "You will indulge me in this, will you not, my lady?"

"But your duties—"

"I have had a belly full of duty. God forgive me what I've done in its name."

Soon we were back in the bustling courtyard of the mightiest fortress in England. My neck ached from peering up at the towering walls. Guards paced along parapets, their halberds glittering in the sun. Thrice, Sir John had to keep me from bumping into one of the numerous workers who kept the fortress running. Once I nearly trod upon one of the ravens the Tower was famous for. In an explosion of squawking and feathers, the great black bird flew into the sky visible above the golden walls.

I wrinkled my nose as we entered a building filled with strange smells and echoes. "Do you have a dragon from the Ethiops here, Sir John?" I regarded the intriguing shapes within. "I am very fond of dragons."

"I am afraid not. But we have a bear that ate a very naughty boy once."

I peered down into the nearest pit, anxious to see this bear. Two lions paced instead, their manes far more scraggly than the stone ones on our gatehouse back home. I chattered with delight, feeling myself the luckiest girl in England when a keeper let me fling a moldy haunch of mutton to wildcats with yellow eyes that glared right through me.

"Do you get to feed the animals whenever you wish if you are the Lieutenant of the Tower?" I asked.

"I do. And all of the soldiers here are under my command. During the rebellion I shot cannons at Wyatt's traitors to help save the queen."

I was not sure if that was a good thing or a bad one. But before I could ask him, Sir John grew grim. "I have other duties not so pleasant. I must accompany prisoners to trial, and those condemned to the block." Sir John stopped beside another pit. I looked in and saw the bear.

"This is the hungry fellow I was telling you about," he said.

"He does not look *very* dreadful." The animal lay on his back, licking his paw.

"May I offer you a bit of wisdom to remember about wild things? Just because you cannot see teeth doesn't mean they won't bite."

⇥⊱≺⇤

NOT UNTIL THREE days later did I peer out of the window in the Lieutenant's lodgings to see the most compelling creature held captive behind the Tower walls: The fair young princess out walking in the Lieutenant's tiny walled garden. She wore a black dress with barely any embroidery. But her hair rippled down her back like a banner of defiance.

"Eppie!" I grabbed my nurse's hand. "Come and look! It is the princess!"

"A real princess? That is a sight I have never seen in all my life!" Eppie laughed, good-natured as ever while I led her to the diamond panes. But the instant she saw the lady in the garden, Eppie shrank from the window as if the guard had fired a crossbow bolt at us. "Come away from there, Nell!"

I pressed my face against the glass to get a better look. "The princess's head seems fastened on tight—"

"I told you to get away from that window!" Eppie snatched me back, squeezing my shoulder until it ached. "I do not want to catch you near that window again!"

From that moment shadows came to live in Eppie's eyes.

At night, in the bed we shared, my nurse tossed and groaned as if the hobgoblin had stowed away in my traveling chest and was poking her through the featherbed with his claws. She began numbering the days until we should return to Calverley Manor. As for me, I could not endure being forbidden something for no logical reason, and I could not forget Elizabeth locked behind walls, nor my father saying someone should set the captive princess free. Unlocking doors and gates was simple, after all. One only had to find the key.

Two Weeks Later

NEASY AS EPPIE SEEMED, MOTHER WOULD NOT HEAR of my nurse and me staying behind in the Tower when there were such fine wares to be pored over in the London streets. The weeks of our visit flew past in a whirl of more shops than I had ever imagined. Jewelers at Cheapside, where Mother let me choose a ring whose tiny cameo face winked as if we shared a secret. Drapers on Lombard Street, their ready-made clothes displaying the latest fashions. Mother swathed me in every color fabric in the world and Eppie insisted on buying me a gable headdress with a velvet bag to hide my hair. As we continued down the street I thought Eppie's words strange and asked what my hair should hide *from*. Eppie would not meet my eyes. She said she meant the velvet would protect my curls from city dust. Already my attention was wandering.

Spices from the pepperers in Bucklesberrie made me sneeze and then Father took us to see London's sights. I gaped, awestruck, at St. Paul's Cathedral and marveled at Whitehall Palace, with a city street running through its center—carts and horses, peddlers and apprentices jostling beneath the queen's very nose. But most delightful of all was the Thursday Father carried me to the house where the wizard John Dee awaited us. Mother and Eppie went off to the apothecary to refill Mother's medicine chest with the herbs and physics people at Calverley would need, so this was a day I had Father to myself.

At first glance Dr. Dee's house seemed cobbled together like the buildings father sometimes helped me make out of playing cards. Bright new wattle and daub sections leaned so precariously against the older part of the house that it seemed as if only a sorcerer's spell could keep it standing.

The wizard who lived within was small and spare beneath flowing black robes. Dr. John Dee's restless hands appeared to pluck magic out of air as he ushered us into rooms filled with scientific instruments much more elaborate than those Father had back home. While Father and Dr. Dee talked quietly in the far corner, I wandered about, surveying all the wonders. A pair of spheres painted in different colors fascinated me, one decorated with blobs, another with white dots and colored circles of varying sizes. Father explained they were made by the great scientist Mercator, one globe mapping the earth and the other charting the heavens. I might have remained transfixed for hours, picking out constellations Father had shown me or attempting to puzzle out how England—the greatest country in the world—could appear so small compared with the sprawling shape that was Europe, where Spain lived. Yet suddenly, amidst the clutter of ink-stained pages and vials of things like mermaid's teeth, I saw something that made my mouth fall open in wonder. A book lay open on a table, revealing a serpentine creature spreading its painted wingspan over two pages, spewing bright-colored flames from its mouth. I scrambled over to it, but Father scooped me up into his arms.

"Hey, ho, Little Bird! Where are you off to in such a hurry?"

"I think I know," Dr. Dee said with a kind smile. "Did you see my book of dragons, Mistress Nell? Books like this were looted from the libraries of monasteries all over England when Henry VIII was king. I thought it would be a shame to let so much knowledge be destroyed.

But in my zeal, I collected two dragon books. Identical. Perhaps you could help me conceal my folly? Would you do me the very great favor of taking this book with you to Calverley?"

"Truly?" I hardly believed my good fortune.

"Really, John." Father objected. "It is too generous. Allow me to purchase it!"

"I won't hear of it, old friend. Mistress Nell will be doing me a service. Hiding my absentmindedness from scholars who already think me half mad. Make these dragons disappear and no one need ever know I have added such a valuable object to my pile of mistakes." He waved at the cluttered table. "Bottles I forgot to label, crushed baskets and coffers beyond repairing. I wish I could make everything on that table vanish."

"I will help you, sir," I breathed. But it was not the dragon book that made my heart pound this time. It was another object all but lost among the mistakes Dee wished to discard: a small iron key. I waited until Father and Dr. Dee turned away to retrieve a manuscript from a locked coffer. They bent over it, engrossed, so neither noticed me close trembling fingers over the key. I could feel its magic, heavy in my hand. I knew exactly which prison this key was destined to open.

That night as I tried to sleep on the lump of key hid beneath the feather mattress, I heard Arabella complain we only had one week left in the city. Surely, I reasoned, that would be time enough to sneak my prize into the princess's hands? But by morning rain settled in, stubborn as I was. Four days slipped past and the strain nearly shattered my nerves. I had not caught so much as a glimpse of my princess and time was running out.

On the fifth day the sun beamed down and I knew I must seize my chance. Easy enough, with Father gone off to study stars with Dr. Dee and Eppie even more distracted than Arabella, who had struck up a flirtation with a handsome guard. Everyone in Calverley's party was trying to gorge themselves on the sweet stuff the city offered before returning to quiet Lincolnshire. Mother and Eppie talked themselves hoarse with the other ladies in the Lieutenant's solar, but even the most scandalous gossip the private sitting room could hold did not tempt me from my post at the window seat near the chamber door. I curled up with the book Dr. Dee had given me, the volume so thick that everyone thought I would be reading as long as the sunlight held. But for once I could not keep my mind on the glorious words. Instead, I watched the walled garden, waiting for my chance. Narrow gravel paths cut sharp corners around beds edged with lavender, a discouraged willow bending over the sundial that marked the slow march of prisoners' time. Smudges of color too wan to be flowers scraped with green tendrils against the walls as if trying to reach the watery bar of light that managed to ooze over the stone barrier. At last the afternoon warmed and I glimpsed the familiar red hair. I set aside my book and stole from the chamber.

Only a scullery maid hauling coppers of water passed me as I crept to the bedchamber, and she was too burdened by her own tasks to notice me. I slipped out of the Lieutenant's lodgings and into the bustle of humanity within the fortress. Never in the weeks I had been at the Tower had I left the Lieutenant's house alone. Excitement filled me at such freedom. A crisp breeze pinched my cheeks as I darted past yeomen guards in crimson livery, their pikes gleaming sharp in the sun. A baker carried a board piled with coarse bread, and cursed me as I ducked beneath the smoke-blackened plank.

I reached the gate that held my princess prisoner. My new headdress felt heavy as I arched my neck back to see how high the barrier towered above me. I knew I could scale it if I dared. Did I? I scrambled up and over the gate before I could change my mind. Slippers scrabbled for purchase on the stone wall, and then I dropped to the ground inside the garden. My heart tripped when the yeoman on guard glanced my way. I was sure he would smell the stink of guilt on me, but he merely turned back to contemplate the musk roses climbing the wall. I peeped from my hiding place, willing the princess to turn my way. As she rounded my boxwood hedge, she appeared conjured by magic, and in that moment, I think, I lost a piece of my heart forever.

The princess nearly stepped on my velvet shoes. "You scared me half to death!" she cried. "How is it that you have come to visit me, little lady?" The princess smiled. "Are you a ghost? Or fairy who stole away from her revels?"

"No. I am a girl," I said, very solemn.

"What is your name?"

"Nell." My hand slicked with sweat where it clung to the contraband I carried.

"I am most happy to make your acquaintance, Nell." The princess curtseyed to me as if I were grown up. "Do you know who I am?" she asked.

"You are the princess they lock in the Bell Tower."

"No. I am only the Lady Elizabeth. Or so my enemies would have me called."

"Then they are blockheads." I was looking at her neck.

She laughed. "What are you staring at, Nell?"

"Your head, Your Grace. I am worried in case it should fall off."

Elizabeth paled. Her long fingers fluttered to her throat. "They took down Lady Jane's scaffold. I am sure—"

"They did!" I assured quickly. "My mother said your head was loose on your shoulders. I was trying to figure out how that might be."

Elizabeth seemed to gather herself up. "I hope to keep my head yet."

"That is why I am here. To help you. I brought you this." I drew my treasure from its hiding place. Elizabeth's gaze leapt from the key to the guard. "Who put you up to such dangerous mischief?" she demanded sharply.

Shaken, I fell back a step. "I did it on my own. I brought you a key so you could open the doors and go abroad."

The sharpness in her face melted. "Where did you get that?"

"It was easy to find once I set my mind to it. Father says I have eyes sharp as a little bird's." I hesitated. "It is a magic key."

"Is that so? Who is your father?"

"He is the wisest man in all of England. He can read Greek and Latin and speak oh, so many languages, and he is teaching them to me." Princess Elizabeth smiled, asking me in Latin if I had read Homer's famous works. In Latin, I told her I was on my very first odyssey to London, though I had not yet heard the siren Circe's bewitching song. But perhaps I had. I stared, transfixed, into Elizabeth Tudor's face.

"That was prettily done," she said in English. "Your father has taught you well."

"He can chart every star in the sky. He is the finest father ever born." Pity welled up. "Your father is King Henry, who cut off your mother's head." The princess's lips tightened. I knew I had blundered again. "I am sorry," I said, passionate with regret.

She knelt down so she could look me in the eye. She took the key gently from my hand. "This is a marvelous gift. I will not forget it."

The guard was now striding toward us. He seemed a veritable Goliath, his halberd in one hand, his brows knit in a formidable frown. Elizabeth stepped between me and the imposing man, and I thought of the rack, and all of us being taken up for treason because of me, just like mother had feared. But I had not told any of the secrets Father had warned me against. Not a single one.

"How did you get in here, wench?" the guard demanded of me.

I tried to master the tremor of fear in my voice. "I climbed."

The guard turned toward Elizabeth, looking sore uneasy. "Your Grace, may I see what is in your hand?"

"A key," the princess said. "Nell gave it to me so I could go abroad." The guard made a sound like he had swallowed his tongue. "You need not fear, good sergeant. It opens a coffer somewhere, I would wager. Not my cell."

"It does not matter what this key opens," the sergeant blustered, his face red as his cap. "This is a serious offense."

"No, it is not," the princess said. "It is nothing more than a child's generous fancy. Can we not let this pass? She meant no harm."

She held the key out to him.

"No!" I cried as the key disappeared into the guard's hand. I flung myself at him. "You shall not take it from her!" But the key was gone. My mother's call from the courtyard barely penetrated my shrieks.

"Someone is seeking the child." The princess caught hold of my arms to pull me off the guard. "Go open the gate and I will do what I can to calm her."

The guard bowed and left us, halberd in hand.

From a distance I could hear his summons, the clatter of iron, my mother's voice sharp with alarm. "Elinor de Lacey! However did you get in here?" It was the voice that usually made her get the switch. I wheeled, and saw mother racing through the gate the guard had opened, her blue skirts flying. "Shame on you for running off!"

Mother stumbled to a halt as the princess scooped me up. I clung to the princess and buried my face in her red-gold hair. When I dared peep between the strands, my mother was staring at the two of us, so silent it shook the foundation of my world. Lady Thomasin de Lacey, Baroness Calverley, *always* had something to say.

"Lady Calverley, it has been years since I saw you last," the princess said. "I had heard of your arrival here. Of course, I did not expect you to visit me."

My mother knew this princess?

"Your Grace." Mother curtseyed stiffly, her damask petticoats making a puddle on the garden path. I could tell she wanted to grab me out of the princess's arms. But even my mother did not dare take such a liberty. "I am most sorry for your trouble."

"You have seen me in trouble before."

"Please forgive my daughter for importuning you so." Mother fiddled with the pomander dangling from her gold girdle. The herbs inside the filigreed ball were supposed to ward off fevers. "Nell is a willful child, your Grace. Given to strange fancies."

"Nell is your daughter?" The princess's brow furrowed. "You are to be congratulated. Nell is a remarkable child. Her Latin is flawless."

"It amuses my lord husband to teach her."

"Father says I am like a hungry bird, gobbling up books as if they were worms."

Elizabeth Tudor plucked a rose leaf from my headdress. "I, too, love learning. You are very fortunate, Nell, to have someone feed your mind so. Perhaps if you study hard and become an accomplished young woman, you could come to court someday."

"We prefer life in the country," my mother said.

"Perhaps Nell will not," the princess responded smoothly, returning her attention to me. "You would make a fine lady-in-waiting, just like your mother did serving my stepmother, the dowager queen."

Mother's jaw clamped tight. "Your Grace, Nell's nurse is also searching, and I have never seen the woman so distraught. She heard a bear in the menagerie once ate a child, and was sure Nell suffered a similar fate."

The princess surrendered me to my mother, but her long, elegant fingers lingered on my cheek. "It would be a terrible thing to misplace such a treasure, Lady Calverley. I remember that you once despaired of being thus blessed. At least you have lived to enjoy your daughter. I wish my stepmother had been so fortunate."

My mother squeezed me tight. "Some were not sorry as they should have been when she died."

The princess winced. "You cannot doubt I grieve for the dowager queen." My mother said nothing and the princess again turned her attention to me. "A position in my household is yours for the asking as soon as you are grown." Her face turned suddenly fierce. "Someday you *will* wait upon me. When I am freed from here. Proved innocent as I must be. Promise me, Nell."

I promised most solemnly.

My mother carried me through the gate the yeoman guard held open, then back to the privy chambers Father's friend had assigned to us. She plopped me down upon the tester bed, a tearful Eppie in her wake. I caught Eppie's hand. "The bear did not eat me! I only went to the garden to see the princess."

Eppie looked as if she would rather I had visited the bear. "I told you to stay away from that woman! Did I not?"

"But she is most wondrous! When I am quite grown I am going to court to be one of her ladies!"

"No!" Eppie shrilled. "You cannot—"

My mother's hand flashed out, striking my cheek with a crack that startled us all. Too stunned to make a sound, I pressed my fingertips to the place that stung.

"Never mention going to court again, do you hear me?" my mother demanded. "Never! You cannot know what it is like, Nell, what can happen to a woman there."

"But I promised Princess Elizabeth—"

Mother grabbed my arms as if to shake loose any threat of defiance. "I am sorry to say it, Nell, but the princess will be dead long before you are grown. It is only a matter of time before her head rolls!" Tears welled up in my eyes as she spun around and strode from the room, leaving me to Eppie's care. I reached my arms out to my nurse, waiting for her to cuddle and kiss away the burn of mother's slap. But Eppie glared at me, her face white, her hands trembling.

"You need to be taught a lesson, you willful girl!" Eppie spoke so grimly it shook me to the bone. "You will remain locked in this bedchamber alone for the night to think of the wrong you have done!" She turned her back on me and walked out the door. I heard the iron bolt slide closed. I had slept in the same bed with Eppie every night of my life, smelling the scent of lavender that clung to her from the bundle of herbs she tucked between her breasts every morning. So it was unthinkable she would abandon me. But that night Eppie was good as her word. Not a soul came up the stairs, not even featherhead Arabella to bring me a candle when night blacked out all light.

I squeezed beneath the bed to hide when the room grew darkest. I writhed in my hiding place, stomach aching as if I had taken one of the fevers mother dreaded, my beloved gown clinging, sticky with sweat in spite of the chill in the room. I had clung to the belief that Eppie would come to help me undress, but as the hours slipped by even that hope disappeared. The bed yawned above me, too big without Eppie in it. Dawn seemed forever away.

Suddenly I heard a scraping sound. A sliver of light peeped beneath the bedchamber doors. Perhaps the guard watching my princess had decided to put me on the rack after all. The bolt slid back. The door swung inward. Father. A sob tore from my throat. I scrambled from beneath the bed and flew at him, nearly knocking the candle from his grasp as I buried my face against the rough cloth of his breeches. Father set the candlestick on a table; in a heartbeat, I was swept up into his arms. "How now, Mistress Magpie. What are these tears about?"

There was no help in a lie. Mother would tell him if I did not. "I took one of Dr. Dee's mistakes and tried to help my princess escape."

"His mistakes?"

"On his table. There was a key. He said he wished he could make it disappear."

"You took a key from John Dee and gave it to Lady Elizabeth?" Father paled. "Did you say the key belonged to him?"

"I made it disappear like he wanted. Doesn't that mean it was my key?"

"Yes, Nell. Thank God." Father sucked in a breath. "You must never tell anyone where you found it. Dr. Dee might be in terrible trouble if you did. A child can make an innocent mistake, but a man known for working magic would be thrown into prison for the same thing."

"I will never tell. I only wanted to let the princess out of her cage."

"That was very brave of you, Nell, but not very wise." Father peered into my face. "You frightened your mother and Eppie worse than I have ever seen them."

"But I had to help my princess. They are going to cut off her head. Mother said so. And I am never to speak of my princess again, even though she made me promise to go to court someday and be her lady-in-waiting."

"Ah, so *that* is where this tempest sprang from. Talk of you going to court."

"Mother went there. You did, too. Why can I not go?"

For the first time in my memory Father evaded my question. I remember the strangeness of it even still. "There will be time enough to speak of court once you are older, Nell. For now, we have but two more days in London. Let us put this unfortunate incident behind us. We will speak of it no more. How would you like to see something so wonderful it will drive all thoughts of your troubles away?"

Father wrapped me up in his thick woolen cloak, the fox fur lining tickling my neck as he carried me, through the silent building, out into the dark courtyard. He spoke to a guard who gave him a lantern and pointed the way up to the Leeds, a narrow walkway along the battlements. I did not know it then, but it was there Elizabeth walked before she was allowed to visit the small garden—her footsteps carrying her from her own Bell Tower to the Beauchamp Tower, where Robert Dudley was being held. How strange, the man Elizabeth would love her whole life spent those same weary hours so close to her, yet another prisoner of the Crown.

"Stretch out your hands, Nell," Father bade me as we reached the topmost part of the curtain wall. "You must hold something for me." I started as something shimmering and mysterious appeared in his grasp. He placed it, cool against my palms, then tilted the object so I could see it in the lantern light, a flat brass disc about the size of a horseshoe, smaller metal cogs fitted on its surface. I ran my thumb across its bumpy face, feeling the etching carved deep in its surface. "Astronomers use it to study the sky," Father told me. "It helps ship captains find their way across the open sea."

"What is it called?" Curiosity blunted the edge of my earlier distress.

"It is an astrolabe. A tool for measuring the heavens."

I looked up at the vast sky, then down at the instrument in my hand. "This astrolabe is very pretty, Father." I repeated the new word to write it on my mind just as he had taught me. "But it looks small to travel so far."

"Your mind will make it reach farther than you can begin to imagine, Nell." Father glanced about to make certain no guard had strayed near enough to hear us, then he boosted me up into a gap in the stone crenellations that looked like the Tower's tooth had gone missing. "Look up at the sky, Nell. What do you see?"

"Stars."

"And what do stars do besides shine, Little Bird?"

"The stars circle around the earth just like the sun and the moon."

"And why is the Church so very certain that is so?"

"Because men are the most important creation in the universe. That is why God put us in the very center."

"So we have thought all these centuries. But what if we have been wrong? Tonight Dr. Dee showed me a rare manuscript called *De Revolutionibus Orbium Coelestium*. Can you translate the Latin?"

"On . . . Revolutions of . . . Heavenly Spheres?" I said so loudly that Father hushed me with a nervous glance over his shoulder. Seeing we were still alone, he grinned at me.

"That is my clever girl! It is a book of theories written by a Polish astronomer named Copernicus. I have set Dee in search of a copy for the two of us as well." Father sobered. "But the book is forbidden. You must not tell anyone about it, Nell."

"I promise." I had gathered up quite a store of secrets on my trip thus far.

"Copernicus made many calculations," Father said. "He believed that earth is not the center of the universe at all. That the earth revolves around the sun!"

"But that is silly! I am quite sure God said . . ." I thought about what Father had said. "Do *you* believe Copernicus is right?" I was not certain who I should believe if it came to cudgel play between my father and God.

"Perhaps we are not as important as we think we are," Father said. "That would be a nasty shock to most people, would it not?"

Then he kissed my nose and I knew he had won.

"Mother would not like it. She says everything we read in the Bible is true. That is why the Catholic priests are wicked. Because they keep all the reading to themselves."

"It is best we keep this theory our secret for the time being. If we tell those who do not understand they will get angry."

"I had a belly full of angry tonight," I said. "It made me feel sick inside."

Father scooped me down from the stones and hugged me against his stiff leather doublet. I leaned back in his arms, the sight of his face comforting me.

"Can I tell you a secret, too?" I toyed with the black strands of his beard.

"You can tell me anything, Little Bird."

"Mother does not like my princess. In fact I am quite sure Mother hates her."

Father said nothing, just leaned his bristly cheek against mine. Then he said, "You know that before you were born your mother served Katherine Parr, our bluff King Hal's last wife?"

"Mother and the princess said she was very kind. King Henry was not. I do not think a person can cut off their own wife's heads and be bluff at all."

"A very astute observation. After the king died, Princess Elizabeth was given into Katherine Parr's care. It was a new beginning, a chance at a better life. Your mother visited me at Calverley from time to time, but mostly she stayed with the dowager queen at the Old Palace in Chelsea, hoping her friend could be happy at last."

"The lady should have been happy with King Henry dead! He could not cut off her head anymore."

"Even when you believe you are safe, life can catch you unawares, Nell," Father said softly. "In the end Katherine Parr suffered more heartache at Chelsea than she'd known at the king's hand. Your mother blames the Princess Elizabeth for that. But the Lady Elizabeth was just terribly young, hungry for someone to love."

"The princess told mother she misses the dowager queen every day," I confided. "Did the dowager queen love the princess?"

"Yes, poppet. With her whole heart. And all would have been well for both of them if the dowager queen had not taken a new husband."

"After all the bad things the king tried to do to her?" I asked, bewildered. "Why would she want another one of those?"

"She fell desperately in love," Father explained.

"That does not seem like a wise idea."

"Love is seldom wise. Katherine Parr made three marriages out of duty. At thirty-five she had been wife to two old men, and then queen to a cruel king. Who can blame her for being greedy for joy after all she had suffered, poor lady?" Empathy filled Father's face in the lantern light. "She married in secret with your mother as witness."

"Did she marry another king?" I asked.

"No, sweetheart. She wed Lord Admiral Thomas Seymour, the Baron of Sudeley, one of the most ambitious courtiers of his age."

"Could he read Greek, Father? Or count all the stars?"

"No, Nell. Lord Thomas had more dangerous gifts. He was handsome and charming, a bold adventurer and skilled at seduction." Father's voice turned suddenly raspy. "You must never fall prey to a man like him, my Nell. I could not bear to think of you at the mercy of that kind of villain. Thomas Seymour destroyed every good and decent thing he ever touched."

Father gathered me close, understanding without words my fear of going to back to bed alone. We watched the sun rise together like an astrolabe of gold over the Thames.

⊹⊱⊰⊹

SIX MONTHS AFTER we left London a messenger rode between the stone lions that guarded Calverley's gatehouse, then into the main courtyard framed by turrets and great redbrick walls. Hearing the commotion, Father and I crossed to the library window. The stranger's livery was unrecognizable, dark with filth from the road, the cloth threadbare beside Father's well-garbed servants in their silver and blue. He was so thin that Mother would have ordered the man to the kitchens to be fed before he so much as spoke. But she was off with Eppie delivering the miller's babe.

"Perhaps it is just as well your mother is afield," Father told me. "Please God it will be our copy of Copernicus from Dr. Dee and you can find more theories to test with your favorite plaything." I had carried the astrolabe about as other girls carried dolls until Mother put a stop to it. But the chance to experiment once more with the beloved instrument delighted me as nothing had since our return to Calverley. After all the excitement in London my home in its quiet Lincolnshire weald seemed quite tame. Father scooped me up and hastened to the courtyard, but the messenger was not from Dr. Dee.

"The man wears royal livery," Father told me as we approached the man and his sweaty roan horse.

"What is your business with Calverley," Father demanded.

The messenger smiled. "I bear a message I am to deliver into the hand of Mistress Elinor de Lacey."

"I am she," I said. The messenger placed a rolled piece of vellum into my hand.

Father ordered Jem to see to the messenger's comfort, then we went back up to the library to read the letter. Father took the missive, broke the seal, an official-looking blot of red wax deliciously bumpy where a ring had pressed into it. I opened the page, but the writing was full of curls and elegant swirls.

"Father, it is the first letter I have ever gotten," I enthused. "Who is it from?"

"The Lady Elizabeth. It seems your princess has left London with her head still attached to her shoulders."

"But how, Father?"

"Her enemies could find no proof she was in league with Wyatt's rebels, so Queen Mary had to release her from the Tower. Who knows what may happen now. Queen Mary's mother had difficulty bearing one living child when she was young. Mary is old. Elizabeth might one day be queen if she is wise and patient." Father considered for a moment. "She would make a fine one, from what my friend Roger Ascham says. Twice she braved great peril, refusing to desert her servants to save herself. She shows great love to those who are loyal to her. People like you."

"Like me?"

"That is what this letter is about, sweetheart. She is grateful for your attempt to free her from the Tower. Someday, when you have a daughter of your own, you can show this missive to her, and tell her of the day brave Nell de Lacey tried to rescue a captive princess. Perhaps it is time I show you a secret place I found when I was a boy. A nook where my father and his father before him hid precious things."

Father carried me to my nursery and showed me how to wriggle a brick near the hearth until it came loose. Behind it lay a piece of blue glass, a lark's nest, and an iridescent peacock feather. I placed my letter in the space beside them.

"Mother would not like this secret place or what I have put in it," I said solemnly.

Father smiled. "Then we must be quite sure she never knows."

Chapter Three

May 1561

CALVERLEY MANOR

I T WAS NOT UNTIL SEVEN YEARS LATER THAT I LEARNED the bitter lesson my princess mastered the moment her mother became a Tower ghost. That life is like the Thames in winter: At any instant the ice beneath your feet can shatter, plunge you into a torrent that sucks you under. Once you realize that hard truth you can never return to blissful ignorance. You spend the rest of your life waiting for the ice to give way.

As the weeklong celebration of my twelfth birthday approached, my father kept the estate buzzing with his promise of a diversion more spectacular than any Calverley had seen. I chafed with curiosity, attempting to spy upon him, uncover the surprise, but he was far too wise for my trickery. He gave me a book sent by his friend Roger Ascham, my own princess Elizabeth's tutor, knowing I would not be able to resist it.

Curiosity pricked me, sharp as the needles Mother used as she and Eppie tormented me with the fitting of new gowns. "Put the book down, Elinor, or we will never get the length of these skirts right," Mother grumbled, taking pins from between her lips. "Do you wish to appear before the Barton children with your hem halfway to your knees?"

"I do not wish to appear before the Bartons at all! They talk of nothing save jewels and gowns and who they will marry one day."

"It is important to consider who you will marry. The future course of a woman's life will depend upon the choice her parents make."

"Your parents did not choose for you. Father told me."

Mother's brow rose in mild displeasure. "My parents were surprised, true. But your father was a suitable choice in every way. He was Baron of Calverley, had wealth enough and ancestors stretching back to Agincourt. He was already known as one of the foremost scholars in Lincolnshire."

"I doubt Clarissa Barton has ever opened a book! Last time she was here, she frightened Moll so with tales of witches that Moll bought a charm from some Gypsy woman and smelled of spoilt fish for days!" Eppie had brought Moll from one of Calverley's outlying farms after seeing the girl's skill with a needle. From the moment of her arrival at the manor, Moll had been so gullible; few of the other servants could resist toying with her. Mother frowned. "Is what Nell says true, Moll?"

Moll ducked her head. Though she was a few years older than I, she was not yet used to the force of Mother's disapproving glance. "It was tales of that witch Nan Bullen Mistress Clarissa was tellin', an' then Jem chimed in, an' all I could see was the witch queen's corpse wanderin' about with her head tucked under her arm."

"You can be sure I will scold Jem over scaring you thus." Suddenly Mother stiffened, remembering some task. "I will return in a minute. Moll, mind that hem you're stitching," she called as she hastened out of the room. "If you aren't careful the edging will end up wriggly as a snake."

"Maybe the witch queen will turn it into a snake!" I snickered. "Surely any self-respecting witch could do such magic. If Anne Boleyn was *really* a witch, why didn't she fly away? Or do a spell to grow another head, just like she grew a sixth finger on her hand? By the devil's magic?"

I could see Moll shiver. "Nay, Mistress Nell! Do not make fun on it. Old Lucifer will snatch you up."

"If he did I would ask him to make a brain sprout in your head! I vow, you believe the stupidest things!"

"Nell, what is this about?" I heard Father's voice from the doorway. He strode into the chamber, a smudge of black powder on his cheek.

Glad to have an ally in logic, I appealed to him. "Moll is claiming Anne Boleyn was a witch. But near as I can tell, Queen Anne got her head cut off for no reason at all."

"She was condemned of witchcraft!" Moll insisted. "'Twas all written down, was it not, Lord John? The charges, I mean."

"Anne Boleyn got condemned for adultery, too, did she not, Moll?" I goaded.

Moll nodded so hard that her chestnut curls bobbed. "With her brother an' lots of other men. The wife o' the king cannot be— be . . ." Moll glanced nervously at my father, then let her voice fall to an embarrassed whisper. "She can't be layin' with other men."

"But King Henry got the marriage annulled before they executed her, didn't he?"

"Aye, and Elizabeth named a bastard."

"So how is it justice to chop off her head for committing adultery against a husband she never had?"

"But he never . . . well, I . . . she was a witch! She cast spells on the king! Made his manhood shrivel up and—"

"Father, do you believe Anne Boleyn was a witch?" I looked to Father, sure he would be proud of my arguments. Instead, he looked a trifle sad.

"I do not know if she was a witch or not. But I do know much evil befell England when she had the king's ear. The king was cruel to his good wife, Queen Katherine of Aragon, and his daughter Mary. Henry would not even let Mary see her mother when the old queen lay dying. People feared Anne Boleyn would see them poisoned. The king had many good men executed for not recognizing Boleyn as his wife."

"Like the man who wrote the book you gave me. *Utopia*."

"Yes. Sir Thomas More. He was not a saint, Nell. Every man has parts that are goodness and parts that are wickedness. But many men who disagreed with the king died so Henry could wed Anne Boleyn and sire princes. In the end, there was only Elizabeth, another daughter, of little use to England's throne."

"Aye," Moll put in, "and she a bastard, an' maybe a witch like her mother."

I stung under the insult to my princess. "At least she has a mind and uses it! She would never run about with a fish head hanging around her neck!"

"Nell." Father's voice was full of disappointment. He looked at the other seamstresses and gestured to the door. "Take a few moments to refresh yourself. As I passed the bake house I smelled fresh bread being taken from the oven."

The ladies scattered, stretching stiff backs, rubbing at their tired eyes as they rushed from the room, fearful my mother would return and order them back to their needles and stools. Moll cast a hurt glance over her shoulder at me. I frowned.

"I was only telling the truth," I asserted.

"Ah, but you did so harshly and wounded little Moll in the process. It was not a fair contest. Your wits are a weapon, Nell. You must not use them against those weaker than you."

"But she smelled of fish heads, and she was saying the most preposterous things!"

"Do you believe in goodness, Nell? Like the kind in Father Richard?"

"Yes. He is the best man in the whole world besides you, Father."

"Father Richard is far better than I will ever be. But just as there is darkness and light in the sky each day, there can be darkness or light in men's souls. In women's souls, too."

"Then you *do* believe in witches?"

"I do believe in evil. One cannot live very long in the wide world without doing so."

"How can we make it go away?"

"We cannot make evil vanish altogether, I fear. But we can try our very best not to be part of it. You can choose not to hurt people if you can help it. Like Moll, for instance. You must be gentle with her. She has come here to Calverley to live far from her family. And she will never get the chance to learn the things you know, you and the Lady Elizabeth."

"Lady Elizabeth is not a witch like her mother. Is she?"

"I cannot say. What I can tell you is that she is one of the finest intellects Roger Ascham has ever taught."

"I wish I could be in the schoolroom with her. You say I must not use my wits to hurt Moll's feelings. I fear I will never get to use my wits at all. Mother says I should think of marrying and such. But wives do not have time to read Aristotle and debate Cicero. Mother never reads anything but her Bible. I wish to be like my princess and study the most difficult subjects in the world."

"Your mother has a fine intellect, Nell. When she was lady-in-waiting to Katherine Parr she studied often, learned much. But someone must tend to things like shoring up the walls of the old castle section of Calverley. Someone must order the joiners to fix the library roof lest the rain come in and ruin all our books."

"I wager Princess Elizabeth is not worried about salting fish and shoring up roofs. I wish I had a mother who—"

"Hush!" Father laid his finger on my lips, stopping my words. "God gave you the mother you have. Surely He knows best. A great girl of almost twelve years old must know that."

"Father, sometimes I am not sure God knows what he is doing at all. When He lets people burn other people up for reading the Bible, and then lets the very same people burn Catholics. Sir Thomas More was a good man about *Utopia*, but a bad man who liked burning people he did not agree with. But then he got his head cut off for disagreeing with the king. It is all very confusing."

"What would Father Richard say?"

"He would say our task on earth is to love God and love one another and try not to squabble over details. God will sort things out in heaven. Perhaps I should begin by sorting things out with Moll."

"That would be a fine start."

I found I liked Moll better once I came to know her. She thought I was the smartest girl she had ever known and promised to ask me before she ever believed in fish-head charms or the like again.

And when Clarissa Barton and her red-faced father arrived for my birthday celebration I told Clarissa that if she frightened Moll I would stick her with a pin.

Clarissa must have believed me, for she ran off to play with the other children arriving from the neighboring estates and left me to talk with father's Cambridge friends.

In the days that followed we hunted Calverley's deer park, ate feasts, and performed a masque where I played the role of Spring with roses in my hair and danced with my dancing master, a tiny, spritely man with a voice that squeaked.

When time came for skittles and hoodman-blind, Mother tried to chase me out to join the other young people, but I hid from her, then slipped into Father's library to listen to the learned men speak.

On the final night of the celebration I sat with my parents upon the velvet draped dais at the head of the Great Hall as servants paraded in with my birthday feast. A trumpet announced the finest dish—a peacock displayed on a silver platter, the bird perfectly roasted, then dressed once again in its feathers so that it looked alive.

I had barely touched the tender meat when the subtleties of spun sugar were brought in, Saint George mounted upon his fine horse, wound away from a marchpane castle on his quest.

I nearly shamed myself by straining up in my seat. "But where is the dragon?" I asked, pulling upon Father's sleeve.

"Dragons are not easily found, you know," Father said with a secret smile. "Perhaps he will appear during the dancing."

But the dragon did not show himself while I impatiently went through the steps of a pavane with dull Sir Charles, Clarissa's father. Nor when there were games set up near the hearth. I would not be drawn into them, searching instead for Father. But he had disappeared and I could not find him.

Suddenly, another trumpet blared, a herald announcing we were all to gather on the field beyond the gatehouse. Father had a special entertainment planned in honor of my birthday.

I ran out into the darkness, far ahead of the other guests. I hastened to where I could see the hillside, where Father was hard at work. Excitement sizzled through the guests like the thin trail of gunpowder Father used to set his fireworks alight. I glimpsed the red smear of Father's torch as he moved to light the fuse. Black powder flared. The sky came alive. Dragon wings spanned the heavens. Fiery squibs and great, golden apples shot from the beast's mouth, setting the sky ablaze. A flaming apple plunged earthward. Then a deafening blast split the night. Flames shot across the hilltop where men were lighting the fireworks' fuses. Our tenants clapped their hands, thinking it part of the display.

I knew better. Even before I heard Father scream.

❧❧ ❧❧

FOR WEEKS WE feared he would die. Between the pain and his blindness he might have been grateful for that final peace. But Eppie nursed him with potions. My mother bullied him mercilessly, demanding that he fight.

As for the daughter the dragon had been conjured for—I hid in Father's study while horror carved up my courage. I might have remained there forever, but Mother hunted me down. "Do you think you do your father any good, starving yourself to a shade?" Mother placed my favorite dishes on the chest at the end of my bed. Just the sight of gingerbread and partridge stew made my stomach hurt anew.

"But what happened to Father is my fault."

"I did not take you for such a fool, Nell!" I could hear her quell the fear in her voice. "Your father is mending now. His sight is gone but his mind is hungry as ever. Feed it, Elinor, the way your father has fed yours for so long!"

I blinked back tears, neither of us able to show the other our heartache. How different things might have been if we had. "I cannot bear to see him hurt."

"You must bear it. You are the one person who can make him want to live." Mother cupped my face, refusing to let me look away. "Since the day you could first name letters upon the hornbook your father bought you at a fair, he has had the raising of you. I have had to fight for scraps of your time to teach you even the barest essentials a woman must know to run a household for her husband someday."

"I will learn it when I must."

"You probably will just to spite me," Mother said. "You've the quickest wit I have ever seen on a maid. But women do not have the luxury of retreating to their library when ugly things happen. We must change the bandages, fill empty bellies. Mend the tears in clothes and in lives. You may not have patience for your needlework, child, but you will be deft at the kind of mending your father needs most." Mother surveyed the shelves packed with volumes precious as jewels. "You will fetch one of these books, Elinor de Lacey, and you will go to your father's bedside and read to him."

Did she long to ask more tenderly? I know she was as lost in her way as I was. Yet what choice did she have besides shoring up the broken places in our lives? "Mother, please do not make me."

"You will show your father that his disfigurement changes none of your feelings for him. You will keep his mind so busy he will not miss his sight. Now go, Nell."

It was the hardest thing I had ever done, entering the bedchamber where Father lay. I clutched a volume of Aristotle against my chest, trying not to let Father sense the horror I felt as I saw his eyes, now gray as marble and as lifeless.

He groped across the covers to find my hand. He raised my fingers to his lips. "I have missed you, Little Bird," he said. And it was

Father's kiss. Father's voice. I read and the books worked magic, just as Mother said they could. Angry red scars melted away with each turn of the page until he was Father. Just my father again.

Yet something in me had changed forever. The ice had broken beneath my feet; I waited for it to shatter again.

Chapter Four

March 1563

TWO YEARS PASSED. I LEARNED THAT OUR NEIGHBOR, Sir Charles, took Clarissa to London to be presented at court. To my Elizabeth, now four and a half years England's queen. I burned with envy, torn between my duty to Father and my own yearning to break free of Calverley's narrow world. I could recite by memory letters I had read to Father, his scholar friends telling of the great minds Elizabeth Tudor gathered around her, discussing advances in science it would take years to record in books that could be carried up the Great North Road to us. I imagined life beyond my cloistered existence, court where intellects were sharper than swords, the world my mother would not speak about, no matter how much I cajoled her.

"Father, what is it like at court?" I asked one day after reading a letter Ascham had sent him.

"That is hard to say. It changes, like the glass in the falcon window, sometimes sparkling so you are entranced by the sight. Other times light pierces your eyes, blinding you. There is much excitement there; the business of the whole world enters England through that gate. Ambassadors, adventurers, scientists, scholars. Rogues and scoundrels as well. The most beautiful, most powerful, wealthiest, and ruthless men England can provide."

"But the queen is a woman. The rule of the country is entirely on her shoulders."

"She has her ministers to guide her, and one day soon, God willing, she will have a husband to take much of that weight off of her shoulders."

"Perhaps she does not wish a man to take the reins of the kingdom from her. Remember when I was learning to ride my pony? Crane hitched a rope to Marchpane's bridle and led me about?"

Father smiled. "You gave him no peace until he freed the rope and let you ride about on your own."

"Elizabeth has ridden on her own more than four years now. I cannot think she would like to be hitched to a lead rope again, no matter which man held on to its end."

Father sobered. "No. It is a frustrating thing when one's freedom is taken away."

I winced, knowing that was exactly what had happened to him. Those rare times Crane could convince Father to come out into the fields, Father now rode the tamest of Calverley's horses, which Crane led as he rode beside him. "Father," I began. "I did not mean . . ."

"You merely raised a well-thought-out point in an argument. Be that as it may, a woman is not able to have such freedom once she has a husband."

"Yet, the ladies at court have more freedom than most?"

"Yes. You would never lack someone to debate philosophy or matters of science with. There are more books in the queen's library than there are in most of England. And the women who surround her have read many of them. Why do you ask?" A line appeared between Father's brows. I could sense the worry in him—that I wanted to leave Calverley, leave him.

Guilt stung. "It is only that Clarissa Barton is in London. I would hate it if she understood things I did not."

The tension in father's scarred face eased. "I imagine you would know more than many women at court. You would like that, would you not? To be more than just the most intelligent girl in Lincolnshire? If you were a fine court lady you could leap all the intellectual fences you cared to—"

"How dare you speak to Nell thus!" My mother snapped, framed in the library door. She did not step into the chamber. It was as if some invisible wall had always held her outside.

Father went rigid. I retreated behind him, alarmed by the expression on my mother's face. "Thomasin," he said with great dignity, "perhaps you should announce yourself instead of lurking at doors. It is a courtesy, is it not, to a blind man?"

It was not enough to deflect her anger. "You are blind in more things than your eyes! Spinning pretty tales to Nell about court when you know I will not hear of her ever going there! Filling her head with thoughts that will only confuse her, make her question her lot as a woman. A wife. A daughter."

"If you would forbid the child to think you are rather too late. She has a mind keen as yours is, keen as good Queen Katherine Parr's."

"And what good did it do either of us in the end? The queen handed her fate to a man not half the wit she was and he destroyed her. And me . . . nothing in my intellect could soften his betrayal. Better never to think at all than to be torn asunder between reason and duty. Nell's life will be running a household, making certain the millers do not grind chalk into her flour, managing servants who may try to cheat her or let her babes wander off. The closest Nell will get to books is making certain the servants dust the volumes so that when her husband is locked up in his library he does not get a complaint of the lungs."

"Is *that* what our life together has been to you?"

Fear rose in me, seeing my parents so angry with each other, so raw.

"Our marriage is exactly what it should be according to the Bible. And it will be the same for Nell. You cannot transform her into a boy who will have a man's freedom. And I will be damned before I allow her to go to court! Talk of your science, your philosophies if you must. But the day she leaves Calverley such luxuries will be at an end. John, you will have to decide upon a husband for her one day. She is growing up and you cannot stop her."

"That does not matter," I shouted as if my defiance could drive back my parents' fury, the way Eppie had once had me shout down the thunder in storms that frightened me as a child. "I will never leave Father," I insisted. But my parents' hard words thundered in the silence, and nothing I did could shout them down.

Yet, in spite of how shaken I was, my father's picture of court entranced me, the letter concealed behind the brick in my wall whispering like Eve's serpent. Forbidden fruit was mine for the taking. All I had to do was ask.

❧❦❧

WHEN SIR CHARLES and his vapid daughter stopped overnight on their return to Barton Hall, Clarissa drove me nigh mad with tales of how she had suffered in London.

"Everyone is so accomplished!" Clarissa exclaimed once Mother took Sir Charles to speak to my father in his library, leaving us alone. "Her Majesty's ladies argued fierce as the men about philosophy and science. I near fainted when one asked what *I* thought of some hypothesis."

It sounded like heaven to me. I loved arguing with Father's Cambridge friends, but as time passed fewer and fewer of them came to visit anymore. They still sent him books and wrote letters, but the travels that once brought them to Calverley no longer took them anywhere near Lincolnshire. It seemed Mother was right. Men could not bear to come face-to-face with Father's pain.

"Before I was presented to the queen my father bought me this book." Clarissa produced a small volume. "*The Three Virtues*. Reading it only made me more nervous. I know you are most fond of books, Mistress Nell. You might as well take it. I never intend to set foot in a palace again."

I glanced through the pages, enough to know Mother would

forbid me to read it. Thanking Clarissa, I tucked it beneath a stack of other volumes so Mother would not see. The presence of the book fortified me during the Bartons' three-day visit. Even Mother was relieved when they left at last. She bustled about the estate on errands postponed while the Bartons were guests. Father had Jem settle him in the library and closed the door for some much-needed relief after Sir Charles's brainless chatter.

The moment the Bartons left, I grabbed my contraband and fled to the nearest deserted chamber.

"Much good this will do me," I grumbled, peering down at Clarissa's volume. "My parents would not even let me go to London for the queen's coronation. If I was denied that pleasure, nothing on earth would move them to present me at court."

My mother had balked about attending the celebration, her dislike of Elizabeth still strong. But Father had insisted it was better to be wise. Queen Mary had died, a great tumor in her belly instead of the babe she yearned for. While Mary Tudor ruled, Elizabeth had endured much at her enemies' hands, and royalty had notoriously long memories when it came to slights. Calverley could not afford to offend a Tudor queen. Every noble family had swarmed to the city for the magnificent ceremony, and I heard told that London was mad with joy that January day. Their Protestant queen: a shining sun to obliterate Spain's dark hold over England. The hated King Philip banished, and with him the Catholicism he and his unhappy queen had tried to force upon their subjects. A proud day to remember in England's history, Father had said. It still stung that I had missed it.

That old bitterness made defying my mother's wishes taste sweet. I opened the book, ran my finger down to the author's name. Christine de Pizan. The book was written by a woman? Katherine Parr had written two books about sin before she died. My mother kept copies beside her bed. But few English women dared to put words in print. Another of the Church's dictums: Females should live to serve their lords and masters. Women should never speak in church. Women must bear children in pain without complaint because we deserved such dire punishment for being the instruments of Original Sin.

The door opened and I thrust my book behind my back, but it was only Moll bringing clean linen. When I let my hands fall back to my sides she eyed the volume wistfully. "A new book, Mistress Nell?" I knew she longed to unlock the secrets encoded in the black print. I sometimes read to her, longing to share with someone my age.

"Clarissa Barton gave it to me," I said, skimming the page. "It is about court."

"Her maid was at table next to me, Mistress." Moll tucked the linens into a wooden chest. "The tales she told took my breath away! All the fine people. I wish that I could see it." I must have looked sour. Moll stammered in her haste to make it right. "Not that I would get so above myself. I know I might as well wish I were queen. Still, I cannot help picturing it."

"Neither can I," I confessed. "Do you want to hear a paragraph about court?" I cleared my throat for dramatic effect. "*A young lady of quality must cultivate the ability to please your mistress at all times.*" I made a face. "I would be happy if I could please my mother once a year."

Moll pressed her fingers to her lips to suppress a laugh as I continued.

"*A lady-in-waiting must exhibit most extreme loyalty at all times and defend her mistress if that mistress is discovered in adultery—even to claiming an infant of her illegitimate pregnancy as one's own.* Exactly how is a woman supposed to manage that deception?" I scoffed aloud. "Stuff a bolster under her gown for nine months and waddle around?"

"Mistress Nell!" Moll exclaimed. "You are devilish wicked!"

"What I am is so restless I feel like I may go mad. I love Calverley and Father and Mother, but . . ." How could I explain longing for a world I had only imagined?

"I suppose that is one thing I can be grateful for," Moll said. "No chance for me to get restless. I've a hundred more tasks to get done before sun sets."

Off she went, leaving me alone. I crossed to the window, a little ashamed for complaining in front of Moll. But I could not help the truth. Once as a child I opened the cages in mother's solar when no one was looking, letting the bright feathered birds fly free. One bird shrank back in his cage, afraid to fly. That was what I dreaded most of all. That kind of fear clipping my wings.

I laid the book facedown on an oak table to hold my place, needing to do something wicked at once. That was *sure* to make me feel better, a sad testimony to my character. My parents did not let me attend the coronation. Perhaps I should see what it would have been like if I had. Shutting the door to the privy chamber, I crossed to the oak chest where Mother kept her most precious things. I opened the lid of the ornate trunk. The double-tailed lions carved on the surface glared in disapproval. But Mother said everything in this chest would be mine on my wedding day. I was only borrowing the gown a little bit early.

I pressed the velvet against me, its soft ermine trim all the more special because it had warmed my mother as Elizabeth Tudor made her coronation journey from the Tower of London to Westminster Abbey in her litter of cloth of gold. The sunshine-hued gown had not been worn since, so it shone, bright as it had on that grand occasion, the emeralds encrusting the bodice sparkling green. I could not resist humming a tune, my feet moving in the gavotte my dancing master had taught me. "Tell me, who do you favor for a bit of frivolous reading?" I asked my phantom partner. "Cicero or Socrates?"

Holding the gown in place with one hand, I approached my mother's silver mirror. I stared, stunned by my transformation. The creature peering back at me was a stranger. I opened Mother's jewel coffer, intent on fastening her emerald cross around my throat. But footsteps sounded in the next chamber. I knew mother's purposeful stride even before I heard Eppie's chatter. The door swung wide, mother entering in a swirl of rose petticoats. She slammed to a halt. "Elinor de Lacey, *what are you doing?*"

My cheeks burned and I fought the urge to stuff the gown behind my back. "I was reading a book and—"

I stopped. What was I thinking, pointing out Pizan's book? I could not have found a better way to raise my mother's ire. She picked up the volume I had left open at the part I had read to Moll.

Mother scanned the page. Her face went still. "Where did you get this?"

"Clarissa Barton gave it to me. I was just pretending—"

"You are far too old to be playing like a child!"

"I am not a child!" I protested. "Most girls my age have been to court! I can only imagine what wondrous things they have seen!"

"I thank God for it! Foolish chits like Clarissa Barton think only real diamonds glitter. They cannot know they are glass!"

"Please, my lady." Eppie tried to intervene. "You cannot blame our Nell for wishing to see exciting places. It is hard to fight the pull of destiny. You can not cage her up like one of your birds! She will sicken and die."

"Do not you dare speak so about my daughter! Nell is mine to protect!"

"She is mine to guard as well, and you know it!" Eppie's chin thrust out of the folds of flesh it was usually lost in. "I have held my peace all these years, but no more. If it were not for me—"

"Be silent, Mistress Jones! Or I swear by the saints I will—"

"Please, both of you," I shouted. Horror and confusion filled me, seeing what my mischief had wrought. "I am sorry!"

"Go to the withdrawing room, Nell. Do not come out until I fetch you."

I obeyed her. What else could I do?

❧ ❧

THE NEXT MORNING Arabella helped me get dressed. But my mother's usually loquacious maid barely spoke to me. When I demanded my own nurse, Arabella said I must speak to my parents about that. As soon as I was decently clothed, I raced down the stone stairs, searching all of Eppie's favorite haunts: The garden where my pet deer, Grace, once doomed herself to exile by eating the herbs mother used to dose the household's ills. The settle by the withdrawing room hearth, where Eppie would doze and toast her aching hands near the fire. The solar, with its sunny windows, where she most liked to stitch.

It was there I found Mother, going over the accounts. The white lawn wrist ruffs edging her sleeves were usually as pristine as mine were blotted whenever I came near an inkhorn. Today mother had dragged her wrist across a damp page. The fact that she had not noticed the stain unnerved me. "I cannot find Eppie," I said.

Mother's hand flexed with such force that it crushed the quill's point against the ledger. Ink bloomed across her precise rows of numbers. "Eppie is not here."

My uneasiness swelled to foreboding. "Did something go awry with Maude's babe?" Eppie delivered all the children on the estate. The smith's wife had borne her child too early, and I knew Eppie had left orders she was to be summoned if trouble arose.

"I do not know where Mistress Jones has gone," Mother said. "But it is time she moved on to another household." My heart sank. "Nell, your behavior of late has shown me that Mistress Jones indulged you far too much for your own good. The fantastical notions she might put in your head—"

"Is this about what happened yesterday? I took out one of your gowns, Mother. *I did.* Eppie had nothing to do with it."

"Eppie is gone. You had best accept that and be done with it. I will find you a suitable maid of your own."

"Suitable? I want Eppie!" I cried, feeling like a lost child.

"Well, you cannot have her. You are never to speak to her again, do you understand me? The woman is mad." Mother laid her quill aside. "Elinor, I know you will not love me for what I have done, but I am your mother. It is my duty to protect you from evil, whether you want me to or no."

"Eppie is not evil!" I cried. "She loves me. Far more than you have ever done! If you keep me from her I will never forgive you!"

Mother looked at me steadily. "Hate me for it as you wish. It will avail you nothing. You will never see Hepzibah Jones again."

I ran to my father, as I always did, sure he would right all the stars in my heavens. How pale he was when I found him in his library, where he always began his mornings alone. Bruised shadows snagged the hollows of his scarred face. His hands cradled a book, his fingers tracing over the binding, feeling its shape, its texture. In the years since his sight was stolen I had often caught Father lifting his precious books to his nose as if the familiar scent of printers' ink and embossed leather could restore to him all he had lost. I poured out my woes. "Father, you will never believe what Mother has done! She says Eppie is evil! But she is not, Father! You know she is not!"

Father laid his book aside. Copernicus, the book we had read together so many times since Dr. Dee sent it to Calverley eight years ago. The astronomer's theory might have applied to me—I was fourteen and so sure I was the center of my very small world.

"Why does Mother hate me?" I cried, certain in my heartbreak that she must.

"Your mother's sin is far different, Nell." Father's hand plucked at his fur-lined gown until it covered his thin white throat. "Perhaps she loves you far too much."

"She would bar me in a tower if she could, keep me from the world."

"Keep you safe." Father groped for me, but I was too distraught to stay still. "You and Eppie love me and you do not try to keep me caged."

"Do you know it is your mother who willed you into being?"

"What?"

"We wished for children. Like most people. Not sixteen like

your poor grandmother gave birth to, but several to comfort us, delight us. Bind us together in a way that the kind of love minstrels sing of never would."

My parents had not been a love match. That I had always known. It still bewildered my father that lovely Lady Thomasin Swift had chosen him for her husband when she had all the gallants court could offer vying for her hand. I thought Father the most wonderful man ever born. Yet he did often try Mother's patience, the two of them different as two people could be.

"Three times your mother conceived and we hoped," Father said. "But three times, the babe was born dead. In her heart, your mother grieved as much as I did. But after we tucked each babe in the crypt, she never spoke of them again. Off she would march to her court duties. Far too soon, we were past the age where we could hope for children. At least we thought so. Then came a miracle, Nell. You."

"Aren't miracles supposed to be angelic? I am far from it."

"Remember what Father Richard used to say when you had one of your fits of anger? That even Jesus lost his temper with the moneylenders in the temple." Father Richard and his family had returned to England when Elizabeth took the throne. He had died last Easter, and I still missed him. Father touched my hand. "From the time you were in your mother's womb you had a talent for mischief, Nell. The month before you were born, you did as the other babes did before you, went still inside her. I gave up hope but your mother would not. She set out on pilgrimage to a holy well near the old Abbey of St. Michael. That is where you were born. I was lecturing at Cambridge. I preferred to be blind to her suffering, and to the crushing blow I feared would soon strike us both down. I was a coward."

"No, Father! Never!"

"She returned to Calverley with the evidence of her great faith. You. Fed by your mother's refusal to despair." His voice softened. "If you could have seen her then, you would not question her love for you."

"It is easy to love a babe so helpless it must do whatever you wish." I sniffed back tears. "It is harder when that child knows her own mind! Mother sent Eppie away! Eppie, who I loved my whole life, better than anyone in the world, Father, except you."

"Indeed, Nell. You have proved my point as I could not." Father cocked his head toward me, guided by the direction of my voice. "Have you ever made any effort to hide how much you loved your nurse, daughter?"

"Should I?"

"Did you ever wonder how your mother felt? Knowing how much you loved Eppie? Loved me? Knowing that in your heart, she would forever be last among us?"

I squirmed as Father pressed on. "The child your mother wanted so badly . . . that little girl's heart was fixed on another woman. It was Eppie's arms you wept in when you were hurt. My lap you clambered onto when you wished to hear a story."

"Mother never had time for such things! She has made Eppie go away because I took out the gown Mother wore when Elizabeth was crowned. It is not rational, punishing Eppie for that! What reason could Mother give you for what she has done?"

"None, Nell." His reply stopped me cold. "She simply asked me to trust her in this decision. I do."

Betrayal burned me, setting loose hard words. "Father, why must you always bend to her will, even when you disagree with her! Please. Do not allow her to banish Eppie just because you cannot bear to fight!"

I saw Father recoil, wished I could recall my angry words. I tried to say I was sorry, but he drew himself up, his voice so calm it startled me.

"Lady Calverley has been my wife far longer than you have been my daughter, and never, in all our years together, has she made a single frivolous decision. I do not know why she believes it is best for Eppie to leave us. But I do know she would never make such a decision lightly."

"She is angry because I was reading a book about court. Mother traveled to court when she was younger than I am now. And you went to the university to learn wonderful things with the most brilliant minds of your age." My voice broke. "Father—"

"You have been the delight of my life, Nell." He sighed with regret. "If you were a son I could enroll you in university. You could master science and philosophy, mathematics and astronomy. Then off I could have sent you, to London to seek your fortune."

Father had often claimed our world was changing so fast it was impossible to keep pace with the discoveries being made all across the globe. Men like Copernicus whose minds could plumb the heavens; the Italian Leonardo da Vinci, whose inventions surpassed even Dr. Dee's wooden beetle: Erasmus, the great Dutch humanist with his revolutionary views on education; and the famous physician and seer Nostradamus, who peered into the future. These were only a sampling of great thinkers whose theories wended their way across the Channel week after week to be dissected by the queen.

England's homegrown adventurers gathered at court as well, men who had sailed to new worlds, discovered creatures I would never see. God alone knew what I might have missed. I had been so isolated in the years of my father's illness I might as well have stepped off of one of John Hawkin's ships into a world as foreign as the Americas.

"Father, I want to stay here and be eyes for you, but sometimes I get so restless. It is not fair that you cannot see. And it is not fair that I am a girl and cannot learn all the things my mind hungers for."

"No. It is not fair, child. But we will have to make the best of what God gives us. Still, things will not remain thus forever. You might write to Queen Elizabeth, a brief note to keep you in the queen's mind. That way, when things change she will not have forgotten her letter to you."

"I will not leave you, Father."

He patted my hand. "But one day, I will leave you."

I did not want to believe him, and yet he proved wiser than I would ever be. During the months that followed, my loss of Eppie faded in significance. For I sat at my father's bedside watching life ebb away. I begged him to stay.

I sat sentry beside the great tester bed where he huddled beneath the heaps of fur-lined blankets that could no longer keep his shrunken body warm. My voice rasped, raw from reading aloud, hour after hour, the one thing that could make him rest. I paused to drink wine from the goblet on the table beside me. The liquid burned my throat not half so much as grief seared my heart.

"Poor Nell," Father commiserated. "Soon you will have no voice at all."

"No, Father. I am fine. I love to read to you."

"And I am too selfish to stop you, even when it would be for your own good. I am storing up the sound of your voice, like squirrels store nuts." Father smiled wearily. "I am saving you up for winter."

I caught his hand. "We have a great many volumes to go. If you could see the stack of books your friends have sent you, you would laugh! There are volumes of medicine and astrology. Mathematics and philosophy."

"You will have to finish them without me."

"But the volume by Erasmus, Father. You must instruct me—"

"No, Nell. You do not need me anymore. I have taught you everything I know."

"Do not say that, Father! I beg you!"

"You beg me often of late. To drink one more spoonful of broth. Swallow that dreadful medicine. Cajole me to sleep, when soon I will do nothing but."

I fought back the lump in my throat. "How could I not? I do not care about anything but you getting well."

"I am weary. Tired of a world without colors. In paradise, perhaps I will see."

"If you do not, I will make God sorry for it when I get to heaven!" I clutched his hand against my face. "Do not go away from me, Father. If you would only *fight* I know you could grow strong again!"

"I have never been good at fighting, as you well know. Your

mother is the strong one. I know you would deny it, but you have always been more her daughter than mine."

"No. You cannot mean that."

"It is the truth. I have no time left to waste on lies. You are alike, Thomasin and you. Intrepid spirits who march right over those too cowardly to keep pace. I have often wondered why she chose to marry me. She was the loveliest sight I had ever seen; with her quick wit and lively tongue she could have had her pick. . . ." His words faded.

"You are tired, Father. You must rest."

"So I can be wide awake for my dying? I have important things to say to you and little time to say them. I am leaving Calverley. But you must leave it, too, Nell. Not long after I do."

I did not care what happened to me in the future. I only wanted to stop time where it was.

"Nell, when I am gone, you must do something for me. You must look behind the loose brick in your chamber. Tucked away in that space you will find a letter to the queen. Jem helped me write it. We hid it when you and your mother were gone. I did not send it. But the money is there for you to hire a messenger to take it to court when I am gone. You are a high-strung filly, Nell. Your wit is too sharp for your own good and your temper . . ." He fretted the fur edge of his coverlet. "You will not send the letter until I am gone, will you, Nell? I could not bear to give up my last ray of light."

"I will stay with you until the end."

"And when death comes where will I be, Little Bird? Unraveling all the mysteries of the heavens?"

"You will know all the secrets of the stars before Dr. Dee does. He will be most jealous of your discoveries."

"Besting the other scholars does not matter so much now. But losing contact with you, Nell, *that* is something I fear. Which is why . . ." He reached beneath his pillow. Something small and gold shone in his hand. "Do you recognize this?"

"It is an astrolabe," I breathed. "Like the one Dr. Dee made for you. But this is so much smaller."

"I had it made specially, when I knew I had to leave you. I asked the goldsmith to string it upon a chain so you can wear it next to your heart. Put it on."

I grasped the necklace, my hands awkward with emotion, knowing that this was Father's way of saying good-bye. I fumbled, then fastened the clasp about my neck.

He touched the chain, his fingers cold against my throat. "There," he said, with a sigh of satisfaction. "Now you will be able to reach me, even in heaven. You must tell me all about the wonderful things you will learn. Tell me you are happy."

Chapter Five

April 1564

PATIENCE IS A VIRTUE I KNOW NOT. EVEN MY STUDIES provided no release from the anguish of losing Father, the finality of his death. I spent my days missing his ready wit, my nights weeping silent tears, racked with grief and uncertainty as I counted the days since I pressed Father's letter into a messenger's hand. I prayed Her Majesty would remember me.

If she did not remember? Then four months after my father's death I would be entombed as well, for my mother insisted on arranging a marriage for me the moment our mourning was done. Without my father to teach me and cherish me, I loathed the home I once loved. The servants hastened about, caught up in my mother's whirlwind of duties, never allowed to falter though my father lay in the chapel crypt.

"The Lenten season is almost here, Nell," Mother warned. "It is time to learn how I keep the wet larder stocked with fish."

"I do not care for fish." My stomach rebelled at the stench of saltwater catch that the peddlers delivered wrapped up in seaweed. The freshwater fish from the holding pond in the garden always tasted foul to me as well. I sated my hunger on Fridays with chunks of white flour manchet and pungent wedges carved from moons of ripe cheese.

"The mistress of a household is responsible to God for both bodies and souls," Mother said. "She must see that her entire manor observes the weeks of fasting. If you will not learn the keeping of fish let us go to the bake house. You cannot make the excuse that you do not eat bread. Not that you eat much of anything at all anymore." She cast a worried glance at my wrist, its bones birdlike. I had nearly starved myself during the weary months of Father's final illness. Mother's voice gentled. "If you would just settle yourself to something useful, daughter, you would feel much better."

"I do not want to feel better!" I snapped. "I want—"

I wanted to be five again, clambering up on my father's knees. I wanted to cry out my grief. I wanted this agony of uncertainty to be over.

Mother stilled for a moment, stared down at the fresh rushes strewn on the floor. Dried rosemary sprinkled amid them released its scent, crushed beneath our feet. Rosemary for remembrance. "I miss him, too, Elinor," she said softly.

You never loved him as I did. I bit back the spiteful words.

Mother sighed and straightened the cluster of keys that dangled from her girdle. Keys to the wine cellar, keys to the coffer where she kept the household coin, keys to the life she wished to lock me into just as tightly.

"Perhaps you could go to the library and organize it," she suggested. "At least then you will not be wandering about the house like a ghost yourself. I will send Moll to light a fire for you."

Without a word I climbed the stairs. I passed through Father's privy chamber, where he had once entertained friends like Roger Ascham and John Dee, through the bedchamber where he died, then to the heart of his world, the library where we spent so many precious hours. Cold struck me, borne of spring winds and the weight in my heart. I had tried to cross the threshold since his death, but the air itself scraped sharp nails across my spirit.

I trailed my fingers along the bindings, then stopped at one that seemed less worn than the others. I drew it out, surprised. *The Three*

Virtues. I was certain my mother had gotten rid of it. Or had she forgotten it in the uproar when she turned Eppie away? Had a servant thought it one more in the endless piles of books and tucked it away on the shelf?

Eppie. The reminder of that terrible injustice shored up my bitterness and for an ugly moment I was glad I might have the power to wound my mother back if the scheme Father and I had hatched came to fruition. Volume in hand, I crossed to Father's chair. As Moll lit the fire, I curled up to read about the courtier's world I longed for. It was there Mother found me hours later, a missive crushed in her hand.

"Her Majesty is eager to meet her newest maid of honor." Mother's voice shook. "How did this come about?" she demanded, her expression a mixture of fury and fear.

"Father felt—"

"Father *felt?* What of things I *know?* You are a child with no more knowledge of the world than the lambs out in that meadow! Are none of the lessons life taught me so harshly of any value to you?"

I dug my fingers into my skirts. "You do not understand me as Father did."

"And neither of you have ever let me forget it, have you? I have always been beneath you and your precious father in wit. Barred from your philosophizing, your debates while I made certain you were fed and warm and the roof did not fall in on your heads." Mother stared down at the missive. "How could he betray me thus? Burying himself alive in this accursed library was pain enough for me, but he had to steal you as well, making certain I lost you to his infernal books! If he were here, I vow I would—"

Her threat faded to silence. Father was gone, far beyond her reach. Only the books he loved remained. She spun toward the shelves, grasped the nearest volume, and flung it into the fire. I cried out, too stunned to move as the flames leapt to devour it. The stench of burning parchment, velvet, and leather billowed into the room as she scooped up an armful of books and hurled them into the fireplace.

Copernicus. I recognized the precious volume that opened the heavens wide to Father and me. I dove toward the hearth, scrabbled in the
flames to save the book, but my mother yanked me out of danger.
Tears streaked her features, black soot turning her face into that of a
stranger. "Be damned to him for this! God in heaven, do you have
any idea what you have done?"

"I have tried to pull myself out of the hell you wish to bury me in!"

"Hell?" Mother gaped as if I were possessed by a demon spirit.
Maybe I was. "What do you think you will find among Queen Elizabeth's courtiers?" She buried her face in her hands. When she raised it
again, it was splotched red. "Your father petitioned Parliament so the
Calverley title could be inherited through the female line. Your father's title will be your husband's to claim if the Crown wills it, as well
as your fortune. And a courtier will gobble it all down, the money,
the land, your body, getting sons to further his ambition!"

I took a step back, buffeted by her words. "I would not wed a
man such as that."

"Courtiers are consummate actors! You would not know his intentions until after he had you safely wedded and bedded. Then the
mask would fall away, too late for anyone to save you. That is not
all! Every time you pass under the queen's eyes . . ." Her fingers dug
into my arm. "Elizabeth is ruthless. Cunning like any other Tudor.
You can never know when she will strike—"

"I will serve as a maid of honor. What possible reason would the
queen have to strike at me? She is one of the finest minds of our age,
Father said. It would not be logical for her to—"

"Father said, Father said! If your father had so much to say, he
might have mentioned your plan to me! I am his wife of twenty-five
years. I had a right to hear it from his own lips! But no. John de Lacey
was ever too much the coward to meet me face-to-face, say something
he knew would anger me."

"He was not a coward!" I yanked away from her. "I would rather
die than—"

"Die? Do you know how many of the people I loved at court

have done just that? Had their head cut from their body? Felt heart-break cleave their chest? Betrayed. Humiliated. Destroyed. Until in the end death's release must have seemed a mercy."

"You speak of Lady Jane Grey and Katherine Parr. What do I have in common with ladies as exalted as that? I wish for no throne."

"You wish for things I know will destroy you! Why did your father not listen when I warned him? He made you fit for nothing, Nell. Not fit to be a wife. Not content to be a woman, accepting a woman's lot in life."

"And what is that?"

"Atoning for the sin that drove Adam out of Eden. Submitting to God's punishment—bearing children in pain, serving man as your master."

"Are you really so certain God holds half the lives he created in contempt?"

"Why else would so many women die bearing new life?" Mother asked with a soul-weariness even I could hear. "I would think a girl as bright as you are would see the truth clearly. Women are lesser beings than men."

"Then why did God make Elizabeth queen?" I challenged. "Perhaps that is the first question I will ask Her Majesty when I am waiting upon her."

Mother's eyes rounded in fear. "You would court disaster? Speak heresy?"

"I will speak the truth." It sounded braver than I felt in the face of her expression.

"You think truth will save you from danger? To survive in a royal court you will have to learn to lie. Lie until you cannot remember what truth is. Lie until it poisons everything you touch." Mother's voice cracked. "Stay here, Nell. Trust a mother who loves you. You will find nothing at court besides your ruination."

For a moment I wavered, an image arose in my mind, a bleak, gray lifetime shut away like one of mother's white larks. "Better that than never to have a chance to be happy at all. Please, Mother. Tell me why you are so set against this. Give me one logical reason I should not go to court. Just one."

"I do not have to explain my decision. You are my child, Nell! Mine! And you will obey me in this!"

❧❧

A MONTH LATER a second summons came from the queen couched in terms Mother dared not refuse. Although defeated, she made what arrangements for my protection she could. She carefully chose the retinue that was to accompany me from my childhood home to London. Twelve armed men, Moll, who was now to be my maid, and Jem and Crane, who were in charge of the de Lacey horseflesh and my baggage.

I had won. I reveled in my victory. Even my mare seemed to catch my mood. My beloved Doucette preened beneath me in her new green velvet saddle, her trappings exquisite against her sleek coat. My own apparel matched her finery. Billows of emerald velvet cloak swirled about my shoulders. A caul of silver thread netting confined my hair. A jet-beaded escoffion with two yellow plumes perched jauntily on my head.

The numerous garments Mother had planned so carefully for my time at court lay stored in Father's traveling chests, their leather-clad lids peaked so the rain would run harmlessly off them. Dried herbs like the ones Eppie once tucked in her bosom were secreted away in the chests to keep the contents smelling sweet.

A locked coffer of jewels and coin I had not bothered to look in was buried deep in the cart that was to be driven by Jem's trusty hand. But I had prepared my writing desk myself, seeing that the elegant drawers and compartments decorated with images of the goddess Diana were well supplied. Quills and parchment. Powder to be mixed into ink. Wax beads and a tiny dipper to melt them above a candle. Tucked in one of the cunningly fitted drawers was my brass seal in the shape of Athena, goddess of wisdom, which Father had let me choose years ago on a visit to Cambridge.

Most precious of all the possessions I carried to my new life was the small chest of books I had cushioned with fresh straw. Tucked within the pages of one of the volumes, a reading list Father had asked Jem to help him write sometime in the weary days before he died. His final gift, so I could continue my studies without him.

I carried so much that was Father away with me. From my mother? Only the breach separating us, wide as any sea. Or so I thought, head-strong babe that I was. I did not guess she sent the sturdiest shield she could find to stand between me and disaster. Ignorance. How many heartsick hours she must have prayed it would protect me.

Doucette pranced, impatient as I was to put Calverley Manor behind us. But as we prepared to ride away, Mother stopped me. She approached my horse, something cradled against her black wool bodice. A book. Something that survived the fire? My heart leapt. But it was de Pizan's *The Three Virtues* Mother pressed into my grasp. The volume that instructed a woman how to survive at court.

"I thought you would be glad to have this. A birthday gift if you will. You will turn sixteen on the road to London."

It was true, in the confusion I had forgotten. Still, I could not conceal my disappointment. "I had hoped this book might be Fa-ther's Copernicus, saved somehow from the flames."

"Copernicus will not help you where you are going, Nell. You will need more practical fare. I read it, recognized the wisdom in the pages, and the warnings. You must beware, Elinor," Mother said as I shoved her offering into my saddlebag. "Do not be rash or hasty or speak without thinking." Her voice cracked. She wrestled it into sub-mission. "Promise me you will not follow through with this mad plan just to prove you can best me. I have told Crane he is to turn back any time you wish it. Even up to the moment you reach the palace gates."

I closed my eyes, imagining the moment I would join the throng entering that glittering new world before me. Scientists bringing their latest discoveries to lay before the queen, adventurers laden with the bounty of new continents, plants and animals and birds no Englishman had ever seen. Philosophers and soldiers, men of daring and intellect. And women who could hold their own among the tangle of new ideas changing the world.

"You will not hear a word of reproach from me if you return home," Mother pressed me, so sincere I felt sorry for her pain. "I swear it on my own dear mother's grave. Once you are inducted into the court, you will not be able to leave unless the queen gives you permission to. You will be under the queen's control for as long as she wishes it. I will have no power to help you."

"I will write to you," I reassured her, regretting the lines in her face, her hair, once lustrous black and now graying. Somehow, in the war between us, my mother had grown old.

She reached for my right hand. Her fingers gently chafed the scar that arced from the knuckle of my smallest finger toward my wrist. For a long moment she stared at that ridge of flesh as if it held all the secrets in the world. "I love you, Nell. You must never doubt it."

Chapter Six

Elizabeth

FEBRUARY 1548

AUGHTERS OF EVE ARE BORN TO SIN. LUST OF THE FLESH waits to devour us . . .

Winter sunlight streaming through the solar windows of Chelsea Manor could not lighten Elizabeth's displeasure at the religious tract Lady Calverley read aloud. But even Kat Ashley, Elizabeth's beloved governess, who sat nearby trying to stitch, was oblivious to the dangerous course of Elizabeth's thoughts of late. Kat did not know the secret her fourteen-year-old charge clung to, hiding its sinful sparkle. Thomas.

Elizabeth frowned at the prayer book cover she was working in silver thread. Her handsome stepfather teased her memory, slapping her buttocks, tickling her, his big hands brushing her breasts. He was her stepmother's loving husband. Elizabeth knew the sensations he evoked showed *her* sinfulness, not his. Had sin been transferred to her while in her mother's womb? She pictured Anne Boleyn's exotic face from a portrait she had seen. The Boleyn Witch. The Great Whore. And what of her daughter? A child conceived in lust so strong it toppled a pope. Elizabeth jabbed her needle through the velvet and bit back a yelp as she punctured her finger beneath the embroidery hoop. A nudge from God, Lady Calverley would have claimed, had Thomasin de Lacey's eyes been able to pierce Elizabeth's innocent facade.

Elizabeth glanced at her stepmother, wondering if she felt that same burn inside when Thomas Seymour was near. The serene Katherine glowed in spite of Lady Calverley's grim reading, blushed with a love that filled Elizabeth with confusion and envy, ugly resentment as well as affection. Four times that day the silk thread Katherine was using had slipped from her needle and she set ten stitches before she noticed anything was amiss. Yet instead of the embarrassment Elizabeth would have felt at being caught thus, Katherine's smile only grew more mysterious.

"Lady Elizabeth," Lady Calverley's voice intruded. "Does today's reading not please you?"

"I am not the one who keeps dropping my thread!" Elizabeth accused, then winced when she saw her stepmother flush.

"You need not scowl, Thomasin," Katherine said. "It pleases me when Elizabeth speaks her mind. I remember when she was far too cautious for such a little poppet."

"I am much grown since then. Forgive me, Your Grace," Elizabeth said, and meant it. "I am restless today."

"And eager for your run in the garden. You love a chase, just as your father did. You need not stay inside, just because I am not ambitious enough for our afternoon game."

Elizabeth's nape burned beneath the veil that hung from her green French hood. The dowager queen was right. Elizabeth loved the chase. And as if wicked thoughts could summon a devil, Lord Thomas entered the withdrawing chamber.

"Husband!" Katherine exclaimed in delight as he swept over to plant a hearty kiss on her upturned face. "What a surprise!"

"I am full of surprises, my sweet. One is being tucked up in the stables even as we speak. The most magnificent stud I have ever laid eyes on. Far finer than any in my brother's stables. I would stake my neck on it."

"Never risk that, love." Worry marred Katherine's brow and Elizabeth could not blame her. A parade of bold men much like Thomas Seymour had supplied gruesome spectacles for London's mobs at the executioner's block throughout her father's reign.

"You and your brother wrestle like schoolboys to see who will be in first place," Katherine said. "What does it matter?"

"It matters to *me*," Seymour said. "Since brother Edward became Lord Protector he and his wife have slighted you too often for me to stomach."

"I do not care about them," Katherine said. "We have each other and now . . ." A look passed between husband and wife that irritated Elizabeth.

"Now *what?*" Elizabeth demanded.

Seymour chuckled. "*Now* I have bought my wife a magnificent stallion to sire meadows full of foals for her." Seymour nuzzled Katherine's neck. Elizabeth imagined how his mouth must feel, his prickly mustache and beard against that fragile skin.

"Thomas! You must not!" Katherine gasped, but she tipped her head to give him better access.

"I cannot help it. I am exceedingly interested in breeding at present." He flashed a devilish grin. Katherine went red as Chelsea's brick walls, and Kat Ashley tittered, while Lady Calverley scowled at the bawdy jest. Sometimes Elizabeth felt her stepfather enjoyed needling the disapproving lady-in-waiting almost as much as she did. Lord Thomas winked at Elizabeth. "I had best make certain the horse is not murdering my stable hands. The beautiful villain stove in a groom's ribs down in Lincolnshire. Lady Calverley's husband can tell her all about it when next she visits him."

"The stallion is a wild one, then?" Elizabeth asked. God knew she had always loved spirited creatures. And when it came to horses, she knew no fear.

"The man who owned the brute meant to slice off vital bits that would make any man shudder in sympathy."

"May I go to the stables to see him?" Elizabeth asked.

"I think you had better not if this animal is uncontrollable," Katherine said.

"I will keep our princess safe. That hell-spawned beast cannot get loose."

"Please, my lady!" Elizabeth bounced out of her seat. "I beg you!"

"Off with you then," Katherine succumbed. "Shall I come, too?"

"Not today, on my life!" Seymour exclaimed. "It is slick outside. I would not have you fall. It is not worth—" He hesitated. "There will be time enough on a warmer day," he amended. "You must have a care, Kate."

Seymour's tender words aggravated Elizabeth. The way he fussed over his wife's fragility. Life had taught Elizabeth to stand strong.

"Your Grace," Lady Calverley began. "Do you think it wise for the princess to—"

Elizabeth fled the room before Lady Caution could change the dowager queen's mind. Seymour followed, his hearty laugh echoing behind her as he ordered servants to fetch her cloak.

Lord Thomas fastened the garment beneath her chin, his fingers lingering against the place where her pulse beat. "I do not envy Lady Calverley's husband her bed. It is cold as a frozen well, I wager, and harsh as a joiner's rasp."

"She makes me feel wicked even when I am trying to be good."

"So you want to be a dour saint like your sister Mary?" Lord Thomas's impudence delighted Elizabeth. "I cannot wait to share this sight with you, my Tudor cub," he said. The wind whipped Elizabeth's hair as they walked toward the stable. "His name is Hades," Thomas said. "The Lord of the Underworld who carried the woman he desired down to hell."

"I know who Hades is," Elizabeth said primly. "Persephone pleaded to be let go. But he ravished her and kept her for his bride."

"That is what your tutors would have you believe. But what if the truth is far more dangerous? If the story took a direction no man would dare mention to a lady."

"But you will dare. You would dare anything."

He grinned in appreciation. "Only think, Elizabeth. What if the lady's protests were for appearances' sake? Because she was afraid others might think ill of her? Perhaps she was as full of passion as Hades was. What if she wanted to be dragged off to his bed?"

Elizabeth knew she should be offended. And yet there was something enticing about sharing things others were not worldly or free-thinking enough to understand. "There is no scholarly evidence of any such thing."

"Do not consider this through the eyes of a child, Elizabeth. Or the mind of a scholar. But as the woman you are. God's blood, lady, you will drive men to madness in time."

Elizabeth feared her heart would beat right out of her chest. She tried to picture her stepmother's gentle features, hold tight to the kindnesses the lady had done her. *Do you wish to be a dour saint like your sister is?* Seymour's question mocked her. Seymour ushered Elizabeth into the stable, and Elizabeth gasped as she caught sight of the stallion, his coat black as devil's wings, his hooves slashing the air. She was glad there was solid wood between her and the beast.

Haunches bunched with muscle as Hades pulled back on the lead the grooms held. "He scents a mare in heat," Thomas whispered, so close to Elizabeth's ear she could feel his breath, hot on her skin. "It is a good thing I had these stable walls shored up, is it not? Or he would tear through any barrier to mount her." As if the mare in the pasture beyond understood, she whinnied, a primal sound that made tiny hairs on Elizabeth's body stand on end.

"He wants to claim her so badly," Lord Thomas said to Elizabeth. "His seed must be planted. It is his whole reason for being. You understand, do you not?"

"Yes." She shivered, watching the mare.

"Some males have seed more potent than other men's. Mine is, princess." Elizabeth gasped that he should say such a thing to her, but he continued. "I have filled the queen's belly at last."

"That is impossible!" Elizabeth felt ridiculous, betrayed. "She is barren."

"I have quickened her womb where three others have failed, one of them a king."

"But childbirth . . . it is dangerous! She is not young."

"I will not let her die," Seymour said, as if he could order God himself. "Of course, the Church commands that I not swive my wife again, until she is churched after the babe is born. That is hard on a man, to have his natural passions denied. I must deny that which I desire most fiercely."

Seymour's gaze swept the area, saw the stable hands busy with the stud. Seymour drew aside Elizabeth's veil, leaned so close she could not breathe. With fierce tenderness, Thomas caught hold of her throat with his teeth for just a moment, touched her skin with the wet heat of his tongue.

Chapter Seven

May 1564

LONDON

I HAD BEEN A MERE FIVE YEARS OLD WHEN LAST I HAD seen the city. Now I was mistress of my own fate. The bounty of all Christendom lay at my fingertips, the finest booksellers, the most intriguing shops. Vendors hawking wares from rosy berries to horn spoons blended into the cacophony of sound. I could buy all the strawberries and cream I wished with the coins in my coffer. Make myself sick on the tart fruit if I wanted. But the one thing I wanted most of all I could never have again. Time with my father. Even London seemed different without his gentle voice recounting tales that made kings and queens from centuries past seem alive. In my mind I tried to imagine how he might describe the scenes we rode past.

Half-timbered buildings cupped the streets like giant's hands, the upper stories jutting out over the road. Signs above every door named each house something witty or whimsical: The Primrose, The Filly Fair. I wondered how anyone ever found a particular shop in this sprawling city. Even the queen had numerous royal residences scattered within London's town walls so the court could move between them when one place became too fouled for habitation. Considering the number of courtiers and the servants necessary to tend their every whim, the queen made frequent use of Hampton Court and White-hall, Greenwich, and Windsor and others as well. With Elizabeth

Tudor's renowned horror of filth the court moved every few weeks. As for Elizabeth's sensitivity to foul smells, I hoped the queen never happened along this street.

The glitter of wealth mingled with abject poverty. The stench of fish from the river and cabbage from the rubbish heaps mingled with the odor of waste from the puddles where chamber pots had been emptied from second-story windows onto the streets below. A gang of richly dressed youths in drunken high spirits jostled to enter an alehouse, pushing a plump older woman aside. But instead of bearing the indignity in silence, the woman thrust out one plump leg, tripping the most obnoxious of her tormentors, sending him plunging into a pile of horse dung.

A pang of loneliness struck me at the sight. The woman reminded me of Eppie. On my childhood trip to the city she had not bothered trying to distract me from the ugliness of beggars and gallows with the artfulness my father used. She had simply clapped her beefy hand over my eyes to blot out anything she did not wish me to see.

Despite my mother banishing Eppie from my life, I never believed she would disappear completely. I had hoped Eppie would smuggle me a reassurance of her love or at least tell me she was safe. But it was as if one of the sea serpents on my map of the New World had sucked Eppie down where I could never find her. If only she were traveling with me instead of Moll, the day would have been quite perfect, I thought, wistful. Yet, Eppie would have been warning me against Gypsies and vagrants. Almost as if my mind had conjured it, I glimpsed a wee flash of crimson and a tiny feathered cap, a monkey capering upon a Gypsy's shoulder. From my vantage point atop Doucette, I saw the monkey sidle up to a rich merchant's daughter and climb nimbly onto her shoulder to kiss her cheek. Moll clapped her hands, reins and all, in delight. "What a charming little rogue!" she cried, not noticing the monkey's naked hand flash out, pluck a pearl from the woman's hair. The cunning creature quickly tucked its purloined treasure into the front of its tiny doublet.

"Oh, Mistress Nell!" Moll enthused. "Is not London the most delicious place? I wish the monkey would dance over to me."

Since Moll had the simple, well-scrubbed look of a country servant there was little chance of that. Yet I did not want to dampen her joy. "You approve of the city, then?"

"I had not known there were so many people in the world!"

"And not one of them acquainted with a basin of water to wash in," I observed wryly as a litter carried by two gray horses nearly overturned a cartload of bricks. "It will take me hours to scrub this filth from my skin. After ten days of traveling on the road I will be fortunate to make myself presentable to a scullery maid at the palace, let alone a queen."

"How soon after we arrive at the palace do you think the queen will summon you?" Moll asked, so twitchy with excitement, her poor horse should have gone mad hours ago. "What will you say to Her Majesty, Mistress Nell? I vow if I were ever presented to her I would be struck mute. Queen Elizabeth is said to be brilliant. A scholar. And sly. In fact, I have heard she is not a woman at all—but a man in disguise."

I frowned like one of the gargoyles on the church carvings—a glare so sharp it could terrify even the most dedicated sinner to repent. "Quiet, for pity's sake!" I warned.

Moll's voice dropped lower. "My sister went to court with her mistress. She heard the queen spends much time alone with Lord Robert Dudley. There are even those who whisper the queen has borne him a child!"

"Which would entirely disprove the theory that Her Majesty is a man, unless there was some sort of miracle you have neglected to tell me about," I observed.

"You are laughing at me, Mistress," Moll said with wounded dignity. "Everyone cannot be as wise as you and the old master."

She turned her attention to the city again. I was left to contemplate Robert Dudley. He had been prisoner in the Tower when we visited there, though I had never seen him. Robert had watched his father, the Duke of Northumberland, and his youngest brother, Guilford, Lady Jane Grey's husband, make the terrible journey to Tower Hill. Some claimed he had found a way to pass secret notes to Elizabeth while they were imprisoned, that they had fallen in love within those dread walls. Even bribed guards to allow them a tryst. But then, people would latch on to the slightest whisper of scandal to share, even if they knew it was a delicious lie.

The thought of meeting Dudley filled me with excitement—Father had told me the queen's favorite was a most exceptional man: canny enough to keep his head, brilliant enough to match wits with England's finest, sensual enough to bewitch a queen, even though he once had a wife tucked away in the country.

Suddenly I noticed my maid's expression, shadowed from our earlier exchange. Father had warned me often it was unfair to lash out with my wit against someone who had no hope to defend themselves. "Come, Moll," I coaxed. "I did not mean to wound your feelings. Your mind is quick enough when you are not making calves' eyes at Jem."

"Quiet! Oh, I beg you, mistress!" Moll hushed me. "Look, he comes this way!"

Indeed, Jem did, weaving his roan gelding against the flow of traffic. He reined into step beside me. "My lady, Master Crane has just returned with news. The queen is lodged at Whitehall at the moment. That is where you must present yourself."

Whitehall. I remembered seeing the queen's chief residence as a child, and hearing my father's tales of how the Archbishops of York had ruled there in the days before Henry's war with the Pope. The structure stood opposite the burned-out ruin of Westminster Palace, symbols of power and destruction set in sharp relief. The buildings that made up Whitehall were crowded over twenty-three acres and had been a gift from Cardinal Wolsey to Henry VIII before Anne Boleyn had destroyed their friendship forever.

In the end, Anne Boleyn's daughter ruled in the palace that had once been Wolsey's own.

I shivered in delight, feeling the history of it all envelop me, enthrall me. Soon I would be safe inside the palace grounds, under royal protection, my hours beguiled by the most exceptional minds England had to offer. Moll's eager questions from moments ago raised a host of my own. When *would* I meet the queen? What would I say to her? Not something that would make me seem a country-bred girl blundering into her first regal occasion. *But that is who you are,* I could almost hear mother say. *A girl from the country.*

We had turned the corner onto King Street when I saw Whitehall Palace rising out of the confusion. The Holbien Gate—with its turrets and chequerwork facade arched across the northern entry, the massive gatehouse wider than several rooms, its windows sparkling. Beyond those gleaming panes lay lodgings for guards, a store of weapons in case of rebellion, and the mechanism Father had once described to me, holding pulleys and ropes the guards could use to shut the gate if needed to keep an enemy out.

The guards themselves stood vigilant at their post, their red livery a perfect foil for handsome faces, shining halberds in their hands to hold the teeming city at bay.

I trembled, anticipation warring with nerves. That gate—built in all its glory to display the power, wealth, and decorum of the English throne—was the entryway to my dreams.

Crane rode up to a guardsman so tall that he seemed a giant. Calverley's beloved Master of the Horse announced: "Mistress Elinor de Lacey, daughter of the Baron of Calverley, come to wait upon the queen."

The guard's massive hand all but swallowed up the summons that had shattered my mother's peace. He noted the royal seal, then regarded me with frank appraisal, displaying the kindest eyes I had seen since I left home. "Welcome to Whitehall, Mistress," he said with a surprisingly graceful bow for one of his size. "I am Sergeant Porter Thomas Keyes. You look wearied from your journey."

"I am."

"I doubt you will get much peace tonight. A new maid of honor is a most interesting curiosity until the court puzzles you out, so you had best brace yourself."

"And exactly where am I to undergo this scrutiny?"

"You must present yourself to Lady Betty, the Mother of the Maids. It is hard to guess where that poor beleaguered lady is, but one of my men can escort you to the Maids' Lodgings and you may begin your search for her there."

"I thank you for your help, Sergeant Porter."

"I will accept your thanks now, Mistress, because later, you may see me as villain. The women you will serve with may look sweet as cream, but they deal nasty scorch marks if left to their own devices. Keep your wits about you when you are in their company, Mistress de Lacey," he said with sudden gentleness. "And give the maids of honor my warmest greetings and good wishes."

I wondered which lady had scorched him, and to whom he sent greeting. Intrigue already and I had not even crossed the palace's threshold. I gigged my horse forward, remembering my mother's warnings. A shadow fell across me as we passed under the arch, then I gobbled up the palace grounds with my eyes. Beautiful gardens spilled before me, grander than any I had ever seen. Courtyards unfolded, one after another. I had entered a world as different from my own as that of the Minotaur that had once thrilled my child heart with delicious fear. But this was no story to escape into, then wake in my own cozy bed. This was real, I told myself. In these grand chambers my future might still be a riddle, yet one I would solve with my own hands.

This was to be my world. *Mine.*

The world of the Elinor de Lacey I wanted to be.

Chapter Eight

Whitehall Palace

HEN MY GUIDE FLUNG OPEN THE DOOR OF THE Maids' Lodgings the chamber with its clusters of beds and chests and women might have been a Roman bacchanal, it was so different from anything I had seen before. I was not used to crowds of women. Perfumes wrestled each other in the stuffy space. Cloth of every color and pattern swam before my dust-irritated eyes. Quilts and cushions, petticoats and embroidered shifts drooped over every surface. Small chestnut and white spaniels fought over confits some lady had abandoned within their reach, while women in various states of undress squabbled trying to be heard above the din.

I could not help but mark the contrast between this room and my own tidy bedchamber at Calverley with its sun-drenched windows, well-ordered chests, and the fresh-scented rosemary Mother insisted be strewn about the rushes.

I hesitated outside the door as the usher announced me. "Mistress Elinor de Lacey of Calverley." Silence fell in an instant.

A thin-faced blonde froze in the midst of boxing her maid's ear; a handsome dark-haired woman stopped trying on a ruby necklace before a polished metal mirror. A dwarf, her back twisted and her head too large for her tiny body, pushed aside the skirt of a vain-looking redhead to pierce me with a hostile glare. I felt as outlandish as the butterflies pinned upon a bit of cork one of Father's friends had sent from Brazil. I curtseyed, aware the travel dust had turned my gown to the dull muck green of Calverley's cow pond.

"So this is the mysterious Mistress de Lacey." The red-haired beauty twitched her skirts out of the dwarf's grasp as if the tiny woman had spit upon the precious damask folds. "Someone had best order our newest maid a bath and comb her hair for lice or Her Majesty will send her back to Lincolnshire before the sun sets."

My cheeks burned. "It is a long journey from Lincolnshire. I would be grateful for a chance to scrub the dirt of the road away."

A woman with honey-colored curls and a face round as an overblown rose bustled over to me. "You had best beware lest Lettice toss you out with the bathwater. She does not tolerate anyone save the queen having hair more glorious than hers. I swear yours is more fiery gold than any I have ever seen. My name is Isabella Markham."

"You were at the Tower with the princess." My father had told me how loyally Markham had served Elizabeth even in the darkest hours. Suffered the terrible uncertainty of that damp cell, then walked from the dread fortress—but not to Tower Green and the block. Elizabeth had been placed under house arrest at the manor of Woodstock. I imagined the reunion the women shared when Elizabeth was no longer a friendless princess, but rather, queen.

Markham's eyes narrowed as if she had traced my thoughts. "You are a cunning little snip." I was not sure whether she meant it as compliment or criticism. "Have you studied the lot of us before you arrived here? Perhaps Lettice is wise to be wary of you."

"I have not studied you at all. I visited the Tower as a child, and asked many questions about the princess. Sir John Bridges and my father indulged my curiosity."

Markham's eyes darkened. "Curiosity can be a dangerous thing at court."

The flame-haired Lettice flounced over to me. "You will find that out for yourself, Mistress, for all of Whitehall will be turning its scrutiny upon you."

"May I present Lady Lettice Knollys?" Markham said, an edge to her voice. "She is quite a great lady here. And not just in beauty. She is the queen's own cousin. Granddaughter of Mary Boleyn, Queen Anne's sister."

It was no secret that Mary Boleyn's eldest daughter, Catherine Knollys, was King Henry's child. So royal blood flowed in Lettice's veins—unless you believed the Boleyn women were something more sinister. There were many who would claim the proud Lettice was niece not only to a beheaded queen, but to a witch. Lettice made a token curtsey; she looked like a more finely drawn copy of portraits I had seen of the queen herself.

"My mother was still near a child herself when Queen Anne was executed," Lettice boasted. "She stayed with Queen Anne in the Tower and walked with her, even to the scaffold. And when Elizabeth was a neglected princess my mother was her most loyal friend. It broke Elizabeth's heart when my mother chose to flee England for the continent, rather than live under Catholic rule."

Many prominent Protestants had left thus during Mary Tudor's troubled rule. But they had flocked back home when the Catholic queen died.

"There is much Tudor blood in this room." Lettice shook me from my thoughts. "Lady Mary Grey's sister, Jane, thought herself royal enough to steal the crown."

I scanned the women, searching for the one who had grown up in the nursery with the ill-fated nine days' queen. I glimpsed a brown-haired lady with great, soft eyes and a sweet yet lively smile. Lettice followed the direction of my gaze.

"You mistake Lady Sidney for Mary Grey?" she snickered. "The sister of the famous Sir Phillip, bred from one of the handsomest lines in England for that bad animal? Perhaps Lady Sidney could hoist Lady Mary onto a table so our new guest can see her."

At that moment, the dwarf who had glared so sourly stalked within a hand's breadth of me. Craning her head back so far back that her French hood seemed like to tumble off, she crimped her lips together.

I swallowed hard. "You are Lady Mary Grey?"

"I am." Her eyes dared me to doubt her. I know she read my thoughts. I had been certain she was a court fool, her task to amuse the ladies with her capering and her jests. But the blood of both Lancaster and York flowed in her torturously shaped body. She was Plantagenet as well as Tudor. Royal as well as disfigured.

I was groping for words to soothe her when the Mother of the Maids of Honor charged up to me with such force of character I had to lock my knees to keep from taking an involuntary step back. "I am Lady Betty," she said, "and it is my responsibility to see you presentable when the queen summons you. It will be no small task from the look of you. Hot water, at once," she barked at a servant. "Nigh on to boiling. And soap and rags to scrub her."

Moll scoured me scarlet with scented soaps and rinsed the dust from my hair to make me ready to take the oath all the queen's ladies-in-waiting must swear: To serve Her Majesty loyally in all things.

I tried not to fidget as Markham laced up my bodice. She ordered Lady Mary Grey to tie the points of my sleeves, which would attach them to the shoulders of my bodice. Lady Mary had to climb on a stool to reach, her thick hands clumsy, struggling with the laces. I remembered how Father felt when people first saw his scarred face. Even blind, he could feel when the staff recoiled from his deformity. I was half tempted to work the laces myself, to save Lady Mary's dignity. And yet, she was bristly as a hedgehog. She even seemed displeased with the gown chosen for the occasion. It had been plucked out by the other ladies once the contents of my trunks were spread across the cluster of beds the maids of honor shared. The five other women whispered among themselves, fingering my garments as if to measure their worth. Measure *my* worth.

An oozing sensation filled my stomach, but I would not let them see my unease.

Lettice Knollys looked down her nose at me as if my gown had been rummaged from the rag bag. "I think it only fair to warn you, Mistress Nell. You have overturned the hive with this appointment to court. There are few posts for young women this close to the queen. The most powerful families in England were vying to win the privilege for their daughters."

"It is an honor to serve the queen's majesty."

"La, yes. It is easy to understand why men throughout England are eager to have someone to whisper in the queen's ear and gain rich appointments for their sons, exalted marriages for their daughters, settle disputes in their family's favor. You have taken this chance from them. There is no telling how long it will take for another position to open. The hive is swarming with angry bees since you leapt out of nowhere to unseat them."

"And no one has a nastier sting than you do," Lady Mary retorted sourly.

"Did I feel some insignificant creature beating its wings?" Lettice grabbed a feathered fan on a chain at her waist and fluttered it close to her catlike face. "Ah. It was only Crouchback Mary. You will learn to ignore her like the rest of us do, Mistress Nell. She is like a pesky spaniel yapping over nothing. We often tread upon her."

"Then perhaps you should watch where you are going." The retort spilled out. I did not cap my folly with my coup de grace— *Looking down that haughty hawk's nose as you do, you should be able to notice a person right beneath your feet.* Yet my insult stung enough without the cream.

Lady Mary gaped at me beneath her silver headdress. Markham and the others reminded me of sheep waiting to see if two rams were about to lock horns.

I forced myself to smile, but it felt more like a grimace. "Of course," I tried to salvage the moment. "I have no spaniel, so I would not know about them."

"Every lady-in-waiting is allowed one." A fresh-faced girl whose name I could not remember tried to ease the tension in the room. "One spaniel and one servant to lodge at the palace."

"Perhaps Mistress Nell has already found her pet." Lettice patted Mary Grey's head. "You two may share a bed. We have to double up, and no one wishes to be Mary's bedfellow. She snores, what with her squashed-up face."

Lady Mary did not even flush. Yet, I could not help but imagine what it might be like to be the object of such scorn.

At that moment, the door to the maids' lodging swung open beneath one of the ushers' hands. A woman of about sixty years, garbed in bright yellow damask, swept in. Brown hair gathered into an elegant gabled headdress. Soft lines feathered an animated mouth and the corners of eyes that seemed both restless and kind. The other ladies-in-waiting curtseyed. I did the same. The woman bustled over to me, her bead-bright eyes reminding me of a jackadaw who has just discovered a diamond in the dirt.

"So, my dear Lady Calverley's daughter has come to us at last!" The woman clasped my hands. "I am Lady Katherine Ashley."

A murmur told me how astonished the others were at the head lady of the queen's bedchamber taking an interest in a lowly newcomer. In the days after Elizabeth's coronation, Father had told me how the new queen rewarded those who had served her in the troubled years before a crown was placed on her head. Elizabeth had summoned her beloved governess to her side, given her the highest rank of any lady-in-waiting. Katherine Ashley had suffered prison twice because of her loyalty to her royal mistress, and thus shared in Elizabeth's triumph as no one else ever would.

"Mistress Nell is nearly ready for the ceremony, my lady," Mary Grey said. "But she fidgets worse than a child and her gown is hopelessly countrified."

Irritation sparked at me. I had made an effort to defend her and now she was maligning me to Katherine Ashley! Perhaps there was a reason the other maids did not like her. One that had nothing to do with her deformity.

"Peace, Mary," Lady Ashley scolded. "Mistress Elinor looks lovely. There will be time enough later to remake her things more fashionably."

My lips tightened. So my gowns were not up to court standards? These garments my mother had labored over and worried over and packed with so much care?

"Look, now," Lady Ashley clucked. "Mistress Elinor has barely arrived and we have already offended her." The woman touched my arm. "Forgive our bluntness. I fear what is considered quite fine in Lincolnshire is not appropriate in London. I shall summon up women to sew for you as soon as the ceremony is over."

I thought of the coin mother had locked in my coffer. Money I had intended to hoard to buy new books. I remembered my mother's fingers, raw from stitching, not because we had no servants to sew for me, but rather, because she had wished to make the garments with which I would start my new life.

"I am quite satisfied with my gowns," I insisted. "My mother made them for me."

Lady Ashley chuckled gently. "Lady Calverley has been away from court too long to know the fashions. Let us begin again, my dear. Forget Lady Mary's unfortunate blunder. She is a tiresome creature at best, and at worst—well, I believe she enjoys prickling things up so others are as uncomfortable as she is."

Lady Mary busied herself applying more pins to my bodice, but I glimpsed a hint of something I had not seen before. Vulnerability?

"Uncomfortable, bah," I heard Mary mumble. "Who isn't uncomfortable with the head lady of the bedchamber barging into the Maids' Lodgings? It is hardly fitting."

"Perhaps that is why no one sent for me as I directed." Lady

Ashley shot Mary a quelling glare, then turned back to me. "I asked to be told the moment you arrived, Mistress Nell. Your mother and I were dear friends in the old days back at Chelsea Manor. And even before, when Katherine Parr was still queen. Those were dangerous times for all of us. I thank God they are over. And now, here you are! My Elizabeth queen and you to wait upon her. Is that not glorious indeed?"

"It is." I put injured pride behind me and warmed to the woman's welcome.

"Yet I swear I would never have guessed you belonged to Thomasin had I not known you were coming to court. You look nothing at all like your mother."

"Father said I was independent from birth, determined to look like myself."

Ashley's features softened. "We were grieved to hear of his death. I met him several times over the years and found him a most knowledgeable man. So bold in his thinking he might have been taken up for heresy had he not been wise enough to remain in Lincolnshire."

"Father was in danger?"

"That is why your mother forbade him to come to court. If King Henry could not ask him the questions, your father could not answer. England lost a great thinker when John de Lacey died. It must have been a sorrow to him that he had no son to carry his studies forward now he is gone."

I thought of the lessons Father had planned out to guide me. Let the world think he mourned having no male heir. I knew better.

At that instant, there was a voice outside the door, the usher booming out my name. "Mistress de Lacey, you are summoned to the Presence Chamber, there to take your oath to the queen."

"Are you ready to reacquaint yourself with Her Majesty?" Kat Ashley asked.

"That is what I have come here for." My heart flipped with anticipation, excitement. I tipped my chin up, proud in the gown my mother had made for me, despite Lettice Knollys's scornful gaze.

Lady Ashley laughed, tucking a tendril of flyaway red beneath my French hood. "It is a good thing for a woman to know what she wants, Nell de Lacey."

"The danger comes when she takes it," someone murmured. Lettice Knollys? Mary Grey? One of the other women who eyed me with curiosity or disdain? I would never know.

Chapter Nine

That Evening

HE RICH LABYRINTH OF CHAMBERS WE WOUND through pressed hot and close with people. Faces blurred. Colors clashed. Rich raiment battled for notice as the nobles and gentlemen and ladies tried to outdo each other in grandness, thus capturing the queen's attention. Yet I did not have to jostle for precedence that day, not even with the finest specimens England had to offer. They split before me, as if an enchanted sword had cleaved the path, and I glided down the Presence Chamber's length. Every eye locked upon me, courtiers taking my measure the same way the queen's ladies had.

What kind of cat is this one? I now know they were thinking. *Is she a nobody like Crouchback Mary, to be ignored? Or is she someone who might displace me in the queen's favor? Let her be a pawn I might be able to use in my own selfish quest.*

My heart lodged in my throat as I made my way toward the cloth of estate, its canopy bright in torchlight. Yet more daunting still was the remarkable woman who sat in a throne beneath it. I thought of Father and the night he had carried me up onto the Tower wall. Never had Copernicus's theory about the sun being the center of universe seemed more absurd. How could anyone believe that we spun around the sun? It was not the center of the universe. She was.

Her whole person blazed with jewels. Her glorious hair shimmered beneath her crown. And her face . . . I hardly dared to look at it, fearing it would blind me the way Father warned me might happen if I stared straight into the sun. Yet I could not resist the pull of that face, layered with strength from the trials she had endured. Elizabeth, cloaked in majesty so overwhelming it was as if God had fashioned her to show his angels, saying "This woman is everything a mortal queen should be." Nowhere in this majestic figure was there any hint of the frightened girl Elizabeth Tudor had been. Before me in royal splendor was a stranger who both fascinated and unnerved me. I curtseyed deep and the queen inspected me. Deliberately, she took my measure. I nearly jumped out of my skin when she spoke.

"And so, you have come to my court at last, Mistress Elinor de Lacey."

"Yes, Your Majesty." I met her gaze.

She gave a small nod, as if passing judgment on a test. "I confess I was surprised to receive your father's request that you come to serve me, Mistress. Lord Calverley attended court only when dragged by his shirt points, as I recall. He preferred libraries and the colleges at Cambridge, as my tutor Roger Ascham did."

"My mother spent much time in the royal household before I was born," I said.

"I remember it well. In the reign of my beloved stepmother, Queen Katherine Parr. Are you ready to serve me as loyally as Lady Calverley did my stepmother, Mistress Elinor? She was with the dowager queen until that lady died."

"It is my deepest wish to serve you with the loyalty my mother showed the dowager queen. My lady mother loved Her Grace very much."

"Yes. Lady Calverley was capable of great loyalty. And stubbornness against those she chose not to like." Elizabeth's eyes narrowed. "She was never good at hiding her displeasure. Neither was I. That is why I was astonished to learn it was your mother's wish to place you in my household."

I swallowed hard, feeling the sensation I would revisit so often at court. That sense of dangling from London Bridge, my fingers starting to slip. "My lady mother was excited that . . ." The lie began to slip out, but I could see the queen's intelligence ready to cleave the truth from me. "My mother was not pleased with my coming here. It was my father's wish. And my own."

"Honesty is a rare quality at court," the queen said. "I had heard there was no small unpleasantness before you left Calverley Manor."

I chose my words with care. "You will not regret bringing me here, Your Majesty."

The queen's nostrils pinched. "Who are you to tell me what I will or will not regret? I will decide the worthiness of those who serve me."

"Yes, Your Majesty. I did not seek to offend you."

"And yet you have. Perhaps I shall see what my trusted advisers have to say about you. Lord Robert?" A man stepped from the crowd. Tall, with a chestnut beard and a horseman's well-honed frame. Lord Robert Dudley, the childhood friend and rumored lover of the queen. I recalled Moll's prattle about the babe the two made together, foolish gossip I was sure, and yet my gaze dropped to the floor, fearing they might be able to read Moll's folly in my eyes.

"What do you think of my newest maid of honor, my lord?" The queen asked Dudley. "As Master of the Horse you have an eye for a likely filly. Is she beautiful?"

Dudley shrugged, barely glancing my way. "How will we ever know? Your Majesty shines so bright, no man will ever notice the poor child."

Elizabeth smiled and in that moment I saw the truth pass hot between them.

"Then I shall bind the girl to me, Robin. And you shall keep your pack of dogs at bay." The queen gestured to the cluster of men Dudley had just left. Handsome, arrogant in their wealth, yet my father had told me the queen gathered only the finest minds around her. I relished the thought of jousting wits with them as others might tilt with lances.

One man stood out even among so fine a display. Black hair gleamed beneath his green cap, white plumes fastening up one side with a pearl brooch. His eyes fixed on me; from his left ear dangled a single earring, a misshapen pearl pale against his skin.

"Mistress Elinor." The queen's voice. Sharp. I jumped, unable to hide the fact that she startled me. "Do you think you can stop gaping at Sir Gabriel long enough to take the maid's oath?" Out of the corner of my eye, I could see him smile, so smug my cheeks burned. "I hope this inattention to duty when faced with a handsome man is not a clue to your future behavior."

"He is not at all handsome, Your Majesty." It was true. Everything about Sir Gabriel was a trifle roughened—his jaw shadowed with a hint of beard, his teeth just the slightest bit uneven. "She does not think you handsome, Gypsy's Angel," the Queen observed. "What say you to that, sir?"

"Perhaps Dr. Lopez could fit her with spectacles," Sir Gabriel replied.

The queen guffawed, setting the rest of the room laughing. "You have wounded one of court's leading gallants, and you not in my presence yet an hour, Mistress Elinor. You are most amusing. A trait your mother never shared."

"I am . . ." An *idiot*. "Your Majesty, I am very nervous."

"If you have managed this much mischief in so short a time, I will be eager to see what you might accomplish in a week. Yet, be wary. You have insulted my gallant Angel. He will demand satisfaction. Sir Gabriel is recently returned to court. I banished him for nearly murdering one of my other courtiers. Tell us, Sir Angel. Will you be challenging my newest maid to a duel since she has wounded your pride?"

"Never! Your Majesty did forbid me after the last one. I am, as ever, your obedient servant."

"Pah!" the queen said, but her mouth curved with sensual

invitation. "You are a bad dog, Sir Gabriel, and you always will be. But you wear my collar."

"Until I die." The knight swept her a bow.

"Let it not be a traitor's death as your father's before you. I remember that your head was to be the next to fall were it not for a royal pardon."

"That narrow escape taught me *some* caution, Your Majesty. You know how fastidious I am about keeping my collars white. Bloodstains can be beastly to get out."

"As Ashwall discovered during the duel when he lost his left ear."

"I hope that in the future he will use his remaining one to listen, Your Majesty."

"You would do well to heed your own advice!" the queen snapped.

Sir Gabriel swept his cap from his head. "I seek to please you in all things. As I hope your new maid of honor will do."

"She does not think you handsome. That pleases me at present. Handsome heads are often the first to roll. Mistress Elinor," the queen commanded, "you will kneel before me."

I did as she bade me, took my oath then kissed the ring of state upon her finger. I pledged myself to Elizabeth Regina. Queen of England, Ireland, Scotland, and France. I was far too innocent to guess what the cost of that day would be.

❦

AFTER THE COURT had supped, and the palace was washed red with torchlight, Lady Ashley signaled the Mother of the Maids that she wished to be left alone with me. Lady Betty gave a brisk nod, then shooed my fellow maids of honor off to their lodgings for the night. "My dear, that was a most unfortunate encounter you had today," Lady Ashley said, her kind face lined with worry.

"I am sorry. The last thing I wanted to do was step wrong-footed where Her Majesty is concerned."

"Your first meeting with the queen went well enough. It was the slap you dealt Sir Gabriel Wyatt's vanity that makes me fear for you."

I remembered how his gaze had followed me the rest of the night. "He treated my blunder as a jest, did he not?" I asked, hoping it was so.

"Mark me well, Elinor. You do not want to draw this man's attention. And claiming a man who has seduced half the women at court holds no allure for you—you might as well have thrown down a gauntlet. He will set out to seduce you, or discredit you, or unearth some secret he can use against you. Sir Gabriel demands satisfaction in blood for slights done to him, because his father was a traitor and his mother a whore. He is not to be trifled with."

"And yet, the queen called him Gypsy's Angel?"

"Gypsy is Her Majesty's name for Lord Robert because he is so swarthy of face. Sir Gabriel is Dudley's man, blood and bone."

"That does not explain the 'Angel.'"

"It is a fine irony. Sir Gabriel will never wear a halo, but he possesses the ability to charm people into confessing things no sane person would reveal anyplace but heaven's gates."

I was unnerved, thinking of the forbidden books tucked in a hidden compartment in my writing desk. "It is a good thing I have no secrets for him to expose," I lied.

"You will have." Wisdom filled Kat Ashley's eyes. "Court breeds intrigue."

"Perhaps if I begged pardon . . ."

"Sir Gabriel would never consider the debt paid unless you announced it to every man or woman who was in the Presence Chamber tonight. And that kind of display the queen would find unseemly."

"My lady mother warned me to curb my tongue once I arrived at the palace or I would find myself in trouble." I remembered the dread in my mother's eyes when she watched me ride away. I had not expected Lady Ashley's expression to mirror hers on my very first day!

"I will never forget the weeks after Lady Elizabeth and I joined the dowager queen at Chelsea." Lady Ashley fingered the gold cross at her throat. "Your mother was there, caring for Katherine Parr after the horrors of her marriage. The queen was thin from strain, pale as the ghosts of the wives Henry killed before her."

My eyes widened at Kat Ashley's boldness. The woman shrugged. "I am speaking the truth. The axe hovered over Katherine Parr's neck from the moment Henry Tudor put his nuptial ring upon her finger. When the queen did not get with child we all knew the king's eye would wander. Once it did, she would go the way of the others. Truth is she would have died, if it had not been for your mother."

"My lady mother?" I echoed, astonished. "What had she to do with it?"

"Lady Calverley saw the queen's great enemy drop a bundle of missives in the garden. Lord Chancellor Wriothesley was looking so fiendishly pleased with himself that your mother—" Lady Ashley made a wry face. "Forgive an old woman's prattle. Your mother must have told you this tale a score of times."

"My lady mother never speaks of her years at court."

Lady Ashley glanced away. "Little wonder." She plucked a loose thread from her sleeve. "There was much to grieve over then."

"Please tell me what happened."

"Your mother brought Wriothesley's papers to Queen Katherine. The bundle contained a warrant for the queen's arrest, signed by King Henry himself."

I pictured mother stumbling across such terrifying documents. I imagined her indecision. She was far too practical not to guess what would happen to her and to my father if Katherine Parr's powerful enemies discovered who had thwarted their plans.

If the queen was sent to the Tower, what trouble would it be to imprison the ladies who loved her? It would not be the first time Henry Tudor condemned one of his queen's loyal servants to the axe. And yet, mother had not done the sensible, practical thing. She had not dropped the documents as if they were afire, left them for someone else to stumble upon. Why had she never told me of her courage?

"The queen went mad with terror when she read the warrant," Lady Ashley said. "I was told her weeping could be heard throughout the halls. But her ladies called good Doctor Wendy to tend her in her distress. He and your mother and Lady Herbert, the queen's own sister, bade Katherine gather her courage. If she could mend things with the king she might yet live."

I tried to imagine going to such a man, pleading for your life. He was her husband. He had taken holy vows to bind himself to her. He had shared her bed. Professed to love her. Promised to protect her. What would I feel if I had been in my mother's place? If the life of someone I loved hung in the balance, in the power of a capricious king who had already sent two wives to the block?

"And so Queen Katherine spoke to the king, brave lady," Kat continued. "She outwitted Wriothesley and the Catholic Bishop Gardiner who hated her. She even held Henry Tudor at bay, vain, cruel monster that he was. She staved off her destruction, but all the court knew she had stayed death's hand only for the moment. Another attack would come, and next time her odds of surviving it would be smaller still."

"But the queen lived." It was fact now, the suspense over. Yet my mother would not have known how her friend's story would end.

"She paid a high price for her reprieve." Lady Ashley paced to the window, stared out at the starless night. "In their quest to bring Queen Katherine down, Wriothesley and Gardiner hunted others who loved the Reformed faith. They found forbidden books, used that evidence to put one of the queen's Lincolnshire friends upon the rack. They hoped to wring proof to condemn the queen from the poor soul. In the Tower's history it had never been done before—to torture a gently born woman. When the Lieutenant refused to carry out the orders without the king's express consent Wriothesley worked that hellish device with his own hands."

My gorge rose at the image her words painted.

"Queen Katherine dared not intercede for Anne Askew, dared not plead with the king to show mercy. She had to sit by, helpless, silent while they burned her at the stake."

I had heard of the Protestant martyr, how they had to carry her broken body in a chair to convey her to Smithfield. Even those eager for the entertainment of an execution had been horrified by what Wriothesley had done to her.

"Did my mother know Anne Askew well? Never once did she say so."

"What would she tell you? We were all ashamed of not speaking on Anne's behalf, those of us who believed in the Reformed religion. We deserved the stake as much as she did. But no one could save Anne Askew, even if they sacrificed themselves."

"I wish I had known what Mother suffered." *What difference would it have made? A* voice demanded in my head. *You would not have remained at Calverley.*

"It was mere luck that the king died before he grew bored enough, or lecherous enough, to draw up another warrant for Queen Katherine's death. Then quickly as it began, the nightmare was over. After the king was buried, we were all sent off to Chelsea."

I imagined the relief that must have surged through my mother, and all who loved the queen. The joy.

"My princess grieved for her father," Ashley said. "She *was* but ten years old. But she bloomed like roses in her stepmother's care, happier than I had ever seen her until . . ."

"Until?" I asked, caught up in the toils of her story.

"Until Lord Admiral Thomas Seymour rode through the manor gates," Lady Ashley said. "He was such a bold rogue. Some say the most magnificent man who ever trod upon English soil. Yet he had one fatal flaw, the Lord Admiral did."

"What was that?"

"He was far too easy to fall in love with. Perhaps if I had watched more carefully then, so much pain could have been avoided." She caught my hand, squeezed it. "It was all a long time ago. I am far more cautious now. Which is why I speak to you so frankly, Mistress Elinor. To warn you of the damage one man can do."

"Call me Nell. Please." I did not know why it mattered so much to me to hear my name spoken as it had been my whole life through.

"Nell, then," Lady Ashley echoed. "I beg you to heed this warning if you never listen to another word I say. Sir Gabriel Wyatt is no man to trifle with. All the court knows that Lord Ashwall got off cheaply."

"The man he dueled with?"

"Yes. If the Angel takes a dislike to you, you may envy his lordship."

"Sir Gabriel can hardly cross swords with a woman!"

"He will duel with wits ruthless as his weapons. When he draws them, Mistress Nell, I fear the Gypsy's Angel might demand you forfeit that which you love most."

The back of my neck prickled. "I do not understand."

"Ashwall was vain of his looks, so the Angel cleaved off his ear. Frances Weller valued his reputation, Sir Gabriel ruined his sister. Whatever Wyatt deems a fitting sacrifice he will claim—your virtue, your honor, your wealth."

"My virtue is in no danger from such a scoundrel," I said. "That I know for sure."

"Here at court you know nothing for certain. Everything is illusion. It turns and turns about until none of us knows what is real."

I thought of home, where honest Crane would soon return to gentling the horses. Jem with his crooked smile, mother who spoke so bluntly I doubted she had ever uttered a falsehood. *For three generations these people have depended upon the de Lacey family for their lives, their crops, their cottages. They depend upon you, now, Nell, in your father's place.*

I remembered the Lacey crest glowing like jewels in the library window. Our family emblem: the hawk, that slight, valiant bird who challenged predators to draw them away from its nest, wolves and bears, hounds and wildcats. That is what I must do as well—swoop and dive, never betraying home by glancing back toward Lincolnshire.

Do not let him know what you treasure, I heard my mother whisper in my head. But Father was already beyond Sir Gabriel's reach. What could that Devil's Angel do? Scrape all the learning out of my brain and burn my books? Yet was that not how they had cornered Anne Askew? Discovering forbidden books in her rooms?

"Lady Ashley, thank you for your kindness to me."

"Your mother and I did not part as I would wish. I regret much that happened during the time we shared the same roof. She tried to warn me of danger then. I would do the same for her daughter."

What had my mother warned Lady Ashley of?

"Now, you must be off to bed," Kat insisted. "You will have a busy day tomorrow, your first full day at court."

I smiled, suddenly exhausted. "Is it possible I only just arrived?"

"It is." Kat surprised me by kissing my cheek. I realized in that moment no one had done so with just that sort of simple affection since Eppie left Calverley Manor. "And you have already won yourself a loyal friend."

I retired to the Maids' Lodgings, plunging into the barely controlled chaos of six young women being stripped by their servants, their clothes being brushed and laid away, creams applied to faces, and bodies burrowing beneath covers.

After Moll slipped my night rail over my head, I squeezed myself onto the very edge of the bed I was to share, rigid with the effort to keep from touching Lady Mary. My new bedfellow claimed the champion's portion of the mattress, her short limbs flung wide. Tonight, I was too troubled to haggle over territory. My head was crowded with all I had learned about my mother. As time toiled on,

Lady Mary did indeed snore, but so did everyone else. If I had been at home, Moll would have been sleeping nearby instead of a room away. I could have let the familiar sound of her breathing woo me to sleep. But tonight, shadows writhed against the wall, the flames reflected from the hearth, and I was haunted by images Kat Ashley had planted in my mind.

The Next Day

I AWOKE NEXT MORN TO THE RUDE POKE OF MARY GREY'S elbow in my ribs and Lady Betty's sharp warning. "The queen does not tolerate tardiness in her servants, Mistress Elinor. And unless I miss my guess you have much to learn."

I leapt up, eager as Moll garbed me in another of the gowns my mother had worried over. A chaos foreign to my mother's orderly household ruled the Maids' Lodgings. Women and servants darted here and there, retrieving gowns, searching out lost earrings, dressing night-tangled curls. But the other maids hastening about had been raised from the cradle to serve in the household of a queen. I had not even paid a *visit* to the court because of my mother's aversion to it. I had read the book Clarissa Barton had given me and gleaned what I could to fit me for life at court. But in truth I had as little idea what was expected of me as my mother had had of the latest court fashions.

All day I was at Lady Betty's mercy, drilled in lessons far more difficult for me to master than Latin: how to serve the queen her dinner upon bended knee; how to replenish her majesty's writing implements, refresh the inkwell, sharpen the quills; how to turn back the royal bed for the royal good night and make it up again once she arose. The Mother of the Maids played the role of queen, while I struggled to get each official detail correct, feeling sick at the thought of blundering. That night, after dinner in the Great Hall with its cacophony of voices and over-rich food, I went to bed with my head aching and dreamed of Lady Betty labeling me hopeless as I snagged the queen's gowns and spilled ink across royal dispatches.

But remaining in my nightmare would have been preferable to facing reality when Lady Betty pounced upon me before dawn, lips pursed in disapproval.

"You are far from ready to attend Her Majesty, yet the queen is determined you will wait upon her this morning. Try not to shame yourself or me."

As Moll's deft fingers fastened my gown I vacillated between elation and dread. Had I not come to London to be near Elizabeth? And yet, Lady Betty was right. I was not ready. To make mistakes before the queen would be humiliating indeed.

Lady Betty escorted me and two of the other maids into the Presence Chamber, where, Lettice whispered, the queen spent most of her working day. People were already gathering in hopes they could get the queen to listen to their petitions. The Usher of the Black Rod guarded the entrance to the queen's private apartments. He stood aside, allowing us access to chambers where only a privileged few were permitted access.

I gaped at the vast portrait spanning the wall of the Privy Chamber, Holbien's masterpiece, an image of Henry VIII and his father, Henry VII, with their queens. The figures were so lifelike, brimming with such absolute power, I felt as if they glared at me, a whim away from ordering me to the Tower.

We wound through the withdrawing chamber, finally reaching the queen's own bedchamber. I hung back behind the others, trying to take it all in. A silver-topped table glittered with morning light, a chair padded with cushions and a jewelry chest ornamented all over with pearls sat in the corner while the gilded ceiling glowed above. A single small window overlooked the Thames, while draperies of painted silk from faroff India curtained the queen's state bed.

As the ladies of the bedchamber drew back those curtains, they revealed bedposts inlaid with woods of different colors and piles of thick quilts—silk and velvet, gold and silver, decorated with embroidery. The queen sat up, maids unearthing her from the coverlets. My heart began to pound.

"Mistress Elinor," Lady Betty hissed. "Are you going to stand there or make yourself useful?"

Jolted as if from a trance, I did my best to follow Lady Betty's harried instructions during the two-hour ordeal of Elizabeth's toilette. I could not help gawking like Moll as the queen applied her enameled toothpick, then allowed Lettice to rub the royal teeth clean with a tooth cloth. I bumbled the simplest of tasks: all but dropping the silver basin I held for the queen to spit in once she was done cleaning her teeth, then nearly spilling the goblet of watered wine when the queen required a drink.

Elizabeth eyed me askance as I helped Mary Shelton tie a pouch about the queen's waist, the container holding her notes, letters, and important dispatches so she could keep them close at hand. "Did Lady Calverley send me a juggler or a maid of honor?" Elizabeth asked me with a pointed glance. Heat burned my cheeks as Lettice Knollys snickered behind her hand. The queen raised one fine brow. "I seem to remember you clambering over my prison gate like a wee monkey, Mistress Elinor. Where is that nimbleness now?"

"I was but a child and most determined to deliver my prize to you."

"I have sometimes wondered in the years since: Did you look at the locks to see what size was needed?"

"I did not think size mattered," I said, smoothing a crease from the loose gown Elizabeth chose to wear that morning. "Mine was a magic key. Or at least I believed so."

"Magic? Did you weave some sort of childish enchantment over it?"

"No. The key came from one of my father's friends, Dr. John Dee."

"Dr. Dee?" Her gaze turned suddenly sharp. "Yet you did not tell the guard of him when you were questioned."

"No. I feared what they might do. A boy had frightened me with tales of torture before I left Lincolnshire."

"Then we both owe him a debt. If you had told the truth neither of us would be standing here now." The queen's face softened and I glimpsed the princess I had loved. "Seeing you fight, fierce as any tiger, to keep the guard from taking the key away made me hope. If a child was so passionate about seeing me freed, others must be as well. I amused myself in the days that followed dreaming of life beyond prison bars, imagining the sort of people I would gather around me once I was free. People who had the courage to fight for me—like you. So perhaps the key was magic after all."

"I am glad of it."

"And I am pleased you are here, Mistress. Almost as pleased as I am that you did not tell my guard about John Dee's magic. Let's you and I conduct an experiment. See if we suit each other now as well as we did then." Her eyes bathed me in warmth. "God knows, we appear as if we should. Our hair is nigh the same hue." She turned from me as others helped her finish dressing. I could only be grateful I was not required to work any more laces or fasten the clasps of any heavy jewels. I stared at the nape of her neck, the skin pale, the bumps of her spine beneath it unbearably fragile. I recoiled, thinking of an axe blade biting deep.

I joined the queen's other attendants, trailing behind her when she broke her fast in her privy chambers, we maids presenting each dish to her upon bended knee. Once her appetite was sated we hastened to the Council Chamber, where the finest courtiers in the land awaited the queen's pleasure. There the queen danced galliards to "work up some heat." It was exercise of the body she craved, but she generated other kinds of heat in the chamber as well—desire in the men who crowded round her, and ambition, headier than the wine her guests quaffed.

Next there was a council meeting where I waited outside the chamber in case the queen needed aught. The strident voices rose and fell, sometimes penetrating into the small closet where I sat,

straining to listen. The work of a whole nation was being con-
ducted beyond that thick door, I marveled. Decisions that would
plot the course of history, consequences that would be felt a continent away.

We accompanied her to the Presence Chamber, the vast room
thronged with people importuning her with their private pleas. I listened to her attending to their cares, espousing the causes of the
lucky who caught her attention, especially the lowly. She met with
ambassadors, deft as any court fool as she juggled the opposing demands of France and Spain and troublesome Scotland.

But the hours that amazed me most were those Elizabeth spent
handling her vast correspondence, the queen dictating one letter to
a secretary while her own royal hand scribed a second letter *and* she
discussed rumors of a winged invention attributed to Leonardo da
Vinci with one of her ministers at the same time.

Self-doubt warred with elation beneath the lacings of my new
blue gown, one of several exquisite garments that were gifts from Kat
Ashley. Delight at being in the center of all things new was tem-
pered by fear of making a fool of myself among such fearsome intellects, a fate I had dreaded beyond all things from the time Father's
learned friends had first come to call. But I had leapt into court's
churning seas of my own accord, I reminded myself. I must navigate
them as best I could.

A week flew past, a flurry of magnificent sights, delightful entertainments. Though I still felt awkward and dreaded my occasional
blunders, I became more familiar with my new surroundings. I was
congratulating myself on surviving a whole day without spilling
anything when I was faced with a challenge I had not anticipated:
I was forced to play my part in Queen Elizabeth's daily exercise.

Her Majesty began every morn with a bout of dancing that would
tire even the most energetic feet, her chosen ladies partnered by the
most athletic courtiers in the land. My own skills were rusted at best.
We had had little heart for dancing at Calverley as my father grew
ever more ill. I had done my best to escape notice at court when

dancing was in the offing. I watched the proceedings from my dim corner, and there was no question whose hand was prized in the dance beyond all others. Once Calverley's beekeeper had taken me with him to the hives. He bathed the wooden box with smoke, then drew off the hive's top, pointing out the bee's queen. The insects boiled about her in frenzy, feeding her honey. That was how the courtiers behaved around Elizabeth, all of them vying for the queen's hand in the dance. But once the men were forced to relinquish her majesty to "Sweet Robin" Dudley, they went in search of other partners. Today Sir Gabriel Wyatt's gaze fixed on me. Appalled, I attempted to duck behind an arras, but there was no escape.

"Mistress de Lacey, our queen has rejected me again. I pray you take pity on a poor Vulcan of a man with no claim to handsomeness."

"Choose another partner, Sir Gabriel. One not likely to wound your toes."

With the flare of a minstrel he swept one hand to his heart. "I know I must seem the fool trying to take the floor with you. But there is an infirmity of the mind I have suffered ever since I was a boy back in Maidstone. When a horse throws me, I must tame it to my hand or be trampled in the attempt. You are a most delightful mystery. I will come to know you, Mistress. That much I have vowed. I have already wrangled secrets from certain sources."

"No one here knows anything about me!"

"You were born and bred in Lincolnshire."

"You are decidedly misinformed." I took great pleasure in correcting him. "I was born elsewhere. In an old abbey near Cheshunt."

"Cheshunt?" Wyatt frowned. "I believe the queen spent some time there after—" He shrugged a velvet-clad shoulder. "It is of no import. What matters is that my sources have deceived me. Fortunate for me, I only passed your maid a counterfeit angel."

"You had best not trifle with my Moll!" I bristled, all too aware of what quick work a dashing courtier like Gabriel Wyatt could make of my romantic maid's virtue.

"You think I bedded your maid to unravel your secrets?" Wyatt grinned. "I gave your maid an angel, my dear. The coin. Counter-feits of that denomination have been flooding our shores from the Low Countries this past year."

I gritted my teeth, furious with him for mocking me, furious at myself for my reaction. "Why do you not go away?" I snapped. "I do not want to dance with you."

"Faith, what is that necklace you wear?" Sir Gabriel stared at my bosom where it rose above the square neckline of my gown. "Is that trinket what I think it is?"

"It is a gift from my father."

Sir Gabriel pinched up the chain between two long fingers and tugged the disc into the light. He cradled it in his broad palm. "This is no gift to make a vain maid preen before her mirror. I would think you should prefer rubies or emeralds."

"This astrolabe is the most precious thing I own."

"The little maid knows what such a scientific instrument is called?" Sir Gabriel shook his head as if I had thumped it with my fist.

"The *little maid* could take measurements aplenty! Maybe enough to prove that Copernicus is right, that the earth revolves around the—"

Sir Gabriel made a show of bowing to Lettice Knollys as she passed. Fear hollowed the space beneath my ribs, and I wanted to cram my knuckles against my mouth to keep any more rash words from spilling out. What was I doing babbling like that? Challenging the dictates of either church, Catholic or Protestant, could be dangerous. But Copernicus's theory flew in the face of both churches. One of the few things both religions could agree upon would be that whoever voiced such a dangerous theory was a heretic and should be burned at the stake!

"Lady Knollys," Sir Gabriel said in a voice smooth with admiration. "You look passing fair today."

"And you look as if you are up to some dastardly scheme. Are you plotting to rid our newest maid of honor of her maidenhead?"

"There is no danger of Sir Gabriel ridding me of anything at all!"

Sir Gabriel tsked lightly with his tongue. "You will have to learn not to leap like a starving bear at whatever bait Lady Knollys dangles, Mistress Nell," he warned. "Our 'Stinging Nettle' thrives on needling people's tempers. It makes her prey careless when she wounds tender feelings."

"You are not the only one whose tender feelings have been bruised this morn, Sir Knight." Lettice gestured toward the couple withdrawn into the stone window alcove. Both Gabriel and I followed the line of her gaze to where the queen and Dudley stood, locked in heated discussion, the rest of those gathered for the dancing giving the pair wide berth. "I fear there is trouble in Eden." Lettice laughed behind one perfect white hand. I knew she had caught me chafing the scar marring my own hand. I had been piercingly aware of the imperfection ever since Lettice had warned me of the queen's horror of deformity. "Of course, Cecil and Norfolk and the rest of the council are delighted."

"Of course," Gabriel drawled.

"Sir Gabriel, you could benefit from Her Majesty's displeasure, if you were not Dudley's man. Truth to tell, your ambition is rumored to be so great, perhaps you are the one who arranged last night's mischief, now I think on it."

"You flatter me. But since I have no idea what mischief you speak of, Lady Knollys, I can hardly take credit for it."

"The queen sent for Lord Robert late last night."

"That is no great news." Gabriel brushed a loose thread from his tawny velvet doublet. "It was to discuss some tangled matter of national importance, no doubt."

"Such as the most inconvenient death of Dudley's wife?" Lettice's upper lip curled in amusement. I felt a twinge of empathy for the poor woman who had died so suspiciously four years past. Some whispered Robert Dudley had ordered his wife murdered, she being the only obstacle standing between himself and a crown. But Father insisted the theory made little logical sense. The queen of England could never wed a man tainted by such a scandal.

"There is no man the queen trusts more than Lord Robert to ease the burdens she bears," Gabriel said.

"Trust is likely to be in question this morning, since even Dudley's devoted servant had no idea where his master had gotten off to last night."

Wyatt shrugged. "Lord Robert is a very busy man. Even a servant of Tamwith's excellence cannot be expected to know of his master's whereabouts all of the time."

"Perhaps matters at the stable demanded Lord Robert's attention," I suggested, wishing she would take her gossip and Sir Gabriel elsewhere. "When our best mares at Calverley are ready to foal, our Master of the Horse practically sleeps in the stalls until they are safely delivered."

"I think Dudley's absence had more to do with mounting mares in heat, rather than safe deliveries. But then, he is a lusty animal. No one knows that better than the queen. Even she cannot expect him to deny his own nature."

"Dudley has another lover?" I knew it was a mistake the instant I spoke.

"Another?" Lettice's elegant brows winged upward.

"Since his wife died," I amended quickly. Lettice was not fooled.

Mary Grey sidled over, so quiet I wondered how much she had heard. "You should look to your own virtue around Lord Robert," Mary said. "He has a weakness for red hair and reckless wits." With a snort of displeasure, Lettice flounced away, Mary Grey following behind her. Sir Gabriel turned to me. His knuckles brushed my skin as he moved the tiny cog on the astrolabe. "It is good you are not important enough to have made any enemies, Mistress, when you would put such sharp weapons as your devotion to Copernicus in their hands." His warning both chilled and burned me. "You need not look so pale. Your secret will be safe with me." Wyatt looked as if he meant it for a moment, then his lips curled. "At least it will be as long as you make it worth my while."

My mouth went dry. "What do you mean?

"In return for my silence, you must grant me a boon. Payment for favors rendered is the way of life at court."

"What kind of boon?" I asked, trying to keep my voice level.

"Two boons, actually. First, dance with me whenever the queen does not choose me to be her partner."

That would be quite often, I thought, since she so obviously favored Lord Robert.

"Answer now, Mistress Elinor," Sir Gabriel demanded. "Will you dance or no?"

"Agreed." The concession tasted bitter. I remembered what the queen had said. *You are a bad dog . . . but you wear my collar.* Lady Ashley's warning whispered through me as well. "I have to dance with someone. At least you are not shorter than I am. You said there was a second condition?"

"That I may call you what Lady Ashley does. Mistress Nell." He caressed the syllables of my name, turned it to music. I felt as if he had trailed his fingers not just across my throat, but across my spirit. "Mistress Elinor does not suit you, although I could imagine you riding into battle beside your man, bare-breasted, as Eleanor of Aquitaine did so long ago. Yes, I can see passion fire up those magnificent eyes of yours. And so our little game begins."

"I was never fond of games. They are a waste of time. One could be reading."

"Something like Copernicus?" His smile faded. "People have burned for less."

The voices in the corner rose, the queen's shrill. The expectant hush deepened in the room, the minstrels plucking nervously at their instruments, waiting for the signal to begin playing their dancing measure. With an oath, Elizabeth stalked away from Dudley, Lord Robert's handsome face surly.

"Sir Gabriel! I have need of you!" The sound of his name rapped out in Elizabeth's regal voice made the Angel leap to attention. Without so much as a glance at me, he strode to her side. "My Horse Master and I were discussing the traits necessary to create a fine bloodline," Elizabeth said.

Wyatt bowed. "I am certain Lord Robert has given much thought to the matter. He has imported horses from Barbary."

"It is not horses I am interested in at present. My councilors are eager for me to marry."

"All loyal subjects wish for your happiness, Your Grace," Wyatt observed with diplomatic care.

"A fine answer," Elizabeth snapped. "Far better than those I hear from my council. I chose you as my example of what I deem worthy in a mate."

I watched something change in Sir Gabriel's face, a keen, sharp edge to him that had not been present moments before.

"You have many virtues, sir," the queen said. "You are a fine musician. A gifted scholar and a ruthless huntsman." Her eyes lit on me for a moment, and I caught a glint of something dark in her. "Add to that your skill in the dance, Wyatt, and I vow you could partner the Three Graces themselves. Which is why you puzzle me greatly in your choice of a partner this morn. Our newest maid stumbles about as if she were a new colt. She is a country-bred child and has only rustic training. Your talent will be wasted upon her."

I bit the inside of my lip, trying to hide my reaction as the rest of the room laughed in approval. Only one face looked even less amused than mine. Robert Dudley's eyes looked furious.

"Lord Robert, come here." The queen crooked her finger at her favorite as if he were of no more import than the spit boy who turned the roasting meat in Calverley's kitchens. "You are most knowledgeable about such matters. If Sir Gabriel were a horse, would he not be the finest stud in the royal stables? Mated with the prime mare, Sir Gabriel would sire a dozen strapping sons."

"That I cannot tell," Dudley said, a vein in his temple throbbing.

"When judging breeding stock the wisest course is to look back into the fruitfulness of that particular bloodline. The Dudleys have filled their nurseries to bursting for generations. I, myself, was one of twelve healthy babes."

"Yet you did not produce a single child with your own wife, sir. Why is that, I wonder? Perhaps the Dudley fruitfulness is not present in you?" The court gaped, silent.

"I beg you will excuse me," Dudley said, each word weighed like lead. "Since it is obvious Your Majesty has no need of me at present."

"I have no *need* of you at all. You would do well to remember that," Elizabeth challenged him. "Go, Lord Robert. I know that Cecil is perishing to add Sir Gabriel's name to my list of prospective husbands."

Dudley bowed and backed from the room, turning at the door and striding out. I felt a presence at my elbow. Mary Grey, back again. "Lord Robert must be in distress," she observed. "He thought his best hound was locked upon your scent."

"I do not know what you mean," I said.

"It has been obvious to the rest of the court Dudley gave Sir Gabriel orders to sniff out your weaknesses. Everyone knows the Dudley faction's creed is to think and hunt as a pack. Still, it seems the young lion may supplant the older one in time. Sir Gabriel is mad for power and will sacrifice anything or anyone to achieve it. Given the chance he may well devour his master one day. He only lacks the right weapon to unseat him. What is worse, Dudley knows it."

The musicians struck up their opening salvo; I watched the queen dance with Sir Gabriel Wyatt, the two as magnificent as the finest animals in the royal stables.

❈ ❈

FOR A FEW days, the balance of power shifted, teetering on the queen's royal whim. Yet before the week was out, Dudley was back at Elizabeth's side. And I was held to the bargain I had struck with the Devil's own Angel. With each leap, each touch of hands as Sir Gabriel Wyatt swept me across the council room floor, one thing was clear. During our fray the morning Dudley almost fell from grace all the rules had changed.

Chapter Eleven

June 1564

HAMPTON COURT PALACE

HREE WEEKS PASSED BEFORE THE QUEEN MOVED US from Whitehall to Hampton Court, the Surrey palace I was most eager to explore. I was lucky to see it at all, Moll informed me while she stitched a rent in the petticoat of my riding habit. Lettice Knollys's maid had told Moll that Elizabeth had avoided the sprawling redbrick structure since she nearly died of smallpox there two years ago. The queen still insisted the air at Hampton Court was unwholesome. But a group of French dignitaries must be entertained, and Hampton Court glittered on such occasions, every wall shining with gold and silver, the woodwork gilded or painted in vivid hues of red and yellow, blue or green.

More exciting to me than the splendors of this, the most elaborately decorated of all the royal palaces, was the opportunity I intended to seize: to test the mystical mirror Dr. Dee had sent my father, the instrument said to reflect the colors of souls, alive or dead. My mother had little use for such superstitions, but Father and I had been fascinated with the shimmering oval from the first moment we unwrapped it. "Who," Father had insisted, "can tell what device might be scientific and which a fool's trinket? One day we will measure things we do not even know exist. Whole worlds must march along beside us, just as the tiny dimple of an ant's hill conceals a bustling city beneath the turf. Why not a world of spirits?"

When I packed the mirror at Calverley I imagined what it might reveal in the place haunted by Henry's dead queens, determined to see if the gleaming surface could reflect Jane Seymour, who had died after bearing the king's only son; Catherine Howard, who ran through the halls begging to be spared the axe; or Anne Boleyn, whose initial still twined with Henry's on the ceiling of the Great Hall. Spectral images mortals could not see, but that could be reflected in an enchanted mirror—so Dr. Dee claimed.

Most enthralling of all, I wanted to explore the magnificent astronomical clock Nicholas Kratzer had built for Henry VIII, a clock with a sparkling gilt face that showed the workings of the universe—the sun and all the planets revolving around the earth, its vital center. The machine told not only minutes and hours, but the seasons, days of the week, month, and when it was high and low tide upon the Thames. I could not wait to beg entry into the great room where the workings of the clock lay hidden, explore the gears and cogs and inner mysteries, discover how the vast timepiece functioned.

But my excursions would have to wait. For we had barely arrived when I was forced to confront the occasion I had been dreading ever since the other maids had begun to babble about the entertainments our royal mistress loved best. I was country born and bred. I had gone on hunts with Father and Mother and their friends. Attended parties where we had tested our skills with crossbows and bows and arrows, or sailed hawks into the sky to make the kill. But in my eleventh year what pleasure I had taken in the hunt vanished altogether because of what happened one fine spring day. I had concocted tricks ever since to hide my loss of enthusiasm, but they would not save me here at court. Elizabeth loved dancing and the hunt above all things, so I knew I would have to face old demons sometime. But I did not realize that by the time it happened my aversion to the chase would cut me to a far more personal level: I would know exactly the panic the hart must feel, fighting to keep ahead of the pack.

Hounds in human form had been circling me as the weeks bled past, courtiers' eyes feral as they tried to discern why I—a nobody—seemed so high in the queen's royal favor. The tale of the key had been bruited about, but it did not change the opinion of most. *"After all, who is Mistress Elinor de Lacey?"* I heard Lettice Knollys say to Isabella Markham. *"Daughter of a baron who avoided court as much as possible. Daughter to a former lady-in-waiting the queen dislikes and makes little effort to hide it."* Elizabeth's courtiers could not resist the urge to pick at threads of my past, trying to unravel reasons why the queen had raised me so high.

As I mounted Doucette for my first hunt with the queen, I feared she would not look upon me so favorably when we returned to the palace heavier by the weight of several kills. Even Doucette, my sweet-tempered mare, sensed my unease and became restive. Or was it the showy antics of the men trying to impress Elizabeth with their rich velvets and magnificent horses that unsettled my mount? I glimpsed Sir Gabriel among the queen's admirers, his laugh ringing out, reckless as his blood red stallion nipped the arse of the queen's mare. Her Majesty's horse squealed, lashing out with one back hoof to catch the stallion in the shoulder.

"Let that be a warning to you all!" Her majesty called merrily. "That is what happens to rogues who take liberties with the ladies! It is a lesson Sir Gabriel should take to heart. Especially since Mistress de Lacey has been trying to teach him just that these many weeks!"

Everyone in the queen's service was bemused by my behavior toward Sir Gabriel. I danced with him, yes. But the instant the musicians fell silent, I made every effort to avoid him. A circumstance that amused Lord Robert Dudley when he threw us together in games of skittles or hoodman-blind.

The scarf pinned about my throat seemed to shrink. Looping both reins around one hand, I fumbled with the amber brooch that held the length of Lincoln green silk in place. The folds loosened but gave me little relief as Lettice Knollys picked her way toward me on her dainty black palfrey. Her riding habit was the color of lapis lazuli. "Mistress Elinor." She ran her gaze over me with a slyness that made me want to squirm. "You have piqued Sir Gabriel's interest and that of Lord Robert as well. You would do well not to pique anything else belonging to a man. My royal cousin denies herself natural pleasures, and she expects her ladies to remain chaste as she does."

"It poses a greater problem for some of us than others." Lady Mary gave Lettice a snide look from atop her own stocky brown horse; she was clinging to her perch like a misshapen cocklebur.

"It is true there are ladies who love the taste of cream." Lettice glanced at Lord Robin, the queen's beloved. Few except the queen were blind to the times Lettice disappeared from her bed. Speculation was rife as to who might be her lover. "Lady Mary, I know it must be vastly tiresome for you, deflecting the assaults courtiers make on your virtue. But if they importune you too much, you can always hide beneath a footstool with the spaniels. Mistress Elinor is not so fortunate."

I was edgy and angry and wanted Lettice far away from me. The brooch I was attempting to refasten "slipped" in my hand. The point pricked the rump of Lettice's horse; the mare screeched in protest and sprang away from us. Taken by surprise, Lettice tumbled from her horse. Lady Mary stared at me with her overlarge eyes. "You are a very stupid girl."

"It was clumsiness. Nervousness on my first hunt with the queen." That much of my excuse was genuine enough.

"Any fool could see you did that on purpose. Mistress, everyone is wondering why you came to court. You do not care for flirtations or fine gowns. I am beginning to think your sole purpose is making enemies."

I meant to protest, but Mary drew the truth from me. "I am glad Lettice fell. Perhaps now she will stay away from you."

For an instant something flickered in Mary Grey's eyes, then vanished beneath a hard shell. "No. She will torment me worse because you interfered. I do not need anyone's pity. The whole world can mock me all it likes. I have the blood of kings in my veins. One of my sisters was queen for nine days. The other, Katherine . . . she is imprisoned in the Tower right now because Elizabeth fears her."

All at court knew Katherine Grey's crime—secretly wedding the Earl of Hertford, a man whose claim to the throne was as strong as her own, then daring to produce a healthy son, an heir of royal blood where Elizabeth had none.

"We Grey sisters have no stain of bastardy to taint our claim to the throne," Mary boasted. "No one, not even my royal cousin, can take that legacy from me."

"Hush, Mary! It is dangerous to speak so."

"You? Lecturing me on what is dangerous? That is amusing." Her expression shifted, as if she were a dog wary of being kicked. She wheeled her horse away from me. In a moment, I saw why. Sir Gabriel Wyatt wound his way toward me through the crowd.

I leaned close to Doucette's neck, fiddling with her emerald velvet-trimmed bridle, fixing all my attention on my mare in an effort *to what?* Lettice Knollys's spiteful voice demanded in my head. Hide beneath a footstool like Crouchback Mary? That spur made me straighten in my saddle, meet Wyatt's eyes.

"Mistress Nell, it seems neither of our horses is in the mood to play well with the rest of the beasts," he said, with a knowing smile. "We shall ride together."

It was not a question, and I knew him too well now to try to dissuade him.

As the company raced through the woodland, I admired his horsemanship. He rode as if he were one with the magnificent animal beneath him. We splashed through streams, leapt fallen trees, pushing each other to new heights, faster lengths, until either of us would have considered a broken neck a small price for besting the other. We passed the rest of the riders, my mare and his stallion outstripping each until only the queen and Robert Dudley surged ahead of us. The hounds bayed sweet music, and then my heart sank as a doe sprang from the underbrush, her eyes ringed white with terror as she ran for her life.

Shouts of triumph rang out as we gave chase. I reined in a little, wishing to be as far to the rear of the party as possible when the inevitable happened. I prayed Sir Gabriel would be so caught up in the fray he would stay at the head of the pack. But no. He checked his own horse, staying close. A crossbolt sang through the air, the queen herself piercing the deer's glossy hide. The doe staggered, blood blooming on her side as her hooves scrabbled for purchase. But even the desperate will to survive could not save her. The doe's legs buckled. My stomach lurched as the animal struck the turf, the dogs snapping and snarling around her, only the Master of the Hounds keeping them from tearing the doe apart.

The Master of the Hunt dismounted and drew his long knife. "And who should have the honor of slitting the animal's throat if not Her Majesty?" He shouted. The doe raised her head, as if she could understand every word. A cry of approval went up from the party. I tried to smile, my hands sweating in their leather gauntlets. I trapped a rein beneath one arm, stripping a glove off with my other hand so I could rub the dampness from my palm. *It will all be over soon*, I told myself as I repeated the process to bare my other hand. The queen motioned to the crowd and it fell quiet. "I have killed many a deer on royal hunts, but today we have among us one who has never ridden behind my royal hounds. One who has pleased me greatly these past weeks. Come forward and take the knife, Mistress Elinor de Lacey!"

Every gaze fixed upon me. *God, no.* I pleaded silently. But there was no escape. A polite smattering of applause broke out. "Your Majesty, I do not deserve such an honor," I averred.

"I say you do." The queen frowned. "Do you know better than your queen?"

"No, Majesty. Of course not. I am most honored."

"Then dismount at once and finish this beast."

Before I could make myself move, Sir Gabriel was standing on the ground holding Doucette's reins while a groom took charge of his stallion. The Angel helped me from my saddle, making it seem as if he were taunting me. I prayed he did not detect my knees shaking as I landed upon the ground. The Master of the Hunt pressed the knife into my hand, the hilt smooth ivory inlaid with tiny gems. I had to clutch the weapon so hard it seemed the carbachons would embed themselves in my palm forevermore.

The huntsman wrenched the helpless doe's head up again, and I could not help thinking it was the creature's last glimpse of sky. She made faint effort to struggle, but the fight in her was gone, her throat with its white patch exposed. There was no escape for either of us now. I forced my hands to move. The blade's edge bit deep, the deer giving a wet, gurgling sound. Hot blood gushed over my hand. *You must not faint,* the warning drummed in my head as whoops of approval filled the air.

"We will all dine on venison this night!" I forced myself to call out. The queen dipped her fingers in the doe's blood. She smeared a streak on my left cheek, then my right. "A brave show you have made today, Mistress Elinor!" she cried. "Now, let us away to find this animal's mate. It will be mercy to kill him as well, will it not?" she asked Dudley and the other men. "You males are forever saying your lives would be worth nothing were I not here to receive your love. We do not want the stag to suffer."

Raucous laughter blurred around me, the men vying for her attention as they galloped off. I cannot remember how I got back on my horse. I believe I rode a quarter of an hour before I feigned the need to answer a call of nature. I climbed down from Doucette, grateful as the music of the hounds faded away from me, the hoofbeats of the other riders softer, until distance muffled them to silence.

Alone, I stumbled to the mossy bank of a stream, sank down to my knees. I plunged my bloody hands into the water, splashed the bracing wetness against my blood-daubed face. I scrubbed at my cheeks with the edge of my cloak, not caring if I spoiled the garment, not caring about anything but obliterating the metallic stench of the doe's blood. But before I could finish, the image of her throat rose in my mind, the bite of blade, the gurgle of her last breath, the hot cascade of scarlet over my hands.

I could hold back no longer. I retched into the grass. Retched until my hair tumbled from my headdress and it seemed my insides should spill onto the ground. Then fingers gathered my straggling hair back out of my way. When my vision cleared, I could see the toe of a man's boot. I was too spent to fight when its owner pressed a silver gilt flask into my hand.

"Drink this." Sir Gabriel brooked no argument. "Do it, Nell. It will rinse the foul taste from your mouth."

I choked, but whiskey burned away the terrible taste, leaving a mellow heat of its own. My stomach did one last flip, then settled back to its natural place.

"There." Gabriel stroked my hair gently. "Good lass."

I swiped my mouth with my hand. "I fear breakfast did not agree with me."

"For God's sake, woman, you have barely caught your breath. Do not waste it lying." He corked the flask, tucked it away. "There is no one here but me, Nell."

"I am better now." I started to climb to my feet.

"You are gray as ash. Sit down before you fall down." He pressed me back to the ground. "You may have hair near the queen's own shade, mistress, but you lack her stomach for the kill. You were wise to hide that from the others. Blood scent is dangerous whether hounds catch it or humans." Wyatt's stallion whickered to my mare. "Easy, Archimedes," Sir Gabriel soothed him. "Steady, lad."

"Archimedes is your horse's name?" I could not hide my surprise.

"This clever lad had an inventive gift for befuddling even the finest masters in my stables, so I named him after the Greek inventor who built war machines to terrorize the invading Romans. He held the invaders at bay for—"

"I know who Archimedes is."

"I would wager anyone who knew of astrolabes should." His stallion nudged him with a velvety nose, demanding to be stroked, as hungry for affection as my Doucette. I remembered the Gypsies at Lincolnshire fair who bewitched my childhood pony. Later I would wonder if the Gypsy's Angel had somehow enchanted me. What other reason could I have had for speaking so honestly?

"I was once able to hunt without a second thought," I confessed, climbing to my feet. Sir Gabriel cupped a hand beneath my elbow to steady me.

"What changed?" he asked.

"The year I turned eleven years old a savage dog got loose near my father's manor house. Our Master of the Horse, Crane, tracked it down. I followed him, though I was not supposed to. When Crane caught up to the dog, it had a fawn by the leg. Crane killed the dog and was knocking up an arrow to do away with the injured deer when I rushed out of the woods and flung my arms around the fawn. It is a marvel she did not kick my brains in."

"It is a wonder your father did not turn this Crane fellow out on the streets for putting you in such danger. I would have."

"I was horrified and Crane loved me. He slung the fawn over his shoulders and the two of us carried her back to the stable and washed the bites with wine. She should have died, and yet, somehow she managed to live. I named her Grace."

"Grace," Sir Gabriel echoed.

"She drove my mother to madness, following me about inside the manor house, stealing pippins from the cook, getting into the garden, tearing the wash off the bushes so she could eat the leaves. When Grace destroyed the herbs used for physicking, mother could bear it no more. She made the gamekeeper take her far out into the woods where Grace would not find her way back. A month later she was dumped on the doorstep of the larder. A 'gift' for my father."

"Perhaps it was some other deer."

"There was no mistaking Grace. Her hind leg was scarred where the dog attacked her. I have never been able to forget the moment I saw her, her throat dark with dried blood. Since Grace . . ."

Wyatt squeezed my shoulder. "Grace. It is a good name for you, as well."

"You surprise me yet again, Sir Gabriel. I never expected you to be kind." He cupped my cheek in one broad palm, and kissed me. Warm, coaxing, then he pulled away. "I am not kind," he said gravely. "I am every bad thing people claim I am. Never forget that, Grace."

His kiss haunted me that night, and every night after, from that moment on. I could not drive the sensation away—feeling stripped bare by the confession I had made to Sir Gabriel. Why in God's name had I done such a thing? Since the day Crane helped me bury my beloved deer beneath Grace's favorite apple tree I had spoken to no one about my pet.

❧❧❧

THE NEXT DAY, when the queen was sequestered with the French diplomats and I was relieved of duty, I attempted to distract myself from disturbing thoughts of the scene beside the stream. I wrangled entry to the tower where the Kratzer clock traced the hours, marveled at the intricate machinery as it whirred, set in motion by the heavy weights that dangled on thick chains.

I returned to the Maids' Lodgings and concealed Dr. Dee's mystical mirror in the folds of my kirtle, then summoned Moll from the servants' quarters.

"Mistress Nell, I dare not be gone long," Moll said as I led her through the palace. "Isabella Markham's maid says there is a most important lady coming to teach us how to prepare ruffs as they do in the Low Countries. There is something called starch which will make the folds stiffen out most elegant."

"Starch?" I scoffed. "Where is your sense of adventure, Moll? Surely you would not rather fuss about how stiff my ruff is than see Anne Boleyn's ghost?"

"If I am to be your maid I would as soon your ruffs be a credit to me," Moll insisted. "Besides, I cannot think it wise to go seeking ghosts. Jem says they can stick to you so you will never be free of them."

"Bah! Jem also claimed the reason Widow Gummidge raised

more cream from her cows was that she dipped a hanged man's hand in the milk bucket. Now hasten along and stay quiet. The gallery should be deserted and we'd not wish to startle any spirits that happen to be lurking about."

With a visible shudder Moll moved closer to me, the tread of her slippers softer on the rush-strewn floor. I glimpsed the entry to the gallery ahead and my grip on the mirror tightened.

"They say that there was a great ugly lump upon Queen Anne's neck," Moll whispered. "A devil's mark."

"If she was so monstrous why would the king have desired her so desperately?" I asked.

"A charm, maybe. A love philter? Some dark witchery. Some say a black owl flew into her chamber and dropped a strangled cat upon her bed the day they chopped off Sir Thomas More's head."

We stepped into the gallery, the long room deserted, hushed, somehow, expectant. I drew the mirror from its hiding place, unnerved by shapes from the trompe l'oiel murals that decorated the walls. Painted tables that thrust into the room with angles that were not there. Cherubs whose wings appeared to unfurl. Sly-faced gods whose hands seemed to blur before my eyes, fingers reaching as if to catch at my skirts. It was a fine place for a ghost if I could just figure out how to make the magic work, I thought, angling the mirror and turning my attention to its surface.

Scarlet flashed against hammered silver. A sudden ripple of what might be black tresses. I glimpsed movement, heard a faint echo. One of King Henry's dead queens?

"Moll, did you hear that?" I asked.

Moll stood, ashen. "Saw it more like. A lady, all white and glowing."

"Was her hair black or brown or fair? It could have been any one of three queens. If only Father had shown me how to use this properly before he lost his sight!"

"Maybe the lady wasn't a queen at all!" Moll cried. "And maybe the old master never meant you to use the mirror!"

"Don't be a goose, Moll! Why would such a mirror exist unless we were supposed to use it?"

"Maybe Lord Calverley was wise enough to use it, and maybe Dr. Dee. But you don't know what you are doing any more than I do! You could make terrible mischief if you do something wrong!"

"What kind of mischief?" I asked, scornful.

"I don't know, but you ought not to be playing at magic you don't understand. It's like flinging sparks into that barrel of fireworks that burned the old master's eyes."

That analogy gave me pause; the mirror's fascination dulled. I thrust the mirror into a pouch at my waist.

Moll touched my arm. "I'm sorry to upset you, Mistress. But all the master's knowledge didn't save him from the fire. This magic—stirring up ghosts and such—it might burn you, too."

I did not answer her, merely started to walk away.

Moll called after me. "It is wicked to dredge up the past. Let it stay buried."

Wise words. I wish I had listened.

❧❧❧

BY THE TIME I returned to the Maids' Lodgings an hour later the chamber was abuzz, the ladies chattering about the special entertainment the Master of the Revels had concocted to celebrate the queen's return to Hampton Court: a masque to take place that very night, a kind of play with elaborate scenery where a select group of costumed courtiers would bring a legendary world to life. I was enlisted to be part of a group of sea nymphs dancing to distract the audience from some shift in scene or character—I could not say which because the Master of Revels did not trust the wagging tongues of maids of honor and made certain we had no notion of any part of the performance save our own.

My costume for the evening's masque—a nymph's fluttering ribbons of gossamer blue and green—did little to drive back the chill of Hampton Court's Great Hall with its great hammered beam ceiling. When we had entered it, no fire blazed in the vast hearths. Only a small wreath of candles in the farthest depths of the room nudged back the darkness, the tiny flames reflected in the hammered silver crags of a make-believe Mount Olympus.

As the hours passed, the Master of Revels drew back one black velvet drapery after another, revealing his creation. The chamber transformed into a wonder of Grecian pillars and splashing fountains amid blue satin seas. Minstrels played celestial tunes from the musicians' gallery overhead, the smell of frankincense burning increasing the atmosphere of magic. Courtiers disguised as gods and goddesses floated through the company like ghosts from ages gone by, while the servants wore wreaths of Bacchus's grapes or Demeter's golden wheat in their hair.

Grateful when my part was over, I tucked up on a pile of cushions between Isabella Markham and Mary Shelton to watch the performance reach its height. The other ladies giggled, ogling the men whose togas revealed hair-sprinkled legs and the occasional flash of bare buttocks. Robert Dudley brought Plato to life, teaching a page boy portraying young Aristotle. Each philosopher set a cresset alight, brightening the world—and the Great Hall—with their knowledge.

Only Elizabeth was awash in the golden glow, the flower-decked throne she sat upon crowning the summit of Olympus. Her role— the goddess Diana, a sliver of jeweled moon sparkling against the sunset of her hair. It fit her—the huntress, eternally virgin, though every man longed to claim her. When each hero approached to worship at her feet, she drove him away with a sweep of Diana's gilt bow, commanding the man choose a lady from the audience to be his consort, the mate who would join him in the annals of history.

Dudley gifted Lettice Knollys with Plato's scroll, mourning that if he were denied the glow of Elizabeth's moon, he would be forced to settle for its pale reflection. Sir William Pickering, Dudley's most pressing rival for the queen's affections, cast Robin a self-satisfied sneer, then sprang from Homer's stylus and stormed across the stage as Hercules. Pickering waged mock battle against his mythical foe: a giant whose face was concealed beneath a mask sporting the Cyclops's eye. Yet as Hercules drove the snarling beast to its doom from a trestle table cliff, I was puzzled to note not only heroes were claiming their mates this night, but the monster claimed a lady as well.

While everyone cheered in delight at Pickering's choice of the respectable matron Kat Ashley instead of one of the court's young beauties, the Cyclops lumbered across to Mary Grey. Her eyes went wide as the monster snatched her up, flinging her over one broad shoulder to carry her to his lair. "That is a perfect match if ever I saw one," I heard someone jeer. "The Devil's child and her demon lover."

"At least the Cyclops has but one eye to look at her." Even in the midst of the masque Lettice could not resist flinging barbs. I tried to blunt my outrage. After all, why should I resent the cruel joke? Mary had been bitter as cheap wine since I had pricked Lettice's mount with my brooch.

The audience shouted encouragement to Pickering, urging him to steal a kiss from the queen's former governess, then Markham, Elizabeth's companion in the Tower long ago, elbowed me in the ribs.

"Look, Nell!" She tossed hair bound with silk water lilies behind her bare shoulder. "See who steps into the light!"

Heralds trumpeted, announcing the final hero destined to step from Olympus's heights. "Come forth, ye noble Pericles, builder of the Acropolis, champion of the Parthenon, ye who raised the city of Athens nigh above the gods."

Pericles, the Athenian general whose wisdom carried Greece to greatness after the first Polypenisian War, the leader who fed the hunger for freedom in men's souls. Homesickness tugged as I recalled my father's worn copy of Pericles's funeral oration, and the horror on Mother's face when he told me of Pericles's great love: a courtesan with an intellect as fiery as his own.

When the curtains of the Parthenon drew back there could be no question which courtier had been chosen to play the Olympian general's part. Sir Gabriel Wyatt circled the company. "I seek a con-

sort with a mind to mate with mine. Tell me, gods, have you fashioned a woman with courage to hold fast to the tail of a comet?
Whom should I choose? A lady wife with unassailable virtue? Can
she bring the light of learning to the Greeks? Or a vestal virgin to
wing me on my way to greatness?"

Sir Gabriel laid his finger along his jaw, considering one prospect
here, another there, leaving nothing but disappointed sighs in his
wake. "No. I care not for the food most men eat. I crave fruit juicy as
the apple Eve plucked in Eden, a pippin stolen far beyond the walled
garden virtue would imprison me in. Is there a woman who craves
learning above a marriage bed?" Pericles demanded. "Who would
dare . . ."

"Dare what?" Mary Shelton asked. I would wager every maid
within the Great Hall wondered the same. Sandal-clad feet stopped
before me. "Who is this vision with the light of learning in her
eyes?" Gabriel asked.

I shook my head, but he was not to be dissuaded. He appealed to
the queen. "I have searched all of the heavens for my worthy mate,
my equal, Goddess Diana. Now that I have found my inspiration my
Aspasia can be no other. Appeal to her in my favor."

The whole chamber stared at me, the queen's eyes most piercing
of all. I tried to discern what emotion I saw in those royal eyes—
displeasure?

I could hear Kat Ashley's warning: *Do not run afoul of the queen
over the attentions of a man.*

"Goddess Diana," I implored. "I beg you command Pericles to
choose another."

Her black eyes were impenetrable. "The man has obviously decided to pursue you. Whether in Olympus or in the deer park he is
eager to spirit you away."

A murmur rippled through the crowd.

"My Aspasia rejects me and I cannot blame her," Gabriel cut in.
"A woman whose mind outstrips even her beauty? I am not worthy
to lay a hand on such a paragon."

"A man who knows his own worth is rare indeed," Elizabeth said in frosty assent. "Such insight must be rewarded. Arise, Aspasia. Aid Pericles in his noble task."

I climbed to my feet, unsettled by the queen's displeasure. Sir Gabriel grasped my hand, his own flesh hot against my icy fingers as he led me to the Parthenon. He plucked a torch from an iron bracket upon the wall, but instead of lighting the final cauldron himself, he pressed the shaft with its bright crown of flame into my palm. I lowered the torch. The flames blazed up. I felt them scorch me—the writhing orange tongues symbols of knowledge, wisdom. But as I glimpsed the queen through the vivid flare I feared I saw something more.

Anger, bright as live coals in her gaze.

Chapter Twelve

Later that Evening

THE CONSORTS MATCHED IN THE MASQUE PARTNERED for the rest of the evening—eating from a single plate, sipping from a single goblet of wine. Sir Gabriel's attention made the queen's mood darken, filling me with foreboding more troubling still.

When at last the revelers began wandering off to bed, Kat Ashley summoned me. "The queen is retiring and wishes you to attend her in the Privy Chamber." She said it so formally that it congealed my dread. "Her Majesty expressly wished you come without delay."

"I shall hasten to her."

"May I escort my Aspasia to her duty?" Sir Gabriel asked.

"You have done quite enough, Sir Pericles, and well you know it," Lady Ashley said.

The Angel helped me to my feet, then kissed my hand. I pulled away and fled from the Great Hall, glad to escape, yet in my haste I got separated from Lady Ashley in the crowd. I had no idea where I was going in this unfamiliar palace. Not wishing to irritate the queen further by making her wait while I searched for Lady Ashley, I looked for a servant to direct me. I saw Thomas Keyes, the Sergeant Porter who had directed me the day I arrived from Calverley. The colossus of a man wore the Cyclops mask shoved atop his head, its eye pointing at the vaulted ceiling. He reclined upon his own store of cushions. Plundered strawberries stained his big hand red.

"Sergeant Porter," I called. "Could you direct me to the queen's Privy Chamber?"

I was stunned when a smaller figure stepped from behind Keyes's bulk—Mary Grey, her gown of pink damask rumpled. "Take her yourself, Thomas. I have watched Mistress Nell with her maps and believe she could chart every border on them until the world ends, but she is hopeless finding her way to the end of the corridor."

"Gentle, Lady Mary," Keyes said. "Mistress Nell is but lately come to Hampton Court. She has much to learn."

"I wager she will learn what matters here the hard way," Mary said. "The workings of court cannot be found in one of her precious books."

"They can," I argued. "There is a volume by a woman named Christine de Pizan. *The Three Virtues.* My mother made sure I read it on my way to court."

Something in Mary's face stopped me. Sympathy? Or did my imagination run wild? I wondered what admonitions Lady Frances Grey had packed off to court with her youngest daughter after she and her husband had gotten their eldest child killed.

"Consult your book later," Mary said. "Her Majesty hates waiting. She is already in a fury over some seditious pamphlet Walsingham delivered to her and last week she went into a rage when William Cecil told her of the queen of Scotland's foolishness. Queen Elizabeth pounded on Walsingham with her slipper," Mary warned. "She could do the same to you."

"Her Majesty would have to have a strong arm indeed to match the beatings I got when my mother was in a rage." I was doing what Eppie had called "shouting down the thunder," my jest an attempt to conceal my dread. I was not certain whether giving in to the impulse before Mary Grey should make me more wary or ease my nerves. I know only that it was the first time I saw Mary Grey soften.

"They beat my sister Jane nigh unconscious when she refused to wed Guilford Dudley. But in the end, what could Jane do but surrender to our parents' will and the will of a man powerful as the Duke of Northumberland? She lost her head for their ambitions, when all Jane ever wanted was to be left in peace with her books."

I started down the corridor through torchlight that set gold threads on the tapestries gleaming. Danger crowded me, thick as storm clouds, a distant rumble of thunder. Keyes shortened his ground-eating stride so I could keep up.

"Nell," Mary called, startling me. I turned; her hands twined together as if to keep from reaching out to me. "Good luck."

I tried to brace myself against the queen's anger as the gentleman usher outside the Privy Chamber announced my presence. I guessed the queen was angry about Sir Gabriel's attentions to me, but I had done nothing to seek them out. Yet did innocence matter when a courtier incurred royal displeasure? *Surely a scholar great as Elizabeth Tudor would be ruled by logic,* I told myself. That calmed me. Elizabeth Tudor's intellect was the main inducement that had brought me to court. Surely I could right whatever was wrong between us with a simple explanation. But the timbre of the queen's reply shook my resolve. "Leave us," Her Majesty commanded.

The ladies of the bedchamber fled, flashing me curious glances as they skirted around the vast bed of state, its curtains even more elaborate than the bed at Whitehall: Cloth of gold paned with white, blue, red, and green velvet. Fretwork ceilings with intersecting ribs dangled pendants picked out in gold. Its shimmer caught in the mother-of-pearl writing table and danced across the curio cabinet laden with musical instruments. Everywhere I looked were symbols of the queen's royal estate, plush velvet cushions and cloth of gold embroidered with crowns and roses, fleur de lis and portcullises. How many hours had women labored with their needles to create such intricate work, the cloth when it was finished as unique and valuable as the finest jewel?

I recognized the figures on one of the fine tapestries that covered the walls to keep out drafts—an exquisite rendition of David, the boy shepherd with his slingshot ready to confront the powerful Goliath. What fire was lacking in the Great Hall, the queen had splashed into her cheeks, her color hectic beneath the white ceruse upon her face. I curtseyed, feeling exposed in my sea nymph's garb. "Your Grace wished me to wait upon you?" It astonished me, how level my voice sounded.

The queen did not answer, merely stalked to a table laden with documents. Atop them sat a pamphlet that looked as if horses had trampled it.

I waited in silence as she held it to the light of a branch of candles and rifled through the pages, ignoring me. After a time, the queen smacked the pamphlet against her open hand. "If Cecil had his way I would spend eternity sifting through such writs, and I would do it gladly if I never had to look upon such wretched filth as this pamphlet again."

For a moment I thought she would fling the offending article into the fire. The queen glared at me over the edge of the ink-smudged cover. "Your reputation as a scholar preceded you to court. My tutor, Roger Ascham, met you when you visited Cambridge with your father. You were about nine years old, or so he said. Shall we see if he exaggerated his praise of you? Answer me this, Mistress. What is the vilest curse a woman can fall prey to?" Her voice chilled to ice.

"There are so many perils a lady must beware of that I do not trust myself to choose just one. I would be guided by Your Majesty in all matters."

"A fine vague answer, that. One would think my Gypsy's Angel had been tutoring you in evasive tactics. Perhaps when you had your rendezvous by the stream?"

Indignation nipped heat into my cheeks. "Nay, Majesty. I swear, by God himself—"

"Hold your tongue. I have heard such vows until I want to retch. I only hope God is as sick of broken promises as I am and punishes the offenders accordingly."

I stared down at my hands.

"What surprise is this?" the queen raised a brow. "You remain silent when ordered? That is to your credit. From what Roger Ascham said of your disposition, holding your tongue cannot be easy."

I clenched my teeth against a reply.

"I had great hopes for you, Mistress Elinor, based on my old tutor's descriptions of your temperament. When you came to court, I thought, 'At last—I shall have one honest voice to count upon.' You disappoint me."

"That is the last thing I would wish to do."

She dismissed my reply with a wave of her hand. "I have heard the same words a hundred times. Yet those who should be loyal deceive me, plot against me. Defy me."

"Your Majesty, I would never—"

"Do not say it!"

A log in the fireplace fell apart as if in warning, hissing and crackling, filling the chamber with the scent of apple wood. "Majesty, I am sorry if I have displeased you, but I cannot think how I did."

She swept a hard glance from my head to my toe, searching for what I could not guess. That black gaze lingered on my scarred hand. "We will test your good faith. I shall pose a question and you shall answer."

Never in the years Father examined my progress in lessons had I felt this sinking alarm.

"If a maid of honor becomes a thief should she be punished or go unscathed because of her station?"

Did the queen believe I had stolen something? "Your Majesty is the best judge of what such a crime deserves."

"Look at this." Elizabeth thrust the pamphlet into my hands. I drew near a taper, scanning the smudged print: "Concerning the Marriage of Lady Katherine Grey." Katherine Grey—Mary's middle sister. "Surely news of my cousin's treachery must have reached even to Lincolnshire?"

"My mother did not allow gossip, and considering her aversion to court, no one spoke of such things. I have heard something of Lady Katherine since I arrived at court."

"They are a rebellious lot, the Greys. Proud and reckless, reeking with ambition because royal blood flows in their veins." Real hate filled Elizabeth's eyes. I averted my own so she could not read my thoughts. There were those in England who thought Lady Katherine would make a better queen than the one who now sat upon the throne. Lady Katherine was unquestionably legitimate and Protestant.

"You know that all those who serve me and all those related to me by blood must have my consent to marry."

"Yes, Your Majesty."

"It is the only way to keep the wolves away from the royal ewes, to curb rampant ambition. Search through history. The moment a monarch names a successor, the country begins to splinter. Malcontents who believe their lot would be bettered with a different ruler vie for power, not caring what ruin they leave the country in when they are through."

The Wars of the Roses were not so far in the past. I knew what battles for power between different branches of the royal family cost England.

"Lady Katherine Grey defied me. Became infatuated with the Earl of Hertford."

The Earl could trace his bloodline to Edward VI, thus was another who—some might claim—was more royal in blood than Elizabeth herself.

"She got herself with child, then flung herself on my mercy.

She claimed she and Hertford were married! Married, by God's wounds!"

If that were so, the babe Katherine Grey carried would mean double peril for Elizabeth: two legitimate contenders for the crown producing a child who carried both their lineages.

"Do you know what I say to their claims, Mistress? I say Hertford and my cousin are liars! Could either of these betrayers produce the priest who wed them?" Elizabeth demanded. "No, I tell you. And their one witness died. How convenient! They pleaded for mercy. Mercy, after the way they had betrayed me! I threw them in the Tower. What kind of fool do they take me for?"

"No one would take Your Majesty for a fool." I imagined Katherine Grey in the fortress where her sister Jane lay buried. To suffer such imprisonment alone would be terrible enough. But to know your lover—husband if the marriage they claimed was true—was locked behind stone walls a little way distant, and that the babe you carried would be born in such a grim place . . .

"Now I have this wretch of a pamphleteer declaring the bastard son Katherine Grey bore is legitimate?" Elizabeth ranted. "Bah! She can rot in the Tower forever. Hertford is lucky I do not take his head for deflowering a virgin of royal blood!"

Fixing my gaze on the pamphlet, I thought of Mary Grey. Did Mary love Katherine? Miss her? Did Mary fear that this sister might suffer the same fate as the first?

Katherine was probably safe as long as her son was judged a bastard. But God help her if the pamphleteer's assertion was caught up by the rest of England. I felt Elizabeth's gaze on me, knew she expected me to speak. "Your cousin Katherine is fortunate in Your Majesty's mercy," I said carefully.

A flicker of something I would later recognize as vanity sparked in Elizabeth's face. "God knows how long she will have it, if fools like this pamphleteer keep spreading lies. Walsingham will find the knave. I will take the hand that wrote this!"

The queen took the pamphlet from me and flung it back on her desk. "Vexing as this matter may be, I did not summon you here to rake over such family coils. I only speak of my cousin's fate because you are an apt student, Mistress. Learn from her mistakes. You would do better to leap into a bear pit in Southwark than trust a man."

"Men do not interest me, Majesty."

"If you have not come to court to seek a powerful husband why defy your mother to come here?"

"I came to be near you." I met her gaze unflinching. "It was tales I heard of you—a woman with learning, knowledge—a mind fine as any man's. Mayhap finer."

"You flatter me."

"I mean only to tell you why I fought to come here. The world is changing so fast, Majesty. I am hungry to understand." My words poured out. "At Cambridge, Father's friends would debate everything from philosophy to science. He would hold me on his lap so I could listen. And when Dr. Dee wrote letters about his discoveries in the years after our visit to London, Father would read them aloud, so I could share in the wonder. Dr. Dee held many magical keys to share back then—keys to the mysteries of the universe. Keys to a wide world of everything I had yet to learn. He even gave me a book on dragons. I near wore the pages to rags. I did so with all my favorite books. I wanted to prove my mind was sharp as any boy's. Mother warned that I must satisfy myself with the station God gave me. A woman must not reach beyond the bonds of home. But after all I had seen in London I could not believe in a God so selfish he would only give men keen minds. If God gave women intellect, then surely He meant us to use it! When I said so Father insisted he could prove it. You were the finest scholar his friend Ascham had ever taught. I strove to be like you from that moment on, Majesty. When Father died, being left in ignorance was like being locked away from light and air. Worse than any Tower cell could be!"

Elizabeth stood, quiet for a long moment. I feared I had been too blunt. Yet she claimed to crave honesty. I had given it to her. She paced to the window seat, where a book lay open atop loose pieces of parchment. An astrological chart, I realized, noting the squared center and the lines radiating out from it. I had often seen the one Dr. Dee had drawn for my father in its place of pride in Calverley's study. The book was familiar, too. *Propaedeumata Aphoristica*, Doctor Dee's effort to explain how the movement of the sun, the planets, and the stars affected events on the earth.

Strange, the queen had been perusing the very things that had made me crave her company. She touched the pages. "Dr. Dee is a friend. Perhaps next time I have need of him I will send you to Mortlake." My heart thudded in anticipation as the queen continued. "I have heard he has cobbled together wing after wing on his house to store the books he's gathered from all over the world. I wish I could explore them, but a queen cannot go poking about a commoner's house. Even a very gifted commoner. But you might delve into his library to find such books as I might enjoy."

"I would be delighted to serve Your Majesty in that way. You could lock me in Mortlake forever, and I would welcome it!"

"You are very young, Elinor." It was the first time she had called me by so informal a name. "How can you know how bleak any cell can be?"

I remembered where we had met—when she was the Lady Elizabeth who seemed to have no hope of a crown. She startled me, grasping my chin and forcing it upward.

"It is not an easy task, being a woman." She examined my face so intently I feared my skin would peel. "I wish all lessons might be learned from books, but there are lessons only life can teach you." She released me, but I did not look away. I could still feel the print of her fingers.

"Your father is dead." The words knifed my heart, more brutal because they were unexpected. Elizabeth's voice softened. "You miss him terribly. It is writ upon your face. He cannot protect you now. But neither can he hold the reins to your future. Your fate is in your own hands and depends solely upon what choices you make."

"I will endeavor to choose wisely."

"Do you think anyone sets out to choose badly? Yet my prisons are full and destined to be fuller still. There are many kinds of prisons. Of that you may be sure."

Elizabeth fingered something at the end of a gold chain—a miniature, I noted, recognizing Robert Dudley's chestnut hair and handsome face. This time I did avert my gaze, feeling as if I had intruded on something private, knowing the queen would not thank me for the trespass.

After a moment she spoke again. "Let me settle one facet of your future right now. Lord Calverley requested I grant you the title that has been in his family these hundred years. I will do so."

Delight rushed through me. I thought of my beloved Calverley—Crane and Jem and the crofters de Laceys had guarded for generations. To win the title meant I would have the power to stay at Calverley instead of losing it to some interloper—protecting the people my father had loved, the farmers, the village folk—that gift was precious indeed. "I will strive to deserve such an honor."

"I hope so. It is a rare chance we two women have. Freedom to shape our own futures. Do not jeopardize it for any man."

"I have no intention of doing so, Majesty."

"Your intentions may not matter. Men are not to be trusted. Once they get you in their power it is too late to save yourself. Yet a woman is under constant pressure to marry. Even a queen is forced to acknowledge her husband as her lord and master." She picked up a terrestrial globe that had been buried among the mess on the table. I wondered if the sphere was one of Mercator's. I wished I could examine it. The queen caught the direction of my gaze. She almost smiled. "You look as if you would like to snatch it out of my hands. Remember in the Tower? You told me your father called you Little Bird because you were so hungry to learn things."

"I am astonished you remember it."

The queen ran her thumb across the globe's surface.

"I sense you are being honest about your reason for coming to court. But now that you are here, you must understand the hard truth. You stand to be heiress to your father's wealth, and will be heir to his baronetcy as well. You will be a tempting prize for any ambitious man to pluck. A man, for instance, like Sir Gabriel Wyatt."

"I do my best to avoid him. I would sooner wed the devil than such a man."

"You would strike a better bargain if you cast your lot with Lucifer. I have known many ambitious men in my life. Men who crave power, wealth, and would do anything to attain them. Sir Gabriel Wyatt is as hungry as any I have ever known and he has obviously taken aim at you."

"He will find me a hard target to hit, Majesty."

"Unlike the doe we brought down this morn?"

I winced, remembering the hiss of cross bolt through air, the thud of its point striking living flesh, the metallic scent of blood as it flooded, hot over my hand.

"Never forget it is the *chase* men prize. Once their prey surrenders, be it in their bed or in the fields, their passion quickly wanes."

I remembered a poem Father read to me, likening Anne Boleyn to a hart. *No lo me tangre, for Caesar's I am, and wild for to hold though I seem tame.* King Henry had defied the pope to possess her. Murdered his friends. Disinherited his eldest daughter. Yet only three years after he wed the black-eyed Boleyn, he signed her death warrant, hungry to wed another. How could any woman forget that grim warning?

The queen took up a goblet, tipped it to her lips. Light chased bright crescents along the moons engraved on the gold cup. "It is my duty to give my ladies the benefit of my experience in the world," she said as she set the vessel down. "Experience earned most painfully. I was once young, like you. Innocent of the traps the heart can lay to snare the unwary."

Pity welled inside me for the bewildered girl she must have been. "I am grateful for your warning, Your Majesty," I said.

"Disregard my words at your peril," Elizabeth said, lost in thought. "The cost can be higher than you can imagine." She pressed her fingers to her temples. "A scholar is not convinced by pretty words, as you well know. A sharp mind looks to actions for proof. Go now. Send Kat Ashley to me. My head is aching."

"Of course, Your Majesty." I felt the gulf that stretched between us, knowing I could never cross it. "It must be a great comfort to you, to have Lady Ashley with you. Such love as a nurse gives is rare."

"I hear grief in your voice. Did your own governess die?"

"I do not know. She and my mother argued over some foolery of mine. Mother dismissed her and I never saw her again."

I curtseyed, then did as the queen bade me, seeking out Kat Ashley. The older woman drowsed near the fire. I touched Ashley's shoulder, shaking her gently. "Your pardon, my lady."

Kat climbed unsteadily to her feet and rubbed her eyes with blue-veined hands. Perhaps her part in the night's festivities had been too much for her. It was easy to forget Kat must be nigh sixty years old. She had waited upon Anne Boleyn when that lady was queen. "Is something amiss?"

"No. The queen has need of you before she retires."

Kat smiled with tender affection. "Her Majesty ever did need me to wish her goodnight. When she was a babe I chased the monsters from beneath her bed so she could rest safe. If only it was as easy to drive away the French and Spanish."

I thought of Hobgoblin Puck, Eppie's creation to keep me from wandering at night. Moved by loneliness of my own, I hugged Kat Ashley. "Her Majesty is lucky to have you with her still. I would give anything if my old nurse Eppie was waiting for me upstairs, to unsnarl my laces and brush the tangles out of my hair . . . out of my life."

"Eppie? That was your nurse's name?"

"Yes. Hepzibah Jones."

"Upon my life, I have heard that name before! She was to aid the dowager queen when that poor lady gave birth. Elizabeth and I were not at Sudeley Castle for the queen's lying in. We were exiled to Cheshunt by then. People blamed me because Thomas Seymour loved Elizabeth. But how was that my fault? He had tried to wed Elizabeth even before he settled on the dowager queen, but the council would not hear of it. Lord Thomas always loved Elizabeth best. Passion such as that must come out."

Kat flushed, as if suddenly aware of her unruly tongue. "You must forgive a foolish old woman her ramblings when woken from sleep. You will not speak of this, Nell? It was a dark, dangerous time. I can only thank God my sweet girl and I survived."

"I will never speak of it," I promised, feeling fragility in the older woman I had not noticed before. I walked arm in arm with her toward the queen's quarters, pretending it was to enjoy her company, not because she was unsteady.

"You must come into the queen's chamber for a moment," Kat urged. "Tell Her Majesty who your nurse was! What a strange world it is, paths forever crossing and recrossing!"

We entered the chamber, Kat's delight masking her weariness. I could not be so blissfully oblivious to the queen's sudden frown when she set eyes upon me.

"I dismissed you as I recall, Mistress Nell," the queen complained.

Kat brushed the queen's ill humor aside. "I insisted she come, my dearest Majesty. I have news that will stun you! Guess who Mistress Nell's nurse was these many years!"

"Nursery matters can hardly have any interest to me."

"Hepzibah Jones! The woman who tended your beloved stepmother!"

The queen stiffened. "I can hardly be expected to have tender feelings for the woman who allowed my stepmother to die."

I hastened to Eppie's defense. "Majesty, I would wager my soul Eppie did everything she could to save the dowager queen. She saved my life and my mother's when all hope seemed lost."

"A veritable miracle worker, was she?" Elizabeth demanded bitterly.

"Everyone at Calverley was certain I was dead in my mother's womb like her other babes had been. But when mother returned from the abbey with me in her arms . . ."

"You were born in an abbey?" Elizabeth interrupted. "Why not at Calverley?"

"My mother went to pray at the holy well, begging God for a miracle. Eppie went to comfort her through another still birth. Eppie used to say that once I was delivered into her hands alive she could not bear to let me go. She had to be my nurse or die."

"And where was this holy well that offered up a miracle?" Elizabeth asked.

"St. Michael of the Angels."

"Astonishing how small the world is!" Kat exclaimed. "Who would have guessed that the midwife who tended the dowager queen would tend Thomasin de Lacey as well! It near strikes me speechless! Of course, it is tragic about your stepmother, my sweet, but the fact that Hepzibah Jones delivered Lady Calverley safely is remarkable—"

"Kat!" Elizabeth interrupted, an edge to her voice. "When one is struck speechless, it usually means a blessed silence."

Unfazed by her mistress's outburst, Kat laughed behind her hand. "So it does. There is nothing more tedious than a foolish old woman, caught up in the past."

"I much prefer the present." Elizabeth sank down onto the stool at her dressing table and began kneading her temples. "My head aches. I wish to be alone."

I curtseyed, backed toward the door as Kat hastened to where the simples were kept for the queen's megrims. Ashley crooned, beginning to mix the dose. "Your Kat shall fix you right up, sweeting. You look pale as if someone walked over your grave."

"Alone, Kat!" Elizabeth snapped, sharper than I'd ever heard her. "I wish to be alone. This is the second time tonight you have not obeyed my orders."

Startled, Kat dropped the twist of paper whose contents she was dumping into the queen's goblet. She fished the paper out, then passed the mixture to the queen. "Forgive me, pet. I did not wish to distress you."

"I am not distressed." Elizabeth shoved Kat's physic away; her hands trembled.

Chapter Thirteen

Elizabeth

I T WAS ABSURD TO LET THE MENTION OF CHESHUNT RAT-
tle her after so many years, Elizabeth scolded herself. Yet,
when Kat had echoed the superstition about going pale when
someone walks over a grave she had raked coals to life, set old fires
ablaze.

Thomas.

She closed her eyes in an effort to blot out visions of that long-
ago day, the laughter, the feel of Thomas's hands on her body as he
slashed her gown to ribbons with his dagger, taunted her with illicit
pleasure. A feminine triumph had blazed in her—triumph over her
stepmother, who was solemn, pregnant, and far past the bloom of
youth. The gullible woman had even helped hold Elizabeth down
as if it were child's play!

Katherine Parr is a fool, Elizabeth remembered thinking at the
time. And yet, if Elizabeth lived to be a hundred she would never
forget the expression on Katherine Parr's face the searing August
day she and Thomasin de Lacey had discovered the two lovers. Elizabeth winced at the memory of how shamed she had felt. Her
bodice unlaced, her shift pulled down beneath one breast, her skirts
bunched around her waist while he lay atop her . . .

Not until she'd glimpsed her stepmother's stricken face had

Elizabeth realized this was no game. Not until Katherine Parr summoned Elizabeth to her chamber had Elizabeth realized what she had lost.

"I do not blame you for what happened." Katherine's eyes were puffy from weeping. "You are very young, Elizabeth. A child, really." Parr's hand had curved, protective, over the bulge where her own babe grew: the evidence of Seymour's love the dowager queen had once rejoiced to see. "You cannot stay here. You understand that."

Elizabeth did, yet it struck her that she was losing the first real home she had ever known. Katherine had been so delighted to be awarded custody of Elizabeth and Elizabeth had been overjoyed to go to her. This sudden break between them would have to be explained, and her stepmother was not one to fall easily into a lie. Fear knotted cold in Elizabeth's belly. "Where will you send me? What will you tell my brother the king? Sister Mary?" Mary would be horrified. Worse, she would feel vindicated that Anne Boleyn's daughter had shown herself as much of a whore as her mother was.

"We will tell no one of what happened here. I have spoken to Kat. She is packing your things. You will go to my stepdaughter's estate at Cheshunt. Lady Tyrwhitt will protect you for my sake, whatever comes." Elizabeth looked at the floor. She could not bear to see the motherly love still marked on the dowager queen's face.

"Elizabeth, please tell me he did not . . . No. Do not tell me. I do not want to know. It is punishable by death, to deflower a princess, and he is the father of my child. You must guard yourself, Elizabeth. Trust those I charge to protect you. Promise me you will be guided by them if your situation grows . . . complicated?"

How could it be more complicated than it is now? Elizabeth remembered thinking.

"No one must tell me if the worst happens," the dowager queen warned. "No one must ever discover or all will be lost—for you, child, as well as for me."

Shame drove Elizabeth to her knees. "My lady mother, I am so sorry. By the time your babe comes you will forget all but your joy in it. Surely that child will prove more worthy of your love than I have."

Katherine Parr had not survived long enough to find out. Struck mad with childbed fever, the gentle queen had raved, accusing her husband of poisoning her so that he could wed Elizabeth. Far away, in Lady Tyrwhitt's care, Elizabeth had sunk into illness, too. She had all but barricaded herself in her bedchamber, spent hours with the curtains closed about the bed, imprisoning her in a feverish haze of guilt and horror, suffering the accusation evident in Lady Tyrwhitt's thin-lipped face. When the message came, telling of the dowager queen's death, Elizabeth knew she had lost the only powerful ally she had, the woman who had loved her and had vowed to protect her.

No one must ever know, the dowager queen had warned. Elizabeth pictured Seymour's handsome face the last time she saw him alive. Saw the passion in him, the hunger. *There is nothing to stand in our way now.* How wrong Thomas had been. The shameful past had poured out when his plot to wed her was discovered. Salacious details pried from Elizabeth's comptroller, Thomas Parry, and from Kat's own lips from cells in the Tower. Elizabeth still cringed every time she thought of the scandal being gossiped about over tankards of ale and the golden goblets of noblemen. Still, there were secrets that remained buried, shadows she could not quite bring into the light.

Logic insisted it was impossible for such ghosts to show themselves at last. But her instincts . . . She dared not discount them entirely. There was something about her newest maid of honor that made her uneasy. Linked Mistress Elinor to places and times and people. But how to make certain it was coincidence, nothing more?

Elizabeth's gaze lit on the astrological chart John Dee had drawn for her. Of course. How did one plumb the unknowable? Consult a man able to delve into realms of spirit, peel back the armor of mortals. A man she had already informed Elinor de Lacey she was to visit. Dr. John Dee. But she would have to be subtle. Dee was a brilliant man. Still, she was tilting at shadows, reason asserted. She wished only to ease her mind, demonstrate how absurd it was to seek ghosts among the living. She crossed to her desk, took up a blank sheet of parchment and a quill.

Queries in the matter of Mistress Elinor de Lacey . . .

Chapter Fourteen

One Week Later

ORTLAKE. THE NAME OF DR. JOHN DEE'S HOUSE made me feverish with anticipation. Mortlake drew the most discerning scholars in the world, men who sat at tables copying valuable texts until their fingers grew so cramped they could not hold a quill. I would gladly have spent eternity in the rooms where he had gathered together the science of ages, old Moorish texts on healing, illuminated books priests had copied centuries ago, and enchantments said to summon angels.

Now, at the queen's behest, I was to see it all as a woman, a scholar. I reached into the leather pouch tied to my waist to make certain the queen's missive to the doctor was still there. I could not stem a sense of self-importance at the waxen royal seal. It was wicked to gloat, but being the queen's liaison to Dr. Dee was grander than anything I had imagined. I wondered what the note I carried contained. Was there was some matter of great import the queen wished to consult Dr. Dee on? Or was she merely sending word that I was to be trusted with the most precious texts in her name?

The groom who accompanied me plucked me from my musings. He pointed out the building with its mismatched wings tacked on at strange angles. "There it be, Mistress, though why any Christian soul would want to enter there is beyond me. Like to be entering the gates of hell."

"More like Merlin's lair in legends of King Arthur." I dismounted so hastily that my skirts caught on my saddle and nearly pitched me into the mud.

The groom caught me just in time. "Truly, Mistress, there be wicked things in there. There is a room he lets just a few of his wizard friends in. I heard they do dark magic, trying to raise the dead and turn tin into gold. No telling what he might do to a helpless woman."

"I will be quite safe. The last time I came here I was holding my father's hand."

The groom looked as if I might turn him into a toad. I imagined my father's amusement at the boy's expression. I could remember Father's delight showing me things forbidden: The scrying balls for telling the future, astrological charts like the one Robert Dudley would eventually have Dee cast to find a propitious day for Elizabeth Tudor's coronation. Jars of strange herbs and dried bits of things like batwing for mysterious brews. And page after page of notations, Dee's effort to find the ancient language Adam used in the Garden of Eden, a pure language that was God's own.

But Father would never come to Mortlake again, I thought with pain. He would never debate new theories. Blinking back unexpected tears, I blundered into someone crossing my path. I leapt back, begging pardon, but my chagrin turned to pleasure as I saw a face much aged, but familiar.

From the blank look in his eyes I knew he had not recognized me. Not that I had expected him to. "A thousand pardons, Mistress." Dee straightened his old-fashioned robes. "My wits were gone a-begging."

"More likely you were listening for angels. Or so my father would have said."

Dee squinted at me. "Should I know you, Mistress? Who, pray tell, is your father?"

"I cannot imagine why you would remember me. I was but five years old when last we met. You gave me a book on dragons that I treasure still."

"Dragons? Is it possible you are my Lord Calverley's little maid?"

"I am! Though how you guessed it is beyond me."

"You made quite an impression on your visit. For reasons beyond the fact that you wanted to break open my scrying ball to let out all the people I saw inside it."

I felt my cheeks heat. "I must have made a pest of myself while you and Father were trying to study."

"You delighted us both. In fact, I told him you were afire with a rare kind of light. I showed him the force reflected in one of my special mirrors. He claimed he had known you were destiny's child from the first moment he held you in his arms."

A chill went through me. I remembered the strange flash in the mirror in the haunted gallery. Had that light not been a signal from a queenly ghost? What if it had come from me?

"Dr. Dee, I have a letter from Her Majesty." I produced the sealed rectangle of parchment. "She sent me to peruse your books, bring her something that will take her mind off of the cares of the throne."

"I would be honored to loan her my texts, but there are some that must remain behind closed doors because they are so rare or so . . . dangerous. Treasures I stow away in my sanctum sanctorium, if you remember from when you were small. A place only a select few are allowed to enter."

Clerics still seriously debated whether or not women had souls. Even someone progressive as Dr. Dee would not want a female pawing through priceless texts. "I am certain I can find something for Her Majesty without disturbing your sanctuary."

"I like to have it disturbed. At least, by the finest intellects I can unearth. Her Majesty is one of few I would welcome there." Dee's eyes twinkled as if he had read my mind. "But I would be even more delighted to share my precious texts with you."

"With me?" I echoed, so stunned I must be gaping.

"I have not forgotten the silvery light that haloed you years ago. And in the midst of all my scientific explorations I have mastered one other valuable gift as well."

"What is that?"

"I can pick out diamonds lost among coal. You, my dear—you sparkle." Not since I lost Father had anyone's praise moved me so much. "There is one condition, however." He looked stern. "You must not shatter my scrying ball." His mouth twitched. "The little people trapped inside it are quite happy where they are."

"Perhaps we could serve them small beer and meat pies then," I said. He took my arm, and led me through Mortlake's door. Scholars glanced up from their tables, blinking at the sudden flash of sunlight as we entered, but Dee firmly deflected all questions as he navigated the crowded room. He opened another door and I glimpsed envy on some of the other men's faces. It pleased me that they were left behind while I was allowed to plunge to the very heart of John Dee's domain.

"You must forgive me if we are interrupted," the doctor said as we neared the final portal. "I am expecting a friend of mine who visits Mortlake often to study my texts. He is a formidable scholar like your father, one of the few who can challenge me in the games of strategy I love. We have an appointment to finish a complicated game I designed involving the heavenly spheres. I fear the scoundrel is going to defeat me."

A man able to triumph over Dr. Dee? I could scarce imagine it possible.

Dee grasped the latch and swung open the portal, revealing the room I remembered from years past. Impressions—just impressions of musty smells, tables piled with instruments I could not name, inventions and experiments half finished. Magical mirrors and books most kings would destroy if they knew a common man possessed them—that was, after they burned the owner at the stake. I rubbed my eyes, trying to clear them. Before they adjusted to the dimness, I heard Dr. Dee's pleased cry.

"And so you are already here, my friend. What a pleasant chance. There is someone I would like you to meet." I blinked hard, wanting to make a good impression on whomever Dr. Dee held in such esteem. But when my gaze fixed on the figure stepping from the shadows I felt as if a donkey had kicked me in the chest.

"Sir Gabriel!" I choked in disbelief.

"Mistress de Lacey." Amusement mingled with the surprise in his gaze. "It does seem that our paths cross again and again. My friend Dr. Dee would say it was fate."

"You young people know each other?" Dr. Dee exclaimed. "How delightful!"

"I would be surprised if Mistress de Lacey thinks it so. Her opinion of me is far lower than yours."

"Then perhaps you should leave off teasing her the way you do your other ladies," Dee scolded. "This is a woman who deserves the highest respect. Why, when she was just five years old she single-handedly attempted a most important prison break. She brought a key to the Princess Elizabeth, so that captive lady could escape from the Tower."

"It was merely a key meant for the rubbish heap and I was only five years old."

"Lord Robert had heard something of the story." I was certain Gabriel's mirth was pure anticipation over the weapon he had been given to torment me in the future.

"Ah, but I doubt even Lord Robert knows that the rubbish heap in question was my own or that Mistress Nell's circumspection probably saved the life of both me and the queen?" Dr. Dee turned back to me. "You have met my lord Robert Dudley no doubt. Anyone in the queen's presence must have. I met Sir Gabriel through that very gentleman. And a more likely mind I had not met since I left Lord Robert in the schoolroom. I was tutor to all the Dudleys, you know."

"I did not."

"There are times I think Sir Gabriel surpasses even Lord Robert in wit, although we must not tell his lordship so."

"Your secret is safe as if it were locked in one of these infernal codes you are forever designing." Gabriel grimaced. "Dr. Dee likes to keep his most astonishing secrets safe, so he has devised his own code to conceal them. I have been trying to unravel this page for well over an hour with no success. But I confess I have a much more intriguing mystery to solve now. How did this lady come to be a guest in this room? After all, John, you claimed it was an honor to be invited here, that I was one in a most select group."

"I have come on the queen's business." I sounded more self-assured than I felt. "Why are you here?"

"Dr. Dee is intent on exploring the labyrinth of my mind. I have a reputation of unraveling people's secrets. I plague the good doctor by anticipating his every move in the complex games we play."

"I suspect you have abilities like Nostradamus, Catherine de Medici's seer."

"Dr. Dee only says that to conceal the fact that he is a poor loser," Gabriel said. "It gives him an excuse whenever I win."

"That may well be," Dee allowed, "but you must wait to prove it until Mistress Nell has taken her leave. I dare not leave her unattended."

"Why?" I asked. "I am perfectly happy to wander among your treasures."

"That is exactly the difficulty. In our former acquaintance you had a fascination for taking things apart to see how they worked. In fact, I would wager before you leave you will be trying to dismantle that clock."

Dee gestured to a metal ball small enough to fit in the palm of a man's hand. Gabriel picked the object up, regarding it. "I collected one much like this when I was a soldier in the Low Countries. I would not trifle with this, Mistress. You cannot afford to replace it."

"Then perhaps, Sir Gabriel, you can transform it to gold once we decipher the manuscript on alchemy you brought last visit," Dee said.

Alchemy? That was a dangerous pursuit indeed, one that could land anyone involved in prison or worse. "Turning metal into gold," I said. "That is a skill I imagine Sir Gabriel would value."

"You wrong us both," Dee protested. "Our hope is that we are not only able to refine metal with alchemy's magic, but also refine souls."

Gabriel shrugged. "It is my lone hope of ever reaching heaven."

But all humor was lost on me as I thought of the risk they were taking. "Is it not dangerous to poke about such knowledge?"

"It is a risk I am willing to take," Dee said. "Discoveries worth making are bought at some kind of price. Your father knew this, Mistress. I think you do, too. In that spirit, let me return something to you." Dee rummaged in a wooden chest. He pulled out a long instrument. "Do you know what this is?"

"A Saint Jacob's staff." My heart tripped as I glimpsed a deep gouge in the wood. I knew how it had gotten there. I had knocked the instrument over when I was playing as a child. It had cracked onto one of Father's strange rocks with the skeletons of dragon-beasts imprinted upon them.

"Ah. I can see you know who this belonged to," Dee said, and I made a desperate attempt to hide the vulnerability I knew must show. "Your father and I took this out to the fields the spring you all came to London. I suspect he taught you how to use it."

"He did."

"Lord Calverley sent it to me after he lost his sight." I could not help myself. I reached out to touch the long shafts, ran my thumb over the scar in the wood. I felt Gabriel's eyes upon me, and I wondered at the Angel's silence. "You must take it, Nell," Dee insisted. "Study the heavens in my old friend's stead."

"I will." I gathered the awkward instrument close, my throat tight.

"You think it wise to trust such explorations to a woman?" Wyatt asked.

"In a perfect world all would be able to learn according to their ability," I insisted.

"Would they use the skills God gave them? And when it came to the fruits of their labor would each person take only what they truly need?" Wyatt turned to Dr. Dee. "I think Mistress Nell has been reading *Utopia*. Has Sir Thomas More's book shaped your views?"

"There is wisdom in what he says."

"Indeed. Save for the fact that he left out one vital force in his calculations."

"What is that?"

"Human greed and ambition." Wyatt sobered for a moment, then turned to Dr. Dee with a laugh. "What say you, Dee? Am I not a perfect example of both?"

"You and Mistress Nell may debate the subject if you wish. I intend to revel in the pleasure of her entering once again into my life. Nell de Lacey, you have come to Mortlake on the queen's errand, but you leave as one of my chosen. You are welcome anytime you wish. Avail yourself of whatever texts or instruments will aid you in your studies."

"You would grant me such an honor?" Tears threatened. But before they could spill free, Gabriel broke in.

"Dr. Dee, are you quite certain it is wise to give Mistress Elinor the run of your library?" Wyatt eyed me as if I were a child with grubby hands. "The lady's head might explode if you fill it with weighty subjects fit only for a man."

"I would match my wits against yours anytime, sir!"

John Dee laughed. "I suspect this is one contest the lady might win." Gabriel protested, but Dee held up his hand. "I told you my mirrors detect light? A sort of energy, if you will?"

"What has that to do with—"

"This woman's is the fiercest I have ever seen. There is something exceptional about her. Something I have wondered about these many years. Some are destiny's children. I cannot say why it is so. Mistress Nell is one of them. I would swear it on my life to any who asked. Now if the two of you will excuse me, Mistress Nell can gather the books Her Majesty sent her to fetch. I must read the queen's letter."

He withdrew to the far corner of the room and broke the wax seal.

I saw the doctor frown.

Chapter Fifteen

Mid-June 1564

URING THE DAYS THAT FOLLOWED I GREW EVER MORE restless. Sir Gabriel's appearance at Mortlake challenged everything I believed about the man, while Dr. Dee's words about the mysterious force that surrounded me haunted me until I peered into the mystical mirror, searching for some hint of what he saw in my face.

God knew, my presence seemed to please the queen less than ever. She had favored me when she had determined to send me to Mortlake. But sometime after, all between us had changed. Time and again the sharp edge of her temper cut me. No service I provided seemed to satisfy. If I carried the train of her gown she claimed I rumpled it. If I fastened her necklace she swore I pinched her skin. She raised subjects well known for their controversy, pushing to gain my opinion, as if testing me in some way.

She quizzed me on religion, demanding to know if I thought it best to root out Popery harshly or curb the dissenters gently so as not to push them into rebellion. She tempted me into dangerous waters, asking what lengths God's anointed ruler should go to in order to preserve peace. Was it just to crush rebellion before it took root? If so, should Katherine Grey not die? And what should be the fate of the woman's son? As for the succession, was it not generous to sacrifice the man one loved most of all, wed him to a royal cousin so his sons would sit upon a throne? All the court had heard that Elizabeth wished for Dudley to marry the Scots queen. Yet was there not a trap waiting for anyone who agreed with her? Her anger at the reality of losing Dudley to Scotland? The enemies of Lord Robert ready to lash back at one foolhardy enough to espouse the cause of Dudley becoming king, even in a foreign land?

Courtiers watched me, waiting for me to lose what little footing I had with the queen, wondering what had caused this shift in her favor. I wondered, too. The constant scrutiny chafed like an ill-fitting shoe, and when evening came with its card games in the queen's Privy Chamber or entertainments where music painted the air, Sir Gabriel's attempts to draw me into arguments in the queen's company only unsettled me the more.

"Mistress de Lacey has spent too much time considering More's *Utopia*, Majesty, to be of any use in debates. Perhaps for discussions you wish to pursue with her she should read Machiavelli . . . ," said he.

I had no doubt Wyatt had committed the author's masterpiece to memory, and so had the queen we both served. Now, I almost felt they were in collusion. As if the queen used Wyatt's gifts to plumb some depth I could not understand.

I waited for my chance to steal away from court duties, slip into the night-shrouded gardens where I could lose myself in calculations, trying to plumb the mysteries of the heavens. My mind itched inside my skull; only solving a puzzle that challenged every corner of my brain could soothe nerves frayed by my encounters with the queen and Gabriel Wyatt.

I had carried out my mission to Mortlake faithfully and delivered Dr. Dee's written reply. So why did matters between the queen and me seem strained?

Perhaps the queen's mood has nothing to do with you. I could hear Father's reasoning. *She may be preoccupied by some other matter and have no patience with maids of honor.* Yet I could not shed the feeling that Elizabeth Tudor watched me more closely, something in her eyes urging me to caution.

⋇⋇ ⋇⋇

EIGHT DAYS AFTER my visit to Mortlake the chance to escape to the gardens arrived—a star-scattered night when I was not serving the queen and Wyatt was nowhere in sight. Slipping into the deserted Maids' Lodgings, I rummaged through Father's traveling chest to find the leather bundle he had carried on astronomical excursions. I added the ungainly lengths of his Saint Jacob's staff for plotting points, and the map of the heavens covered with notations in his spidery hand. I placed the bundle on the bed, adding a corked bottle of ink, parchment, and two freshly mended quill pens.

After donning my old mantle of tawny velvet and strapping pattens on my feet to protect my slippers from mud, I paused before the gilt-framed looking glass. What mystic force had John Dee seen in me? I wondered again, glimpsing not the slightest hint of light. Only my astrolabe gleamed in the candlelight. I reached behind my nape to unfasten the chain that held the instrument. The gold disk slipped as it so often did when I removed the necklace to bathe, and I barely caught it before it rolled beneath a stool. I pinned the chain to my waist, so I would be able to use the instrument once I reached my destination without risking its loss.

Praying I would encounter no one who would detain me, I tucked the leather bundle under my arm, then hastened toward the nearest garden door. As I stepped into the night, torches spun haloes of light, reclaiming wobbling circles of lawn from the darkness so pleasure seekers could find their way through the labyrinth of walled gardens. I could hear muffled voices, the sound of laughter—lovers who had stolen away to some secluded corner, seeking privacy for their lovemaking? Or courtiers plotting the best way to gain royal favor?

Thrice in the past I had stumbled across Sir Gabriel while on some errand in the gardens. Another time I had surprised Lettice, her lips kiss swollen, while a man with an uncanny likeness to Robert Dudley retreated through the nearest garden door. But the haven I sought tonight was seldom favored by anyone—a spot near the kitchen gate with the clearest view of the sky. I made my way toward the Base Court where the kitchens lay, the gardens boasting fat cabbages and frothy carrot tops instead of flowers. Herbs for cookery and simples and for strewing smelled sweet.

Laughter echoed from the scullery as servants polished coppers, wiped plates clean. It would be hours before the kitchen staff could drop onto their pallets to sleep. I was sniffing the faint scent of roasting meat when someone called my name. Startled, I wheeled around to see a boy of about nine racing toward me, his jerkin dirt-stained, cheeks wind-burned from hours in the sun.

"Mistress, wait, I pray you!"

My stomach sank as if I had been caught in thievery. Perhaps my reaction was not so strange. I *was* bent on stealing something precious and rare at court—time alone.

"What is it?" I asked.

He snatched off his dun felt hat, regarding me as if he expected me to cuff him for his impertinence in addressing me. "Be you Mistress Elinor de Lacey? Your hair looks red, but there be an uncommon lot of ladies around here with the same."

"I am Mistress de Lacey. Who asks for her?"

"That I cannot say." The lad hitched up his stocking. "Only this be a most important message. I am to be paid a whole guinea if I bring you along quite secret like."

Wariness surged inside me. What message could be so important that someone would offer such a sum? Who might be rich or rash enough to send it? Sir Gabriel maneuvering to get me alone? I frowned at the boy, remembering the queen's warnings. "How did you know where to seek me?"

"I was told to look where the stars shone brightest. You'd be peering up at them." Whoever sought me knew my fascination with astronomy. That made me more uneasy.

"The man who sent you . . . he was not a tall gentleman, with dark hair?"

"It were not a man at all." The lad peered at me with eyes round as the coins he had been promised. "It be a *lady* who asks for you, Mistress. She said you would appear some clear night if I kept watch. Since tonight seemed perfect, I sneaked her in the servant's gates when I was fetching swans to be plucked for the queen's dinner."

A woman was seeking me? Surely this mysterious visitor could not be mother. She would enter the palace grounds with the same pomp I had. Unless something had gone dreadfully wrong back home in Lincolnshire. It seemed a wild flight of fancy, yet who else could be seeking me here? The possibility of unnamed peril spurred me. Not wanting to be slowed by the equipment I carried, I hid my leather bundle beneath a bench, where no one would find it. I scrabbled at my waist to find Father's astrolabe. Holding it tight as a talisman against God knew what, I followed the boy through the maze of walled gardens. My pulse drummed as one shadowy enclosure spilled into another. Tall wooden posts bearing carved animals glinted, gilt in the moonshine, the royal banners clutched in paws or hooves fluttering like ghosts. A distant fountain burbled a haunting melody, the shadows seeming to conceal my worst fears.

By the time we reached our destination, my fingers felt numb from clutching the astrolabe so tight. My gaze probed otherworldly shapes, shrubs trimmed into creatures—a griffin, a stag, a dragon with wings outspread. At first I discerned no human shape, but after a moment a figure separated from the darkness. Enveloped in a black stuff cloak, the lady did not possess my mother's active, birdlike frame. Rather, someone short and stout stretched arms out to me. Even before her cloak fell back to reveal her face, I guessed who my visitor was. "Eppie!" I cried, hurtling into my beloved nurse's arms.

Eppie crushed me against the bosom where I had cried childish tears, sweated out winter coughs, and snuggled to sleep. Even now, her warm lavender scent drove away any threat of nightmare. I laughed, I cried, the sweetness of our reunion piercing deep. "Oh,

Eppie! It has been a hundred years since I saw you last! Where have you been? I am so glad you found me!" I was too delighted to wonder why she finally *had*.

"When I heard you were at court I could not believe it. Some men on their way to a bear baiting stopped at my sister's inn. Dudley's men they claimed to be. Talked about the new maid of honor— red-haired, wondered how long before she caught their master's eye. 'Sweet Nell' they named her and I thought . . . I feared . . ." She stroked my hair with calloused hands. "Dear God, how could she thrust you in such danger!" Suddenly Eppie's eyes widened with alarm when they fell on the boy. "Pay him off! Mary, Jesus, and Joseph, what he might tell—"

Fear scratched my nerves with tiny claws as I scrabbled in my pocket for a coin, pressed payment into the kitchen lad's hand. "What is your name, boy?"

"Posthumus Thomas, Mistress. I was born after me father got crushed under a miller's cart."

"Posthumous Thomas. Run along now."

"I'll not forget you, Mistress!" He goggled at his good fortune. "I'll not forget you *nor* the lady who sent me to find you!"

I heard Eppie whisper, beneath her breath, "God save us all."

Clutching Eppie's hand, I tugged her deeper into the palace grounds. "Eppie, what is wrong?"

"I would not have come if I could think of any other way. Would have sent my sister. But I could not—her poor babes . . . I would not leave them motherless."

"You are not making sense, Eppie. Come to the Maids' Lodgings. I will have Moll heat you up a lovely flagon of ale and send to the kitchen for something to eat."

"Not the palace." Alarm stitched her voice. "No one must see me. I have news that only you must hear." A torch flared. Eppie cringed, startled as a wild animal. For the first time I got a good look at her face. What I saw turned my blood cold. Haggard, haunted, she looked as if she had not slept in weeks. She clung to the shadows as if she were hunted. Perhaps a little mad. I remembered my mother accusing Eppie of being just that. Eppie darted a glance over her shoulder. "Hasten! They may be after me even now."

"Who might be after you?"

"I always watched for it, dreaded it would come. She has eyes everywhere. Hurry, let us secret ourselves away. There is much to tell and I must be gone before any save the kitchen boy know I was here."

My mind leapt to the only person I could think Eppie might wish to hide from. "Mother is still at Calverley. You need not fear."

Eppie stifled a strange laugh. We retraced the path Thomas and I had taken, through walled retreats and blocks of flowers and white sand that reminded me of a chess board stretching from the palace walls. At last, we stepped into the nook where I had hidden my bundle.

Eppie ferreted about the shrubbery, searching as if she feared some invisible army might pounce. Finally I could bear it no longer. I grasped Eppie's hand and pulled her to a stone bench, forced her sit. Eppie clutched my fingers, and I was surprised to find I held my astrolabe as she pulled me down beside her. She clung to me so tight that the gold disk dug deep. My breath hissed between my teeth at the pain. Starting at the sound, she wrenched my palm upward, peeling open my fingers. The astrolabe glinted. "What is this?" She looked as if the disc concealed the tiny people I'd once imagined were trapped in Dr. Dee's scrying ball, tiny hands noting every word she and I spoke.

"It is a device for measuring stars. Father gave it to me before he . . ." Even now, I could not say the word *died*.

"The good master . . .'twas his then? No evil can lurk inside it. No strange magic. He would not hurt *you*. Even if he curses me from heaven."

"Father curse you? How could you even imagine such a thing?"

"Deserve it, some would say. Say it myself on the darkest days. I swear I would change things if I could, tell him the truth. But your mother knew. She insisted . . ." Eppie's voice cracked. "I was so certain she would keep you safe."

"Safe from what? You make no sense." I could not shake the strangeness of that. Eppie had always made the best sense of anyone save my father. But I had been so young then and Mother . . . The back of my neck prickled.

"This place, Nell! You must get away from this place before it is too late." Eppie glanced at the palace walls as if they were jaws waiting to snap shut on us both.

"But I have just begun to find my place. I am studying with Dr. Dee, and—"

"You must not let him look into your eyes! Him with his devil-skills as a seer. He is the queen's creature now and he will betray you!"

"There is nothing to betray! Eppie, let me slip into the palace, bring you a posset to calm you. You are overwrought. Seeing menace when none is there."

"It is everywhere! Lurking in shadows, watching me. Even at the Silver Swan."

"Your brother-in-law's alehouse? The one you meant to visit when we came to London?"

"How could I after what I saw at the Tower? Once I realized the danger, I dared not leave you." Eppie plucked at the ties of her cloak, as if some specter was cinching it tight. "But once your mother drove me away from Calverley where else could I go?"

"Why did you never write me? I am sure one of the servants would have smuggled your letter to me."

"She might have had me murdered if she knew where I was. A mother might do anything to see her child safe."

"You cannot possibly mean you feared my mother might murder you?" I recoiled from Eppie, not wanting to see deeper signs of madness I now suspected might be there. "I know you and Mother parted badly. You were both angry—"

"I have no time to debate this! Not when they might have followed me." Eppie shuddered, her busy eyes searching the shadows. "Last night the people I've dreaded finally came searching for me. Three fine gentlemen swaggered into the alehouse prying with strange questions, watching with eyes that could peel the very thoughts from the mind. My sister knew they were up to some evil. She put them off. Sent them back to the palace. God knows what powers their mistress might have invoked—a witch's daughter. Familiar of sorcerers like John Dee."

"You are speaking of the queen? But what would Her Majesty want with you?" Images flashed into my memory—the queen's gaze black ice. Was my mention of Eppie the reason for the chill between Her Majesty and me? Did Elizabeth hold such a grudge over Katherine Parr's death that she sought revenge? Dismay filled me. I pressed my fingers to my lips. "Oh, Eppie! I fear the visit from the queen's men might be my fault! I told Her Majesty you were my nurse and she spoke of Katherine Parr."

Eppie clasped my arms so tight they ached. "What else did you say, Nell? Lives depend on what you recall!"

My stomach coiled tight. "The queen blamed you for Katherine Parr's death in childbed. I told her I would stake my life that you did all you could to see the dowager queen safely delivered. You were the finest midwife in the land. A miracle worker."

"A miracle worker?"

"That is what Father claimed. I told the queen I was not expected to survive. My mother's other babes had died in her womb. But you made certain I lived, even when all the rest of the world believed I was dead."

Moonlight filtered through the trees, revealing Eppie's eyes stark with terror. "What did Her Majesty say when you spoke thus? Did she ask any questions of you?"

"I cannot remember it all. I told the queen I was born in what used to be an abbey, near the well of St. Michael."

"She cannot know! But she might suspect . . ." Eppie crossed herself with a shaking hand. "The danger is greater than I feared. But if a rabbit runs the fox will chase. The only armor I can give you is the truth before it is too late."

"The truth about what?" I could almost feel her mind unhinge.

Wind fingered a banner. The rustling sound made me jump. "Eppie, you are scaring me!"

"I will frighten you a good deal more. It is time you learned the truth about your birth."

"Father told me."

"Your father?" she scoffed. "And what did he know? Your mother and I, we kept secrets from Lord Calverley. We may burn in hell for it."

"What kind of secrets?"

"About where you came from. How you came to be at the abbey."

"It was run like an inn, Father said. Desperate people stayed there to pray for miracles."

"Your mother had no hope of a miracle! All I prayed for was to keep her alive once the babe was delivered dead! But the waiting was so long, the hours tedious. Other women who lived near St. Michael's heard of my skill, sought me out when they needed help. I never could have guessed what deviltry that would lead to." She sucked in a deep breath.

I chafed at the old scar along the side of my hand, listening.

"The night before you were born, someone knocked on the door of your mother's apartments. I opened the door. Masked strangers blindfolded me, then bundled me into a coach that took me to a house in the country. They did not remove the blindfold until I was in a richly appointed bedchamber where a very fair young lady lay suffering birth pangs.

"She was very young, this lady, dazed and frightened. It broke my heart, the way she stayed silent as birth pains tore at her. For two days she labored. Finally I had to wrench the babe from her womb or both mother and child would die. She should have screamed the lot of us deaf, the ordeal was so rough. The damage to her womb was such she would never deliver another babe. I went to console her, show her the healthy child she had borne. But before I could put the babe to her breast, one of her ladies made to suffocate the poor wee thing beneath a pillow."

My stomach lurched at the image of that pitiful babe struggling for air. "How could anyone murder a babe? Did you not try to stop it?"

"They might have killed me, too. They were masked. The affair so furtive I knew I was in peril. They snatched me into the coach so quickly I barely had time to grab my bag of instruments. No one at the abbey knew where I had gone." I pictured Eppie in that strange room, imagined how vulnerable she had been, how helpless.

"It is not the first time I had seen someone try to take a new-born's life. It happens far too often. Mothers unable to face raising a bastard. In grand homes, murder done to save the pride of a noble name. In simpler cottages, a babe is sacrificed so there is enough food for other children to survive. I cannot imagine the guilt those who kill such innocents must carry. But on this night fortune smiled on the unwanted babe. Before the servant snuffed out the last spark of life, the fair lady started to wail like a wild thing. The servant rushed to her—to silence her, to comfort her—I know not which. But the instant all eyes were upon the mother, something drove me to peep beneath the pillow at the child. You peered up at me, so solemn, so . . . alive—"

"*Me?*" I recoiled. "What are you saying?" Nay. Every part of me rejected it. "I am my father's daughter. Everyone always said so! Even when we visited Cambridge and I recited my lessons!" I blinked back tears, remembering how proud I had been when Dr. John Dee had said farewell, the dragon book in my hands. *You are your father's daughter, little Nell. You will not be satisfied until you have drained every drop of information on these fierce beasts there is to know.* Eppie moved toward me. I cringed away.

"You were like Lord Calverley in your love of learning, Nell. But when you looked into the mirror did you see Lord Calverley's eyes? His nose? His chin?"

I looked no more like my swarthy, small father than a fox resembles a crow. "I was the babe the fair lady wished to kill?" I asked, knowing it was true.

Eppie nodded. "There you lay, your tiny mouth gasping for

enough air to cry. Before you could do so, I slipped you the sugar teat I kept to teach reluctant babes to suckle, then I tucked you into my bundle, claiming I would give you a proper burial. By then, the mother who bore you was in hysterics. The servants blindfolded me and hastened me out of the house to the waiting carriage. I was ter-rified you would cry, betray us both. But you lay inside my bag, so silent, trusting me even then. By the time we reached the abbey my nerves were ragged with fear someone would check and make cer-tain the babe was dead. Perhaps it was prayers that drove the thought from their minds. My prayers or a spate of even more des-perate ones.

I found your mother alone, on her knees. Her water had broken, and it was murky with death like all the times before. I told her not to despair. God had answered her pleas for a child. Not the way she ex-pected, but answered it, nonetheless. I opened my bag in the candle-light and told how they tried to suffocate you. She snatched you up into her arms and the look on her face! She loved you right then, so fiercely she barely felt the pain of delivering the child she had car-ried. 'Show her to me, Eppie,' she pleaded when agony gripped her. 'Show me my perfect daughter.'"

My throat ached. So she had thought me perfect once. Her own babe lay dead in her womb, so in travail my mother had clung to me. She had needed me then, to drive back the pain, to grant her hope. My mother, vulnerable to pain and fate and God's cruel whim. Needing *me*. Lying to her husband so she could keep a child who was not her own. I wondered how soon she had regretted the choice she made, realized I was anything but perfect.

"I did not know what danger I had put you and Lady Calverley in," Eppie continued. "Not until five years later when you pulled me to the solar window of the Lieutenant's house to see a real princess walking in the garden. The very same fair lady I had tended."

I reeled, feeling sick, scarce believing my own ears. I could think of no catastrophe more devastating than what she had already told me—that I was not John de Lacey's child. Yet this news flung me into a peril so vast I could scarce comprehend it. "You cannot mean that I am . . . Eppie, that is *impossible*!"

Eppie gripped both my hands in hers. "You are the Virgin Queen's daughter."

"Nay!" I pulled free, backed away. "You are mad! My mother was right to send you away!"

Pain crumpled Eppie's features, pain and iron-hard resolve. "I would bear insanity gladly if it could keep you safe. But what I tell you is the truth. I swear it on my husband's grave." Eppie's husband had died in King Henry's French wars, and she had never loved again. "What is more, I have proof what I say is true."

"Proof?"

"The most certain kind of proof, at least to the woman who bore you. But only she would recognize it as such. She is not likely to ever forget it." Eppie drew something from inside her bodice, a scrap of cloth she pressed into my hand. I stared at dark velvet in the glow of a torch, the silvery embroidery glittering in the moonlight.

"What is this?" I asked, wary as if it were steeped in poison.

"A bit of cloth from the bed curtain in the chamber where you were born. I snipped it off when no one was looking." Bed curtains. I thought of those in Elizabeth's chamber here at Hampton Court, laboriously stitched by hand, each design unique as the patterns frost etched on wintry window panes. Such curtains were valuable as jewels, put in wills and passed on as legacies through generations.

The truth in what Eppie had said shook me. Weeks before an impending birth, a woman was shut away from the world. Anyone who spent her confinement in a bed luxurious as this scrap came from would never forget the pattern stitched on its curtains. "My mother knew whose daughter you say I am?"

"I told her everything at the Tower when you disappeared."

"You could be lying. Mother is not here for me to ask."

"Think, Nell. Why did we lock you in your room? Leave you there alone? For slipping away from me? You had done so before and been let off with a scolding."

I remembered with burning clarity my mother's stricken face when Elizabeth Tudor had swept me into her arms. I remembered the door to our Tower bedchamber slamming shut, mother and Eppie leaving me alone. To punish me, I had been so certain. Now my imagination ran wild, pictured two women who loved me, terrified at the secret they had discovered. Was it possible? Could that explain so many things?

Yet Eppie must have been mistaken. Nine years had passed between our visit to the Tower and the day that Mother banished her. Perhaps the imagination that had once conjured up Hobgoblin Puck had invented a far more menacing monster? Yet there could be no question my mother feared Eppie's fantasy might be true, otherwise why had she reacted so violently when the messenger arrived from court? I recalled the frantic burning in Mother's eyes as she crushed the missive in her hand, the queen's seal like a gobbet of blood.

A rustling nearby startled us. Eppie and I sprang to our feet. Something tugged my petticoat. For an instant I feared it was a hand ready to drag me before the queen. I spun around. Heart hammering, I searched the shadows, met only Eppie's eyes, so round with fear the whites glowed. "It was only the wind," she said. "Or God himself warning I must leave before we are discovered." Eppie clasped my face between her work-roughened palms. I flinched from her touch, but she held firm. "Nell, you understand what I have told you? You know the danger you are in?"

"Yet it does not make any sense," I protested, desperate. "A woman with child would have a big belly. How could she have hidden it? You should see her at court—every moment of her life under scrutiny. She could not keep such a secret."

"I do not know how she managed to do so, child. I only know that she did."

"If Mother would have told me, I would have stayed at Calverley."

"This secret means death to whoever knows it. That is why she did not tell you. That is why we must never meet again."

She took the snipping of bed curtain from my numb fingers. Tucking the scrap in the cloth bag at my waist, she stretched on tip-toe to kiss me. "Be careful, my wandering princess," she whispered. "May God shield us both."

A heartbeat later, she was gone.

My mind churned. *God in heaven, was it possible what Eppie claimed was true?* I dared not believe her. And yet so many things Eppie said laid siege to my doubt. I ran, ran from that insistent battering through the darkness, my skirt catching on the topiary, the griffin's claw, the dragon's wing. My hair tore loose from my headdress and tumbled down my back. Pain knifed into my side, tears streaking my face. I tripped over something, skidded to my knees. Shoving myself back to my feet, I searched the garden, desperate to find someplace, anyplace safe, where I could think. *And where would that haven be, you fool!* Truth mocked me. *It does not matter if Eppie has lied. The merest whisper of this rumor could spell disaster for you. And if—God forbid—her tale is true, it could topple the queen from her throne.*

I flung myself to the ground in a shadowy nook, huddled there, my arms wrapped tight about my knees, my whole body trembling. *Oh, God, how could the world careen off its axis between one breath and the next?* I stifled an anguished sob.

I wanted so badly to believe that Eppie's story was nothing but the ramblings of a broken mind and yet, how could I do that when so many fragments from my childhood had never quite fit: the appearance of my face in the looking glass, my coloring so foreign from my parents'. I was as different from them as if I were a cuckoo dropped in a drab sparrow's nest. And yet, it did not mean anything save that I was not their natural child. My mother could have been any of a score of wealthy women with red hair. *Look at Lettice Knollys,* my logic argued. And yet, was not Lettice the queen's own cousin? I rocked myself in terror, remembering the pamphlet the queen had raged about—Lady Katherine Grey locked in the Tower, separated from her husband. Helpless in a cell with a son whose blood was so royal he could threaten England's throne.

Every noble at court was vying for power, eager to determine who would inherit the crown should Elizabeth fail to produce an heir. If one of those ruthless men caught wind of this rumor about me it could hurtle me into the center of some mad conspiracy that would cost me my head. The ambitious Stuarts, the haughty Howards, they would see me as nothing but a tool to use for their own ends. Robert Dudley would be ecstatic to have such a pawn in his power. The features of the queen's favorite rose in my mind—Robert Dudley's auburn hair, his shrewd eyes, a man so far gone with ambition some said he had murdered his own wife to open his way to the queen's bridal bed. He would see me as his main chance to triumph over his enemies or perhaps to seize the prize he had lusted after for so long—leverage to force Elizabeth's hand, become husband to the queen, her lord and master and England's king. How had Mary Grey warned me against the man? *The Dudleys think and hunt as a pack . . . and Lord Robert has set his best hound upon you.*

Wyatt. My blood ran cold. If Sir Gabriel ever discovered the tale about my birth I would be exactly the weapon he needed to exceed the power of everyone surrounding the queen. Even his master, Robert Dudley.

As for the queen herself—every day of her life Elizabeth battled the legacy her mother had left her. Anne Boleyn, the King's Great Whore. To protect the honor of her name, she would crush anyone connected to such a dangerous lie. And if what Eppie said was true— what price would the queen be willing to pay to be rid of the evidence of her own shameful secret? I closed my eyes, remembered the doe's throat dripping blood, saw it transform into my own. What would the death of one maid of honor be in comparison to the peace of Elizabeth Tudor's entire realm?

"Nell!" The sound of Gabriel Wyatt's rough voice struck me as if I had summoned the devil himself. He strode toward me, the person above all others I dreaded to see. Terror drove me to my feet, an irrational fear he could read the truth in my eyes. What had Kat Ashley told me? The reason he earned the name "Angel"? *He possesses the devil's own gift for charming secrets people would only tell at heaven's gate.* Gabriel caught me by the arms as if he knew I planned to flee. He shook me firmly. "Nell, you struggle like a wild thing. Hold still."

"Why can you not leave me alone? Let go!"

"Not until I get the truth from you. Who was that person I saw you with?" Horror turned my knees to water. The man had been spying on me! How much had Sir Gabriel seen? Heard?

Think, Nell, think, a voice screamed inside me. *If he had heard what Eppie said, he would not need to question you thus. Use your wits. He cannot read your mind!* A flash of pale satin skirt swept past one of the windows cut in the garden walls, a man's laughter ringing out as some gallant chased after his lady. I latched on to that laughter as my own salvation. "You want to know who I met in the garden? My new suitor. Perhaps I should have him drive you off."

"Your new . . ."

"My lover!" I flung back at him, defiant. "A man who is everything you are not. Noble. Honorable. A man of integrity, honesty."

A muscle in Wyatt's jaw tightened, then smoothed so quickly I thought I had imagined it. "You found an honest man here at court?" His eyes seemed to pierce secret places in my mind. "Perhaps we should display him with the other curiosities in the menagerie at the Tower. Who is this paragon?"

"It is none of your affair. I wish only one thing from you. Leave me alone."

"You are lying. You have no lover."

"I do! I do! Tell the whole court! Then I could go home!" My voice cracked as I pictured the lions on the gatehouse, my mother bustling about, her keys all a-jangle, Father's library with its stained-glass windows, his crest turning to liquid jewels in the sun. But I did not belong there any more than I belonged here at court. I had no home.

I yanked myself free of Wyatt's grasp. He caught at my waist, but I flung my weight against his grip, heard cloth tear as I wrenched free. Desperate to escape him, I raced through the gardens, the shrub-carved creatures unfurling shadowy claws to catch at my sanity. I was not wise enough to wonder why he did not pursue me.

Chapter Sixteen

The Same Night

ATHER'S FACE ROSE BEFORE ME AS I FLED, SCARRED not only from the flames but by a far more devastating betrayal. Seeing me for what I was, a bastard his wife tried to pass off as his own. I struggled to comprehend it: Lord John de Lacey, not my real father. The man who had taught me so patiently, cherished me, coaxed my mind to soar . . .

"Father," I cried, picturing his wise, gentle eyes before the fire seared them. "I do not know what to do."

Oh God, I thought with a sick jolt. Father's papers, his instruments. They still lay hidden beneath the garden bench. I dared not go back and risk encountering Wyatt again. Pressing my hands against my stomach, I sought out the nearest page, a ruddy-faced lad with a crooked front tooth.

"I need you to run an errand for me," I said. "Retrieve something I've forgotten." I described the bundle and the bench where it lay hidden. "Deliver it to the maids' quarters and I will make it worth your trouble."

The lad doffed his cap, then set out at a run. I groped for the one thing of Father's I could still touch—my astrolabe. My fingers scrabbled at the place where I had pinned it so carefully in the Maids'

Lodgings, but even the chain was gone, torn from my waist some-time during my flight. It felt as if God's hand had reached down from heaven to snatch it away. *Why should you have such a treasure? John de Lacey does not belong to you. He never did.* The truth knifed through me, severed the bond that had anchored my whole life. And a new question battered me: If Lord John de Lacey was not my father, then—God save me—who *was*?

I made my way back into the palace. When I reached the Maids' Lodgings they seemed empty. I sagged against the door, groping to find the snippet of cloth Eppie had tucked into my cloth bag, wish-ing to hurl the scrap into the fire. Obliterate the one bit of tangible evidence from this night's madness, as if that could banish her claims to the realm of nightmare. But before I could rid myself of Eppie's "proof," Mary Grey slid out of the shadows where her spaniel had made a nest, ready to whelp any day now.

Heart hammering, I stowed the embroidered bit of velvet back out of sight. I should have guessed Mary would be there. She had hovered over the bitch for a week now, as worried as if the dog were her daughter instead of her pet. But why could Mary not be somewhere else tonight? Perhaps playing skittles with friends in the gallery or somewhere in the garden meeting a lover? The absurdity of either notion struck me: The other ladies barely tolerated her. And as for a lover . . .

"There was a page come looking for you an hour past." Mary wiped any lingering softness from her expression. "I told him you had run off to the garden."

My imagination leapt to the worst possible circumstance. I dared not face Elizabeth Tudor right now with Eppie's words still a fresh wound. "Did the queen require me?" I prayed it was not so.

"Lord, no," Mary snorted. "Her Majesty seems to crave your company about the same as she does mine of late—like a bout of Saint Anthony's Fire."

"Then who sent for me?" Sir Gabriel, perhaps? I wondered. Was that why he sought me in the gardens? Thank God he did not stumble upon Eppie and I sooner. Or had he?

"How should I know who sought you?" Mary said. "Contrary to simple folks' belief, the demons who twisted me in my mother's womb did not see fit to give me evil powers. If they had, I would have made Lettice's hair fall out in great clumps by now. Preferably in Robert Dudley's bed."

I did not even grimace, let alone smile. My clashes with Lettice seemed a thousand years ago. Mary peered up at me with a suspicious eye. "You are not taking a fever, are you? I have seen plague victims look better than you do."

A frisson of hopelessness rippled through me. If Mary could tell something was amiss, how would I ever hide my emotions from courtiers more cunning? The wolves would close in if they scented blood. I fought to smooth the edges from my voice. "I have a megrim. Nothing more."

"You had best keep it that way." She looked no more convinced than if I had claimed I had risen from the dead. "I have seen the way men look at you. If it were not for their fear of Gabriel Wyatt's sword, you would have a dozen suitors by now. You would do better to catch the sweating sickness than get with child, that I can tell you. The court dogs may whelp as often as they like, but Her Majesty does not deal well with blossoming bellies among her ladies. Whether they are married or no."

"Babes are expected when a woman marries. Why should the queen object?"

"My royal cousin expects to be the center of the universe for anyone she loves. A babe tends to steal its mother's affection. I do not speak from experience, of course. My mother loathed me, and Her Majesty would be delighted to get rid of me. If I were a dog, the queen would have drowned me long ago."

A hopeful light flickered in Mary's eyes, and I realized with a jolt she was trying to get me to laugh. God knows, the other maids would have found her words amusing. But I looked at Mary Grey as if seeing her for the first time.

All England knew Mary's lineage was more royal than Elizabeth's own. What's more, Mary bore the treason-stained name of Grey.

"Mary, you must be careful," I warned, aware of how vulnerable she must be despite the hard crust life had forced her to grow.

"You are a fine one to urge caution! I am not the one getting mysterious messages from God alone knows who."

"No. But you are sister to a woman the queen has great cause to fear."

"Katherine is no threat to the queen locked up in the Tower! What can she do in her cell?"

"She does not have to do anything at all. There are others beyond the stone walls determined to plead her case." I expected some reaction. Mary had seen what havoc such plots could wreak. I pressed on. "I am only trying to tell you what I saw. When I met with the queen after the masque, she showed me a tract proclaiming that your sister's marriage is legitimate and her son . . ." I let the words trail off, knowing they were too dangerous to say aloud. But Mary showed no such fear.

"Katherine's son is rightful heir to the Crown? If Mother were still alive she would be delighted. Unless, of course, Katherine loses her head as Jane did. That would be the end of all our family's hopes. Even my lady mother did not have any delusions a crown could be made to fit my head. Someone twisted by God's own hand."

Most would agree that God had cursed Mary. The Church was clear enough—such tragic crippling in body or mind was proof enough God's wrath had fallen on those such as Mary Grey. And yet, should she be condemned for her gnarled body any more than I should be because I was bastard born? Circumstances neither of us had any power over? I wished I could ask my father. Grief twisted inside me. As if Mary sensed my pain, she turned back to the spaniel, offering me space to wrestle my dragons in peace.

"There is a letter arrived for you," she said. "It bears the Calverley seal."

A letter from my mother. Already our correspondence was painfully stilted. How would I ever put pen to paper again? What would I say to the woman who knew my whole life was a lie, then had let me charge headlong into a lion's den?

My dear lady mother, I began my reply in my head. *Nay, not my lady mother. My lady liar is much more apt.* I crossed to where the letter waited. I could not bring myself to touch it, my mother's seal dangerous as Father's firework dragon.

Mary moved toward the hearth, where the fire crackled. She took the iron poker from the flames and plunged it in a flagon of ale. The liquid sizzled as it warmed, filling the chamber with its warm, yeasty scent. When the bubbling ceased, she set the iron aside, then crossed to me, flagon in hand. I accepted the drink gratefully, praying it would steady my nerves. Did my eyes betray me?

"I used to dread opening my mother's letters as well." Mary's voice had gentled. "If I ever have a daughter, I swear she will not. She will be glad to hear from me." She bent down to scoop the spaniel into her arms.

I sipped the ale Mary had given me, her act of kindness moving me as she started toward the door. "Mary." My voice cracked. "I do not mean to drive you from the room."

"Do not fret." She smiled, and she looked almost beautiful. "I have a place to go."

My throat tightened as the door closed behind her. I took up my mother's letter and thrust it into my writing box. Mary had somewhere to go. I had nowhere.

❦

MY OWN MOTHER wished me dead. Day after day, every time I looked into Elizabeth Tudor's eyes, I pictured the babe I had been, imagined being completely at her mercy. I could see the pillow growing larger, blotting out light, air, life. If she had been capable of murdering an innocent babe, how much easier would it be to kill me now?

I scarce ate. Dreaded sleep. With sleep came nightmares, all defenses swept away. I trudged through the days as they spiraled into weeks. Time was not weighed down with the stones that seemed to compress my chest. I still rose at dawn. Moll still laced me into my gowns. I still danced every morning in the Council Chamber and waited upon the queen when she required me. Nothing was different. Everything was changed.

I mapped the landscape of Elizabeth Tudor's features to measure against mine. I listened for the merest inflection of her voice, the shift of her moods, fearful.

Thrice, my mother had written to me, each letter more worried. *Are you well, child? The city air is noxious. Have you need of anything?* Can you scrub my mind clean as you do Calverley's stained-glass windows? I wanted to beg her. Wipe away the words Eppie said to me? *Then I would not know the truth, Mother, and you would not fear I might be daughter to the queen.*

I tried to grab tight to my anger, but the edges frayed with my loneliness. Would it be so terrible if I were to go back to Calverley? Anything would be better than court, this feeling as if the floor beneath me might crumble at any moment.

I glanced across the chamber to where the queen's ladies gathered in the twilight. Isabella Markham's fingers plied the strings of a lute. Mary Grey sorted a rainbow of embroidery threads Lettice Knollys had tangled in a fit of impatience. The queen stitched a tapestry, pausing now and again to bid Kat Ashley pop a strawberry into her mouth, releasing its sweet scent into the air.

Suddenly, I felt the queen's gaze hard upon me. "Leave off playing, Bella," Elizabeth commanded with a hint of petulance. "I weary of such a melancholy song. Mistress Elinor looks pensive enough these days."

Lettice preened, catching glimpses of her new russet silk gown in a nearby looking glass. "Perhaps she is missing Sir Gabriel, absent these many weeks."

That, at least, had been a blessing. I put aside my own stitching, the piece as snarled as my thoughts of late. "I am much relieved he is gone."

The queen pursed her lips, stained from the berries; the uncertain light gave a chalky cast to her features.

"Sir Gabriel will be gone all summer," Kat Ashley observed. "It is a hazard of being one of Lord Robert's most trusted men. His lordship sent the Gypsy's Angel on business, to oversee the transfer of the estates he gained with his new earldom. Then Wyatt is to ride to Maidstone and oversee the building of his own house."

Kat smiled, her delight in Dudley's good fortune evident in her kind face. Few others in court were pleased that the queen had endowed her favorite with the earldom of Leicester, her goal to make him noble enough to marry the troublesome queen of Scots. Yet even as Elizabeth draped the ceremonial robes around him she had not been able to resist her own attraction to the man. She tickled his neck before all those present, solidifying the Scots queen's resolve not to wed her bastard cousin's leavings.

I did not care about such royal machinations. I was only glad Sir Gabriel had more important tasks to pursue at present than discovering the identity of my visitor that star-scattered night in the garden.

The queen flashed me a pointed glance. "I cannot abide a woman mooning over some absent man. It makes my head ache. Perhaps Mistress de Lacey would fetch a book and read to us. She must have skill at it. I remember Roger Ascham mentioning that she read to her father after he lost his sight. Did you not, Mistress de Lacey?"

"I did, Your Majesty." I crossed to retrieve the book she indicated. The volume from Dr. Dee's library lay in the shade of a fragrant bunch of lilies William Pickering had sent the queen just that morning as a love token. With trepidation I regarded the pages left to read, dreading the time I must go to Dr. Dee's again, Eppie's fear of him infecting me, making me shudder at the prospect of confronting the alchemist's intuitive gaze.

The queen paused in her stitching to pluck the choicest of Pickering's blossoms and tuck it into the bosom of her gown. "My tutor admired your father, Nell. Ascham claimed it astonished him that Lord John could digest such huge amounts of learning and store it in such a small vessel. Your father was quite short, was he not? And swarthy?"

I kept my eyes on the book. There was no denying my father had been both. "He was, Majesty. Small in body, yet mighty in wit."

Kat Ashley chuckled. "He was small and dark and Thomasin, well, she is like a sparrow. Tell us, Mistress Nell, are you a cuckoo dropped in their nest?"

I fought to keep my voice light. "I am as God made me and my parents do not object. Perhaps I am like my grandfather." Suddenly portraits I had seen of Henry VIII splashed into my head. My courage wobbled. "Who can say?" I finished, shifting my eyes to where the other ladies sat on cushions, watching our exchange. "Look at Lady Mary's pups. Some are black and some are red. They have no power to choose."

Elizabeth frowned. "It is a most intriguing science, guessing which traits will appear in a breeding. There must be some order to it we have not yet discovered."

Grateful for the distraction, I tried to fix her attention on science. "We may unravel the mystery someday. I think we live in great times. Who knows what might be revealed if the right man does look for it." Yet another blunder. My cheeks heated.

"Perhaps I should have you speak with Walsingham. My old Moor says much the same thing when my cousin queen in Scotland vexes me." Elizabeth mimicked her sober Puritan spymaster's voice. "*Who knows what might be discovered?* As for a man keeping watch over my throne, I could have no better. Walsingham would interrogate a lark for stealing a crumb if he thought it a danger to me. Yes,

I am most fortunate to have such a man in my service, even if his methods leave me cold."

Mouth dry, I tried to judge whether the queen spoke warning to me or was merely praising her most cunning servant. If she were warning me, time to escape this coil might be running out. It would be worth risking an attempt to escape from her service. Once I was away from court she might forget whatever suspicions niggled at her. I had to take that chance. I crushed the book tight in my hands.

"Majesty, when Lady Ashley spoke of sparrows, it made me think. I am missing the de Lacey nest most sorely. Do you think it possible I might return home for a visit?"

An affronted spark lit Elizabeth's gaze. "You have duties more important than serving your queen?"

"Not more important. I am my mother's only child, Majesty."

One brow raised, ceruse paste cracking near her eye. "And yet, you were so eager to come to court that you defied her, if I remember rightly."

I dropped my gaze to the red leather cover of the book I held. "I am ashamed to recall that is so."

Kat Ashley spoke up. "Do not fret, Nell. There is little a mother would not forgive a beloved daughter." She gazed, heart-full, at Elizabeth. "Nor, by God's mercy, is there much a daughter refuses to forgive a foolish old woman." Regret years old clouded rheumy eyes.

Elizabeth patted Kat's blue-veined hand, and I remembered how Kat Ashley had been forced to make a record of Elizabeth's shameful encounters with Thomas Seymour. Yet it was obvious Elizabeth loved Kat still, without caution, without blame. Did the queen wish to please her old governess? Or did she use Kat's concern as a ruse to get what she plotted all along? I would never know for sure.

"Kat is right," the queen said. "Duty should be rewarded in all things. I cannot spare you, Elinor, but I could invite your mother to court for Christmastide this year. Would that please you?"

I froze. "I do not . . . what I mean to say is that I am grateful for Your Majesty's kindness, but Calverley is a great estate, and—"

Elizabeth scowled, not bothering to veil her displeasure. "It can hardly take more care than ruling a nation, and even I am able to celebrate Christmas. I will send a royal summons at once. Surely six months should give Lady Calverley plenty of time to discharge her duties. I am determined she will join me come December. I have much to ask that only she can answer."

My knuckles stood out white against the leather binding. I fought to keep my face from showing fear.

"Now read, Mistress. Read," the queen snapped. "You make me quite fidgety, leaping to and fro. First wanting your mother, then thinking her too busy to wait upon her queen. A great honor for any subject, mind you."

"I am aware of that, Majesty."

"Good. Kat will tell you it is not wise to try my patience. I lost all will to master my temper during the weary time I spent prisoner in the Tower. Listening to the workmen hammering on a scaffold frays a woman's nerves. It is an experience I hope none of you ladies ever suffer." She included them all with a sweep of her hand—Isabella Markham and Mary Sidney. Lettice and Mary Grey. Yet the queen kept her gaze pinned upon me. I had to force myself to breathe.

After a moment that seemed to last forever, Elizabeth retrieved her stitching. "But on to happier thoughts, Mistress Elinor," she bade me, her voice still holding a hint of frost. "Christmastide and your mother, here at court with you. Now you may thank me." She offered me her hand to kiss.

"Thank you, Your Majesty." How I squeezed the words out through a throat choked with fear, I do not know. I brushed my lips across her cold, white fingers.

I wished to escape the Virgin Queen's snare.

Instead, I was the bait to lure Thomasin de Lacey into the Tudor lioness's den.

Chapter Seventeen

December 1564

S UMMER VANISHED QUICK AS A FAIR-DAY RIBBON STOLEN by stiff wind. The court traded summertime London's plague-ridden streets for an orgy of pleasure at the finest country estates in England. Peer after peer played host to their queen.

We maids of honor jounced along in Elizabeth Tudor's wake, part of the jumble of carts and litters that carried the queen's household, the awe-inspiring spectacle displaying an entire royal court on the move. We clogged rutted roads and drew flocks of village folk come to press almond cakes and meadow flowers into their beloved queen's hands. Bewildered, I tried to fit the shape of the people's Elizabeth against that of the cunning stateswoman I had come to fear. Her graciousness to the grubbiest farmer, her patience as she listened to whatever petitions they brought her, and her tender compassion to those cursed with troubles astonished me. In spite of my wariness, I admired her when she was powdered with travel dust, listening intently to simple cares.

Yet as soon as we arrived at the next grand estate, the Elizabeth Tudor I dreaded emerged again. Each entertainment must be more extravagant than the last, the queen's most powerful subjects expected to beggar themselves to win royal favor.

I teetered on the knife's blade of the queen's cunning, never knowing when I might fall. When we were engaged in scholarly pursuits she challenged my powers of reason to the very limit, fascinated almost against her will. At other times she watched me, her eyes brimming with mistrust. I tried to convince myself my imagination had run wild: Elizabeth Tudor was capricious with all her ladies save the increasingly frail Kat Ashley. And yet, none of them posed the threat to the throne that I did. They did not wake every morning knowing the queen they served would order their death if she unearthed an old woman's rumor, or recognized the scrap of bed curtain hidden in my writing desk's most secret drawer.

Why had I not destroyed such damning evidence? Because some part of me wanted to show it to my mother. Use it to cross the uncharted passage between my present and my past, an astrolabe of silver stitches that might reveal where I came from.

One relief in this time of uncertainty—Sir Gabriel Wyatt remained absent from court, setting the other ladies buzzing with curiosity as to what improvements he was making to his estates and to Robert Dudley's. Wyatt was planning to take a wife, rumor said. I could breathe more freely once knowing I did not have to encounter the Gypsy's Angel prowling around every corner.

Still, once court returned to London and the queen's own palaces, dread thickened in me again. And as December loomed, I felt the queen taking a tender interest as to when my mother would join us.

"On Christmas Eve," I told Her Majesty, according to Mother's last letter.

Mother's letters had grown increasingly tense and anxious, as if she could sense trouble and needed to assure herself that I was well. Despite her desire to see me I detected uneasiness, too, as if she were about to step out on an icy staircase where she had taken a bad fall. My mother was wandering into a tempest and there was little I could do to warn her. A letter might be intercepted by one of Walsingham's men. Any hint of trouble between the queen and I might be just the spur his agents needed to delve deeper into my past. On

the thirteenth of December, fat flakes of snow smothered the garden. I wished I could deaden my foreboding as well. The queen
summoned me to wait upon her, and I hastened to her Privy Chamber where she sat examining a strange crystal sphere. "Mistress
Elinor, guess who has come to bid me Christmas cheer."

A cupboard door moved, revealing a familiar figure in dark
robes. I dropped my gaze. "Happy Christmas, Dr. Dee."

"I have asked him to predict my fortunes in the coming year. It
was quite enlightening. So intriguing watching him use his gifts. Yet
one gets distracted when it is one's own future being foretold."

"I do not foresee the future, Your Majesty," Dee corrected. "I
only read what the stars have to tell."

"And yet, what astonishing secrets you uncover. I have seen Dr.
Dee pluck amazing things out of what seems thin air. And so, I
thought, would it not be fascinating to watch him cast someone
else's horoscope? Try to unveil their future? Their past?"

Unbidden, my hands curled together, my fingernail catching
upon the proud flesh of my scar. "I think that a very fine idea, Your
Grace. I will fetch Isabella Markham at once. She will make a perfect
subject."

"I know too much about her to make such a reading entertaining. I prefer it be someone I have known a shorter time. Someone
with a mind to challenge Dr. Dee." Her lips thinned into a smile.
"I have chosen you."

My pulse tripped. "No, Majesty. I pray you would not."

"What? Such a devoted scholar unwilling to delve into the mists
of her own fate? I cannot understand it. Surely an innocent maid
like you has nothing to hide? And you cannot say such things make
you uncomfortable. You have been acquainted with Dr. Dee even
longer than I have. Your father's friend."

"Mistress Nell, in my experience it is best to accept Her
Majesty's generosity at once and regard it as the honor it is." Dr.
Dee looked wary as he approached a table laid out with volumes of
star charts, pens, and quills. The queen placed upon it the crystal

sphere. The scrying ball, I noted with a chill. Mere possession of such a thing could condemn its owner to the stake. Yet Elizabeth did not recoil from the object. I remembered Dee's efforts to foretell a propitious day for her coronation. Had that mystic question led to others until the embattled queen's fascination with seeing her future outweighed even the stain of dark magic? And if the situation shifted, would she shrink from bringing the full power of her crown to punish those whose skills she once sought?

I approached the table and sat down. What choice did I have? Dee took the bench next to me, his scent a comforting blend of ink and parchment and dusty books. A scent like that of my father. My eyes stung at the irony.

"Actually, I did Mistress Nell's star chart long ago, at her father's urging. It was strange, a most memorable accounting and one that gave me pause."

"Pause?" the queen echoed. "Why?"

"Saturn promised she would be gifted in sciences. A strange reading for a girl. Mars predicted conflicts ahead and yet—a great partnership. A congress of minds."

"Who is this partner?" the queen demanded. "A man?"

"I cannot say. I am not even sure whether they will be ally or foe. That is yet to be decided. But the strangest thing was the position of one of the constellations, a trickster who ushers in both dark and light. Draco the dragon. That is why I gave you the dragon book, Mistress Nell."

I flinched. "My father was blinded by a dragon."

"What?" The queen queried sharply.

"A firework he had created for my twelfth birthday. It was in the form of a dragon. It exploded and ignited the whole hill where he was setting off the display."

"Troublesome beasts, dragons," the queen said. "Ones every good knight should set out to drive from the earth."

Dr. Dee smiled. "Dragons do not really belong to the earth,

Majesty. They are meant to fly. Yet I would guess that even dragons sometimes need the right instrument to help them find their way back to the sky."

"I am more interested in Mistress Nell, Dr. Dee," the queen said. "I wish you to attempt the scrying ball."

Dr. Dee nodded. "Place your hands upon the scrying ball, Mistress Nell, let your essence seep within it."

The queen leaned closer, her eyes sharp. "Dr. Dee tells me that often in secrets of the mind success depends upon the openness of the subject."

I cupped the sphere as if it were melting glass. I tried to think of anything except what might betray me: Eppie's tale, the haggard cast of her face. And yet rather than blocking the condemning images, they flooded into my mind. What would happen if Dr. Dee was able to discern the truth? How would I know what he told the queen once I left? My mother was even now on her way to London. She might be outside the city walls, outside the palace gates. And I, all unwilling, might even now be betraying her secrets, condemning her along with myself.

Dr. Dee cupped his hands over mine on the ball. "Look at me, Mistress Nell. You have nothing to fear."

"Look at him!" The queen demanded. My gaze snapped to his. I felt as if I were falling into someplace dark. A tunnel. A cell. Before I struck the bottom, Dr. Dee startled me, pulling the sphere from numb fingers. I trembled, waiting for him to speak.

"Mistress," Dr. Dee said. "I vow your father would be most disappointed. You are the dullest subject I have yet attempted. Majesty, I fear Mistress Nell is very young. Perhaps we might attempt another reading when something happens in her life worth probing."

I hardly dared count my good fortune. "You saw nothing?" Elizabeth demanded.

"Guilt over her father's accident, but that is the burden of a dutiful child and can be of little interest to either of us."

"But you claimed there is a light about her. A fierce light you saw in your mystic mirror."

Dee shrugged. "I mistook it for something important. It was not. The light I saw was what Mistress Nell would be to her father after Lord Calverley lost his eyes."

"You may leave me, Mistress," the queen said. "Go join the other ladies decking the halls." I left the room much shaken. Was it possible I had deceived the greatest mystic in England? Or was Dr. Dee telling her my secret even now? More astonishing still, had John Dee seen all and risked the queen's wrath to shield me? *Do not fear.* Dee's voice seemed to whisper in my mind. And yet, how could I do anything else?

❧·❦·❧

I CURLED UP in a window seat apart from the other courtiers milling around the gallery. An open book lay forgotten in my lap as I peered out the mullioned panes to the road my mother would ride. Suddenly, across the room, I caught a glimpse of cloak flung back over familiar broad shoulders. I readied to make my escape as I had so many times in the three days since he had returned, but this time Sir Gabriel was too fast for me, blocking my flight from the alcove.

He wore a crimson velvet cap and his cloak was as green as the emeralds around the queen's throat that morning. Silvery fur edged the folds, and I knew where the twin to that fur had gone, his gift to Her Majesty. "I had this imported from the Russias," he had told the queen. "The pelts are much thicker there. I like wearing wolf because it reminds me that there are always predators about."

"Ah, but does it protect you against the predator you are closest to?" The queen's eyes shone with delight. "My new Earl of Leicester is looking quite thunderous since your return."

"Lord Robert? A predator?" Wyatt had seemed all astonishment. "Surely you cannot mean to warn me against him, Majesty. The predator I am closest to is right here."

Sir Gabriel tapped his chest with a grimace that set the ladies laughing. But it was not Wyatt's usual grin. Somewhere on the road the Angel had lost his smile.

"Greetings, my lady Grace."

I resented his reminder of the hunt where I had retched my insides out. But I was too weary to lock swords this day. "My name is Nell, as you know."

"Forgive me for cutting off your escape, but you have a talent for vanishing whenever I am around."

"Then perhaps you should leave me in peace."

He drew closer, leaning against the wall a hand's breadth from where I sat. He smelled of winter fires and warm stables, not the perfume other men wore.

"There is something I am anxious to show you. I am conducting an experiment, growing a strange fruit a sailor stole from a Spanish ship returning from the West Indies. It is called a pineapple." He took what looked to be a yellow half-moon with a harsh brown rind from the leather pouch affixed to his waist. "Taste it," he said, offering the fruit to me. "I cut into it just this morning and saved some for you."

"I am not hungry."

"The yellow meat tastes sour and sweet at once and seems to bite back. It reminded me of you. Are you not curious?"

I hesitated. My curiosity seemed a pale shadow of what it had once been. Yet I was still enough the girl raised by a scholar to take a tiny bite. The flavor burned with sweetness, too intense, like the court around me.

"What think you?" he asked. "I plan to take some to Dr. Dee. Perhaps you can arrange to join us at Mortlake. Between the three of us we can learn much about this fruit. See if it has healing properties, or might be used for a dye of some sort. Would that not please you?"

His words surprised me. There was kindness in them. And an understanding of me that had not been there before.

I shrugged. "My time is much taken up by my duties. Better you should pursue the matter of this fruit on your own."

Wyatt's gaze strayed to the window. "Are you waiting for the stars to come out? A winter sky can be beautiful as a spring one."

"I do not study skies at all anymore. I have everything I can do to keep track of things here on the ground." I fingered the naked hollow of my throat. "I lost my astrolabe in the garden all those months ago." My father's gift was gone forever.

I had recovered my father's instruments and his precious celestial charts. But I could not carry them with me every step, a talisman to remind me of the safety that was once mine. A safety built on lies, I reminded myself with brutal honesty.

"I thought you valued the necklace much," Gabriel said. "Perhaps more than the Saint Jacob's staff that Dr. Dee gave you. And then, you were almost moved to tears."

I dragged the tattered remnants of my pride about me. "There are far more important things to lose." *Like your father. Your mother. Every piece of who you are.*

"I liked it better when you hissed at me like a cat," he said, so soft it almost sounded like tenderness. "You are far too silent now."

"People here talk too much. They wield words like knives. No one tells the truth."

"I will."

"You are the worst conniver of them all! Everyone I know has warned me against you. Kat Ashley. Mary Grey. Even the queen herself. The cunning of a Gypsy, the face of an archangel. What could such a man as you want with me?"

He regarded me, solemn. "I swear, I cannot say."

"Is my virtue the prize you seek? Tell the world that you've claimed it." I thought of the queen's wrath once he did so. "Other maids have surrendered their maidenheads to courtiers and are none the worse for it unless they get with child. Just stay away from me is all I ask."

"I cannot. You are too thin, too pale." The pearl earring glimmered, taking on a dragon shape of light and shadow against his skin.

"I have worn myself out dancing for joy while you've been gone."

"You will not drive me away by wounding my pride. It seems with you I have little." His jaw tightened. "Something is not right with you. I can sense it. And I am not the only one. Even Lord Robert has spoken of the change."

"Extend my apologies to your master. I am sure you will soon find some other intrigue to occupy your time. A real intrigue instead of a maid of honor who dislikes your company and misses her home."

"Perhaps that is some of it, but not all. You look as if . . . almost as if someone has broken your heart. But I know you have no lover. I made certain that was true."

Fear threaded my nerves, reminding me too vividly of Gabriel's face when he'd caught me in the garden, demanding to know who Eppie was, what she had said to me. I still did not know how much he had heard that night, nor could I question him. I dared not risk stirring his already dangerous curiosity any further. Instead I locked onto anger, as much as I could muster. "So you continue spying on me. And you wonder why I despise you?"

"I do not wonder that at all." Laughter echoed from the far end of the gallery where the queen's fool capered about—a dwarf named Thomasina.

"Nell, I can tell something is amiss between you and the queen. Just know there are few things that cannot be mended at court if you have the right friends to help you."

My knuckle brushed the binding of my book. "You, sir, are not my friend."

"No. I am not." Something flickered in his face. Pain? Frustration that I had not succumbed to his legendary charm? I did not guess.

"I am busy with my reading," I said, touching the pages. "It is a most interesting tract I borrowed from Dr. Dee." I recalled my last encounter with the astronomer, the sensation I had felt, as if falling into his eyes. "The book is difficult. It takes all my concentration to decipher it."

"I can certainly see why." Sir Gabriel took up the volume, turning it in my lap. The print had been upside down. I slammed the book shut, waited for some burning jibe. I could expect no less, considering the opportunity I had given him. "Perhaps your mother can help you with the translation," Gabriel said. "I was surprised to hear she is to join us this Christmastide."

"My mother loathes this place and the queen knows it."

Gabriel regarded me a long moment, his face intent. "I will plague you no longer. I have pressing business to attend. I have just remembered it."

I did not reply, just turned my face back to the window. It was not long before I caught a glimpse of movement in the garden below, the flash of a jaunty feather in a ruby red cap, the flutter of emerald green velvet, faced with silver wolf.

Where was he going? To make note of everything I had said? To consort with Dr. Dee or unravel the secrets in my words, searching for something that might betray me?

❧❧❧

MOUNTAINS OF GREENERY trundled into the Great Hall in carts from the countryside, until it seemed all of England must be stripped bare this Christmas Eve. Holly with its spiked leaves sported berries like drops of blood. Evergreen with its piney scent whispered of Calverley's hills. Leathery bay leaves, boxwood, and holm oak waited their turn to be bundled into kissing spheres or garlands to deck Greenwich's Great Hall as all the queen's ladies labored to make this the merriest festival ever.

Thrice I had slipped and cut my hand as I snipped off bits of green. I nearly jumped out of my skin as Mary Grey bustled up with an expression disgruntled as I had ever seen on her face.

"You are a menace to the whole season." She groused so loudly that Isabella Markham, Elizabeth's current favorite lady-in-waiting, laughed from across the room. Mary removed the scissors from my hands. "Let me take those before someone loses a finger."

Startled as if she had slapped me, I gave her gnarled fingers a pointed glance. "Do take them if you think you can do better." Venting my hurt did not take the sting of her sharpness away. Mary and I had managed not only a truce of sorts these past months, but something that tiptoed near friendship.

"Your mother is come," she whispered. "Thomas sent word. He will keep her at the gatehouse as long as he can."

Shame welled up at how I had lashed out. "But why would he do that?"

"I asked him to. I always preferred to know when my mother was swooping in."

Frances Grey was the kind of mother who might have devoured her own young. Looking at what she had done to her three daughters, it might have been a more merciful end.

"Thank you." I squeezed Mary's hand.

"Do not be doing that!" She jerked away, sounding for all the world like she was furious, then she hissed. "You are supposed to stomp away in a temper."

So she had even planned a way for me to quit the circle of ladies, won me time to gather my wits, prepare to face my mother alone.

I left the hall as if I were in a temper. This first meeting with my mother since hearing Eppie's claims would be the hardest thing I had ever done. It was evident Mother had forgiven me for the way I left Calverley, but who could say how she would feel hours from now? My willfulness had dragged her back into the intrigue she had escaped. And yet, the lies she had told, the false life she had woven for me . . .

My heart raced as I hurried to the door, almost upsetting servants bringing trays of the fruit suckets the queen so loved, confections dusted with sugar soft as new-fallen snow.

I exited the door leading from the Great Hall and raced down the steps. Without bothering to grab pattens or cloak I hastened into the courtyard. Snow welled over the edge of my slippers as I rushed toward the gatehouse. Snowflakes stung wherever my skin was bare, but I scarce noticed, my gaze locked on the banner that rode gusts of wintry wind. The Calverley lion that had guarded me all my days, my birthright. Now, even the heraldic beasts seemed to show their fangs in disapproval.

The curtains on Mother's litter were drawn back, the interior empty. A jolt of panic made my ruined slippers even fleeter. Had the queen ordered my mother taken for questioning the instant she arrived?

No. I glimpsed a tiny figure in a serviceable gray cloak. She stood in the glow of a lantern under the roof that spanned the gatehouse's two towers. Thomas Keyes' mammoth hands held a coffer I recognized as my mother's physicking chest, while a young yeoman of the guard allowed my mother to peer into his throat. What on earth? I wondered, trying to make sense out of the situation. Back at Calverley mother prided herself on nursing our ill crofters. Nothing was more likely to consume her attention than someone in need of her skill. But how on earth had Thomas Keyes guessed that?

"It is not so very red, Sergeant Porter," I heard mother say. "Yet a putrid throat is painful. Boil the herbs in this pouch into a hot tisane, sweeten it with honey and—"

"My lady?" I called. I did not add "mother," the word awkward on my tongue.

Even so, she spun around at the sound of my voice, all but dropping the infusion of herbs into the snow. "Nell?" Her cry was so glad I wanted to turn and run from the welcome in her face. Father would have eschewed formality and scooped me into an embrace. For an instant, I feared my mother might do the same and I was uncertain of my own reaction. But she approached me with all the dignity of a baroness encountering her daughter before the eyes of the world. Embraces would come later, when we were alone. I was glad of that little time to compose myself.

"Arabella," she called, summoning her maid. "Fetch Mistress Nell a cloak out of my trunk. It is freezing out here. She will catch her death."

Keyes intervened. "Please, my lady Calverley, allow me to see your daughter warm." He swept off his own cape, settling it around my shoulders. It was so long it pooled on the ground in a crimson puddle. "I would hate to have Mistress Elinor take sick or carry fever back to the maids' quarters. I can gather it up once my shift here is done." It could only be Mary Grey he would recover it from; the other ladies would hardly give the "commoner Cyclops" a civil good morrow.

"I thank you," Mother said, with a wry smile. "I had hoped life at court might make my daughter a trifle less impulsive, but I can see it has not changed Nell at all."

Resenting her for picking at me about not wearing a cloak seemed absurd under the circumstances, but it provided a familiar island in the tumult that raged inside me. I wished I could beach myself on that island and rest. But before I could, my mother caught my hand in a grip that conveyed more than she would ever allow herself to put into words.

Tears sprang to my eyes. I bit down, hard on the inside of my lip, praying the pain would drive my emotions back behind the dam that had contained them for so long.

"Come, sweeting," my mother said. "We have much to talk about."

The child in me longed to bury my face in her lap and weep. The Nell forged in a crucible of lies and betrayal could only say: "We do." How I had changed in the months we had been apart. I knew fear now, and self-doubt.

"Have you made any friends among the ladies-in-waiting?" Mother asked as we made our way toward the warmth of the palace. "My affection for Katherine Parr and Kat Ashley was the only precious thing I found at court."

"I have not much time for friends," I evaded. "Elizabeth is a demanding mistress, and you know how I am. I always did prefer to be alone with my books."

Mother tsked, then smiled. "You always were just like your father."

"Do not say that," I cried, voice raw.

"What?" My mother exclaimed, surprised.

"Do not say I am like him!"

A gust of wind pelted us with snow crystals, making our cheeks burn. "Let us go inside, Mother. I will order hot ale for you and a bite to eat. You must be iced through and famished after your travels."

Mother looked at me, a crease appearing between her brows. "The Nell who left Calverley would not have noticed such things. You are much changed, daughter. Thinner. More reserved."

It was not until Mother was divested of her snowy garments and toasting her stocking-clad feet at the fireplace in the deserted maids' chambers that I dared broach the subject that infected every corner of my mind. I had tried to compose my questions a thousand times, but they knotted on my tongue.

"Eppie found me," I said. "She told me wild things about my birth."

Mother clutched her stomach. "You are *my* daughter."

"Do not lie." Tears burned. "Your face tells the truth! You did not bear me."

"I am not denying that!"

"You brought me home and told Father I was his child. That is why he loved me. If he had known the truth—"

"John knew."

"You told him?" Possibility rushed in: If Father had known and loved me in spite of my birth I could let go of my greatest terror, that he would have rejected me. "Eppie said you kept it secret."

"I did not need to tell John de Lacey you were not of my womb. He had eyes to see, Nell, and the keenest mind God ever put inside a man. Even when you were a babe you were fair of face, with a red-gold cap of curls. So hale and lusty no one could look at you and believe you'd been snatched from death's door. Our other babes, your sister and brothers buried in the crypt, they were spindly, wizened, brown little things like John and I. Your father knew. When I started to tell him, he kissed my lips shut, said how beautiful you were, or how bright. He would hold you up into the light from the window in his library—he took you there even as a babe—and he would speak to you of stars and myths and dreams."

Tears brimmed over my lashes. It was so like Father, I knew Mother's tale was true. "But I am not his daughter. I never was. You *both* lied to me then."

"And how did we lie, Elinor de Lacey? God placed you in our arms more surely than if he had seeded you in my womb. What drove me to go to that holy well? What impelled Eppie to come with me? And that night, when those masked people knocked upon the abbey door . . . How had they come to know Eppie would be there?"

"I do not know."

"I do," Mother said fiercely. "God went to a great deal of trouble on our behalf, Mistress, and if I were you I would not quibble over loose threads, but be grateful." Her voice broke. "As grateful as I am that He did!"

"Mother, there is more. Eppie says that . . . that the queen is my . . ."

"Hush, Nell!" Mother pressed her fingers to my lips to stop the words. "That part of the tale is *not* true. Mistress Jones is mad! I should have turned her out the instant she told such a lie!"

I peered into my mother's face, desperate to believe her. "If you should have sent her away, why didn't you?"

Mother flinched. "Because you loved her so. Because . . ."

I knew in that instant, felt my heart sink. "Because you were too just to condemn her for what you feared might be the truth."

"Nell, I—"

"When the queen heard that I was born near the holy well of St. Michael and that Eppie was my nurse, things changed between us. I could see something in her eyes."

"Elizabeth Tudor has spent her whole life being hunted by one wolf or another. She imagines danger behind every corner. You have the red-gold hair of a Tudor rose, but what does that signify?

Henry was a lusty man and had mistresses aplenty. Nor was he the only red-haired man in all of England. Why, then, could you not get your coloring from some sprout started thus?"

Why did I sense there was something more, something she was hiding? "What you say is possible, but you cannot dismiss Eppie's claim entirely. I can see it in your eyes. How could Elizabeth have concealed being with child, Mother? Would not her belly have shown? Look at how the servants chattered about the scandal with—"

We both started at the sound of the door latch. It opened, Lettice Knollys sweeping inside. "Lady Calverley!" She dropped my mother an arrogant curtsey. "Welcome to court! I believe you and my mother are near an age. Was she Catherine Carey then?"

"Your mother is a good and gracious lady by whatever surname. And a brave one. She was but a child when she kept vigil with Queen Anne in the Tower, even walking with her to the scaffold."

"It was her duty as the queen's own niece," Lettice said. "Or was it duty to her natural father she felt?"

All England knew Catherine Carey Knollys had been conceived during Henry's affair with Mary, the first of the Boleyn sisters he had bedded. And yet, to have the woman's own daughter making jest of it was more than my mother could stand. "Your mother was one of the bravest women I had the privilege to know. You would do well to model your behavior after hers."

"That is what my father is forever saying. But since there are no queens being beheaded at present I must shift for myself however I can. It is nearing time for the queen's dinner, so Nell had best come along with me. Today she gets the great honor of holding a fine linen cloth for the queen to spit in."

Lettice hoped to prick my temper, but I had more important matters on my mind than my position in the order of service we were to provide.

"Run along, Nell," my mother bade me. "We can finish our discussion in private later." She gave Lettice a pointed look. But where would we find such privacy at court?

❦ ❦

IT WAS NOT until three days had passed that I was able to steal my mother away, into a closet near the queen's chapel. By then, the strain was etched about her eyes, and I could see the cogs in her mind whirling. I had watched her solve a thousand problems over the years at Calverley. Some part of me still believed she could do the same even here. "I have been worrying this difficulty over and over in my head," Mother said. "Trying to puzzle out how it might have been possible for the princess to hide such a condition."

"And it is not possible, is it? The authorities interrogated her servants and they testified to it all—every humiliating incident with Thomas Seymour. There is no way something so earth-shattering could be kept secret."

"I wish I could tell you that was so. But the more I think on it . . ." Mother pleated a fold of her black damask gown. "Nell, during the years Edward reigned people were not certain she was King Henry's daughter. King Edward was a healthy boy. We all believed he would marry and father heirs of his own. Elizabeth was unimportant. She was not closely watched in Katherine Parr's household. Katherine believed those she loved were as good and honorable as she was. It never occurred to her that her husband would seduce her stepdaughter beneath her very nose."

"But playing bawdy games is different from stealing a princess's virtue."

"Seymour was arrogant enough to risk all for the prestige of bedding a king's daughter."

I flinched at the thought such a man might have sired me.

"When the dowager queen and I discovered Seymour atop Elizabeth that August I cannot tell you how stricken we all were; Elizabeth, too. She was painfully young. If Katherine Parr suspected the girl was with child, she would have moved both heaven and earth to shield her. I always knew that she did not banish Elizabeth to Cheshunt out of spite or to punish her. She sent the child to the care of her trusted stepdaughter in order to protect Elizabeth from Thomas Seymour."

I tried to imagine what the women must have felt.

"Once Elizabeth arrived at Cheshunt she fell desperately ill, a sickness that confined her to bed. Months she suffered, I always believed stricken with guilt. The dowager queen was a mother to her, you see. In the months that followed, the two even wrote to each other. Katherine showed Elizabeth's letters to me. Letters of a desperately penitent child starved for love. I think there were times I could have happily murdered Thomas Seymour in his bed."

"The princess was lodged at Cheshunt. Is that not near the place where I was born?"

"It is."

My nerves tightened with dread. Had I not boasted of just that location to Sir Gabriel soon after we met?

"Now when I think of those months my heart aches for her. Back then, my heart was far harder. She had wounded my beloved friend. Even if Katherine could pardon her, there was a part of me that could not forgive her. Now that I have a daughter of my own I better understand." My mother touched my cheek. "Do not look so guilty, sweet. For once this is not one of my criticisms. It is only an explanation."

"But she could not hide in her bed from everyone. Her servants of the body would have seen her swelling belly when they bathed her. Dressed her. Surely they would have exposed her secret? And to great personal gain in Queen Mary's reign, when the woman would have given much to be rid of her Protestant sister."

"Is it so impossible to think that good people might be inspired to help a child left so unprotected? Especially if Katherine Parr asked them to? The queen inspired great love and loyalty in those whose lives she touched, and it is likely that few people dared enter

Elizabeth's chamber when she was ill. There is no way to predict how deadly an illness might be. Plague, consumption, a putrid sore throat . . . any such infection can kill. If there was a plan to protect Elizabeth, the conspirators would take care few would see her. And who would have suspected Thomas Seymour's seduction of the child? It was not until Katherine lay dead and the blackguard pressed his suit for Elizabeth's hand that the world learned of the affair. By then any child would have been long born and discarded."

"Do you not mean murdered?" I wanted to retch.

"Yes. Murdered. Were it not for one woman's courage and a babe tenacious of life." Mother drew a ragged breath. "That is, if events happened as I now imagine."

"If they did, then Elizabeth ordered me to be destroyed. Like a pup born with its mouth cleft."

"Perhaps. Or perhaps she was told you were born dead by those who wished to protect her. But even if the worst is true and she had a hand in ordering your death, even I cannot think too harshly of her. Imagine facing such a thing at fourteen. The terror of a child already named bastard by her own father, her mother beheaded, her stepmother aware she had been tumbled like a milkmaid. Elizabeth must have been half wild with horror, and denied the truth as long as possible. Eppie told me that she had seen cases where women were forced to lie with brutal men and were so traumatized that they did not suspect they were pregnant even when the pains began."

"That is hard to believe."

"Your father believed that the mind protects us from calamities too great to bear. For Elizabeth, what greater calamity could there be? The good news is that there is no way for anyone to prove for certain this tale of Eppie's is true."

"But—" I stopped.

There is, I had meant to tell her. A *scrap of bed curtain stitched in silver.* Yet if mother knew it existed, she would see it destroyed. *I* should have done so myself, stuffed it into the flames long ago. It was the one tangible piece of where I had come from, held the key to who I really was. Once it was gone, it could never be replaced. I looked away from mother's eyes, shining with love, with protectiveness.

"Mother, I am sorry. About defying you. Coming here. I did not understand."

"I never wanted you to face this. I was afraid you would blame me. I was a coward."

"No! Not you! Not ever!"

"Yes, Nell. A coward. I always knew your love for me was not on solid footing the way it was with your father and Eppie. I clung so tight, afraid of losing what bit of it I had, that I put you in danger."

Blunt, my mother's words. A lifetime of wistfulness, watching others gather up the love she had risked so much for, longed for during pregnancy after pregnancy. And yet, to tell her that I had loved her the same would be an insult to her honesty.

"I am sorry," I cried.

"I am not. There. I have said it. It is all in the open now, like a wound that must have air to seal it properly at the last."

In that moment I saw a different mother from the one I had known. I saw the woman who had been a rock for Katherine Parr when all of court had been shifting sands. I saw courage and strength and love. Most of all, love.

"We will survive this trial, Nell. You and I. Together."

I wanted so much to believe her. "What if the queen guesses? What if someone finds out? When Eppie came to the palace she said the queen's men were seeking her. She seemed so rattled I half believed she was mad after all."

"Only you and I and Eppie know her tale and no power on earth would compel any of us to tell."

I should have known the danger of tempting fate with such confident words. I should have remembered Kat Ashley had broken, told of Thomas Seymour's licentious deeds when the right pressure was used. Within the Tower's dread fortress, far stronger wills were broken every day.

Chapter Eighteen

December 25, 1564

HRISTMAS DAY DAWNED WITH GLOWERING GRAY clouds that even the festive decorations could not banish. It was as if my fears pressed at the windows, trying to catch a glimpse of battles still to be joined. I had seen skillful jousting during the months court was in progress, yet never between two fearsome combatants wearing silken skirts. Instead of charging horses at each other in the lists, my mother and the queen chose the chapel after Christ's Mass as their venue. But the spectators who gathered after the service watched with that same eagerness I had witnessed in the pavilion, people attempting to guess which contender would draw first blood.

It was obvious the court knew of the queen's long-standing dislike of Lady Calverley. Some, like Lady Ashley, had actually witnessed the scandal that had forever planted Elizabeth Tudor and the loving friend of Katherine Parr on opposite sides of battle lines. Imaginations brewed all sorts of possibilities, the speculation that had marked my first weeks at court boiling over anew. Why had I been chosen as maid of honor when so many more powerful nobles battled to win the privilege for their daughters? And now the even more intriguing question presented itself: Why had my mother been invited to London when such bitterness stood between the queen and the Baroness of Calverley?

My mother stayed as close to me as she could after the service, slipping through the crowd until she was near my place with the queen's other maids. As Elizabeth prepared to exit the chapel ahead of her courtiers, the queen paused to regard the carved wooden Christ child placed upon the altar for the day.

"What fear His mother must have known when she bore Him in a stable," the queen observed. "Stealing the babe out from under the nose of a vengeful king and then fleeing with God's own son to Egypt! It is no small feat to raise such an extraordinary child. I cannot imagine how one would do so."

Secretary Cecil smiled. "Someday, Majesty, you will find out. When you give England an heir. A fine strong son."

Hands clapped, voices murmured in the crowd as a hearty round of approval rippled through those nearest her.

"Yes," the queen said. "A son." Elizabeth's own mother had died for want of one. Had Anne Boleyn produced a healthy prince, there would have been no trial for witchcraft and adultery, no beheading on Tower Green, no parade of other wives haunting Tudor palaces.

Elizabeth coughed behind her beringed hand. "If you remember rightly, Cecil, my stepmother, Jane Seymour, died giving England a prince. Childbirth is dangerous business. More difficult still, raising heirs to be proud of. Look at the whelps scrabbling over the French throne. It remains to be seen whether Henri Valois and Catherine de Medici produced even one in their vast litter worthy to wear a crown."

"That will not be the case with Your Majesty," Robert Dudley cut in. "No one can have any doubt that you would be an exemplary mother. You are a most doting godmother to . . . how many babes now?"

"I fear I lose count and am too full of holiday spirit to puzzle it out. But I observe mothers closely. Make a study of the science, one might say. For example, our recently arrived guest Lady Calverley."

The queen glanced about the party until she found my mother. "Come forward, Thomasin."

My mother brushed past me to wend her way toward the queen.

"You have a most remarkable daughter," Elizabeth said. "What is your secret in raising her?"

My mother looked somehow taller in her sober black gown. "My methods are simple enough. A steady diet of Latin and the classics, exercise in clean country air, and a hearty dose of good sense. In short, a childhood much like the one you had, Majesty."

"You would know all about that, Lady Calverley, would you not?" Elizabeth gathered up the chain at her waist that held her pomander ball. She raised the scented sphere to sniff it. "You were seldom far from my last stepmother's side. You accompanied her after she was widowed, and were present when she wed again. Far too soon for decorum's sake, considering her late husband had been King of England."

"Your opinion about their marriage was not always so disapproving, Majesty."

Elizabeth dropped the filigreed ball, its chain rattling. Her face went still as marble. A crackle of anticipation set the crowd on alert and my hand knotted beneath the folds of my gown. What was my mother thinking, speaking to the queen so?

Mother smiled as if not noticing the queen's displeasure. "It is fortunate you and I are grown women now, Majesty, and know opinions often change with time. Age gives us wisdom. Thank God we are not held accountable for youthful folly." Suddenly I sensed what Mother was doing—laying the groundwork for the case she would later present to convince Her Majesty to allow me to return home. It was a great gamble to offend the queen, but no greater than remaining here.

"I find myself curious. What wisdom have the years granted you, Lady Calverley?"

"They have shown me that I am not a woman made for grand settings. I seek peace on my husband's estates and wish only to have my child nearby."

"Your child did not want your company the same way," Elizabeth said with some pleasure. "She defied you to serve her queen."

I winced, but mother did not betray the pain that must have cost her.

"I pray Elinor has served you well, Majesty. But that does not save a mother's heart from missing her most sorely."

"Nestlings must fly, whether one wills it or no. I find her quite useful in scholarly debates and questions of science. Just the other day we discussed my Catholic subjects' unruliness about religion, debated whether harsh measures were needed to bring them to heel. Some of my ministers would crush them sharply. Your daughter said one cannot drag an animal to the trough and force it to swallow something that does not nourish it. A cow cannot be expected to eat what a hawk might. But both may live together in the same meadow."

"Nell has a fine mind," Mother agreed. "She inherited it from her father."

"And what do you think I inherited from mine?"

The queen regarded Mother with wolfish intensity. I could hear the echoes of pain decades old, wounds left by those who insisted that Elizabeth was a bastard sired by the musician Mark Smeaton.

"You are a fine scholar, a gifted musician, regal in bearing, and have the love of your subjects. In face, of any of his children, you are most like Great Harry."

Elizabeth looked pleased.

She did not feel Mother shudder, or discern the reason behind it.

❖❖❖

CHRISTMASTIDE AT COURT. My mother had seen many, this would be my first. Feasting and mummers would fill days and nights, Morris dancers frolicking in bright apparel, their hobbyhorses and Saint George's dragon drawing laughter from young and old alike. Boys who sang like angels would fill the musician's gallery in the Great Hall, but I doubted we would notice, however sweet their song.

Twelve days of rejoicing Mother and I would be forced to endure, each with its own tradition: Christmas with its grand feast, then the Saint Stephen's Day hunt, when the poor fox was pardoned. New Year's Day with its long-anticipated exchange of gifts. The festivities would not end until Twelfth Night, when the decorations were burned, a chunk of yule log saved so it would protect the house from fire in the year to come.

As time crawled past it was as if Mother and I snatched each day from the fire, like we did raisins in the game Snap Dragon. Nipping the dried fruit with quick fingers from the blazing bowl of brandy someone had set alight. Our greatest hope? Once the queen was sated with roasted brawn and softened by gifts from her courtiers, Elizabeth might be willing to let me leave court. When time came for my mother to return home, pray God, I would ride out of London by her side.

Resolved as my mother was that this would be so, my own optimism sank further as each night passed. The queen demanded I wait upon her, seldom allowing me far from her side. Was she jealous of my mother drawing my attention? Or was the queen's remarkable behavior something more strategic? A way to keep both de Lacey women close enough to catch us off guard when the time came to make her thrust?

As I prepared myself for the New Year's festivities, thrice I tipped over bottles strewing the table before my looking glass. I stained my sleeve with wine, and muttered an oath when Moll dropped the hairbrush in my lap, snagging the satin. Mother gently motioned Moll aside and took the brush, drawing it through my hair in long, soothing strokes. I could remember her performing such a task only rarely. That made the experience all the more precious.

"Do not fear, sweeting. A few more nights, then all will be well," she encouraged as she set the brush aside and began rubbing the hip-length strands with red satin to polish them to a sheen. I wished I could believe her. But the moment we entered the Great Hall I could feel a charge in the air, the kind that seized Calverley's hilltops just before lightning split the sky.

Rivers of candlelight illuminated the walls, loops of greenery draped every rail, and dangling from the ceiling were gay ribbons. The crowd pressed close, fighting to see the wondrous, rich gifts courtiers offered to their queen. Even I was transfixed as fantastical clocks, exquisite jewels, and gowns encrusted with gems were unveiled. As Robert Dudley approached the queen the whole room strained forward. That moment, something tugged at my skirt. I turned, expecting someone had trod on my hem. Instead, Mary Grey smiled up at me, her brown hair caught back in a white French hood trimmed with silver. My mother gave her such a warm smile it touched me. "Happy New Year, Lady Mary."

Mary curtsied. "Lady Calverley. I hope you have gotten some sleep since you've taken my place as Nell's bedfellow. She is terrible greedy when it comes to the covers."

"This from the smallest woman at court, who takes up more space in the bed than Thomas Keyes would!" I said. "Add to that Polly and her pups, and it is a wonder I even get a sliver of the feather tick!"

"You see what I must endure," Mary said to my mother, then passed me a packet.

I looked at it in surprise. "What is this?"

"Open it," Mary urged, eager as if the gift were for her.

Shame stung me. "I do not have anything for you."

"I did not expect you to." She meant it, no rancor in her tone.

I tugged at the wrapping, unveiled a pair of stockings. They were an exquisite blue, thick and warm. I had seen just such a color when we ladies had been stitching with the queen. The silk yarn had been pillowed in Mary's lap, her fingers awkwardly wielding four thin ivory needles. Mary had started the project over and over, her tongue stuck out just a little, her brow furrowed until it all but disappeared. I lifted the socks into the light. "Did you make these for me?"

"I tried them on Polly but they made her slip on the floor. I only give them to you because she would not have them." Mary made a face so comical it should have made me smile. "I grew weary of you waking me up in the night with your cold feet."

"Mary, I—"

"Yes, yes. I know. You are overcome with gratitude. Tell me later. I must steal away. I have another gift to deliver and I am certain the queen will not miss me." Mary waved at the mass of courtiers that swarmed around Elizabeth, the nearby tables groaning with rich gifts. "If anyone asks tell them I was stricken with a headache or drank too much wine or some such."

"But you look more pink-cheeked and glowing than I have ever seen you," I observed, noting how her eyes were sparkling.

"Please, Nell. Just tell them . . ." Mary broke off with a chuckle. "Oh, you needn't bother. If anyone notices I am gone it will just be an excuse to toast their good fortune!"

"Mary!" I exclaimed.

"You know it is true. But I do not care tonight. I doubt I will care what they think of me ever again!" She gave me a quick hug, then darted away, her tiny form swallowed up so quickly I could not catch her, say the words that suddenly rose up in my mind: *Be careful, my friend. For despite the commotion the queen sees far more than we will ever know.*

"Poor creature," my mother said softly, looking where Mary had disappeared.

"Do you pity her because she is dwarfed?"

"No, though her size gives her trouble enough for a lifetime. I have sympathy for Mary because I knew her mother well. We were girls at court together and even then Frances was the most selfish, haughty woman I ever met. Three daughters she had in the years since then, and she twisted them all through her ambition."

"Father said when Jane Grey was a girl she lived with Katherine Parr at Chelsea."

"Such a solemn child she was, all huge, worried eyes and freckles on skin far too pale." Sadness shadowed Mother's face in stark counterpoint to the gaiety around us. "But her mind was hungry as yours, Nell. She would have been happy locked in a quiet garret somewhere as long as she had her store of books."

I felt a jab of jealousy, imagining this quiet, perfect child. And yet, Mary claimed they had beaten Jane to force her to wed Guilford Dudley. She must have had a strong will as well.

"Do you know what Frances Grey did after Lady Jane died on the block?" Mother demanded, bitter. "That vile bitch carried Mary Tudor's train. The train of the woman who had executed her daughter. If Frances could do such a thing without plunging a dagger into the woman's chest, I can only imagine what evils she must have dealt your wee Mary. And yet, Frances survived it all—stealing a crown for her child, seeing it ripped from Jane's head. Two rebellions and her husband and daughter dead upon the block. She even married her Master of the Horse mere weeks after her husband was executed. Frances managed to thrive when far better people were trampled by fate. There are times, Nell, I wish I were more like you. With a list of questions to take to God on judgment day. There is so much I do not understand."

She took my hand beneath the fall of our sleeves, and I was glad for the warm press of her fingers as we wended our way toward the dais where Elizabeth sat, her face aglow with the delight of an overindulged child. A mechanical toy made of gold gleamed in her hands, a unicorn perched atop a mountain of cabochon jewels while a maiden reached to touch the mythical beast.

"Look, you! All of you!" the queen cried, working its mechanism. The unicorn's delicate gold forelegs buckled, kneeling to kiss the maiden's feet. "See what Lord Robert has given me? How can any of you bid me marry when it would deny me the worship of such a magnificent creature?"

"Say the word and you shall exchange it," Dudley said. "A creature of fantasy for a man of flesh and blood who would be faithful to you forever."

Lettice tittered, other maids hiding giggles behind their hands. The laughter echoing through the rest of the chamber was stiff, ended far too sharply. I glimpsed Sir Francis Walsingham and Robert Cecil, both scowling. Behind them, I recognized another familiar figure ranging through the crowd—Sir Gabriel Wyatt, garbed in his finest raiment, the pearl dragon dangling from his ear. His gaze caught mine. Held. He had not troubled me while my mother was about, yet small, mysterious things had begun to happen. The finest bits of marchpane found its way to our plates, a new pair of gloves appeared when I mislaid a pair. A book was delivered upon the subject of botany, a segment marked on propagating unfamiliar plants. I remembered the pine apple and wondered. Who but Wyatt would know to tempt me so?

Yet such silent acts of generosity were over; I could tell from his expression. I fought the instinct to flee. It was pointless to attempt it in such a crush of humanity, all straining to get closer to the queen. Instead, I held my ground, feeling braced by the presence of my mother beside me. "Lady Calverley," he said, bowing so low I glimpsed the tender nape beneath his tumbled curls.

"Sir? I do not believe we have met." My mother said with a curtsey.

"I am Sir Gabriel Wyatt."

"Wyatt?" My mother's eyes narrowed, but there was a softness to her mouth. "From which branch of that family do you come?"

"My grandfather wrote poetry to Queen Anne Boleyn and lived to tell of it. My cousin led the rebellion to keep a Spanish king from the English throne. My father died a traitor's death for fighting along his side and I was condemned to die as he did." It was more than Sir Gabriel ever shared with me.

"Why were you not executed?" I asked.

"Nell!" My mother tried to hush me.

Sir Gabriel's lips crooked in a ghost of his old smile. "It is a fair question. And I like your daughter's bluntness above all things. Almost." I felt the word like the trail of fingers across skin. It nearly made me retract the question. But Sir Gabriel glanced down at an object in his hand. "You ask why I was not executed at my father's side?" He met my gaze so levelly it astonished me. It was as if I were seeing him, truly seeing *him* for the first time. "When a chance of escape was offered me I took it. Saved my life as best I could. I was far hungrier for life than to die a noble death. I am much too selfish to make a good martyr, Mistress Nell. Do you not agree?"

"I do."

"Ah, something we can agree on. Your daughter and I cross swords often, Lady Calverley. I have brought her a peace offering during this season when the lion is to lie down with the lamb." He thrummed his fingers upon a leather-bound book. I regarded it warily. "Do not fear, Grace." The pearl dragon shifted against his skin. "It will not explode when you open it."

"Sir Angel!" The queen's summons cut through the jabber of the crowd. I jumped, startled. The queen rose from her throne in radiant splendor. "What is that intriguing object you hold in your hands? Doubtless a gift for me?"

Gabriel flung his cape back over his left shoulder. "Majesty—"

"Sly boy! You know I love books above all things! Give it to me at once!"

Gabriel shifted, suddenly looking uneasy. "This gift would not please you, Your Grace. It is not worthy."

"I will suffer none of your false modesty," Elizabeth preened with a merry toss of her head. "What is the book about? Is it philosophy? Some classic translation you have bought from Dr. Dee? Tell me at once, sir!"

Gabriel held the volume closer to his chest. "It is nothing save a collection of very bad poetry, Majesty."

"I shall be the judge of that. Who is the poet?"

Did I see reluctance in Gabriel's features? And around his mouth something more? Embarrassment? "I am," he said.

The queen clapped her hands. "Love poems from my Gypsy's Angel? And shall we guess who inspired them? She batted her lashes like a moonstruck girl. Little wonder. Nearly every man at court had tried to woo her thus, in verse or in song.

"Majesty," Gabriel said, "I pray you—"

"No more excuses. Come stand here beside me and read so everyone can hear." Gabriel cast me a cryptic glance, then did as he was commanded. Standing before Elizabeth, he opened to a page inked in what must be his own hand.

> "My lady Grace, how fleet you race across the meadow fair,
> While I, in thrall, do watch you blunder into tangled snare,
> Dreading huntsman's lance or arrow tipped with death, I
> cannot rest.
> I beg you let me turn its point away from your sweet breast.
> I, a beast no woman has yet tamed, nor even hath been
> tempted.
> From Venus' pleasure-charms all know I be exempted,
> Yet to your hand, fate led me, by shining path to follow,
> While stars might give you light, sweet Nell, I offer my
> tomorrows."

Few who had watched his pursuit of me could doubt who the Angel's "Nell" was. He could not be sincere, the poem one more tool to unnerve me. Yet, his words echoed through me as if I were a bell struck by a sexton. As for the rest of the vast chamber, a sudden hush blanketed it. I felt the questioning of my mother's gaze, the speculative glances of courtiers. Even through the white paint on the queen's face all could see her flush with humiliation.

The queen's lips pursed. "It would be a pity to lose the hand that writes such fine poems, Sir Angel."

"I would strike my hand off myself rather than allow it to distress you, Majesty."

"Do not put me to the test. Nor test the virtue of my maids of honor, do you hear? I advise any lady of mine not to believe a word that comes from your mouth—or your pen. In fact, I remember well warning one particular maid about you. It would make me most unhappy if I discovered she had not heeded me."

Gabriel grimaced. "The maid you speak of is a pillar of wisdom, Majesty. I can assure you she trusts me not at all."

"Mistress Elinor?" the queen summoned me. "Relieve this poet of his offering and give him the set down he deserves. Now, is there not another present for me?"

She turned back to the table of gifts as Sir Gabriel approached me. I watched him wend his way through the crowd, his shoulders broad, his gaze strange. Bright.

I held my breath, not knowing what to say, feel. "Are you mad, writing poetry to me?" I said at last. "The rumors will run wild!"

"That is what rumors do best, Grace." He shrugged. "I did warn Her Majesty that my poetry was vile. But there are many blank pages that follow for you to fill with writing far better."

"You should not have written such things about me."

"I must have been making rather too merry with the Christmas wine. Perhaps I can redeem myself with what is pressed between the book's pages. It is a marker of sorts to help you keep your bearings. It is often difficult at court to find your way. You must remember to look up if you are to see the sky." He grasped my hand, turned it palm up, then he slid free something caught in the book's pages. A chain poured in a delicate gold waterfall to pool in my palm. A moment later something heavier thudded softly atop it. I stared in disbelief at the wheels and gears of my father's astrolabe. They were bent, scratched, but the instrument was miraculously whole, unbearably precious.

Mother looked at it. "Is that the necklace your father had made for you?"

"Where did you find this?" I gasped, clutching the astrolabe close. Suspicion dawned. Where indeed? Would this not be the perfect key to unlock all my reserve? "Did you have my necklace all this time? That night in the garden—did you take it?"

He scooped my hand, kissed my curled fingers, astrolabe and all. Then he took the chain up and fastened it about my neck. Frozen in a welter of emotion I glared up at him, trying to see past his facade. He smiled as if he knew.

"Happy New Year, Grace," he said softly, then bowed and strode away.

I wheeled to watch him, nearly crashed into my mother. "Elinor, why does he call you Grace? What is this about?"

"Nothing. Everything. I lost my astrolabe the night Eppie came. He saw us in the garden and after . . ."

Mother paled. "Jesus, Mary, and Joseph, tell me Sir Gabriel did not overhear."

"I do not know what he heard. I dare not ask him. He would not tell me the truth even if I did. He is Dudley's man, blood and bone. I know where his loyalties lie."

Mother gripped my hand. "That man suspects something. A hound on a blood scent is a dangerous animal." A line of Wyatt's poetry ran through my head . . . *I, a beast no woman has yet tamed*. He was a beast, wounded and wily, tortured but ruthless. I peered down at the leather book, the words upon the pages incantations meant to tempt me. To what? Allow him to charm caution from me? Let him steal, not my maidenhead, but secrets that could cost me my life? And what if he *had* gotten my astrolabe that night in spring, I reasoned. What if Wyatt had been waiting for the perfect time to return it to me? Throw me off guard? Win my gratitude, my trust, entice me to betray Eppie? My mother? Myself?

The thought stalked me as the night wore on, people milling around, comparing the queen's gifts. Mary had told me Elizabeth's gifts to us would be delivered by messenger, plates and cups weighed carefully to match our importance in her eyes.

The last thing I expected was for one of the heralds to find me in the crush. "Mistress Elinor de Lacey?" he said. "Her Majesty wishes you to attend her at once."

Was I to feel the lash of the queen's temper because of Gabriel Wyatt's poem? There was no avoiding the royal summons. I approached Her Majesty, my mother hovering in my wake. "You wished to see me?" I asked her, feeling curious glances from those nearest us in the crowd.

"Indeed," Elizabeth said. "I have something special for you on this, your first Christmas at court. Give me your right hand."

"Majesty?" I curled my fingers, could feel the scar thick in the crease at the edge of my palm. Still, what could I do but extend my damaged hand for her inspection?

Elizabeth drew a ring from her own finger, then made great show of slipping it onto mine. It fit perfectly, the moonstone glimmering in its setting of gold, changeable as fate. When I tried to withdraw my hand and curtsey, the queen held on tight.

"I have often noticed these many months that you are hesitant to show your hands. This one seems quite lovely except—" Her fingers skimmed the raised flesh above my little finger. She turned my hand to examine the puckered skin. "This scar is quite dreadful. It is a pity you are disfigured so." She ran her thumb along the mark. "When did this happen?"

My cheeks burned. "I have had the scar as long as I can remember."

The queen turned to my mother. "Lady Calverley, do enlighten me. Surely you can explain how your beautiful daughter got such a wound?"

My mother stepped half before me, as if putting her body between me and the queen. "It was a kitchen accident, Majesty." I could feel what it cost Mother to keep her voice level. "Nell was ever curious and reached up for something shining on the table. A knife fell. It could have been far worse. I thank God it did not sever any of Nell's other fingers."

"Other fingers? Did I miscount?" Elizabeth pulled my hand as she examined first one side, then the other. "No, Mistress Nell has five fingers like the rest of us. Where is the finger the knife severed?"

The terrible silence that fell between my mother and the queen was frightening.

I heard mother suck in a breath. "What finger was severed? A fine question, Majesty. I was merely flustered by the favor your majesty showed my daughter and misspoke. I meant to say *any* fingers. Of course Nell has five fingers," she continued. My mother was babbling. My mother never babbled. "What other number could there be?"

Never had I seen my mother so rattled. Something momentous had occurred right before my eyes and I did not know what it was.

Later, as revelers wandered off to sleep, my mother led me from the Great Hall. We wound through the palace, past red-eyed servants who had made as merry as their queen. Thrice I started to ask where we were going, but mother glanced about as if she feared the figures on the Flemish tapestries we passed could write down every word we spoke in their hearing. At last she led me into a gallery so deserted we might have been the only people in London.

Mist swirled beyond the windows overlooking the gardens. Mother and I slipped into one of the nooks where we could see any other wanderers before they might happen on us and overhear . . . *what* I did not know. Only that something terrible had happened when Elizabeth Tudor had slipped her ring upon my hand. I fidgeted with the moonstone, twisting it around my finger.

We curled up on a bench and I tucked my feet beneath me to warm them, the fires on the vast hearths neglected and dead. Even after my mother checked one more time to make certain no one could hear us, she hesitated, picking at the cuticle on her thumb. The tiny clicking sound of her nails grated. "Whatever you wish to tell me, just say it," I pleaded. "What happened that has upset you so dreadfully?"

Mother looked up from her ravaged nail, a tiny line of blood smearing her skin. "The queen took pointed notice of your scar. That may be a calamity indeed."

"Why would a childhood accident be of any interest to the queen?"

"It was no accident, Nell. The wound that scarred you was made on purpose."

"Someone hurt me on purpose?" I felt a lurch of disgust. "Who? The masked servant who tried to smother me?"

"No. Eppie and I did. To save you, disguise you. To make certain no one could link you to the child who was supposed to be dead." Mother picked up my right hand so tenderly it terrified me. "When you came to me, Nell, you had a mark upon you that could betray us all. A sixth finger right here." She ran her thumb over my scar.

"A sixth . . ." My stomach sank. "Is that not the mark of the devil?" I shuddered, remembering the tale I had over heard as a child, witches burned alive in the fires of Smithfield.

"The devil? Bah!" My mother kissed the ugly ridge of flesh. "What superstitious nonsense! Such traits appear sometimes in certain families, passed from mother to child like a hooked nose or a claw foot. Yet it is unusual enough to mark someone in a way that particular family can recognize. It is not foolproof. More than one bloodline can produce a certain trait. It is just a greater likelihood that one might surmise a link when that trait presents itself. Do you understand what I mean, Nell?"

"That someone of my blood had a flaw like mine. Someone you fear. Mother, who else was marked that way?"

"Anne Boleyn."

I felt a terrible clarity, remembering one of the servants chattering that there was some reason Anne Boleyn wore sleeves that covered her fingers, that there were whispers of a defect she was trying to hide. But I did not care about queens or styles of dress or gossip then.

"No," I whimpered. "It cannot be true." The woman who had rent England apart, shattered the hold of Rome, bewitched a king, destroyed her . . . Anne Boleyn, Elizabeth Tudor's mother, had had a sixth finger like me?

"As I say, such traits can be scattered about an area. Through cousins or grandparents, or other relations. Eppie and I had seen such markers in the past. But until the day Eppie recognized Elizabeth in the Tower, we did not know what the finger meant for sure. We only knew to disguise you and to keep you truly safe we must remove such a distinguishing feature so no one else might see it. So I held you in my arms while Eppie heated a blade over the fire and then severed that finger from your hand."

"No. I do not want to hear this." Bile rose in my throat.

"We had no choice. Eppie's 'fair lady' would recover from her ordeal. Once she had her wits about her, who knew what might happen?"

"But I could have died if the wound had turned putrid!" My whole life I had heard my mother warn people thus. The tiniest wound could spread poison, red streaks climbing from the wound to the heart to cause fever and delirium and agonizing death.

"You would have been dead already if they had gotten their way." Mother pressed her hands to her stomach as if fighting not to retch. "Jesus, God, I will never forget that terrible day. Trying to comfort you while I flattened your tiny hand on the table. Eppie taking up the knife. I was singing you a song my mother once sang to me and you were gurgling, so happy and wide-eyed, when Eppie did what had to be done."

I cupped my left hand over the old scar as if I could rub the mark away.

"You screamed, and the blood . . . so much of it from such a tiny babe."

I pictured a tiny newborn like the ones Mother and Eppie had brought into the world at Calverley. Pink-and-white creatures with hands smaller than rose blossoms and skin so tender it seemed the merest brush of anything rough might scour it clean away. I tried to grasp the truth from those first days of my life. Marked from birth as granddaughter of the Witch Queen, one mother ordering servants to smother me, the other mutilating me in a way that could have resulted in an even more terrible death.

As if she could read my thoughts, my mother stared at her own clasped hands. "I did the best I could to get you safe through the healing. I pressed a cloth to the wound to stanch the bleeding until Eppie could turn her blade white hot in the fire. She lay the glowing metal against the raw flesh, searing the poison out, closing the wound. Once it was done, I thrust you into Eppie's arms and ran to the chamber pot to retch."

I had seen my mother face farmers with legs crushed under cart wheels, women burned when their skirts caught fire. Never once had she shown any sign of weakness. Even when I had tumbled off my horse, blood flowing down my face, she had not flinched. And yet now I could imagine her so clearly, weak from childbed, her skirts spattered with my blood as she heaved up raw horror.

"I cannot say how long I lay there on the floor. I only remember the feel of the stone on my cheek. The sound of your wails, the knowledge that I had betrayed your trust. I was supposed to protect you and yet I held your tiny hand down while . . ."

Tears coursed her cheeks. "When I managed to climb to my feet and weave my way back into the bedchamber, Eppie had quieted you. I do not know how. You huddled against her breast, your little body shuddering with every breath you drew, your cheek wet with tears. I went to take you from Eppie's arms, but when you saw me you started to cry. You were wary of me. How could I blame you? I was supposed to keep you safe."

"That is what you were trying to do."

"It seemed from that moment on you cried whenever I held you. You were so tiny that I knew you could not remember the terrible thing that happened that day. At least that was what Eppie told me. Perhaps guilt made me nervous when I held you. Guilt soured my milk. That and fear you would be snatched away. My breasts dried up. By the time we reached Calverley we had to hire a wet nurse. And week after week, I felt this wall grow tall between you and me. While you and Eppie grew ever closer."

My mother turned toward the window, the veil on her headdress obscuring part of her face. I did not need to see it to know her features were taut with pain.

The morning she sent Eppie away flashed into my memory. I had stormed into my father's library, half wild with grief and out-rage, demanding that he summon Eppie back. I had been so certain my mother did not love me. Father's expression had been so wise, sad as he tried to show me my mother's pain. Told me how desperately she had longed for a child. Then been forced to watch that child shower affection on him and her nurse, while Mother got only what scraps were left. Now that I knew what Mother had suffered for me, I felt ashamed. "I am so sorry," I whispered. "Why didn't you ever tell me?"

"What?"

"About how much you wanted me? What you suffered, longing for a child."

"A child should not be coerced by such a heavy weight as my hopes and disappointments. Even a child's heart should be theirs alone to give."

"But every time I hugged Eppie, kissed Eppie, it must have hurt you."

"I cannot say I did not wish I was the one with your arms forever twined around my neck. I did what I could, found ways to keep you close by me. Lessons in a woman's duty. Picking at you so that you had to do the task again and again so you had to stay with me. It was no wonder you came to resent me."

What could I say? It was true.

"By the time I realized I was driving you away it was too late," she said wistfully.

"You made a poor bargain when you took me in. Willful, careless little fool that I was. And once Eppie told you who the fair lady was, I became a danger to you and Father and everyone at Calverley. You must have felt regret you'd ever laid eyes on me."

"Never!" She protested, so fierce I had to believe her. "I only wish we might start over. I would do things so differently. I would spend time playing with you in the orchard, make you laugh, join you and your father in the library when he was teaching you lessons. But the time for that is past."

"No, Mother. No, it is not. I want to learn now, all the things you have to teach me. I want you to show me how to keep a wet larder and blend herbs in the still house, and I want to know about what it was like for you when you were at court."

"I was much different from you." Mother's gaze clouded with memories. "My parents could not wait to have a daughter in a queen's service, prepared me to be a courtier from the time I could speak. Yet I sickened of the intrigue quickly once I came to the palace, learned to fear the power men held. I know your father wondered why I wed him. He was nothing like the gallants who buzzed about me. But he was the truest thing I found, a simple stone in all that false glitter. Something solid to build a life on."

"But Father was a dreamer. You always said so."

"His dreams were of comets in heaven, of philosophies that could raise men up, not ambitions that could cast them into the straw strewn on the scaffold. I watched so many die there. Sir Thomas More and that tragic child Catherine Howard. Pawns sacrificed in the king's marriage games. It was a miracle Sir Gabriel's grandfather did not suffer the same death because he wrote a poem to Anne Boleyn." I remembered the expression on her face when Gabriel had spoken of the man.

"Sir Gabriel looks much like his grandfather," mother said, "but rougher, somehow. Do you care for him, Nell, as he cares for you?"

"No!" I shrank away from feelings I would not name. "The man does not care for me at all. He merely likes to torment me."

"With poetry? And returning the necklace your father gave you? That seems more like kindness to me."

There were other instances as well, kindnesses I had chosen not to notice. The way he tended me during the hunt and again when those surrounding the queen were engrossed in discussing questions of science. Times when I was anxious to add my own theories he had cleared the way for me to speak, then listened with a secret smile.

"He prowls around corners," I reminded myself. "Like the wolves whose fur he wears."

"I do not think he has always been wild. He is more like a hound once cherished, who has been cast into the wild and learned to survive. I am glad to see in spite of that Sir Gabriel keeps some fragment of his grandfather's poetic soul alive."

"How can you say that? There is nothing sensitive about—"

"At first glance you could not see such qualities in Thomas Wyatt either. But in spite of the raucous revels the king and his friends thrived on, Thomas treated me gently when the court felt too rough. I loved him for it. A girl's calf-love."

"Did he care for you?"

"Heavens no! He had no eyes for anyone save the queen. But I would stake my life he never touched her. He was a good man, Wyatt. Sensitive. Kind. Not fit to be flung into the bear pit that was Henry's circle of friends. Never underestimate the cruelty of this life, Nell. How quickly you can be sucked under its shifting sands. God alone knows what is true and what is not. What lengths ambitious men and women will go to in order to win the power they crave. It is a sickness. One that eats away the soul. I have not told you much of my life with Katherine Parr. What few know is that I was with her when she delivered her babe. And when she went mad with childbed fever."

"That must have been terrible for you."

"Worse still, I guessed truth. That she wished to die, even before she entered her confinement. The pain of living with Seymour's betrayal was too great. And yet, who can say for certain how she died? Thomas Seymour tried to wed Elizabeth before he married Katherine, and then again after his wife's death. If he *had* managed to rouse the princess's passion, who can say what he might have done to be free so he could wed her?"

"What are you saying?"

"That before Katherine Parr died she claimed her husband had poisoned her so he could wed Elizabeth Tudor and tame a princess in his marriage bed. She was delirious with fever, and recanted it later, but . . ."

I recoiled, feeling filthy at being spawned by such a betrayal, the product of adultery. It was hard enough knowing I was not John de Lacey's daughter. But if the blood in my veins was that of Thomas

Seymour, who had seduced his stepdaughter beneath his pregnant wife's nose, it was more terrible still. "Are you sure I could not be Robert Dudley's child?" I pleaded, trying to fend off my horror. "At least then I would be a child of love, not ambition, scandal, heartbreak. No one knows when their love for each other began. Is it not possible?"

My mother brushed a strand of hair from my cheek, tenderness softening her gaze. "I do not know who your parents are for certain, Nell. I know only this—Eppie claims you are Elizabeth's daughter. If that is true the queen might guess what that scar on your hand means. Thank God she cannot prove it."

I thought of the bit of cloth with its glimmer of silver thread, my lie to my mother heavy on my conscience. I should burn the evidence now, I thought. Destroy it the first chance that I got.

"I want to go home." My voice broke. "Take me home, Mother. We can pretend none of this ever happened." I clenched my hands together, the queen's ring biting into my finger. I pulled it off, wanting only to be free of everything it stood for.

"It is too late for that, Nell," my mother said, sliding the moonstone back onto my finger. "I cannot make this go away no matter how much we both wish I could. Elizabeth has made it clear she intends to keep you close at her side. And if she suspects what the scar signifies, she will be even more determined to watch you closely."

"I am no good at concealing how I feel. I never was."

"You can learn anything, Nell. You are John de Lacey's daughter." Her words cut deep. "No, I am not."

"You *are*! Use the discipline your father gave you. Study how to deceive even someone wily as the queen. You will have to be more careful than ever before until we can find a way to cut you loose from this coil."

"We could run away. Just slip out in the night and—"

"Where would we go? Even now the queen's men might be watching us. If we run we will look guilty. No, we must use our wits,

Nell. I have been thinking, planning, praying, and I believe I have puzzled out what course we must take."

I must have looked pathetic, gazing at my mother as if she had the power to save me.

"After Twelfth Night I will take my leave," she said. "We will part without a fuss, for the queen will be watching for any hint of weakness."

"I do not think I can."

"You will behave as if my visit was overlong and you are glad I am gone. I will return to Calverley and you will return to your duties. Act as if you have not a care in the world. When next winter comes I will send word that I am gravely ill. Elizabeth can be compassionate in such cases. Please God, she will send you to my bedside."

"Next winter is forever away! Why must we wait so long?"

"You are a fine rider, Nell. You know the danger of rushing your fences. If we act too quickly our chance is lost forever. We must be patient, wait until the queen's suspicions are quieted. Perhaps you will be home by next Christmas."

"I loathe Christmas now." I would never again see garlands and kissing boughs without remembering all this season had cost me. "I will loathe winter until I die!"

"Hush, now." She touched my cheek. "If winter seems bleak to you, look forward to spring instead. Imagine your daffodils and the new lambs. I am so sorry you will miss them this year."

"I would trade all the springs ever to come if I could take this past year back. If I could do it all again, I would heed you, Mother. I would be the kind of daughter you wished for. I must have been such a disappointment to you."

"Hush!" My mother grabbed my arms, shook me, hard. "You are everything I could hope my child would be. Brave and bright, loyal and loving."

"How can you possibly think so?"

"It was writ in your father's eyes whenever he beheld you and in Mary Grey's when she gave you her gift. In Eppie's love for you and in mine. You will survive this, Nell. You are stronger than you know."

"No, you are the strong one. Father always said so. I am afraid."

"I am, too, my precious, precious girl," Mother said, gathering me tight in her arms. "But this must be the last time we say it." I clung to her until courage born of her honesty poured strength into my limbs. I squared my shoulders, looked into her eyes.

"Spring," I said.

Chapter Nineteen

January 1565

THE HALLS LOOKED NAKED, BEREFT OF CHRISTMAS finery. The garlands and bunches of greens we had labored so hard to weave had been stripped down at midnight and thrust into the fire to burn once the Twelfth Night revels were done. Any faint hope the queen might let me depart with my mother vanished with the pine-scented smoke from the chimneys. Lettice claimed the queen was so eager for my mother to depart that Elizabeth would have ordered a January gale to blow Lady Calverley all the way to Lincolnshire if the wind heeded royal command.

Mother and I lay awake in bed our last night together, knowing come morning she would have to leave the palace and I would have to stay. More sobering still, we must make the whole court believe we were glad it was so. I tried to recall the freedom I once felt when I shed my mother's presence, counting myself lucky to escape her criticisms. I attempted to school that relief into my expression the following day as I watched her pass beneath the arch of the gatehouse in her litter emblazoned with the Calverley hawks and lions. But now I knew the raw places in her spirit, what she had suffered for me, what she had sacrificed, and all I could feel was shame and grief and a desperate longing to know her better. The strong, pragmatic, brave Thomasin de Lacey I had never troubled myself to understand.

The courtyard boiled with confusion, parties setting out for estates scattered all over England. We members of the court would be leaving Greenwich, too. Twelve days of Christmas revels had left the palace filthy from too many people, too many servants, too many animals, the kitchens and chamber pots in sore need of cleaning. By the time the last Calverley retainer had disappeared through the gate my face felt ready to crack from the effort it took to keep a smile upon my face.

Drawing my cloak tight beneath my chin, I started back toward the stairs leading to the Great Hall, swishing my skirts in the way I had seen other ladies do as evidence of their delight. The performance seemed pointless. In such a welter of confusion I doubted anyone would notice—unless the queen had put Walsingham on alert. Sir Francis had eyes and ears everywhere. Any glimpse his minions might catch of me today must show me merry as a spaniel let off its leash to run.

I started across the courtyard, barely able to see through a brittle icing of unshed tears. A hand caught me from behind, yanking me backward. I saw a blur of manes and haunches followed by the hard, jouncing box of a new coach. Its driver waved his fist barely an arm's length from my nose, and I was dismayed to realize he might have run me over. I turned to thank my rescuer, saw the wolf's-fur trimming of Sir Gabriel's cloak.

"Have a care, Grace. It is madness out here today. You must keep watch where you are going or you will be trampled beneath the wheels."

It seemed such a straightforward warning on the face of it. So why did I sense he was hinting at something more? I forced a bright laugh. "I fear I got distracted trying to think what mischief to get into first now that my mother is gone."

"Is that so?"

I groped for one of my old complaints. "You cannot know what it is like with Mother just waiting for me to make a mistake."

A fleeting shadow crossed his face. "No. I suppose I cannot."

"Believe me," I insisted. "Her absence will be bliss."

"Careful, Grace. When someone at court begins a claim with 'believe me,' it is likely they are lying."

I feigned outrage. "How dare you imply that?"

"I only mean to put you on your guard. Any man canny enough to survive in this court must be a student of human nature. They will know you are up to some trick just as surely as I do."

"The only trick I want to master is disappearing when you are around. It is obvious I need more practice."

"What you need is an ally. Someone strong enough to shield you from whatever tangle you are in."

"You imagine things. Next you will be claiming there is a dragon in the sky."

"This is no game, Nell. The stakes are high, more than you can afford to lose." I caught hold of my astrolabe. The treasure Gabriel had restored to me. "I know you have little reason to trust me," he said. "But know this. I am fascinated by you in a way so new I cannot describe."

"That is for certain. Spare the art of poetry and never attempt to do so again."

He winced. "I even managed to appall myself. But that did not keep me from observing the sword that divided your mother and the queen that same night was far sharper than some long past quarrel. I know it. And you are thick in the middle of this battle."

I shrugged. "My mother is gone now. What can it matter?"

"It matters. I can feel it." A bitter edge sharpened his voice. "You have been at court long enough to know why people call me the Gypsy's Angel."

I sought some shield against him. An insult. "You dig around in the muck to drag bones from the midden heap and carry them back to your master. But you are wasting your time with me. There is nothing to find. You will come away from your search looking like a fool. Why do you not do something noble? Something honorable? Something admirable with your life instead of licking Robert Dudley's hand?"

"Perhaps I should try licking yours."

"You disgust me!"

"No. You only wish I did." The truth thudded into my chest. "Nell, whatever went wrong that night is so dire that the queen will not even speak to Lord Robert about it."

"The queen has advisers wiser than Robert Dudley."

"Wiser, perhaps, but not more trusted, more beloved."

I thought of the two of them—their passion for each other was there for the world to see in their eyes. I longed to be born of that passion, something far cleaner than the murky seduction of Seymour.

Sir Gabriel reached toward me, his fingers brushing my throat as he scooped up the gold chain, the bent astrolabe sliding down into his grasp. "I meant things to be so different when I returned this to you. I hoped I could win your trust."

"Was it a gift or a bribe?"

He smiled. "Both."

"Where did you get it? How long did you have it? You never answered my questions."

"I searched the ground like a beggar who had lost his last shilling. I traced every step I made that night I followed you."

"So you admit it!"

"I tell you the truth in hopes you might do the same for me. I let it be known among the gardeners that I was searching for something I lost. That I would reward whoever brought it to me, recompense greater than what the trinket was worth."

"So you were willing to lay gold down to buy my gratitude? That is a merchant's bargain, not a reason I should trust you."

Wyatt drove his fingers through his hair in exasperation, knocking his hat askew. "If I merely wanted to buy your goodwill I could have had any goldsmith in London make the necklace's double and saved myself a deal of inconvenience! I offered the reward because I knew the astrolabe was precious to you. A gift from your father."

"Why should you care?"

"I should not. God knows I never have before. But my mother once loved stars. And . . . Christ's wounds, never mind! You wish to be left alone with your trouble? Fine. I have far too much of my own."

"Angel!" A call rang out from across the yard, another of Dudley's entourage trying to gain Gabriel's attention. "Will you come to the tiltyard with us? We thought to take a run at the quintain if the ground be not too slick."

I had seen the men tilt in the practice yard before, riding full speed at the apparatus mounted upon a pole, a target on one branch and a weighted sack on the other. Gabriel dragged his tongue over his teeth, considering before he turned back to me.

"You know, I cannot imagine anything more pleasant than driving a lance into the shield. Perhaps if I am lucky the weight will swing around so quick it will hit me in the head. I might forget all about you, Grace."

"I shall go to the chapel at once and pray that is what happens. Do you think God answers prayers to crack open someone's head?"

"I do not know. God and I have not been on speaking terms for a very long time."

"Fortunate God."

Gabriel's features shifted, solemn. "Fortune is slippery near the queen, Grace. Time is precious. Let me help you."

For a heartbeat I was tempted, pulled into his eyes. Just as fast, the connection snapped. I dragged my gaze away from his and gestured toward Dudley's other men.

"I believe your friends are waiting for you."

"You are cruel, my lady Grace. To cut at a man who wishes to serve you thus. Perhaps you have been taking lessons from the queen. She would be proud as if you were her own daughter."

A dizzy haze engulfed me. Wyatt could see it. I struggled to regain control of the fear inside me, tried to crush the words that wanted to rise. *What do you mean, Like her daughter? What do you know?* "I endeavor to be like Her Majesty in every way."

"And you are," Wyatt murmured. "The truth is heavy, Grace. It will tumble out." His gaze pierced me a long moment. "I will be ready when it does."

❧❦❧❦

IT ASTONISHED ME, how swiftly I started to lie. Lie to the other maids that I was delighted my mother was back in Lincolnshire. Lie to myself that I would be able to return to my old life and forget this year ever happened. Lie that Sir Gabriel Wyatt had not seeped into my heart, invading my thoughts like wine colors water. I should have been more alarmed than ever after the way the Angel and I parted in the courtyard, the words he spoke, the *knowing* in him. He insisted that my secret would come out and he would be ready when it did.

Ready for what? I wondered for the hundredth time as I slipped across the January-slick courtyard toward Whitehall's stable late one night. *Ready to take advantage of my vulnerability? To use my secret to his advantage?* That was the logical conclusion.

Yet, what was it about his steady gaze that haunted me as sleepless nights crept past? Was it a dark enchantment, a spell like the one a Gypsy had used on my pony so long ago, to cure its fear of water? What if I grew so much in thrall to the man that I stepped off the bank and was drowned beneath currents under the Tower Bridge?

I clenched my hands around the sticky lumps of sugarloaf I had smuggled from the Great Hall after the court had dined and bent my head into the wind that tugged my hood from my hair. But I never questioned whether it was worth being battered by the cold to sneak the tidbits to Doucette. For a week now, the warm, hay-scented stable was the only place I could breathe, the mare daintily nibbling treats from my palm, my cheek buried against Doucette's arched neck.

Even on nights like tonight, when Sir Gabriel's place at table had been empty, my thoughts about him gave me no peace, the subtle change in him a loose thread I picked at even though it could unravel my tenuous hold on my emotions. I could not forget my mother's description of Sir Gabriel, not as the wolf I had named him, but rather, an adored hound suddenly beaten and flung into the wild to fight for survival.

I found myself watching him when we were in the same room, picturing him as a boy. He could not have been much older than fifteen when his father made the journey to Tower Hill. Had they shared the same cell or had the guard separated them? If apart, had he been allowed to say good-bye? How had Gabriel gotten the news his father was dead? Had it devastated him? Or had every fiber already been concentrated on trying to save his own life? A Herculean task he succeeded in. But at what price?

And what of Gabriel's mother, the woman who loved the stars? The only thing I knew about her were rumors she was a whore. During the first clash between Sir Gabriel and me, Kat Ashley had claimed it was so. No small insult, considering what was whispered about Elizabeth's own mother—that Anne Boleyn had bedded her own brother. Yet I had discerned no contempt in Gabriel when he'd spoken of the woman who bore him. None of the reactions one might expect of a son to the woman who had disgraced his family name. More puzzling still, I sensed he understood the value of my astrolabe because of *her*, recognized the scratched gold disk was irreplaceable.

Something had altered between us. I could feel it in his touch when we danced, see it in the way his eyes searched my face. More unsettling still, I could not keep from tallying up his kindnesses to me since my mother had made me aware of them. Pomegranates he split with his dagger to offer me the sweet fruit. Books he claimed he had tired of, and pressed into my hands. The satisfaction he could not quite hide those rare times he managed to surprise a laugh from me with some irreverent observation or command my attention through some insight so learned it startled me. He was a scholar indeed, one of Dr. Dee's chosen. *Do not underestimate him, Nell,* I cautioned myself as a drowsy lad with chilblained hands sprang up from his place near the stable door to open it for me. *Wolf or hound, Sir Gabriel is still unpredictable, dangerous. A wild thing turns on anyone near it to save its own skin. And yet,* a voice inside me whispered, *John Dee trusts him with his most dangerous secrets.*

The night-quiet stable wrapped me in warmth, the scent of horses, leather, and hay reminding me of Calverley and the hours I had spent in Crane's tender care. A lantern dangling from an iron hook in a rafter cast uncertain light, mellowing the wood to silver and the hay to strands of gold. Halfway down the line of stalls, I heard the hollow sound of shifting hooves. Doucette thrust her head over her stall gate to whicker a greeting. "Can you not sleep either, my beauty?" I crooned as she nibbled my sugar, mannerly as a duchess. I stroked her nose the way she liked it. Before she could nuzzle me further, I heard the commotion of someone arriving in the courtyard I had just crossed.

The stable door flew wide and I heard a voice over the flurry of hoofbeats as the person rode in. "You, boy, saddle a fresh mount for me. Have it ready for me by the time I return and I will reward you most handsomely." The figure flung himself from the saddle and in the wavering lantern light I glimpsed silver wolf fur and black hair. Gabriel. He started to charge past me when suddenly his gaze locked on my hair. He slammed to a halt. "God's blood," he swore, startled as if he had stumbled on a devil or an angel, I could not tell which. "You."

"Sir Gabriel." I felt as if he had sucked all the air out of the stables.

"What are you doing out here?" He scowled. "There is no way you can know."

"Know what?" I asked.

"Lad!" Gabriel barked over his shoulder. "Hasten with that horse. The lady I seek is already here."

"You were looking for me?" I backed away a step, my shoulder bumping against the wall of Doucette's stall.

Gabriel smelled of cheap ale and heavy perfumes. His hair was tousled, and there was a smear of what looked to be a woman's white makeup on his breeches. How it had gotten there I could not guess. "Does anyone know where you are?" he asked.

The back of my neck prickled, and I hesitated. It hardly seemed wise to tell him not a soul would know I was missing until tomorrow morning. Mary had a filthy cold, so I had given her our bed, and offered to find somewhere else to sleep, beyond the maid's lodgings. To save Moll the trouble of tracking me down in some as of yet unspecified place, I had told her not to bother with readying me for bed. I would find someone else to undo my gown.

"Of course people know," I lied. "Why should it matter?"

Gabriel glanced around, but the only ones in the barn were the two of us and the lad putting tack on a restive bay. "Nell, where is Hepzibah Jones?"

Eppie? Terror iced me.

"You must tell me where to find her."

"Find who?" I balked, trying to buy myself time, think what to do.

"You know damned well who she is! The woman in the garden! Your old nurse."

He knew who Eppie was. What else had he managed to uncover? Was this a trick? Some way to get me to admit to meeting Eppie? Did Gabriel hope that by frightening me this way he might startle me into confessing something more?

"I have not seen my old nurse since I was fourteen," I lied. "My mother banished Eppie from Calverley because the old woman ran mad."

Gabriel dragged me into the shadows, his face so close to mine I could feel the chill on his skin. "Damn it, Nell, we've no time for games. Walsingham is sending his men to arrest her."

I stumbled back, horrified. "How would you know such a thing?" I reeled, knowing I had blundered. I had not questioned why Walsingham would order her arrest, only demanded how Gabriel knew the spymaster had done so.

"I was reveling with some of Walsingham's men at a brothel.

The sergeant bragged he was to drag a woman to Tower Prison for Walsingham himself to question."

"It cannot be Eppie."

"Every moment we waste arguing is one less we have to reach her. I would not have wasted time riding back here, except I could not get the soldier to tell me where they planned to find her. You are the only person who might know."

His words thrust through me. Why would the Gypsy's Angel wish to foil Walsingham's plan, if a plan existed? To do so would be political suicide if the spymaster found out. Whereas if Gabriel's intent was to lead Walsingham's men *to* their quarry, what better way to make me confide it to him than to prey upon my worst fears? That way I might tell him of Eppie's whereabouts. I was the only one outside Eppie's family who knew she lived at the Silver Swan.

I edged away from Gabriel, searching for some weapon to use against him. "For all I know you weren't even outside the palace walls!" I challenged, stalling. "What gate did you ride through? And where was this brothel you supposedly patronized?"

"In Southwark. The Cock and Bull. I rode through the postern gate. I bribed the guard to keep it open until I ride back through."

I caught sight of the brick grooms used to hold the stable doors open when summer turned stifling. I let the panic overwhelm me—an emotion real enough—let my legs collapse beneath me.

Gabriel cursed, lunging to catch me before I struck the ground, but I rolled to one side, my fingers closing around the rough brick. Fear shot uncommon strength into my arms. I swung the brick in an arc, striking Gabriel in the side of his head. He gave a cry, fell half across me, his big body driving the air from my lungs.

"Sir?" the stable lad called in alarm. "Sir, is something amiss?"

"He fell, struck his head," I said as I struggled to push Gabriel off me. "Go fetch some cold water to splash his face."

The lad bolted out of the stables, leaving the door flung wide. I grabbed my chance. I wrestled the freshly saddled horse to the mounting block and scrambled astride the bay's back. I drove my heels into its sides and the animal sprang into action.

Cold wind snapped my hood against my cheek. Clutching the reins in one hand, I yanked the fabric up over my head, then clamped my chin down on the bunched material to hold it in place. Leaning over the horse's neck, I cantered toward the postern gate, praying Gabriel had not lied in this much, and that it would still be open for me to ride through.

I saw smears of orange torchlight, the dark mouth of the arched opening. Heart hammering, I prayed. It was open! I closed my eyes for a second, thanking God. The guard waved me through, and I heard the gate grinding closed behind me. London engulfed me. I knew thieves owned the darkness, cutthroats and brigands and whores selling their wares. The curfew was long past, and any watchman could challenge me. If anyone at the palace got wind of my flight from Whitehall . . . I shuddered, imagining what it would be like to be hauled before Elizabeth Tudor, have her demand to know what a royal maid of honor was doing racing about the city at night. What if Walsingham had other spies keeping watch while Sir Gabriel tried to trick me into betraying Eppie's whereabouts? What if someone was following me even now?

I glanced over my shoulder. Behind me the world was a blur of shadows. As for the pounding in my ears—I could not tell if it was hoofbeats or the drumming of my heart. How could I even find the Silver Swan? I had never been to the place, only knew it lay across the Thames in Southwark. What if I became lost in the labyrinth of streets? Who among the denizens of night would I even dare to ask for directions?

Hopelessness dragged at me, but one thing I knew for certain: Eppie was in danger. I clung close to the edge of the river, using it to guide me until I caught sight of the lights from the houses on London Bridge. When a watchman stopped me, I told him my sister was like to die in childbirth if I did not fetch a midwife to save her. I begged him to tell me where to find the Silver Swan, then followed his directions, thanking God that Father had drilled the skill of memorizing into me.

Twice I took a wrong turn, losing myself in alleyways that smelled of raw sewage and rotted meat. I retraced my steps, fighting back tears. Then I glimpsed landmarks the watchman had given me. Two more turns and I would be there.

I rounded the last corner, saw cresset torches blazing, a dozen horses waiting outside what looked to be an inn. My heart leapt as I glimpsed the sign swinging from chains above them—a swan's arched neck. I reined my horse to a stop and flung myself off, relief flooding through me. I had found the Silver Swan. I would see Eppie safe! I was still two houses away when the inn door flew open, a crowd spilling into the night. Soldiers garbed in crimson, inn customers clothed in fustian. A plump woman and a cluster of children sobbing, clinging to the skirts of the person the soldiers were hauling away. Torchlight illuminated a white headdress, a haggard, beloved face.

Eppie. I choked back the scream that rose in my throat, knowing I dared not utter her name. If anyone caught me here Walsingham would have all the proof he needed to condemn Eppie and me to the queen. Gabriel had been telling me the truth. The knowledge struck hard as the brick I had wielded. If I had trusted him, he might have known where the Silver Swan was. I would not have wasted time asking for directions. I would not have gotten lost. We might have reached Eppie in time to warn her.

I pressed myself against a wall as the crowd from the inn railed at the soldiers, neighbors who knew Eppie and her family roused out of their houses by the noise. Walsingham's men jostled Eppie toward the horses, lifted her up before a burly soldier. Eppie's tormented gaze caught mine across the space that separated us. I saw her eyes go wide with terror, recognition.

The soldiers spun around, following her gaze. He must have seen my stricken face. "Over that way!" Eppie's captor waved a beefy arm in my direction. "Seize whoever that is!"

The crowd scattered, as if afraid he might order them captured next. Half a dozen soldiers started wading through the press of people. I hastened to where I left my horse. Alarm rocked me: the animal was gone. An equine snort sounded in the alley and I took a chance, plunging into the narrow opening, not knowing whether I was rushing toward escape or a place the soldiers could trap me all the more easily. I suddenly slammed into what seemed a wall. Pain shot through my nose, but a hand muffled my cry before I could utter it.

"Quiet," Gabriel rasped as he flung something over my head. I felt wolf fur against my cheeks. "Not a word or I cannot save you."

Grabbing a flask of ale from somewhere on his person, he dumped the liquid over us both, the stench making me choke. He clamped his arm around me so tight he nearly suffocated me in the folds of his cloak, then he jerked me forward none too gently, weaving his way through the alley.

"Halt in the name of the queen!" one of the soldiers pursuing me roared. Gabriel swerved us around until I knew we must be stumbling toward the man instead of away.

"This is a surprise, my fine fellow!" Gabriel greeted in a slurred voice. "Were you not with Sergeant Perkin at the Cock and Bull tonight?"

"I was."

"What are you doing frolicking about here?" Gabriel gave a most convincing stumble, treading on my toe. I bit back a cry of pain.

"Careful, my sweet," he said. "Keep your feet out from under mine or you will make me trip into the good soldier, here, and he will 'rrest us both." Gabriel gave a sloppy laugh.

"Someone fled this way. My captain ordered me to seize whoever it was."

"A wench shoved past us. Did one not, my pet?" Gabriel nudged me. "Wait! Do not answer." He turned back to the soldier. "No one must recognize her voice. Her husband is suspicious already. He's likely to murder her if he finds us out. I have been tippling at her fountain."

"I am sorry, but I must insist on identifying your lady friend."

Gabriel seemed to stumble, knocking into the soldier, flinging the man off balance. Gabriel shoved me behind him and I heard the metallic ring of sword ripped from scabbard. Through an opening in the folds, I saw Gabriel's sword glitter. "This lady is not the person you seek," he said, his voice lethal as his blade.

The soldier leapt back in surprise and I saw him draw his weapon. "My sergeant will be the judge of that." Metal clashed, the two circling, thrusting, parrying. I heard a tearing sound; the soldier yelped in pain. I knew Gabriel's sword tip had struck true.

What would happen if Gabriel killed one of Walsingham's men? The queen had warned Wyatt never to use his sword thus again, threatening he might lose his hand. But before the soldier's wounds got grimmer, the sounds of battle brought others rushing to the alley. One soldier carried a torch. "What goes on here?" A commanding voice shouted, a man on horseback blotting out the light. "Seize that villain!"

"Sergeant! Hold. It is me, Sir Gabriel Wyatt."

"Wyatt?" The officer gigged his mount closer. "What the devil? What is this about? You dueling with a soldier of the Crown?"

"The man insulted my honor." Gabriel thumped his chest with his fist. "He refused to take my word."

"Sergeant, I was chasing someone down this alley," the wounded man explained. "I demanded to see Sir Gabriel's companion and he drew his sword."

"It is a bad habit with me, I confess." Gabriel shrugged ruefully. "The queen herself has chastened me for my readiness to cross swords. But there was no help for it this time. I had to fight. You see, your minion wished to unveil my mistress, but the lady has a very jealous husband who would strangle her if he ever found her with me again. I could hardly take the chance that such gossip would get back to him."

The first soldier protested, but Gabriel cut him off. "I seem to re-member telling you about my lady's charms while we were reveling tonight, Sergeant. There is a certain trick she learned at the court of France . . ." I saw the officer shift in his saddle, his mouth pursing as if he were imaging some pleasure.

"Ah, yes," he said lewdly. "How could I forget? Perhaps I should peek beneath what veils her, just to reassure my underlings. Surely you could not object to that."

I held my breath, knowing even one glimpse of me could mean disaster. Gabriel shook his head in regret. "I am afraid I cannot agree to even so reasonable a request. I gave the lady my word as a gentleman that I would conceal her from all eyes. And that is what I intend to do. Sergeant, I beg you to pause. Reflect upon what I said earlier tonight. Did I not tell you I was leaving the brothel to seek her out? Indulge in French delights? I am loath to draw any more blood tonight. But I will if I am forced to."

Silence stretched out, our fates in the balance. Skilled as Gabriel was reputed to be with a sword, even he could not hold off a dozen armed men.

"Watkins," the sergeant snapped, "put up your sword."

I heard the sound of a blade being sheathed. "Watkins and Smith, ride north to see if you can overtake this fugitive. The rest of you, let us deliver the prisoner to the Tower."

I could see a blur of motion, glimpsed Gabriel making his bow. "I will not forget you indulged me in this matter." I heard a jangle of coins as the Angel poured some from his purse. "Do let me pay to see Watkins has his wound looked at by a surgeon. I prefer the queen not know about our little contretemps. She frowns upon violent encounters and I have already tried her patience on that score. But women have little stomach for such things. What can you expect even from a queen? Even so, it would be most inconvenient if she carried out her threat to take my hand. I am fond of riding and wielding swords and far more pleasurable pursuits where my fingers are quite adept, eh, sweetheart?"

I grunted what might have been an assent.

"Indeed," the officer said stiffly. "You would do well to take your lady friend somewhere private to indulge in those pursuits rather than disrupting an official arrest. I bid you good night." I heard the scuffle of retreating feet growing fainter.

I felt as if I were suffocating, my chest ready to burst. I turned toward the wall, shoving back the thick folds. "Eppie," I whispered, heartbroken.

"Hush," Gabriel warned. "We cannot risk anyone hearing you. I have the horses tied on the next street." He led me through the darkness, my eyes burning with tears. A sob rose in my throat as he lifted me up onto his horse. He swung up behind me, cradling me in his arms, the bay's reins tied to the saddle somehow. I could not speak as we wound through the streets, retracing the path I had ridden such a short time ago. By the time we reached the postern gate I felt as if I had been beaten.

He guided the horses in and threw enough coins to the guard to keep him quiet. Gabriel handed off our mounts to the stable lad and then lifted me into his arms. He carried me to his own lodgings above the tiltyard. I was too devastated to protest.

"We must have a private place to speak," he explained. "Somewhere no one can listen." He maneuvered the door open, took me inside. A single torch blazed, the fire crackling merrily. His manservant clambered up sleepily from a cot near the hearth, but Gabriel bade him leave us. The servant did so, closing the door behind him. "I thought that you were trying to trick me into leading Walsingham's men to her," I admitted. "But they knew where she was."

"Walsingham would not strike unless he knew where his quarry had gone to ground. Flailing about searching would only give the fugitive warning to run."

And Elizabeth Tudor's cunning "old Moor" had outwitted far more wily prey than my nurse. "It is my fault Eppie was arrested," I wailed as Gabriel set me upon his bed. "If I had listened to you . . ."

"We might not have gotten to her in time anyway." He drew the crewelwork coverlet around my shoulders to warm me. I winced at the sight of the injury I had dealt him—an ugly purple bruise swelled the left side of his face, a slash cutting him from his brow to the line where his hair began.

"There is no use in tearing yourself to bits over things that cannot be changed, Nell," he said. "No one knows that better than I do."

A chill wracked me in spite of the fire crackling on the hearth. It was a simple room, but comfortable. Linenfold paneling enriched walls bare of even a painted cloth to keep back the drafts. Some strange plant with spiked green leaves sat in a pot on the window ledge, straining as if reaching for the sun, while a brace of chairs padded with cushions were positioned opposite each other, a bowl of dried apples on one of the seats. A table strewn with writing implements sat near the window and a branch of half-burned candles reached waxy fingers toward the arched ceiling while a round gold mechanism similar to the one I had seen at John Dee's whirred noisily. Every other surface in the chamber reminded me of Mortlake as well, crammed with books of all sizes and shapes.

My mind filled with images of a far more intimidating residence— gold-hued stone walls, the Tower's maze of cells. I imagined Eppie thrust behind barred doors, with no light, no hope, a prison like the one they had used to break Kat Ashley. I could barely force words from my mouth. "What will they do to Eppie?"

"I do not know. If she were a gentlewoman she would be safe; though they tortured Anne Askew, the horror of it still sticks in the people's throats."

"I could go to Walsingham," I said, wild with the need to save Eppie from Anne Askew's fate. "I could tell him . . ."

"Tell him what? That you may be Elizabeth Tudor's daughter?"

I reared back as if he had slapped me. "You know? How?"

"I heard you and your nurse that night in the garden. Every word."

He had known the truth these many months. When he gave me the astrolabe, when he wrote me the poem, when he disappeared while we were on progress. He knew. I remembered the strange ring of promise in his voice as he vowed to be ready when my secret tumbled free. God help me—ready how?

I was completely within his power. "So you know my secret," I said. "What do you mean to do?" Of all the nightmarish possibilities storming through my head, nothing prepared me for the next words Gabriel uttered.

"I mean to marry you."

"Marry me?" I leapt up from the bed, shaking off the folds of cloth. "Did I scramble your brains when I hit you with that brick?"

"Not entirely." He grimaced, the wicked gash puckering. "But it was not for want of trying. Nell, this is the only way I can think of to protect you."

"Protect me? What possible good could such a marriage be? It will infuriate the queen even more."

"Perhaps at first. But there is a chance in time it might ease the queen's fears. She might hesitate before striking down her own daughter. That hesitation, combined with my connections, might be enough to spare you. Elizabeth knows I am Dudley's man, and if there is one person in England the queen trusts it is Lord Robert. If it comes to crossed swords Lord Robert would vouch for my loyalty. It is one thing to strike at a country-bred girl with no powerful friends. It is another to strike at the wife of Sir Gabriel Wyatt."

"I can take care of myself."

"Do not make empty boasts, Grace. It is a sure sign you are afraid."

I was more than afraid, I was terrified. "What are you going to do? March up to the queen and ask for my hand?"

"She would never give it, suspecting what she must. We will marry in secret, and keep it so until I can think how to present it to her in the best light."

"That is your plan? Everyone knows the queen goes into a fury when courtiers deceive her thus! She threw Katherine Grey and her husband into the Tower when she found them out!"

"Only after Katherine's belly swelled with a son."

"Is that what you hope to do? Get me with child so you will have two pawns to help you gain power?"

"No. A child would only complicate things. Expose us before we are ready."

"Ready for what? To buy Dudley's favor? Or am I to be offered up to the Howards or, God help me, the Queen herself? Surely you cannot be picturing a halcyon marriage, the two of us growing old on your estates?"

"I can think of worse ways to spend a life. Nell, I do not know how this gamble will play out. I can only promise you I will do what I can to see that Mistress Jones has some small comforts in her cell. A decent bed to sleep in. Good food. Warm clothes."

"I do not love you," I said, trying to bite back any weak tears.

Gabriel turned away. "Love is fleeting. But our minds, Nell, those we keep forever. If we bind them together, just think how strong we will be."

I thought of John Dee, his voice in the Queen's chamber. *I foresee a great union of minds.* Was Sir Gabriel Wyatt the partner foretold? Yet Dee had not said if this partner was to be ally or foe.

"I will arrange for a priest. Send word where you are to meet us tomorrow."

"And if I refuse?"

"That is your choice, Grace. But before you do, use that logic you are so proud of." Gabriel closed the space between us, his face intent. "I did not put anyone you love in danger. You put yourselves there. Eppie, when she was foolish enough to say Elizabeth bore you. Your mother when she let you come to court. And you when you defied her to contact the Queen." The truth slipped between my ribs like a knife. "If our bargain goes awry I will likely end up just as dead as you will."

"Why would you take such a risk?"

He turned away, and I could see the bruise darkening his cheek, the jagged edges of the gash that ran from his left brow to his cheek-bone. "Do you know my cell window looked out over Tower Green?

I saw poor Jane Grey die. She was such a tiny thing. She meant to be so brave, but when she knelt down, she could not find the block."

I imagined the terrified sixteen-year-old groping about her, her eyes already blindfolded, blotting out the last sunlight she would ever see.

"It is not a pretty way for anyone to die, Nell. Especially a woman." Silence stretched between us. Horror at the picture he painted spun its web in my head. After a moment, Gabriel spoke. "Now, perhaps I should see you back to your own bed before someone realizes you are missing."

He opened the chamber door.

❧ ❧ ❧

As we neared the door to the main palace, he stopped long enough to tug my hood back up to hide my face. "That is better," he said. "I would not wish the guard on duty to think you have been out making merry. My wife cannot be thought light of virtue."

"Why not?" I fired back, wanting to wound. "Your mother was."

Gabriel's eyes went wide, his hand jerked up and for a moment I feared he meant to strike me. I wished he would. Then I could cling to my anger, my pain, instead of remembering his tenderness on our flight from the Silver Swan, his sorrow when he spoke of Lady Jane Grey. After a moment he let his hand fall back to his side. He rolled his shoulders as if his neck was stiff. "I would be careful not to rouse my temper," he warned so I could barely hear him. "I fear it is a most unruly beast."

I remembered the tales Kat Ashley had told of vengeance he had wreaked.

"Nell, I wish I could undo the dark work of this night, but I cannot. And—strong and brave as you might be—neither can you. Your mind is sharp, Nell. Mine is, too. Pledged together, we can hone them into a weapon mightier than any sword. Unless you can think of some other plan."

I tried, God help me. I tried. It was a gamble to wed him, but once he was my husband he would be deceiving the queen. He would have almost as much stake in my secret as I did. Add to that his fealty to Lord Robert, the one man the queen might trust should things grow even more tangled. Would Robert Dudley plead for Gabriel Wyatt's wife? Could Dudley turn the queen's wrath away from me? Banish her fear? More importantly, would he if we were somehow cast upon the queen's mercy? I could not guess. Yet what Gabriel said was true. I would be stronger standing with the weight of Dudley's name behind me, with Sir Gabriel Wyatt's fate tied to mine. Stronger than I would be standing alone.

Chapter Twenty

The Next Day

TRIED TO BLOT OUT THE HORRORS OF EPPIE'S ANGUISHED face as Walsingham's men dragged her away, to quell Gabriel's voice as he insisted I marry him. Father's voice echoed from my memory. *You must promise me you will never fall prey to such a man as Seymour was, Nell. I could not bear it . . .*

"Father, I wish I knew." Knew what was the Angel's mask and what was Gabriel's true face. Could be certain what his motives were—to protect me as he claimed or, like Thomas Seymour, to advance toward some grand aspiration. Like a crown? Any bid for a crown made on such a shaky claim as mine would be suicide. And yet, men had been known to take mad risks before. Perkin Warbeck, an imposter who pretended to be Edward IV's long-vanished son, had been crowned king in Ireland. Malcontents flocked to his standard before Henry VII's armies cut him down.

I clasped my astrolabe, held it, praying for that mystical link Father had promised me. *Oh, Father, help me! I don't know what to do.* The metal warmed. From my hand, or in ghostly comfort? I wished I knew. But if I hoped for some ephemeral whisper of Father's voice to answer, there was none. Only the crackle of the fire.

Eventually, I splashed cold water on my face and peered at my reflection in the mullioned window while Moll dressed my hair.

The woman who stared back at me appeared infinitely older, the flesh beneath her eyes bruised with exhaustion, her gaze raked with grief. How on God's earth was I going to survive attending the sharp-eyed queen? Endure my daily routine of dancing and lute playing, stitching and reading aloud, acting like any other maid of honor—a carefree, entertaining girl.

Discerning my real identity and deciding how much risk I posed to her throne must be one of Her Majesty's most weighty concerns at present, or at least Sir Francis Walsingham's most pressing worry. I wondered if Elizabeth had spent as tortured a night as I. Had her spymaster met her before dawn to inform his mistress he had Eppie in hand? Had Walsingham promised he would soon present Her Majesty with one more diplomatic pouch, this one containing every word Hepzibah Jones confessed during *questioning*? What did they hope to achieve by persecuting a poor old woman? Merely to ferret out any source of scandal before it took root? Or did they hope to smother the truth forever the way my natural mother attempted to smother me?

"Nell?" Mary Shelton called from the doorway. "You had better hasten or the queen will be angry. You know how she hates when we are tardy for the dancing."

I smoothed the net of seed pearls over my hair one last time, their subtle glow reminding me of another jewel, the misshapen dragon pearl that forever dangled from the lobe of Gabriel's ear. Would he expect to be my partner? I wondered as I exited the maids' rooms in Mistress Shelton's wake. How would it feel to be touched by him, knowing what now lay between us? Worse still, would Walsingham be watching my every step, weighing every expression on my face to see if it revealed horror at Eppie's capture? Walsingham could not know I had looked on; I must not betray otherwise.

Mistress Shelton and I entered the chamber to the sound of musicians tuning their instruments. I prayed Gabriel would be absent. He had a priest to find, one foolhardy enough to officiate at another courtier's secret wedding. But a moment later I saw Robert Dudley, Earl of Leicester, deep in serious conversation in the far corner of the room, Gabriel's dark head close to Dudley's ear. Wyatt's gaze locked on mine; he crossed to me, bowed low. *Keep quiet,* his eyes warned. *Not a word about last night or the lady involved.*

Did he think I would march up to Walsingham and question him?

Gabriel strode from the room, Dudley staring at me so long and hard it seemed as if the seed pearls netting my hair should melt. Had Gabriel confided in his master? Was it possible he had already set in motion some plan in which I was to help the Dudley faction's cause? I turned to where William Pickering, Dudley's most threatening rival for the queen's favor, was standing. I would have him partner me, wanting to lose myself among the other dancers. But before I could secure Pickering's hand, I glimpsed the man I now feared more than anyone.

Sir Francis Walsingham's features seemed carved by unsympathetic hands, the dour planes and angles far from handsome, his eyes cunning as Machiavelli. Plain black garb marked his Puritan leanings. His lack of wealth and jewels—the bright plumage other courtiers wore as marks of the queen's favor—were testament to Her Majesty's ambiguity where her spymaster was concerned. She trusted Walsingham without question. Knew the worth of his particular skills. Yet all who saw them together knew the queen did not treat her "old Moor" with the same warm affection she did Cecil. I had spoken to Walsingham as most of the maids did—as seldom as possible and with only a few polite niceties. But today the spymaster was determined as he caught my eye. He glided toward me with a thin smile. "Mistress de Lacey."

"Sir Francis." I trod on my hem, my curtsey awkward. Walsingham reached down to unhook the cloth from where it had snagged on my slipper. "No, Sir! Pray, you mustn't."

"But I am certain the blame for your mishap lies at my door. I have the most unfortunate affect of making people nervous. It is a difficult job keeping the queen safe."

"Surely you need not worry here, with those who love Her Majesty best."

"You would be grieved to know how close to Her Majesty some threats reach." Walsingham regarded me with hooded eyes. "In fact, there might be one matter you could help me unravel, though I regret pulling you away from the dancing."

"I cannot imagine what help I could be."

"You could be helpful in an investigation I am carrying on at present. One that disturbs her majesty greatly. We do not wish the queen to be disturbed, do we?"

"Most assuredly not."

"Good. I will find this interview so much more convenient if you and I agree on that." Walsingham offered me his arm. He led me to a nearby closet, a tiny private room where no one would overhear us. The chamber was outfitted with a small table and chair, writing supplies precisely arranged, and a spindle-thin secretary whose mouth reminded me of the keyhole in a lock. Unaccountably I remembered some text Father and I had read once about a sultan who had his private secretary's tongue ripped out so the man could never tell state secrets.

"Charles, this is Mistress de Lacey, who has graciously agreed to talk with me this morning." The towhead tugged on his cap in deference.

"Pay no heed to Charles." Walsingham waved his hand. "I always keep him near to take down people's words for me. My memory is not as sharp as it once was."

More likely Walsingham employed Charles so he could use the writings later to trip up his prey. As for Walsingham's memory, intellect burned in his gaze. It was obvious he had been planning to waylay me if he had this scribe waiting.

"Now to the matter at hand." Walsingham shut the chamber door. "Last night my men made an arrest the queen found most disconcerting."

"Did they?" I knew this was coming, yet it slammed into me with the force of a fist. I struggled to keep from showing it.

"It was an Englishwoman. A midwife who tended the Dowager

Queen Katherine Parr after the Princess Elizabeth was gone from Chelsea. Your mother served at the same household."

"My mother served Katherine Parr until that good lady's death."

"Then Lady Calverley would have known Hepzibah Jones. In fact, was not that woman your nurse?"

"It is true." I knew self-preservation meant I should hold myself aloof, not ask questions. But I could not help myself. "What charges did you lay against the woman?"

"Witchcraft."

The word nearly made me retch. They tortured witches to drive out the devil or to save their souls, then hung them before a jeering crowd. I pictured my beloved Eppie, the arms that had comforted me bound, her legs kicking as the noose strangled her. I averted my face from Walsingham, unable to suppress a shudder.

"Mistress de Lacey, in the years Mistress Jones was in your family's employ, were there any signs of sorcery? I am told she did much work in the surrounding neighborhood, brewing potions and such."

"She was a midwife. A healer. Her simples were to ease people's sufferings or cure them from diseases."

"And you are an expert in such things? You would know the difference between a tisane that hastens labor pains and one that poisons the babe in its mother's womb?"

"No, I cannot tell the difference. But Eppie loved every babe she delivered. She would never hurt one!" A mistake. A dangerous one. Walsingham steepled his fingers and tapped them against his mouth. Charles's pen scratched across the page.

"Did you see any wax dolls in Mistress Jones's possession with pins thrust into their bodies?"

"No!"

"Had she a cat or some other creature forever near her? A familiar?"

"Of course not! Do you think my mother would have placed me in the care of a witch?"

"One would hope not. Yet desperate women go to such fiends every day, requesting potions to make dead wombs fertile or dash unwanted babes from their body. And there are more sinister practices. You have heard, perhaps, of certain goings-on at Sudeley Castle when the dowager queen was in childbed? The lady spoke of being poisoned?"

"By her husband, Thomas Seymour, not by Eppie! Eppie has delivered countless babes. She saves lives. She doesn't take them!" Silence fell. I feared I had gone too far. And yet I had to defend Eppie. "Sir Francis, I have known Hepzibah Jones most of my life. She is no witch. She is the most tender nurse any child could ever have."

"Then why did your mother turn her away? I have it on good authority that Mistress Jones's departure from Calverley was not a pleasant one."

"Eppie told you that?"

"I could hardly trust the testimony of an accused witch, could I? She might say anything to spare herself. I have made inquiries. That is all you need to know. Now I would like to hear your version of the tale."

I drew a deep breath, knowing Walsingham lured me onto a path littered with sinkholes that could suck me down between one word and the next. "Mother and Mistress Jones argued. They disagreed often enough. This time Mother turned her away."

"I see. Perhaps I should question Lady Calverley. She might remember more details . . . for example, the fact that she claimed Mistress Jones was mad?"

My heart fell. "Eppie grieved at leaving me. What nurse would not? But I had simply grown too old to be tended by her. You have children, Sir Francis. You know that the time comes for them to put away childish things. Even nurses they have loved."

"It is a painful time for everyone—the parents, the child, the nurses or tutors who have helped nurture them."

"Mistress Jones is the kindest soul who ever lived. It pained her to part with me, that was all. I beg you, Sir, believe me. She is no witch. Can you not let her go?"

This time it was Walsingham who turned away from me, paced

toward the window as if he craved a lungful of wholesome air. The sort Eppie could not find anywhere in London's Tower. "Your loyalty does you credit, but it has been years since you last saw her. Children think the only life their elders ever lived was the time spent with them. Yet there were many years before you knew Mistress Jones and many years after. Other lifetimes, so to speak. It is my duty to uncover the truths from those times as well. Until I do, I regret that Mistress Jones must remain in the Tower."

"Sir Francis, if you would only—"

"Thank you for your help, Mistress de Lacey. May I call upon you again if any more questions arise as the case develops?"

"Of course." What else could I say?

"Now, I must send you back to the dancing or Her Majesty will be most unhappy with me for unbalancing the couples. However, I fear your most ardent admirer will not be partnering you this morning. Sir Gabriel and the Earl of Leicester were arguing over some matter of business. Wyatt stormed out as if he were ready to do murder. I wonder what distressed him."

I remembered Gabriel's face, so hard. Shrugging, I tried to brush Walsingham's probing aside. "How would I know?"

"Sir Gabriel had a nasty gash in his face. From brawling again, no doubt. The man has a talent for getting into fights. Her Majesty is running very short of patience on that score. Wyatt should have a care or the consequences may be grim. Perhaps you could caution him, Mistress de Lacey? Be a gentle voice of reason."

"Why should I try to change his nature? I have no interest in the man."

Walsingham crossed to where Charles was sprinkling sand on the inked pages to dry them. "I am relieved to hear it." The spymaster shook sand from the first page, examining the writing. "There is a reckless streak in Wyatt that will undo him one day."

An image flashed to mind—Gabriel weaving as if he were drunk, the hiss of his sword being drawn, the cry of pain from the soldier as steel bit deep. What would have happened if the Sergeant had refused to call off his men? Gabriel and I would have been taken to the Tower as well. I curled my fingers into my palms to hide their trembling.

Sir Francis flicked a grain of sand off of his pristine black sleeve. "An heiress like you cannot be too careful, Mistress de Lacey. Wyatt is determined to build up his family estate since the queen returned it to him. He does not merely wish to restore the old buildings, but intends to build quite grandly, carry out plans his father made. Of course, it will cost a great deal to undertake such massive construction. There are men making wagers about how quickly Wyatt will take himself a rich wife. There was talk of Wyatt wedding Lord Downing's widow, and she is near sixty."

Walsingham's claim made me feel sicker yet. Did the man guess Gabriel was off arranging a wedding even now? I would be a prize for a courtier so greedy he would marry a woman old enough to be his mother!

"Perhaps you have not heard Lady Downing's sad story," Walsingham continued. "Her last husband kept her a virtual prisoner, locked away in a room in the country for years. But then, I have heard of more harrowing experiences still. Men poisoning a wife when she became inconvenient. There are rumors Thomas Seymour may have done so to the dowager queen."

I remembered my mother's story, Katherine Parr racked with fever, raving that Seymour had done just that. Surely Gabriel's plans could not follow Seymour's bent? Could Gabriel be that ruthless? Hadn't Thomas Seymour wooed Katherine Parr with painful sweetness? Promised her love, then betrayed her? "Sir Gabriel will be at the practice field later." Walsingham interrupted my musings. "The ladies are going to place wagers on the men as they tilt with the quintain."

The ladies placed wagers on everything—tennis matches, games of skittles or cards. None would wish to miss seeing the handsomest, most skilled men at court display their prowess with the lance. Perhaps I could plead an aching head to escape it.

"Have you heard that Lord Robert is planning a tournament

for the queen's birthday come September?" Walsingham asked. "Rumor is Wyatt is determined to win."

"I can only hope he will be disappointed," I said.

"Ah." Walsingham's eyes widened. "If you care enough to ill-wish Wyatt, you are not as indifferent to the gentleman as you would have me believe."

I edged instinctively toward the door. "He annoys me greatly, that is all. Now, if you will excuse me."

"Mistress." Walsingham stopped me. I turned back to see his face, dark, somber. "May I call you Elinor?"

"Yes," I said, though I was thinking of the room deep in the Tower, where truths were ripped from unwilling souls by red-hot pincers or the ropes of the rack.

"There is something about you that reminds me of my own daughters. Sons have the power to battle the world, but a girl . . . no matter how learned she is or how brave—the world can be cruel to women. A father's greatest fear is that some peril will overtake his daughter and he will not be able to protect her."

My chin bumped up a notch. "My father prepared me well. I can take care of myself." But I could not take care of Eppie. I could not shield my mother. I could not see into Gabriel Wyatt's soul, know if it was dark or light.

"It is a brutal world, Mistress Elinor," Walsingham said. "I did not make it so. Sometimes I wish I could turn away from what is necessary, but I cannot. We will speak again once I unravel this matter with Mistress Jones. I am sure of it."

God help me, so was I.

Chapter Twenty-One

The Same Day

OURS LATER WE LADIES TRAMPED AFTER THE QUEEN through the January gardens to the practice field where the men, the court's finest athletes, had gathered to show off their battle skills. A forest of lances, horses, grooms, and swords thronged the area. Some courtiers paired off, honing their swordsmanship. Others sat astride fierce warhorses that plunged and reared. Breastplates and helms glimmered in cold winter sun.

Women trickled along the sidelines in pools of vivid colors and soft furs. We wandered about to watch the various contests, calling out encouragement to particular favorites. I stared into space, the field a blur, my face feeling as if it might crack from the effort it took to mirror my companions' enthusiasm. I was not the only one whose mind was burdened with far more serious matters than which handsome courtier would triumph today. Though the queen made a show of watching Robert Dudley as he prepared to take up his sword and fight, I caught her gaze on me time and again, her eyes hooded, her lips compressed above the soft ermine that framed her face.

What was she thinking? Did I imagine a new intensity in her gaze? Last night's horrors must be written on my face. "Mistress Elinor, come stand beside me." The queen's command startled me. "I do believe

Lord Robert is about to teach the Gypsy's Angel a lesson in swordsmanship." My gaze jumped to where Gabriel stood, stripped to his cut-leather doublet and breeches despite the weather, the wind tugging his dark hair as he tested the blade of his sword with this thumb. "Would you care to place a wager on which man will triumph?"

"It will be a futile wager if we both choose the same champion, and I would not bet against Lord Robert for the world."

Elizabeth nodded. "A wise decision on your part."

"Your Majesty, shall I send a groom to fetch a brazier to keep you warm while the men show you their skills?"

"Devil take it!" Her sudden irritation made my breath catch. But I was not the one who had incurred her displeasure. Elizabeth was glaring across the field at Gabriel. "What mischief has that fool Wyatt been about now?"

"Majesty?"

"Look at that rogue's face! He is mass of bruises again! Mistress de Lacey, fetch Sir Gabriel to me at once."

There was no avoiding her command. I picked my way across the field to where Leicester and Wyatt circled each other, graceful as if in a dance. Their swords clashed, Gabriel parrying each flash of blade with ease; I hovered on the sidelines, fearful that if I distracted them, one might slip and wound the other. If that happened, the queen would not be amused.

"Pardon me, gentlemen."

Pickering, who lounged against a nearby post, winked at me and pushed himself upright. "Hold, enough!" he shouted. Two blades froze midstrike.

"What the devil?" Lord Robert grumbled.

Pickering made an exaggerated bow in my direction. "I was afraid the lady might get skewered by one of you. She has some business here."

"Mistress de Lacey?" Lord Robert said in surprise. I wondered again how much he knew about my situation.

"I am come from Her Majesty. She wishes to speak with Sir Gabriel at once."

"Have you been reduced to a page, Mistress?" Lord Robert asked.

"I do what the queen bids me."

"Obedience is a fine quality in a woman," Sir Gabriel said. "Albeit a rare one." He handed his blade to a squire, then bowed to Dudley. "If you will excuse us, my lord, we will finish this contest later." I started back across the field again, but Gabriel seized my elbow, then rolled his eyes at his companions. "Do you wish to be trampled, Mistress? Or would you prefer to cause an accident so that some man gets hurt?" Gabriel maneuvered us both out of earshot. "Lord Robert claims you and Walsingham disappeared for a considerable time. Is it true?"

"Why should Lord Robert care who I talk to? I am none of his concern."

Gabriel's fingers tightened on my arm. "Do you *want* to end up in the Tower?" His gaze swept the area, making certain no one could hear. "It will do your nurse no good if they put you in the cell next to hers," he snapped.

"There was no point in pretending I did not know her or love her when Walsingham questioned me," I insisted. "He already knew she had been my nurse! Half of Lincolnshire would have told him that."

"There is still no reason to make the inquiry any easier for him. He will uncover dangerous evidence soon enough. The longer it takes him to do so, the more time I have to figure out a plan."

"From what Sir Francis said, you are up to your neck in schemes already, trying to find enough wealth to build your traitor father's house. I am certain the widow Downing will be most disappointed when she hears of your marriage." A destrier ran at the quintain, the smack of lance into shield startling me so badly I bit my tongue.

"Marriage is a business proposition," he reasoned. "The widow will not blame me for choosing a more lucrative one. Which brings me to the point. I have arranged for our little outing on Thursday next. Lord Robert is planning to take the queen on a hunt. There is some sort of entertainment to follow. They will be gone all day and far into the night. I have already begged off—an engagement with the builder who is working on my estate. You plead ill health to get free of the other maids. A litter will be waiting by the north gate to bring you to the rooms I have secured."

We had gotten near to the queen. Gabriel closed the distance between them. "Your Majesty." He swept her a bow. "You desired to speak with me? I would not have damaged Lord Robert very badly had you allowed our match to continue." He slanted her a roguish grin as if his anger of moments before had never existed.

"It is not Leicester who concerns me at present. It is the condition of your face." She grasped Gabriel's chin and yanked it toward her like a tutor at the end of patience. "What devilment have you been about now?"

"It is nothing, just a trifling accident."

"You have an appalling number of those. And most of the time they involve another courtier's sword or fist." Her tone pulled her ladies' attention from the action on the field.

Gabriel grimaced. I could see his gash pull, noted a wince of pain. "I suppose if I told you I walked into a door you would not believe me?"

"Save your charm for my ladies," the queen said with a wave toward the women around her. "They may be fool enough to believe you. I will have the truth, Sir Gabriel. Who have you been fighting with? By God's blood, if you have cleaved off any my courtier's ears or fingers or even the fastening off their doublets I will beat you senseless with my own two hands!" The queen cuffed Wyatt on the shoulder. He fell back a step, whether from surprise or from the force of the blow I could not tell.

"I am too embarrassed to confess under these circumstances." He darted a glance at those now listening. "But if we withdraw from listening ears and Your Majesty vows to keep my secret . . ." he let his plea trail off a moment. "Otherwise I will never be able to show my face in the Great Hall again."

"I promise nothing!" High color washed over the queen's angry face. "Who were you brawling with?"

Gabriel managed to look as if he wished the ground might swallow him. "A lady, Majesty, who did not find me charming at all." The other women jostled closer.

"A lady?" The queen echoed.

"Indeed it is true, Majesty. Your own Mistress de Lacey."

He had called me reckless? Did he intend to spill out the whole story of what had happened in the stable last night? All save our flight to the Silver Swan?

"I cannot tell you what she struck me with," Wyatt continued with mock sheepishness. "I can say that any hope I had of wooing has been pounded out of my head."

Elizabeth wheeled on me. "Is this true?"

"Yes, Majesty." I swallowed my nervousness. "I struck him with a brick."

The queen tilted her head to one side, regarding me for a long moment as if she were seeing me for the first time. "*That* was as worthy a service as any maid of mine has ever done for me."

Gabriel shifted his feet, looking much abashed as he glanced around at the tittering women. "Now that you have humbled a knight of the realm completely, might I return to the war games to reclaim at least some fragment of my honor?"

"Honor?" Elizabeth snorted. "You Wyatts have little of that. Do not think I take your trifling with one of my maids lightly! I grow weary of your unruliness. Vex me one more time and I will teach you a lesson more crushing than Mistress de Lacey did."

"I am properly terrified."

"I doubt it. But someday your recklessness will cost you dear. I have my eye on you, Sir. Forget that to your peril." Gabriel backed away from her, then turned and ran across the field with lithe strides. Horses nearly trampled him, sword points slashing close.

He did not seem to mind disaster closing in all around us. But I had glimpsed it as Walsingham's scribe wrote down my words. And I sensed it in the queen as Elizabeth Tudor watched the Gypsy's Angel lope heedlessly away.

Chapter Twenty - Two

Elizabeth

A Day Later

ELIZABETH RUBBED THE BACK OF HER NECK, GRATEFUL the council meeting was over, ready to have Robin send to saddle her favorite mare and secure the birds so they could go hawking. And yet, hunting had not had its usual appeal of late. Her heart no longer soared with the falcons, fierce, untouchable. Elinor de Lacey had reminded her far too keenly how it felt to be the prey.

"Your Majesty."

She looked up. "Sir Francis."

"I have news to impart to you alone."

The queen waved her hand at the other ministers who were gathering their parchment, quills. "Leave us," she said.

Lord Robert's eyes narrowed. William Cecil started to speak, but Elizabeth glared at them, driving them to join the others exiting the Council Chamber. Once the door shut behind them, the queen bade Walsingham speak.

"I wished to report that we have the subject of our search lodged safely in the Tower. Now we have only to decide what to do with her."

"Discover any tales she might have to tell about Nell de Lacey's birth and about the scar on the girl's hand. I must be certain there is no link to me."

Walsingham raised one brow. "If you could be more specific . . ."

"I will tell you all I can." Elizabeth paced away from him. "There are shades from when I was exiled to Cheshunt, ghosts summoned up by my feverish brain in that place. The people who tended me, the months I suffered there . . . they blur together as if a nightmare. I was little more than a child then, so ill. There were times I even wished . . . well, death will come for us all in time. Hepzibah Jones haunts me from that time, makes me fear . . ."

"Fear what? Tell me, Majesty. I would die to keep you safe."

"And kill to secure the same end."

"If necessary. Is there something you remember about the Jones woman?"

"I do not remember, but sometimes I dream . . . hellish dreams, Walsingham. I wake feeling as if someone had scraped my very soul from my body."

"Surely it is some strange humor of the blood. After all Your Majesty endured it is little wonder your nerves are shattered when you think of those terrible times."

"Nell de Lacey and Hepzibah Jones bring those times back to me. They flood me with poison, churn inside me until I feel half mad myself."

"There is no need for you to endure such. Send the girl away."

"No. The situation is too unpredictable. I need her here, under watchful eyes."

"Sometimes when a situation becomes too unpredictable, it is best to act subtly. Accidents happen. People die of strange fevers. Fall down stairs and break their necks."

"How dare you fling Amy Dudley's death in my face! It *was* an accident. The incident was thoroughly examined, and Lord Robert was acquitted of all charges."

"Indeed, Lord Robert was a most fortunate man."

"Was he?" Fury bubbled up in the queen. "In that one fall Amy made certain I could never wed the man I love."

"That result was either tragic or fortuitous, depending upon your point of view." Walsingham did not flinch. He was the one among all her councilors who never did.

"Do you think it is a pleasure to be alone?" Elizabeth raged. "To be denied the comfort of a husband in my bed? To carry the weight of a kingdom without a strong shoulder to lean on?"

"I am merely observing that people disappear and sometimes the world is safer for it. Would I could make the Queen of Scots vanish."

"God's anointed queen? How dare you presume."

"She would not scruple to rid the world of you if she had the power. We must make certain no one gives her the weapon necessary to depose you."

"Indeed. We can decide what to do with our captive later. For now, I wish you to be on the alert for anything unusual. If there is some irregularity in Nell de Lacey's past, we must uncover it."

Walsingham frowned, considering. "In fact, there was something unusual at the arrest of Mistress Jones. Sir Gabriel Wyatt wounded one of my soldiers."

"What?" Elizabeth stiffened, remembering the gash on his face, his claim Elinor de Lacey had wounded him.

"Wyatt was in the area with his mistress. Apparently the woman has a jealous husband threatening to murder her. Wyatt drew his sword rather than let the soldiers get a glimpse of her face."

"That is reckless even for him."

"Is it not time Sir Gabriel's temper was checked, Your Grace? You have certainly given him warning enough to stop his brawling. This offense is grave, and yet . . ." Walsingham stroked his beard.

"Yet what, Sir Francis?"

"I cannot help but wonder who this mysterious woman was. And why the Gypsy's Angel risked so much to shield her."

"Some foolish notion of chivalry?"

"Perhaps. But I will probe more deeply in case it is something more."

Chapter Twenty-Three

February 1565

COME THURSDAY I DID NOT HAVE TO PRETEND I WAS ILL. The thought of Eppie imprisoned and the uncertainty of the marriage I was about to make was enough to turn me pale and wan. Moll and I huddled in the room where the queen's ladies could be quarantined when they had fever, my loyal servant in a welter of concern. Sounds of confusion rose in the courtyard below and I went to the window to watch the gaily dressed court ride out on their day's adventure. The queen, garbed in purple, should have been in high spirits. But even from a distance I could see the quick, impatient thrust of her arm toward her groom, the rigid set of her spine, her fine gray hunter sidestepping as if her tension flowed down through the reins.

For a moment I even imagined the queen glared at my window. I ducked out of sight, heart hammering until the party left. The moment they disappeared Moll laced me into my plainest gown so I might blend with simple Londoners.

"Mistress," Moll said. "You will get in trouble with the queen, running off like this. If she discovers you are not sick—"

"It is a chance I have to take. But you will be safe enough, Moll. I will not tell you where I am going. That way, if anyone questions you, you will not have to lie. Just say you were weary and fell asleep over your mending."

"That will not stop me from worrying over you! All this secrecy frightens me, Mistress. Last week you came in late, looking as if you had ridden through hell. And every day since you look so pale it breaks my heart. I know I am but a servant, but I am a loyal one, and true. I wish you would tell me what is troubling you."

"It will all sort out in time." I did not clarify what that meant: That I would end up with my head on the block, locked up in prison, or married to a man I feared to love. Whichever way my fate turned, I would be bound forever as Gabriel Wyatt's wife.

I scooped up Moll's fustian cloak, a disguise to conceal I was highborn. Moll adjusted its voluminous hood over my head to make certain no red-gold hair could be seen. I looped her basket over one arm, looking for the world like a servant girl off to do some errand for her mistress—I hoped.

Slipping through the back ways of the palace seemed to take forever, clinging close to the walls, my head bowed, eyes downcast. When I reached the litter outside the north gate I climbed in on shaky legs, then drew the painted leather curtains shut, blocking out the London sights as a strange groom set the palfreys on each side of the litter into a jarring walk. Clasping my hands, I prayed in phrases so broken I doubted even God could understand them. But God did not stoop to answer me; the yawning chasm of silence deafened me to all but my own desperation. Too soon the litter lurched to a stop. A groom came forward to pull back the curtain. "This is our destination."

Our destination? And where exactly was that? I felt tempted to ask with a wild kind of irony. I had no idea where the litter had brought me. I only knew I wished to be almost anyplace else. Clutching the folds of the cloak under my chin, I passed the servant a coin. The groom bobbed his head in thanks. "You are to go upstairs. Third chamber to the right."

Squaring my shoulders, I forced myself to enter a townhouse, a trifle shabby compared to the fine homes court visited. I walked through a hall strangely empty of either people or furnishings. Then I climbed up the stairs. A row of doors opened off the corridor. I knocked upon the third. It flew open, an arm sweeping me into the chamber in a rush. Panic jabbed me as someone swept off my hood. I saw a harsh, familiar face, a bruise somewhat faded.

"You came."

"I did not know I had any other choice."

"There is always a choice." Gabriel unfastened my cloak and I shrugged it off my shoulders, my eyes taking in the chamber where I was to become a bride. Unlike the barren hall below, this suite of rooms was obviously occupied. The common area boasted a hearth of marble veined with blue. Fire crackled behind iron fire dogs shaped like wolves. Walls paneled in rich oak linenfold were polished a mellow gold, while a faded tapestry depicting the rape of the Sabine women covered the western wall.

A table was laid with platters of fruit and bread, cheese and sweetmeats and a bottle of what looked to be wine. A branch of unlit candles stood beside a single chair painted green and red, much of its former glory rubbed away. An elaborately scrolled *W* was still visible on its back. I might have stared at that single letter forever if it meant I would not have to face the conflicting emotions the Gypsy's Angel raised in me.

"May I introduce you to the priest who is to marry us?" Gabriel asked. I looked up as a figure stepped from the shadows, the holy man's feet stirring up the fresh rushes that strewed the floor. "Mistress de Lacey, this is Father Ambrose Larkin. He has been a friend of the Wyatt family these many years."

"Back in the times when we spoke of the reformed faith only in whispers, and had to hide our belief in it," the ruddy-faced priest said. "Long before you were born, Master Gabriel. A scrawny, wailing scrap of a lad you were. Your brothers were disappointed you did not skip out of the cradle immediately to play ball."

Wyatt had brothers? I thought, startled. Why had no one mentioned them? And if they were older than he, would they not be the ones to inherit their father's estate?

Gabriel smoothed the soft ruff around his throat, the Holland linen seeming all the more white contrasted against his dark blue doublet and sun-browned hands. "Mistress de Lacey is not interested in tedious family tales. And I can never disappoint Dickon and Hal again. So perhaps we might proceed."

"Forgive an old man his ramblings." Father Ambrose flinched at Gabriel's tone. "Let me begin again. Good morrow on this happiest of occasions, Mistress. Might I wish you a lifetime of days exactly like this one?"

Gabriel interrupted. "Father, we have little time and are anxious to be wed."

"Certainly, my son. If you will summon the witnesses."

Gabriel went to what must be a privy chamber. "Keyes, Tyrell. It is time." Two men appeared—one the sergeant porter who played the ogre the night of the masque. The other Sir Gabriel's manservant.

Keyes grinned. "So I am not the only man to fall recklessly in love."

I was too unnerved to question the kindly sergeant. This marriage was based on necessity, not on love. I wanted to beg Mary Grey's good-hearted friend to get me away from here. But what point would it serve? Better to face the inevitable like Tyrell, who stood silent, only a beading of sweat above his upper lip betraying his unease. Little wonder he was rattled. Witnesses would face the queen's wrath if we were discovered.

Father Ambrose cleared his throat. "Sir Gabriel, if you and your bride will stand before me and take hands, we may begin."

I tried to hide my fists in the folds of my gown, as if that could delay the inevitable. Wyatt gently dragged my fingers out of hiding and gripped my hands in both of his. I stared at our locked fingers, unwilling to meet the Angel's gaze.

Long, tapered fingers enveloped mine, Gabriel's palm broad, his nails squared off at the ends. They were hands a sculptor would pay to carve onto a statue of Apollo or Odysseus. Soon they would be the hands of my husband. The man who had the right to my lands, my wealth, my body. The priest must have prompted us on the marriage vows. But it was only Gabriel's voice I heard, rough as though it were a race he was determined to win. I repeated the words required of me, remembering all of the queen's dire warnings. *It is a rare chance we two women have . . . our fate in our own hands . . .*

Not anymore, I thought as Gabriel took his ring, slipped it first to the knuckle of my thumb, next to my first finger, then to the middle one, and lastly pushed the cold metal circlet firmly to the base of my fourth. Each motion matched with his voice claiming me in the name of the Father, the Son, and the Holy Ghost, Amen. I stared down at the circlet of tiny emeralds now glittering from my wedding ring. It was done.

Father Ambrose beamed. "May I be the first to congratulate you, Mistress Wyatt?"

Elinor Wyatt. That was my name from now on. Elinor de Lacey was no more.

Keyes wished me happiness as he raised a glass in a wedding toast. After downing their wine he and Tyrell exited the chamber. Gabriel passed the priest a purse and hastened the holy man out the door behind them. I heard the latch click shut. Silence pressed my chest, Gabriel's ring heavy on my hand. Gabriel stood for a moment with his back to me. I wondered if he, too, could think of nothing to say.

"It is done," I said, retrieving my cloak from the chair where Gabriel had tossed it. "Perhaps I can catch up with Sergeant Keyes so he can see me back to the palace."

Gabriel's hand caught mine before I could pick up the cascade of rough russet cloth. "You cannot leave yet."

"The ceremony is over. We are wed. Man and wife."

"Not entirely. I will not risk this marriage being annulled. Until we consummate the union, our marriage would be far too easy to dissolve."

"Can we not pretend that we—"

"No." He said so fierce it startled me. Noting my reaction, he softened his tone. "You will be my wife, Nell. For good and all. We will rise or fall in this together."

Gabriel crossed to the table, poured a goblet of wine. He pressed it into my hand. "Drink this. It will help you to relax when I bed you."

But the thought of relinquishing any fragment of control made the prospect of what was to come even more unnerving. I pushed the goblet away from me. "I do not want it."

"As you wish." Gabriel gestured to the door leading to the privy chambers. My feet felt heavy as I moved through a sparsely fur-nished second room, then into what was a bedchamber someone had obviously taken trouble to prepare. A tester bed stood against one tapestry-covered wall, the bedposts patterned in the same gilt and green and red that the chair in the common room had been. Initials twined the columns and were stitched onto the bed cur-tains. H and A. I wondered who they stood for. Not King Henry and Anne Boleyn. The W was again picked out in gilt at the head of the bed.

Coverlets and pillows in a rich Lincolnshire green mounded the expanse of mattress, the damask embroidered with the device of a maiden rising up from the center of a rose. A motto: "The happiest" was stitched upon it in Latin. In counterpoint, a griffin spread its wings across the other pillow, with the legend "Honor above all."

The words pierced me with sadness. I traced the elegantly stitched words. "I feel ashamed to touch these. Our marriage makes a mockery of both honor and joy."

"Our marriage is no worse than many. Few wed for love. Most do so to get heirs, add to their estates. To build life on a solid foun-dation."

"Ours is built on shifting sands."

"That is true, but only for now. Life is full of more unexpected turns than the labyrinth where the Minotaur once dwelled. We can both hope for more secure footing in the future." He crossed to me, crooked his finger beneath my chin. "I do regret the way we have begun. When I imagined our wedding night, I wanted more than this."

"I'm astonished you imagined anything but the properties you would gain."

"I suppose I have been guilty of your charge. That is what marriage meant to me. A union based on advancement and of course, to save myself from hell. What was it Saint Paul said?" His mouth lifted in a cynical smile. "It is better to marry than to burn?"

"I will reserve judgment on that. At present I am not certain I agree with him."

"We will come to know each other in time. I hope one day you will find me not reprehensible as a husband. We are both ruled by reason, unlike those who are slaves of passion. Even your wedding ring attests to that. It is engraved 'Let Reason Rule.'"

I chuckled without mirth.

"Nell, I do care about you. Perhaps more than is convenient. I mean to use every skill in my power to make sure you are satisfied when we arise from this bed."

I folded my arms tight around myself. "I wish you would just get it over with."

"You do not wish that and neither do I." Loosening my clasped arms, he untied my sleeves, and slid them down past my wrists one by one, his calloused palms rough against my skin. "I have seen the way you look at me. Heard your breath catch when I touch you in the dance. And when I kissed you by the stream during your first hunt there was sweetness in it for us both. There can be sweetness between us again."

He unfastened my gown, his knuckles brushing my spine. He pressed a kiss to my nape. "Confess it," he urged me, "if only to yourself. Have you not imagined what we might be like together?"

I clutched tight to sorrow, rigid self-control, trying to wall out any feeling but that. Yet stiff as I tried to hold against him I could not lie to myself. I *had* wondered what Gabriel Wyatt's hands would feel like on my body when the other ladies whispered about their lovers. I had imagined kisses flavored with the danger of the Gypsy's Angel. With a few soft tugs my kirtle and petticoats pooled upon the floor; my stays followed. I scrambled into bed, pulling the coverlets between us, not caring if he thought me a coward.

The wretch smiled, almost tender, as if he understood, then focused his attention on his own clothing. He did not turn his back to me as a gentleman would, only made quick work of his doublet, shedding his stockings, boots and breeches. Once revealed, his fine silk shirt showed patterns of diamonds pressed into it, tiny pillows of fabric Tyrell had painstakingly pulled through the small slashes cut into Gabriel's doublet.

I could have closed my eyes as he reached for the hem of his shirt to strip it away, but the naked male body was a mystery to me, and I could not resist seeing the whole of what I had heard discussed by the other maids. Light from the window warmed his skin a golden hue. He stood before me, a denizen of some seductive world I had never ventured to before: Hades when the Lord of the Underworld first climbed into his reluctant bride's bed. Had Persephone come to love her dread lord? I wondered. The myths said only that she returned to her mother each spring. And yet, had it been difficult for Demeter's daughter to resist the pull of currents older than time? With measured strides Gabriel approached the bed. Our bed, now. Our marriage bed. He grasped the coverlets in one strong hand. I was too proud to resist when he tugged them away, exposing me to his gaze.

"Do not be afraid to let yourself want me, Nell," he urged as he lay down beside me and pulled me into his arms. "It is natural, this fire between us. Instinct that has peopled the world for thousands of years. A scientist like you must want to explore the place this craving leads us to."

For as long as I could remember my curiosity had been both my greatest gift and my most dangerous curse. And yet, to let reason be overpowered by passion seemed a dangerous gamble. I could feel sensations already heating my veins. I did not want to notice how warm his skin was, how different from my own. I did not want to feel an unexpected freedom when he drew my shift off. I felt naked in far more than my body as he stared at me. He scooped my astrolabe from where it laid between my breasts.

"I am a skilled lover," Gabriel said, turning the disk over in his hand.

I gave a nervous laugh. "At least you are an arrogant one."

"It is no boast." He let my necklace fall back against my skin, traced the slender river of chain down the slope of my breast. For a moment, I could not breathe. "I can give you great pleasure in our marriage bed if you have the courage to let me."

"I want to resist you."

"I know." He looked somber for a moment, and I could not stop the fine tremor that shook me as he skimmed my nipple with the tip of his finger. "But this is not a battle one of us must lose, Nell. Stubborn as we are, in bed we can both win. Your body is willing. And mine . . ." He chuckled wryly. "My lance has been couched and aching for you a very long time. Can we not put my theory to the test?" He laid my hand on his naked flesh. Contrasts struck me, hardness, velvet skin, coarse hair tickling my palm. He groaned as my fingers explored, my curiosity racing to meet his hunger. His mouth found my throat, my cheek, my chin. We battled most sweetly in the hours that followed, and I learned these new lessons as quickly as I had any other. Before he thrust into my body he covered his lance with a pale sheath, ribbons on its open end, his voice gravelly. "'Twill guard you from conceiving a child."

He settled his hips between my thighs and drove himself deep. I cried out in surprise, pain, as he tore my maidenhead. But as he began to move inside me some mystical alchemy occurred, turning pain to pleasure—tempting me to pretend the practical metal our marriage was based on glittered with just a touch of gold.

Sated and sweating, we rolled apart from each other and I

faced reality once more. I still feared to trust him. The Gypsy's Angel deceived in many things. But in one matter he told me true. We snatched pleasure out of pain that day, at least for a little while.

All too soon, he roused me, dressed me deft as any maidservant, even brushing and pinning up my hair so no one would guess what mischief we had been about. "You are as apt at this as Moll," I jested feebly. "Where does a man learn such skills?"

"In a court full of romantic intrigue can you not guess?"

I looked away, remembering the hungry way Lettice Knollys and several of the other women had looked at him. "Oh. Well, that is in the past."

"No it isn't."

His refusal struck me to the quick. I spun around. "What do you mean?"

He peered down at me with a mixture of defensiveness and regret. "My life must seem to go on exactly as it did before. Not a ripple of change for Walsingham's spies to detect. I cannot suddenly transform into a monk."

"But you will not be celibate at all. You will sleep with me. Your *wife*."

"I cannot wait to bed you again, sweet, but it is too dangerous for the time being. I must visit my mistress." Jealousy streamed through me in vivid hues.

"You tell me you are going to sleep with harlots before the sun has even set on our wedding day? It seems a strange pronouncement from a husband."

"That depends whether you want a faithless husband or a dead one. If I suddenly forgo pleasures of the flesh I will bring suspicion down on both of us. It will be blood scent to wolves." It was true, and yet that did not cool its sting.

"Perhaps you are the wolf I should worry about."

"Perhaps." Gabriel's jaw tightened. "But I am a wolf who upholds his end of a bargain. Last night I met with a guard from the Tower prison where your nurse lies."

My heart leapt, dashing away all thought of the other woman who would soon bed my husband. "You have news of Eppie? Tell me!"

"She is alive." He did not add "for now." "Oxenham agreed to carry food to her, blankets. For a ruinous fee of course."

"Will he smuggle a letter to her? Sneak me in to see her? If I am hooded and veiled no one need know who I am."

"No."

"Gabriel, I beg you. I won't care how many mistresses you take if I can see Eppie."

"I can buy food, Nell. A fire for her hearth. But if I took every piece of gold, every acre of land, every brick and jewel we both own I could not buy you passage into her cell or pass her a letter written in your hand. Not and keep either one of you safe."

It was true. I knew it. For a moment I felt foolish, like a reckless child. "Gabriel, this guard . . . did he say . . ." I hesitated, my mind filled with horrors I had heard of, dank cells, the ropes and chains determined men once used to break the body of Anne Askew. "Have they hurt her, Gabriel?"

"She is alive. That is all he knew. Perhaps we can learn more in time."

"You will tell me if you do. Not knowing is the most terrible thing of all."

"I thought the same thing once," he said. "But that was a very long time ago."

❧❧❧

IN THE WEEKS that followed fear stalked me as the hours stretched long. From the guard we learned little. Mistress Jones had been questioned, moved from a comfortable cell into a miserable one with the damp and the rats to loosen her tongue.

From the queen's actions we learned even less. She summoned me to serve her as usual. Ordered me to read aloud. Wove tricky questions through our conversations as deftly as she pulled gold thread through the altar cloth we ladies stitched. She pricked my pride by listing Gabriel's attentions to other women, a torment that shredded my already ragged nerves even further. Was it intentional? Her cruelty? Or was she trying to comfort me in her way? I could not be sure. I hid my heartache when she claimed I was lucky to escape him. All men were faithless in the end, the queen affirmed. I should pity the foolish woman Wyatt seduced into becoming his wife one day.

I forced myself to be careless and gay, locked in my cage of deception. Only with Gabriel could I allow real emotion to show. At first I pressed him for any news of Eppie. Later, I sought him out for other reasons as well. Jealousy when I smelled unfamiliar perfumes on his clothes. Torment at the knowledge that nearly any woman at court would be far more practiced in pleasing my husband in bed. I cannot say exactly when our private world shifted. I only know in time I sought Gabriel out because I wanted to.

He made me presents of books he collected, hoping to distract me for at least a little while. Stretched my mind with volumes of ancient wisdom from the spice countries and new discoveries from rich lands across the Atlantic where Spain, France, England, and Portugal now scrambled for power. He gave me books so poorly reasoned out he knew they would anger me, or perhaps make me laugh at their muddled logic. One day he left a coffer with a clock in pieces, daring me to try to fix it. Not since Father had anyone demanded my mind reach so far, and I was grateful for it.

One February night I caught him alone in a corridor, glimpsed the brooch pinning his cloak. Initials twined in gold, first H, then the A I had seen embroidered on the curtains of our marriage bed. "Who were they?" I asked. "The happy woman and the man with honor?" Gabriel stiffened. I wished I had said nothing.

"I suppose you must hear it soon enough. Better it come from me. The initials belong to my father, Henry Wyatt, and my mother, Alison."

I remembered what Kat Ashley had said about his parents when first I came to court. His father a traitor, his mother a whore. It grieved me, how far they had fallen from the mottos they once held dear. I could only imagine how much their disgrace pained their son.

"You say nothing. You heard the tales people tell."

"The court is full of tales. Not all of them are true."

"The ones about my parents are. My father did turn traitor against Queen Mary. He would not have a Spanish king sit on the English throne. And my mother—she bedded a man named Sir Albion Ferris while my father lived."

Ferris? Had I heard that name in some discussion between my father and his Cambridge friends? "Did not Albion Ferris help the Duke of Norfolk execute the rebels? My father said the man was as vicious as his master. Power-hungry. Vile."

"Ferris was all those things and more. He never forgot a slight and would plot his whole life to seek revenge."

Katherine Ashley claimed Gabriel followed a similar code. I shoved the thought away, then asked: "Ferris had a grudge against your father?"

"No. It was my mother Ferris loathed. When she was a maid, presented at court, they called her Alison the Virtuous. Which meant, of course, that all King Henry's favorites were eager to debauch her. Charles Brandon wagered that Ferris could not deflower her. Unfortunately Brandon did not specify it must be with her consent." Gabriel's mouth crooked up, even though his face looked grim.

"You smile at that?" I asked, confused.

"My mother had been raised with a pack of brothers who liked to fight as much as I do. When Ferris attempted to rape her, she wrenched the man's own dagger out of its sheath. It was a long while before the knave could use his offensive parts again."

"I am glad of it."

Gabriel braced one arm upon the wall. "I could imagine you doing the same thing. In fact, I considered having Tyrell line my codpiece with lead the day you came to wed me." Gabriel's smile did not reach his eyes. "Brandon guessed my mother was responsible for Ferris's injury, though he had no proof. The suspicion was humiliation enough. Ferris waited his chance for years, patient as any spider. Then he struck."

"What happened?"

"He made a devil's bargain. My mother was to be his whore before all the court for as long as my father was alive. And she was to make certain my father knew it."

"She should have killed him."

"Ferris used a pretty weapon to force her to his will. If she complied with his wishes, he promised to secure a pardon for me from the Duke of Norfolk. My brothers had died during the first clash of Wyatt's rebels against Queen Mary's soldiers. My father was merely awaiting his execution. I was all my mother had left."

I thought of my own mother, her courage, her fierce protectiveness. "Of course she did what Ferris commanded. She must have loved you very much."

"She did. I was her favorite, you see. Reminded her of her brothers, forever spoiling for a fight. But I did not love her after I was let loose from the Tower. I accepted the reprieve she gained me because I wished so much to live. But I hated her for shaming Father. Shaming me. I did not learn she had done so to save me until months later, after Father's head was on a pike on London Bridge."

I shuddered, my childhood curiosity about those grisly warnings haunting me even further. The Lieutenant had told me the reason they lasted so long. They boiled the heads in tar so it took longer for the flesh to fall away. What would it be like to see someone you loved hoisted high in shame? Ravens plucking at his eyes?

"My mother sickened in the months after, poisoned by my hate and by the weight of Ferris's bastard in her belly. Had her brother not come three days before she died, I might never have known why she did the things she did. She confided in him and he carried the truth to me as she lay in her bed, her body bloated with that monster's child."

Gabriel arched his head back, shut his eyes tight. I stole up behind him, put my arms about his waist, giving what little comfort I could. Gabriel sucked in a slow, deep breath. "I begged her for forgiveness. But she could not grant me absolution, no matter what she said. I had believed such horrible things of her, Nell. Despised her and let her see it. But she smiled at me, so tender. Said she would forget all if I would swear one vow to grant her peace. I would have promised her anything."

"What did she ask?"

"That I not kill the man who raped my mother, tortured my father with tales of her unfaithfulness. If I cut Ferris down I would pay with my life. Her sacrifice would have been in vain."

"Your promise must have given her some comfort."

"I cannot imagine why. I broke it three months later. Bribed a Fleet Street whore to lure him into an alley, where I killed him one tiny cut at a time. The way my father must have suffered. The way my mother . . . so you see I am a devil, not to be trusted. I broke a deathbed vow to my own mother."

"I do not blame you. I could not have borne seeing that beast going about his life, gloating over his triumph."

"I vowed no other man would slight any Wyatt again without paying at the point of my sword. You once told me not knowing is the most horrible thing imaginable. I tell you there is something worse. Knowing someone you love surrendered all for you. And you did not deserve it."

Chapter Twenty-Four

April 1565

ARCH SWEPT PAST WITH SHEETS OF RAIN AND promises of lambs scattered on distant meadows. One dark night in late April as the rest of the court gambled at cards, Gabriel came to seek me. "The chapel," he whispered. "Meet me."

I knew from his face the news he carried must be bleak indeed.

I waited a bit after he disappeared, then slipped from the chamber and dashed toward the chapel. Before I could reach it, a voice hissed my name. I looked around, but the corridor seemed empty. Then Gabriel beckoned me from the partially open door of one of the many rooms kept for nobles' use while at court. I hastened in and he bolted the door behind him. I could tell the chamber had not been occupied for some time. Holland cloths draped furniture, filling the room with ghostly shapes in the flickering light of the taper Gabriel held. "Did anyone follow you? See you passing this way?"

"No. What is it?"

"I needed to get you alone, but I dared not take you to my chambers or your own. We should be safe for the time being. No one would think to look for you here. These are Lord Ashwall's rooms, and that bastard hasn't been to court since I lopped off his ear."

"Please, Gabriel," I begged. "Just tell me what is wrong."

"Mistress Jones is dead."

"No!" I jerked away from him, shook my head in denial. "That is impossible."

"I wish to God it was. Oxenham claims the Tower guards speak of little else."

"Eppie dead?" I choked out. "Why did you not tell me she was ill? I could have brewed a posset. Sent her an apothecary."

He gripped my arms as if to keep me on my feet. "No medicine on earth could have helped her. She was not sick."

"Not sick? Then why . . . ?" Dread wrenched tight at the hell in Gabriel's eyes.

"Do not make me tell you, Grace," he pleaded, soft.

"Tell me!" My voice rose on a note of hysteria. "Tell me, Gabriel, now!"

He clapped his palm over my mouth, glanced at the door in alarm. "Quiet! Christ, Nell! Do you want to bring Walsingham's spies down on us?" Ever so slowly he withdrew his hand from my mouth, but he did not release his hold on my arm.

I was shaking as if I had been cased in ice. "Tell me," I rasped.

"They put her on the rack. Tried to break her there."

"God, no!" I pressed my hand to my mouth. Gabriel maneuvered me to a bench before my knees buckled. "Did she . . . She must have told them everything. Who could suffer torture and not do anything to end the pain?"

"We do not know that for certain." Gabriel sat down beside me and clasped my hands in his. "No one but Walsingham and the torture master know what she revealed. We must be vigilant. Brave. We may survive this yet."

"At what price?" A sob rose in my throat. "Eppie died for loving me."

Gabriel chafed my fingers as if trying to press life back into them. "You did not put Eppie on the rack, Nell. Walsingham did."

"Because I was too headstrong to stay at Calverley. If I had never come to court, I would never have mentioned Eppie to the queen.

Gabriel . . . if Walsingham resorted to torture, then do you think what Eppie said about my birth is true?"

"Perhaps. But perhaps not."

"Why else would the queen's spymaster hunt a simple midwife?"

"I wonder that myself. But we do not know all the circumstances, Nell. Perhaps Eppie told someone else of her encounter with the "very fair lady" and that person carried the tale back to the queen. Mere rumor can pose enough of a threat to bring a ruler down. The queen knows the danger of well-placed rumors in unscrupulous hands. Her mother lost her head because a musician broken by torture swore he had bedded her."

"Eppie must have fought so hard to keep the truth from Walsingham. If she had revealed all, they would never have tortured her. She died trying to protect me."

Gabriel kissed my brow. "She loved you very much."

"I called her mad . . . I called her a liar."

"It is little wonder. The information she gave you still sounds fantastical."

"If it was fantastical then why arrest her?"

"For all her temper the queen is cautious to a fault. She drives her councilors mad with her indecision when it comes to matters like this. I know Her Majesty has been cool to you of late. But I have seen Her Majesty look warmly upon you as well. She respects you, a woman whose intellect can match her own. She admires your honesty. You told her from the first your mother did not approve of you coming to court. While other women play games to win her favor, you do not."

"I am too busy trying to stay alive! As for honesty, I shed that long ago. I badgered my father to secretly write the queen on my behalf. I deceived my mother. Dear God, I wish I had never come to court! I am sick of the intrigue, the lies. Acting as if all is well, trying not to flinch whenever I hear the guard drawing nigh me, even though they might be coming to take me to the Tower. Behaving as if all is goodness and light when I know the queen is plotting against me. Looking at her and wondering if she carried me inside her womb, if she felt me move, felt the life in me, and then ordered some servant to smother me. Maybe even Kat Ashley—Kat Ashley who is so kind to me . . ."

"I know how you must feel, Nell."

"No, you do not! I have to brush the queen's hair and fetch her books and smile even while she talks of you and your women!"

"Nell—"

"I do not feel like a wife! I feel alone and scared and helpless, knowing I might die tomorrow. And it might be better for you if I did."

"Nell, for God's sake."

"It is true! Anyone who is linked to me is in danger. Who might be next on Walsingham's list to torture? My mother? You?"

"He will not torture a peer of the realm."

"He could kill you, Gabriel. What if your life is the forfeit?"

"Then you would be a merry widow," he tried to tease.

I knotted my fist, pounded it upon his chest. "Do not mock me! I have already lost one person I—"

My voice broke. I could not finish.

Gabriel caught my wrist. I could feel his heart racing. His lashes dipped down, as if to shield feelings so raw he dared not let me see. "My death would grieve you?"

I wanted to rage at him. I wanted to pull away from emotions inside me, be safe. But who knew what time we had left? Even now Walsingham's men might be coming to lock us up in Eppie's place. *"My death would grieve you?"* His question reverberated through me. What could I say but the truth? "Yes."

Gabriel kissed my temple, nudged my face upward until he could reach my cheek. His lips were warm with life, a gift I knew was far too fragile, fleeting. I wrapped my arms around him, held tight as if the two of us were caught in a gale. My lips sought his, and I wept as I dragged him down to the floor, then onto my body.

The skill he'd brought to our first bedding was gone, his body urgent as we both attempted to drive back horror with one life-affirming act. This time when he drove inside me there was no time for caution, no sheepskin barrier between us. He could not keep me safe.

I cannot say how much time we lay together. But when we heard footsteps beyond the door Gabriel went rigid. I held my breath. The instant it was quiet again he scrambled to get me back into my clothes, his face hard with self-disgust. "We should not have stayed away from the queen so long. Someone will be looking for you."

God help me, how I wished that were true the way it had been when I was a child, when arms eager to gather me close waited behind every doorway and I had no doubt that love was there for the asking.

I fought for composure as I entered the queen's chamber a quarter hour later. "Mistress Nell," the queen said. "Where have you been off to?"

"I fear that there was a private matter, a woman's matter to attend to."

"Ah," the queen nodded. I felt her eyes follow me the rest of that endless night.

❧❧❧

THE DAYS THAT followed were a blur of grief and deception. I stumbled through my duties, trying to hide what I knew: That Walsingham had Eppie's blood on his hands and that Elizabeth Tudor, the queen I had so admired, the woman who might be my real mother, had given permission for the torture that had ended my nurse's life.

I hated the queen, hated her spymaster, hated myself. Could barely drag myself through the day, until everyone from Lady Betty to Kat Ashley to even Lettice Knollys wondered at my sudden decline in health. It poisoned me inside, thinking the queen must know the reason why, be watching, waiting. At night, I tried to stem my weeping until all were asleep, but there were not enough tears in the world to wash away the guilt I felt, or the terror.

Uncertainty tore at me like the beak of the giant bird who was Prometheus's tormenter, ripping me open night after night, making me doubt my own courage. If I could not even bear imagining the horrors Eppie had faced, how would I endure my own trial by fire if should it come? And the odds of that trial coming grew more ominous by the day. Why hadn't Walsingham pounced already? I wondered, listening at every moment for the sound of guards marching to escort me away. More to the point, how would I outwit Walsingham when I could not even fool Mary Grey into thinking nothing was amiss? My failure to deceive her was evident in the soft store of cloths I found one night when I slipped my hand beneath the pillow.

Even Gabriel wrenched at my tenuous hold on sanity. I could not reach him. He had closed a gate heavy as the Tower's own between us. To protect me, I reasoned, while a cold voice whispered within me: *to protect himself*.

Night after night I huddled in the bed I shared with Mary Grey, in the chamber full of maids of honor and snuffling small spaniels.

I had never felt more alone.

May 1565

IRONIC THAT ANOTHER WOMAN'S SUFFERING SHOULD grant Gabriel and me a brief respite, delay the hounds we feared were closing in upon our heels. On the fifth of May, Isabella Markham hastened into the Maids' Lodgings, exhausted and discouraged.

"You look a fright," Lettice observed, her nose wrinkling in disapproval.

Isabella groaned. "It is my lady Ashley. She was stricken last night and can scarce sit up in bed. The queen is heartsick and even Her Majesty's own Dr. Lopez does not know what may be done to put Lady Ashley at ease. I have tried every trick I know, but I only make her more restless. The queen actually hurled a book at me. Someone must go to the sickroom and attempt to soothe both of them, but I cannot think who to send."

After what the queen had done to Eppie, part of me was glad to know Elizabeth Tudor felt pain. Then I remembered Kat Ashley's kindness to me. "I could distract Lady Ashley," I volunteered. "I read to my father for hours at a time after he went blind."

Isabella Markham sighed. "I wish you luck with it."

I selected one of Father's volumes, then went to where the sick woman lay. The queen had ordered servants to move Kat Ashley to a chamber near to her own, fitted out with a tester bed spread with the finest linens. There, with every comfort love and wealth could provide, lay Elizabeth Tudor's childhood nurse, lines of suffering etching her face. I pictured Eppie's final days, imagining horror, filth, knowing I had abandoned her to her fate. It took all my will to keep my outrage from showing on my face.

"I hear you had a storm-tossed night, my lady," I said as I approached the sickbed.

Lady Ashley's hand fluttered. "I have been a great deal of trouble to everyone I fear. I feel as if someone placed an anvil on my chest and my limbs ache."

At least no one has ripped them out of their sockets, a grim voice whispered within me, as I shifted the heavy embroidered bed curtains out of the way. They were decorated with exotic animals like those I saw in the menagerie so long ago. Vines and trees and lushly stitched flowers created a jungle where the colorful creatures dwelled. With deftness cultivated while caring for my father, I slid a bolster beneath her knees, fluffed a pillow behind her shoulders and drew a snug shawl under her chin.

"I am here to amuse you," I said, tucking the blanket around her feet. As Kat settled back into the nest I had made she sighed.

She gave a wan smile. "You are a good child to do so. I fear Her Majesty has frightened everyone else away. She is most worried, bless her."

I did not trust myself to answer. "I have brought the tales of King Arthur. Perhaps hearing of his quests will while away the hours." I opened the first page.

In time the tight-drawn skin on her face softened, her eyes closed. She did not sleep, but she was lulled by the tale, and when a gentleman usher opened the chamber door for the queen hours later, Kat Ashley looked the better for my being there.

I saw the queen start at the sight of me. Felt her unease. Perhaps she was wondering if I knew of Eppie's fate. If I might take some sort of revenge.

"Mistress Nell has made Camelot come quite alive," Lady Ashley said. "I vow I am tempted to walk to the window, peer out to see if Sir Gawain is riding up to the gate."

"That is a fine idea," I said. "Movement will keep your muscles from growing stiff, and sunshine can revive you as it does the flowers."

Elizabeth regarded me warily as I helped Lady Ashley to a chair near the window, where a block of spring landscape could cheer her.

"I wish I might keep Nell with me whenever I cannot sleep," Lady Ashley said. "She does not knock about disturbing things and making me fretful."

I saw conflicting emotions cross the queen's face, could imagine how torn she must be. Kat must have recognized her reluctance as well.

"I beg you, Your Majesty, indulge me in this," Kat pleaded. "Something in the child delights me. Reminds me of the old days when you were young."

My red hair felt like a banner of guilt, and I wondered if the queen was considering the likeness between us.

"As I recall, they were dangerous days, and comforts were sparse," the queen said.

"There were happy days even amid the troubles. You loved me well then, best in all the world."

"I still do." Elizabeth turned her eyes to me. There was grief in them, helplessness, rage, and a warning that chilled me.

Let her suffer as I have suffered, as Eppie suffered, I thought. Yet there was one fatal flaw in that plan: Kat Ashley would have to suffer as well.

As the summer slid past I could not bear the kind woman's pain, or ignore the queen's tender care of the only mother she had ever known.

Once again the strands of Elizabeth Tudor's life twined with my own. She stood by as helplessly as I had while her beloved nurse grew ever more ill, just as I had when my father was dying. Even a queen cannot command death to retreat. As spring greened into summer and the whole countryside thrived with life, Lady Katherine Ashley withered away, and all the physicians in the queen's household could not force her to get well.

I could have succumbed to bitterness since the queen was able to sit by her nurse's bed and spoon broth into Kat's mouth, while away her dying hours by sharing memories to make Kat smile. Elizabeth had the chance to tell her nurse how much she loved her, say goodbye. Comforts the queen's watchdog, Walsingham, had denied me. Even so, I felt no joy in kind Kat Ashley's pain. Nor could I help but pity Elizabeth.

I still had my mother. The queen had never really had her mother at all.

No matter what estate we visited on progress or what palace the court lodged at, Elizabeth's pattern remained the same. Every night after the business of state was concluded, Her Majesty would enter Kat's chamber, hold Kat's hand, speak to her of the day's events. We discussed the movements of the stars, the wellspring of art blossoming in Italy, men like Michelangelo and the great inventor da Vinci.

Early one July morn while I sat building a cathedral out of playing cards, the queen came in, fragile somehow in her embroidered night robe, shadows beneath her eyes.

I rose, balancing the last stiff rectangle against one of the spires. "Your Majesty. I did not expect you until tomorrow night."

"I could not rest. I heard something that reminded me of a tale the Spanish ambassador once told me. It regarded a miracle cure worked on King Philip's only son two years past. The prince had taken a blow to the head. The finest physicians in Spain tried everything they could think of. Applied holy relics and charms to the wound. The pious throughout Spain flogged themselves as a plea for God to spare him. A man named Vesalius wished from the beginning to trepan the boy."

"Drill a hole in his head to let out the poison?"

"Exactly." Elizabeth looked surprised at my knowledge, but I had heard Mother and Eppie discuss such a procedure, yet both felt the risk of infection too great. "At last in desperation the king ordered Vesalius to perform the procedure. He drained a good deal of pus from the wound. The prince lived. Do you think there might be some cure that the physicians are missing? Something that would help Kat?"

"My mother often lances wounds that are swollen and angry. But you cannot trepan a wound you cannot see."

The queen hugged her arms about a waist still slim as a girl's. "Do you think she is in pain?"

"The doctors are dosing her with soothing teas, and she complains little. You are doing all you can to help her."

"Would I could do more. There are those who loathe the anatomist's work, dissecting human beings, even criminals who earned their execution. I have heard many churchmen claim it is an abomination and I understand the horror of it. Yet, what if such grim searches could reveal the secrets that would save one like Kat?"

"The more scientists learn about the body the more likely they'll be to heal it."

"Spoken like John de Lacey's daughter. I am certain Thomasin does not share your view."

"In science Father always said there must be mistakes before there can be great discoveries. He believed God gave us the ability to reason and expects us to use that reason to solve life's mysteries. Else why would we be so curious?"

Elizabeth's eyes narrowed, and I felt the force of her will upon me. Felt angry with myself for bringing up such a subject. Was not my curiosity what she must fear most of all?

"Such hungers of the mind can be fatal, Nell," Elizabeth said. She touched the card cathedral I had been building. I watched it teeter, the whole structure threatening to fall. "Curiosity can bring any world you build tumbling down."

❧❧❧

I THINK ELIZABETH surrendered to the inevitability of Kat Ashley's death thereafter, and turned her thoughts to whiling away the patient's weary hours instead. The queen had servants bring whatever novelties she had to hand that might distract Kat during the weeks in bed. Exquisite instruments came to rest on shelves so I could play for Kat and sing at her whim. Seven ivory and gold flutes that made the sounds of different animals distracted her during one sleepless night, the two of us attempting to identify which beast the cry came from. The queen's own ivory chessboard was brought for Kat to play upon and we cast the silver dice upon the backgammon board late into the night. But in time the games became too tedious. Even Kat's needle grew too heavy, and she fastened it into the tapestry piece she was working on and laid it aside.

One night the queen entered, her face icy pale, tense with waiting. Death was coming. We all knew it would not be long. "Kat, is there aught I can get for you?" Elizabeth asked, and I marked how strange it seemed—the queen asking such a question.

"There is something. My coffer. Nell, bring it. Most precious gift the queen ever gave me . . . tucked in very bottom."

Elizabeth nodded to me and I went to the far side of the chamber, scooped up a pearl-crusted box. I set it on the bed between them and opened the coffer's lid, wondering what kind of treasure it might hold.

The queen rummaged through it, drew out a pair of velvet slippers no longer than her palm. A tiny rose was stitched in gold upon the worn blue cloth.

"My first dancing slippers," Elizabeth whispered. "I remember you snipped off the pearls."

"Had to return them to the Royal Wardrobe. But slippers were beyond repair and too small to be of any use. You said I must keep them, lest I forget you. It was as if you knew somehow how many of those you loved you had yet to lose."

"Not you. Even when they tried to take you away."

"Will you tuck them in my shroud when this is over? I cannot be without them."

Feeling their grief too private for me to intrude, I withdrew to the far side of the chamber where my writing box and books lay, close at hand for those weary hours when Kat was sleeping. But the pain reached out to me across that divide. I know the queen wept. I was weeping, too.

I stood at a table, tried to write to a letter. At length, the queen crossed to stand beside me.

"Kat is asleep. You write to your mother?"

"Yes."

"Have you told her of Kat's illness?"

She already knew the answer, I was certain. Walsingham had read every missive I wrote. I laid my pen aside and turned to look at the queen. "My mother cares much for Lady Ashley. I know she prays for her to find peace."

"Peace," Elizabeth echoed, running her thumb over the tiny slipper cupped in her hand. "These might have fit you had you tried them on that day you tried to rescue me from the Tower."

"I frustrated my poor dancing master. He did his best, but my parents did not push me overmuch. I was to stay in the country, as you said the day Sir Gabriel wished to partner me."

The queen fell quiet. I expected her to leave. Instead she whispered. "I have never known a world without Kat."

I cannot say what drove me to risk it, but I dared to squeeze Elizabeth's hand. No words would come. The queen's thumb swept the ridge of my scar. I could feel the truth she must know, an insurmountable barrier between us. I released her, looked away.

Next morn, Katherine Ashley was gone.

❦ ❦

IN A WAY, the queen's grief was a gift to me. It allowed me to pretend Kat Ashley's death was the source of my own sorrow. I could weep for both women—Eppie and Kat—openly. My affection for Kat was real.

Who could imagine after all the suspicion between the queen and me that an even stronger bond would forge between us against our better judgment? Not a mother's bond to her daughter. That would have been too dangerous for canny Elizabeth to ever risk. And her part in Eppie's death made such feelings on my part impossible. Yet the queen had relied upon me against her will. Part of her relied upon me still to share her grief, speak of Kat's last days.

Shattered as Elizabeth was, Walsingham dared not importune her too strenuously as the queen tried to recover. He could not press her about the dangers of the Scots queen or Catholic Spain—or me. Elizabeth Tudor, who had withstood so many storms during her life without flinching, was so brittle with grief now that all who served her feared for her health. A terrifying prospect, since she had no heir and refused to name a successor to follow her on England's throne.

The court remembered far too well that when Her Majesty had smallpox two years earlier she had proclaimed Robert Dudley be Lord Protector of her realm if she died. Now, more than ever, Dudley ruling was unthinkable.

In the face of more pressing woes, what danger did I pose, at least for the time being? Walsingham thought me ignorant of Eppie's arrest, let alone her death. There would be time to strike at me when the queen's mind cleared. Or was it possible Eppie had kept her secrets in spite of what Walsingham did to wrench them away?

❦ ❦

As SEPTEMBER NEARED, bringing with it the tournament Robert Dudley planned to celebrate the queen's birthday, I began to hope that Gabriel was right. We might survive this crisis after all. Yet as the day of the tournament approached, another peril threatened. I was curled up near the fire with a volume of poetry Gabriel had loaned me, tracing the words he had scribed on its flyleaf—*Gabriel Wyatt of Wyldfell Hall. From his mother on his birthday. He is 8 years old.* I was picturing him at that age, a head full of black curls, his long-lashed green eyes, a gangly boy chasing after his two older brothers. Secure in his parents' love. A boy with a quick temper, yet sensitive, too. A boy his mother could offer a book of poetry to, and know it would delight him.

It made me ache for his mother, knowing she had seen his poet's soul harden, prison and grief and rebellion driving the dreams from his eyes, filling them with the cynicism and dark skills that would fit him to be Queen Elizabeth's Gypsy's Angel.

Strange, that I was imagining that black-haired child when Mary Grey bustled into the room, glancing behind her as if she feared someone might be following her. "By God, it is hard to catch you alone!"

I shifted on my red cut-velvet cushion. "I cannot think of anything we can't say before the other maids."

"I can. It is four months since you had your courses," she said abruptly.

"Why should my cycles matter to you? What are you? The laundress's spy?"

"You are not the first of the queen's ladies to get with child. The fact that you have a husband will not cool the queen's wrath when she discovers you."

My heart skipped beneath my pearl-trimmed stomacher. "I do not know what you are talking about." I heard a shout of greeting in the corridor outside, then the sound of footsteps marching. My nerves tightened and I realized just how intently I had been listening.

Mary glanced at the door. "We have no time to dance around this. Thomas told me everything."

Heat flooded my cheeks, outrage sharpening my voice as I levered myself to my feet. "He vowed to keep it secret! And yet he is blabbing to whoever he likes?"

"No. He confided the truth to his wife."

"His wife? Someone said she died years ago."

Mary's voice sweetened, touched with a musical quality I had never heard in it before. "I am Thomas's wife, just as you are Sir Gabriel's."

"You cannot be serious." I gaped, disbelieving.

Mary flinched and I knew I had hurt her. "You think me such a shrunken, ugly thing, devil-cursed and twisted in body, that no one could ever want me? Why should I be surprised at that? I believed it, too, until Thomas changed my mind."

"It is not your stature I speak of! You are cousin to the queen! Royal blood! You must have Her Majesty's permission to wed or she will throw you and your husband in prison the way she did your sister!"

"I doubt the queen would bother. Katherine and Hertford are both perfect in body, with royal blood. Once they produced two healthy sons Elizabeth had reason to fear they might become pawns to threaten her throne. I am no threat to anyone."

"But Mary—" The dread I felt about being discovered myself mingled with my fear for her. "I am afraid for you."

"Faith, I believe you are!" She did not grow prickly in defense. Instead, a smile spread over her face and she reached out to squeeze my hand. "Nell, all will be well with me. Thomas is a commoner, and I am as far from queenly as it is possible for any woman to be. For once I am grateful for it. No dwarf could sit upon any country's throne. Elizabeth may be angry when she discovers us, but she will accept our marriage in time. We only wish to be left alone, raise Thomas's children. Truth to tell, the queen will probably seize Thomas and kiss him for ridding her beautiful court of my ugliness."

I surrendered to impulse, stooped down to embrace her. At first she leapt back, startled as a pup that has been struck too often. But Thomas Keyes's love had wedged open the gate she kept shut against the world. She held out her arms. I gathered her in. She felt tiny as child in my grasp. "I wish you much good fortune," I said, and meant it.

"Keep it for yourself. You will need it as your belly begins to show."

"My belly?" I echoed, startled.

"You are with child."

I pressed my hands against my stomach. "I know I have not had my courses, but it is only because of the strain from Kat's death. I remember my nurse telling women it wasn't unusual to skip a month's flow when their nerves were rattled."

"One month. Perhaps two. But four? Besides, you wince when Moll laces your breasts tight beneath stays, and I have heard you retching of a morning."

"Anyone would with the strain I've been under." My voice sounded hollow even to my own ears. But Mary was right. Panic rocked me the way it must have shaken the woman who bore me—a sick dread of being discovered.

"You are about to undergo a great deal more strain," Mary said. "Unless . . ." She fidgeted with her sleeve, unable to meet my eyes.

"Unless what?"

"Unless you wish to see a woman I have heard my mother speak of. Old Grisel brews a posset that can expel an unwanted babe from your womb."

I cringed, recoiling from the thought but feeling tempted at the same time. If I was carrying Gabriel's child, it would be one more excuse for the queen to lash out.

"Grisel is wife to an apothecary in Spitalfields and serves as midwife."

I remembered Eppie's tales of how hard she had studied to help women labor with as much health and comfort as possible. But this . . . Had Eppie known of such dark secrets? Practiced them? "Your mother spoke of destroying a babe in front of you?" I asked Mary, shocked.

"More times than I can count. From the time I was in the nursery I heard her say that if she'd known I'd be born a monster she would have had Old Grisel kill me thus."

I pressed my hands tight against the place where my child might lie as if to keep it from hearing.

"I know it is hard, Nell, to speak of murdering your babe thus. But I tell you this because I care what befalls you. The queen's temper is more unpredictable than ever since Lady Ashley died, and while Her Majesty's gallants may swive in secret then beg pardon and be forgiven, women have the wrath of God rained down on them and are banished for good and all. Speak to Sir Gabriel about your difficulty. He is a most practical man. I predict he will agree it would be best if this pregnancy dissolved."

Would he? Gabriel's features swam before me, the consummate courtier, a man who had fought his way back from the brink of ruin. Would he be willing to put all he had gained in jeopardy for a child as yet unborn?

Mary must have seen my dismay.

"You are young and vigorous." She tried to comfort me. "There will be plenty of time for other children when it is safer."

How could anyone be certain of that? My terror warred with something surprising, something new. A healthy babe was growing even now in my belly. A miracle my mother had been denied. Life. Then, something strong, sweet, filled me with awe. "Surely a man would not wish to destroy his own child," I said, as much to myself as to Mary.

Mary's voice softened with empathy. "I have lived at court far longer than you have and have seen the worst the human spirit can do. I have watched and listened to see who managed to survive. It is said Jane Rocheford was desperately in love with George Boleyn, but when her own life might be forfeit she testified against him, sent him to his death on the block. When my sister Jane was condemned, and my father faced a traitor's death, my mother scrambled to lick Queen Mary's boots, anything to save her own skin. I think she loved Father in her way. Even if she did not truly ever love Jane or Katherine or me. She told me her first loyalty must always be to herself."

"What are you saying?"

"There is no point in sacrificing yourself once a battle is lost. Do not count on anyone to sacrifice themselves for you, Nell. Not husband, mother, sister, or friend. We courtiers are raised from the cradle to keep an eye to the main chance and to surrender when we must, live to fight another day. Sir Gabriel is a courtier, every bit the match for Robin Dudley; maybe even the Duke of Norfolk, who sent two nieces to the headsman's block to please a lecherous king."

"I do not believe that," I protested. "Gabriel is—"

"Wyatt has spent every moment of his life since he walked out of the Tower alive attempting to reclaim all his father lost He will not tolerate anything or anyone—even his own child—getting in his way. I only say this to save you the pain of discovering it on your own."

"Mary, you must promise me something. You must swear you will not tell Thomas or Sir Gabriel about this."

"The child? You will not be able to keep it secret much longer. Sir Gabriel is bound to figure it out."

"Then I must take care to avoid him." How simple my resolve sounded. Mary was not fooled.

"That will not prove to be as easy as it sounds. He will know something is amiss."

"I will think of some way to explain it. Just promise you will not betray me, Mary. I will do anything, pay any price you ask." She should have been angry at me. Outraged.

"You called me friend," Mary said with great dignity. "That is payment enough."

Chapter Twenty-Six

September 1565

MARY HAD FORCED ME TO FACE TWO FRIGHTENING truths: I carried Sir Gabriel's child and he might wish to kill the babe before it drew first breath. The morn of the tournament threatened rain, clouds crowding over the tiltyard as if they were common folk trying to get a view of the festivities to come.

For weeks I had been afraid to meet Gabriel's eyes.

I made certain I was never alone, used my wit to cut away his pride before the other ladies. He retaliated without a word, focusing on his latest mistress, the lovely Douglass, Lettice Knollys's rival and friend. He danced with her until she was breathless, flirted whenever I was around. Only Mary knew what was amiss. Each night she stroked my hair while her spaniel, Polly, nuzzled her small, warm body against the slight bulge where my unborn babe grew.

I feared that the other maids with their voracious appetites for scandal would guess something was wrong, would wage campaigns to gain my confidence, hoping to discover a tidbit they could use against me. But I had grown adept at deception the months I had tended Kat Ashley under the queen's very nose.

As Her Majesty's birthday celebrations commenced, I gave a fair imitation of pleasure. We ladies traipsed after the queen to the gaily decked tiltyard, most women hoping a knight would claim her as his lady before all the court. My energy was spent keeping the smile pinned to my face and my banter light, though my heart felt raw indeed.

Douglass and Lettice flaunted the favors they had selected and tried to predict which man would bear their colors. Douglass waggled the extra sleeve she had chosen. "Sir Gabriel will look fine with my red satin fluttering from his lance, will he not?"

Lettice laughed. "You have decked the knight's other lance often enough of late."

Douglass slid one hand over her breast. "He's grown quite fierce about it the past few weeks. But then, he and the Earl of Leicester are at war of late. Perhaps that is why the Angel is in such a temper."

Gabriel and Dudley at war? I had not noticed. Still, I wondered what had spurred the argument between them.

"It is as if Sir Gabriel is trying to beat back a demon," Douglass said. "But he can use my body as his exorcist any time, he gives me such pleasure." Her words cut me and she knew it. Mary cast me a worried glance, then trotted ahead to tug Douglass's skirt.

When the woman turned to flick her away, Mary warned, "You had best watch your tongue. If the queen catches wind of what you've been about she will send you to the Maids' Lodgings and you will miss the joust entirely."

"How sweet," Lettice sneered. "The gargoyle defending her bed-fellow. But all the court knows Sir Gabriel no longer gives a snap for you, is that not right, Nell? Did you even bring an extra sleeve to give away?"

"No. I brought one of my miniature books to fight off boredom." My ruse to keep from watching the combat when Gabriel entered the lists.

As we neared the tiltyard the sun broke through, turning the pennons into a fluttering rainbow. At the far end of the lists caparisoned horses and men in full armor appeared like a scene straight out of the time of King Arthur. We climbed to the royal box and arranged ourselves on cushioned benches around the queen.

Lord Robert, magnificent on his black warhorse, reined to a halt before Elizabeth and then humbly begged her favor. The queen gave him a fluttering Tudor green ribbon. A girlish flush rose in cheeks too pale of late. One by one the contestants approached the lady of their choice. I did not want to mark Gabriel's progress as he drew closer while Douglass licked her lips as if she could taste my husband's kisses. A disgruntled William Pickering took Lettice's yellow ribbon since Leicester had reached the queen before him.

Douglass preened as Gabriel spurred his horse to the royal box. No combatant looked finer, not even the queen's own champion. Jealousy burned in me as Gabriel's blood bay danced sideways. Gabriel's armor was not intricately etched like other courtiers, no gold chasings or marks of heraldry. Yet he seemed more dangerous for the simplicity. A hawk among a flock of peacocks.

I braced myself for the pain of watching my husband flaunt his passion for his mistress. Instead Gabriel guided the stallion until its hooves scraped the sand before me. "Mistress Elinor?" His green eyes burned. "I ask most humbly: Will you do me the honor of allowing me to wear your colors into the lists?"

He was forcing me to speak to him. I could see it in his face. "I do not have any to give you." Those closest to me roared with laughter, passing on what I had said to those not near enough to hear. But they scrambled words until the pavilion buzzed with the news that Elinor de Lacey had told Gabriel Wyatt she did not have any favor to "give the likes of you."

Queen Elizabeth added to the mirth from her place beneath the gold cloth of estate. "So did you not bring some trinket for any champion, Mistress Nell? Or is it our Angel in particular you intended to leave a-begging? No matter. Sir Gabriel must choose another lady. Perhaps the enchanting Douglass would oblige?"

"If Mistress Nell will not have me for her champion, I will take no favor at all."

"That's not what I said!"

My protest was lost in the thudding of hooves as he galloped away from the box. The other men each carried some bit of ribbon or sleeve or nosegay a lady had honored them with. I cringed, knowing I had set Gabriel up to be tormented. He rode as if Lucifer himself spurred hot behind him. Each time Gabriel thundered down the lists his lance struck home, thrice driving men from their saddles to the sandy ground. The wooden shield painted with the Wyatt wolf edged higher, a squire keeping score until only two shields hung above the rest: Gabriel's and Dudley's bear and ragged staff. But as squires helped William Pickering limp off the field the queen grew agitated.

The queen nudged me with her slipper. "You have put Sir Gabriel in the very devil of a temper by rejecting him. I shall not be amused if he damages Lord Robert."

"Look!" Lettice cried as the last two combatants rode forth to see who would reign champion of the day.

I tried to calm my heart, but it thundered like horses' hooves as the men charged their mighty stallions down the lists, their lances couched, their helmets gleaming. The impact as they struck each other's shields made the very ground shudder, both lances splintering, Lord Robert nearly unseated. The queen pressed her fist to her mouth to keep from crying out. Both men rode to their end of the lists, taking a second lance from their squires. Again they charged. Sir Robert nearly faltered. I tried not to feel pride in Gabriel's skill. Tried not to care if he landed on his back in the sand. But I could not stop the question swirling in my mind. *Why had Gabriel singled me out? Taken such a reckless chance?* I fiddled with my astrolabe, wishing the contest was over. They circled their horses on either side of the flimsy barrier between them, Lord Robert signaling Gabriel to draw near. Both men shoved up their face guards, so they could see the other. What was Lord Robert saying? I wondered. What could he possibly have to tell that was so important it could not wait until after their combat was finished? Even the crowd was growing restless.

"Gentlemen, this is a joust, not a meeting of the Privy Council," the queen called.

Dudley saluted her, wheeled his horse and cantered to his end of the list. Gabriel seemed frozen, staring after Lord Robert until Leicester had taken a fresh lance from his squire. Jibes rang out, demanding that Gabriel either take up his lance or forfeit. God knew, he looked more stunned than he had all day when he had been struck with mighty blows. What was the matter with him?

Just as the queen was rising to her feet to call out to him, Gabriel jolted to life. He spun his stallion around, but the masterful control he had shown all day crumbled. He nearly dropped the lance his squire handed up to him. Forgot to lower his guard over his face until the lad called out warning. When the queen dropped her kerchief to signal them to spur toward each other, Gabriel drove his mount forward a few seconds late. The lance swung down into position, but Lord Robert was already upon Gabriel, Dudley's own weapon solidly couched, steady.

The men came together with an earth-shattering crash, their stallions bellowing. I screamed as Dudley's lance struck Gabriel's chest, flinging him backward through the air. He seemed to fly forever, his arms flailing. He slammed to the ground with a force hard enough to shatter iron. No man could suffer such a fall and live!

Shrieks of horror echoed around me, but I barely heard them. Heedless of the queen watching, I scrambled from my seat, stumbling past the gentlemen pensioners guarding the royal box. Gabriel's squires were running toward him. Even Dudley seemed appalled at how violently his Angel had fallen. In a blur I saw Leicester dismounting, awkward in his armor. But I raced in front of his horse, flinging myself down beside Gabriel, who laid terrifyingly still, his helm twisted at a sickening angle. Dear God, had he broken his neck? Was his last living memory of me his humiliation? My stomach lurched as his squire fought to wrestle the helm from his head.

Hands grasped me, firm yet gentle, pulling me away. "Come, Mistress. Give them room to work." Robert Dudley. I struggled against his grasp.

"Is he dead? Please, God do not let him be dead!"

Gabriel's squire had unbuckled the breastplate, pulled it free. He pressed his ear to Gabriel's chest. "He breathes!" The youth shouted. "Sir Gabriel breathes!" But as another lad wrestled off his helmet Gabriel looked ashen indeed. Someone brought water, splashed it on Gabriel's face. Thick black lashes fluttered. Yanking free of Dudley, I grasped Gabriel by the sweat-soaked leather of his doublet. "You are not dead!" I clutched him close.

"My babe," Gabriel mumbled. "Is it true you carry my—"

I pressed my hand to his mouth to stop the words, knowing I had already perilously betrayed us. I turned, saw the queen leaning forward in the box, her body rigid, her beringed hands gripping the rail. Elizabeth's accusing glare pierced me. But I had no time to castigate myself for my recklessness in flying to Gabriel's side. He might be bleeding inside where even the finest doctor could not reach him.

"Sir Gabriel has taken a fearsome blow to the head," I said in the commanding tone I had heard my mother use in countless crises over the years. "Carry him at once to his rooms. Summon the physician." A flurry of movement erupted as people leapt to obey my commands. Surprised, grateful, I followed the men who carried Gabriel from the field. His rooms were just above the tiltyard, quickly reached.

They laid him upon his bed, the faithful Tyrell and several other squires working the tangle of leather straps and buckles to get him out of the rest of his armor. The moment they were done I sent them away on errands to buy us a moment alone.

Gabriel looked so pale, his curls so black upon the pillow. "What were you thinking? Asking me to give you my favor?" I demanded. Gabriel ignored my question, catching hold of my hand. Sometime during the day's contests he had cut himself, dried blood smearing his knuckles.

"Lord Robert said a spy told him you were carrying a babe." I tried to pull away, think what to say, but he held on tighter still. "It's mine, isn't it, Nell?" His voice cracked. "Why did you not tell me?"

Something in his gaze smothered any lie. "I was afraid that you would want to kill it in my womb. Mary said it could be done."

Pain crumpled his features. "You believed I would do such a thing?"

"Considering all the other peril we are in? What else would you do?"

Gabriel tried to lever himself up. Agony flashed across his features and he clutched his arms across his ribs. For an instant I feared he would tumble back into unconsciousness. "What else would I have done? I would have gotten us all away from here. Someplace safe. But now . . . Christ, Nell. Now Dudley will know the child is mine. It is obvious he knows I have deceived him as well. He will have to separate his fate from ours to protect himself from the queen's fury. Dudley will tell the queen and she will have to act."

To act on whatever evidence Walsingham had gathered against me. Act against her suspicions, out of fear. But there was no real proof for her to condemn me. Even though the queen must guess what the scar on my hand signified, it could not be proved without a doubt. The condemning extra finger was gone and the old wound merely proved I had been injured. There was only one piece of evidence that could not be refuted if Elizabeth *was* the fair young lady who had stared up at the star-scattered bed curtains in her travail.

"There is something I must do." I kissed his brow. "I will return quick as I can."

Gathering up my skirts, I made my way out of his chambers, fled down stairs scattered with the curious, with servants and an herbalist, even a red-faced doctor on his way to tend Lord Dudley's favorite.

I hastened through the gardens, my skirts caught up so I could run. At last I slipped through a little-used entry, raced up steep stone castle stairs to the Maids' Lodgings.

Only Polly the spaniel was there to greet me. I nudged the dog out of my way and went to the chest that held my writing box. Hauling the inlaid desk out, I placed it on the nearest bed, then fumbled with the catch that opened the secret compartment. It seemed to take forever for my shaking fingers to spring the latch, but at last the secret door popped open. I thrust my fingers into the narrow compartment, wriggled my fingers deeper into the tiny space.

Only smooth wood met my touch.

The scrap of velvet bed curtain was gone.

Chapter Twenty-Seven

Later That Day

WAS NO LONGER NAÏVE ENOUGH TO HOPE ONE OF THE other maids had been prying about my desk. They would not bother taking a scrap of fabric. Only one man could know its significance. Sir Francis Walsingham.

Eppie must have told all when he tortured her upon the rack.

Oh, God, why had I not burned the scrap the way I knew I should?

I closed up the desk's compartment and stowed it back in my trunk. Shutting the lid, I paced the chamber, trying to think what to do. I could not run, but neither could I wait here like a helpless fool. I could not solve this puzzle on my own. There was only one person who might be able to help me find a way to escape. I must go back to Gabriel. Warn him.

I started toward the door, glimpsed my face in a looking glass, my eyes wild, my face flushed. Step one foot outside the chamber looking like this and I might as well light a signal fire to alert Walsingham I knew what he had stolen from me. I had already made enough of a spectacle of myself today, racing out to the lists when Gabriel fell.

I leaned closer to the looking glass, smoothed my hair, but no matter how I tried to pinch color into my cheeks, my eyes still held images from hell. I forced myself to walk with some measure of decorum, even paused to greet Thomas Keyes when I stumbled across him. But once I reached Gabriel's room all my subterfuge seemed absurd. Two guards dressed in crimson stood at the door with halberds in their hands.

"We have strict orders from Lord Robert that no one may enter," one said.

"Please," I begged. "If you would grant me but a moment."

"I am sorry, Mistress. Perhaps you may see Sir Gabriel when he is better."

I bit my lip. "Has the physician seen him? Is Sir Gabriel well?"

"I am only the guard, Mistress. I cannot say."

My knees shook as I forced myself to move away. Was it possible that Gabriel had taken a turn for the worse after I left him? I could remember mother explaining that sometimes there were torn places deep inside the body that bled until the injured person died. Hard as the lance had struck Gabriel, violently as he had landed upon the ground, was it not possible he would suffer such a fate?

I blinked back tears. I wanted to flee the palace. I wanted to storm into Gabriel's rooms. I wanted to turn back time, give Gabriel my favor, somehow make things turn out differently. But how could they? Dudley knew I was with child. He guessed it was Gabriel Wyatt's. Walsingham had Eppie's confession. There could be little question of that now. He would not have presented his report to Elizabeth until he had every fragment of information gathered. Hadn't Walsingham told me he did not allow anything to distress the queen? But now he had the scrap of bed curtain that could extinguish any shadow of doubt if Elizabeth was indeed my mother. And it was no one's fault but my own. How long had he had it, I wondered. Had he discovered it long ago? Before Kat Ashley grew ill? Had he kept it, biding his time until the queen's private anguish was over? Sparing me until he could see Her Majesty was recovering? I would never know. I only knew I had not opened the compartment since the night I first hid the scrap of bed curtain away.

Despair overwhelmed me as I thought of Gabriel, injured, trapped in his chamber, under guard. The thought of him suffering imprisonment, even death, because of my folly was unbearable. *You need not fear he'll suffer once he sees he cannot save you,* I could almost hear Mary say. *He escaped the headsman's axe when his own father died.* That was his mother's doing. It was not Gabriel's fault! I argued with myself, fierce, frightened. Gabriel would not betray—

That depends on whether you want an unfaithful husband or a dead one . . .

Gabriel's words from the day we were wed. What would I give to keep light in his eyes, that devil's smile on his lips? What would I give? Anything. The truth jolted me. Anything except our child. But how could I protect our child? Get us away from here? That is what Gabriel said he would have done. Gather my small belongings and flee . . .

And where would you run? reason demanded. *Walsingham will hunt you to the end of the earth. A woman with a belly full of child cannot keep ahead of pursuing hounds for long.* No. I could not run. I could only go back to the palace, make my way to the Maids' Lodgings, and wait.

When I reached the chamber, Mary was there, her headdress askew, her spaniel whining at her feet. "Nell, I wished to tell you first before Lettice or Douglass, the nasty cats! The queen is furious over your display at the tiltyard. She has ordered you to stay in these rooms until she summons you."

"It will be a relief not to have to face the rest of the court." I collapsed onto a carved wood stool. I did not care if Mary saw me shattered.

"Lord Robert and the queen were closeted a full hour together alone. Then Walsingham entered. When they exited—I have never seen the queen so angry." Mary hugged her arms tight about her. "It frightened me. I came right away to warn you."

I could imagine her, skirts caught up, tiny legs flying as she tried to outdistance Lettice. At the best of times, Mary sometimes had difficulty breathing. Running like that, it was little wonder her face was scarlet, dripping with sweat. That she had pressed herself so hard for me touched me deeply. I blinked back tears, knowing she would not welcome that brand of gratitude. "You would do better to keep away from me, Mary. Join the other maids wherever they are. I do not wish the queen's anger to fall on you."

Mary trembled, scooping up her frantic spaniel. Polly snuggled against her mistress, close as she could get. "I would not leave you even now, except I fear for Thomas. He thinks Walsingham's men have searched his rooms."

So they were spying on Thomas Keyes as well as on me? "Walsingham must have been very busy indeed," I said.

"Nell, I am sorry to leave you. But Thomas . . . Please understand."

"I do, Mary. Go. I would not have you caught up in this."

Mary hesitated, obviously torn. She crossed to me, thrust Polly into my arms. "You must take care of Mistress Nell now," Mary told the little spaniel. "I would not leave my friend alone."

I should have protested her sacrifice. I knew how great it was. Instead I gathered Polly to me. I could feel the spaniel's heartbeat, the warmth of her small, silky body.

THE NEXT DAY the queen sent guards to escort me to the Council Chamber.

The place where Gabriel and I had danced so many times was deserted now, a vast, hollow cave that magnified my fears like a malevolent echo. Within stood the dread triumvirate I knew I would have to face. Lord Robert paced the room like one of the Tower menagerie's lions, his auburn hair disordered as if he had torn at it in frustration, his handsome face sharp with suspicion. Walsingham waited a few paces away from his queen, and I could not forget what he had said the day he questioned me about Eppie—that he had a daughter like me. But the sorrowful, almost fatherly expression he had regarded me with was gone, the spymaster's face was now as grim as the portraits of death painted on church walls when plague first decimated England.

Most daunting of all, the queen stood by the tiny window, her face terrible in its stillness, every fiber of her being under fierce control.

I crossed to this woman whose hair I had rubbed with a length of red silk to bring out the shine, this scholar I had debated with long into the night. I had known the most intimate details of her existence, but the hard-eyed monarch before me seemed like a stranger. I stopped before her, dropped into the deepest curtsey I could manage. But my swollen breasts and my thickening waist made me awkward. Or was it something else that unnerved me? The familiar sound of Gabriel's tread as he approached the chamber from the corridor beyond. I fought the urge to go to him. What shelter could we give each other now? Instead I determined to hold myself with the dignity befitting even secret royal blood.

Gabriel entered the room and attempted to sweep Her Majesty a bow. He winced and clamped his arm against his left side. His lips compressed in a tight line. No trace of empathy softened the queen's disgust. "Sir Gabriel, you have much to answer for."

He straightened his shoulders in spite of his pain. "Yes, Majesty. I do."

"Half the men on the tiltyard overheard you make a most infuriating claim. When I questioned the Earl of Leicester he confessed he has known for some time you planted your bastard in Nell de Lacey's belly."

"Strange my lord Dudley never mentioned the subject to me." Was he trying to incite the queen to fury? I held my breath, knowing what storm would come.

"Do not try any of your sly evasions with me, Sir! Debauching a maid of honor in my care is a transgression I will not tolerate!"

"Your Grace is to be commended for tending to their virtue with such care. Just let me say I hold the lady's honor as precious as my own. She is my wife."

"Your wife?" Dudley exclaimed. Hectic color flamed in Elizabeth's cheeks. Any hope we had of softening that revelation or of enlisting Dudley's aid was gone.

"I married Nell some months ago," Gabriel said.

"Married her?" Walsingham turned to me. His brows lifted a fraction, betraying a faint hint of surprise. It was an experience I would wager he had not had often. "Mistress Elinor, is what he claims true?"

"It is." I fidgeted with my astrolabe, hoping its familiar gold weight would steady my nerves. How could Gabriel seem so calm?

He regarded the spymaster with a steadiness that astonished me. "I have witnesses to prove we were wed if Her Majesty requires them."

"Do not you dare address me with such insolence!" The queen's temper blazed. "You deceived me. Plotted against me. How dare you make a fool of your queen?"

"I am the fool, Your Grace," Gabriel said. "Mistress Nell made one of me. She tempted a man who has prided himself on being a masterful courtier to do something he knew was inexcusable. Her virtue was unassailable and I was most taken with her. I have no resistance when it comes to temptation."

"You can save your fairy stories, Wyatt! I know the kind of man you are! Where is this priest who married you against my will? I vow he will suffer the consequences of his actions." Father Ambrose's features rose in my mind, so gentle as he told tales of the boy Gabriel had been. Fear for the old man filled me. Surely Gabriel would not name him! The Angel softened his voice.

"I can hardly produce the good Father if he is to face your wrath, Majesty. The fault in this matter is mine alone."

"Produce him or suffer the punishment for fornication!" the queen roared. "Both you and your whore."

Gabriel's smooth facade cracked. "The lady is my wife."

"The lady is a fool! I warned her to beware of you! But no. She did not listen. Instead, she plotted against me."

"No, Majesty!" I protested, clasping my hands to keep them from shaking. "I swear on my soul I did not."

"Quiet, you stupid girl! And make me no oaths! You have already shown you are willing to deceive me!" The queen swung back to Gabriel. "Tell me, sir. What did you hope to gain from this marriage?"

"What most men do: A handsome dowry and God willing, an heir."

"Do not toy with me, you treacherous whoreson." Gabriel went still. I knew he was thinking of his mother. How he held back a sharp retort I would never know. "Walsingham claims you have been plotting treason!" Elizabeth accused.

"Treason?" A muscle in Gabriel's jaw ticked. "Never, Majesty. I am your most loyal subject."

"Then it is a miracle I still have a country to rule! Did you hope to blackmail a queen with some wild story a madwoman spread before she died?"

Panic dug cold fingers into my chest. "No one believes the ramblings of a mad woman," I protested.

"Perhaps not," Elizabeth countered, "but you seem quite sane, Mistress. In fact, all my court raves about your intellect. That is what makes you all the more dangerous. Tell me, Elinor de Lacey Wyatt. Exactly who do you think you are?"

I searched for words to calm the queen's fears, perhaps elude the snare closing all about me. "I am a country-bred daughter from Calverley Manor." I forced myself to meet her gaze. "I wish only to go back home."

"Surely there is more to you than that!"

"There is." I glanced at my husband. He was watching me, steady as a wolf with a band of huntsmen circled around him. "I am Sir Gabriel Wyatt's wife."

"God's blood!" Elizabeth dashed the candelabra from the table. It clattered to the floor. "Would I could wrench a straight answer from you with my own hands!"

"It is true, Majesty. I would not trade the title of wife. Not even for a crown." I prayed she would see the truth in my eyes.

"Traitors are never in danger of enjoying either marriage or a crown," the queen threatened. "And as for your *husband*, do not count on him to hold loyal. Men are most unreliable when the right pressure is applied, and Sir Gabriel is my most pragmatic courtier. I do not have to search far to find a charge to level against him. He has broken the law, dueled twice against my express warning."

"Your Majesty has forgiven such trespasses before," Dudley put in. I wondered if he were defending Gabriel in some small way, or if the earl was merely cautioning her that such a charge might be challenged.

"The arrogant son of a whore compounded the offense by challenging one of Walsingham's men," the queen said, returning her glare to me. "On your behalf, Mistress Nell, I might add. At the inn where the witch Hepzibah Jones was taken into custody."

So the queen knew all. Only Dudley looked bewildered.

"Majesty," the earl said. "I do not understand. Who is this Hepzibah Jones and what has she to do with Sir Gabriel and Mistress Nell?"

The queen whirled on him like a fury. "Who do you think you are, my lord? It is not your place to question me!" I saw Lord Robert's cheeks darken in humiliation as Walsingham stepped in.

"Her Majesty has been lenient with violent displays in the past, but Sir Gabriel knows what punishment law demands." I bit the inside of my lip until I tasted blood.

The queen closed in on Gabriel, grabbed him by the wrist. She shook back the ruffle that edged his cuff, the sun-browned contours of his hand seeming suddenly vulnerable in the trap of Elizabeth's white fingers.

"He has such a graceful right hand, my Gypsy's Angel. It is the hand of a swordsman, a dancer, a poet, a musician. How will he do any of those things once his hand is severed, Mistress Nell?"

My stomach roiled in horror. "No, Majesty! I beg you, do not—"

"*Hurt him?*" The queen cut in with a snarl. "Is that not what you cried to the squires when they wrenched his helmet from his head? Sometimes pain is necessary if a queen is to rule."

Walsingham shuffled his papers, crossed to where writing implements were laid. "The queen, in her great wisdom, will grant your husband this much, Mistress. Sir Gabriel will be master of his own fate. To save his hand he needs only to tell us what wickedness his wife has been concealing from his queen. Or perhaps, Mistress Wyatt, you will write your own confession to save him, that is, if you love your husband at all."

Did I love Gabriel? I suddenly feared how much. I wavered on the brink of flinging myself on the queen's mercy. But even then I could read the dark truth in Walsingham's eyes. If I confessed all I knew to Elizabeth out of fear, how could she be sure I would not reveal the same information to gain some reward? She would be compelled to destroy anyone who knew Eppie's story. Gabriel might lose not only his hand, but his life. Another life would be snuffed out as well. Our child's.

It was a fiendish test, not unlike the ones accused witches were put to when they were tied hand and foot, then flung into a pond. If they floated they were condemned to hang. If they drowned they were judged innocent. No matter what the verdict, the accused was dead. Minutes crawled by filled with the ticking of clocks and the maddening sounds of Dudley pacing.

"So you choose to defy me." Elizabeth's eyes glittered hard as the diamonds clasped about her neck. "You Wyatts were always a stubborn breed. Perhaps another visit to the Tower will loosen your tongue, Sir Gabriel. It has broken far more honorable men than you."

Walsingham crossed to the door, rapped on it with his knuckles. Gabriel slipped his arm around me as the guards spilled in. How many times had I seen them in their dashing crimson livery? There was a time I had no idea how menacing they could be.

"Majesty," Gabriel said, "I pray you will realize in time we are your loyal subjects."

"We mean you no harm," I added, my voice breaking.

"Harm the queen of England?" Elizabeth's bosom swelled with outrage. "You are having delusions of grandeur, Mistress! I do not tremble before trifles like you! You and your ill-got husband are nothing! I will crush you beneath my heel in an instant if you drive me to it!"

"I trust we will not," Gabriel said.

"Trust? That is a fine word to hear from the Gypsy's Angel! You have lied your way through half of England and bedded a score of women along the way! And now you refuse to give me the information I require? A loyal subject has no secret from his queen! I am sick to death of loyalty such as yours!" She swung her arm toward the door, rings glinting on the fingers she was so vain of. "Get out of my sight!"

"As you wish, Your Grace." Gabriel bowed, and I heard his breath hitch. I prayed his rib was not broken. The point could puncture a lung, let it fill with blood. But I could only curtsey, and battle my urge to tell the queen all she wanted to know.

Walsingham caught my eye, his fingers steepled, almost as if in prayer, his lips compressed, eyes hooded. What was he thinking? Could anyone really tell? He possessed a labyrinth soul, and no one had solved its mystery yet. I knew full well I would face him again. Someplace darker, more frightening. Then any pretence of politeness would be stripped away.

Gabriel and I turned to the door and the guards marched us from the chamber. Through the palace the guards took us, past gawking courtiers, their expressions eager as rats, feeding on the promise of scandal. I glimpsed Mary Grey almost hidden by the sea of skirts. But she said nothing. She had learned how to restrain her emotions in the most brutal of schools, watching her sisters fall, first studious Jane, then Katherine, the headstrong beauty. Katherine, who had been imprisoned when she was with child, like me.

The September air struck me with a chill as we walked out into the night. Perhaps the last time I would ever breathe it, free. The gardens of Greenwich Palace filled with ghosts for me. It was here Eppie had sought me out, desperate as she told me truths that shattered everything I had believed about myself. In a royal garden such as this my mother had found the warrant Wriothesley had dropped, her discovery saving Queen Katherine Parr's life. And Gabriel—he had searched for Father's astrolabe in just such a place, retrieving the treasure I thought lost forever.

I shuddered as the smell of the river filled my nostrils, the faint stench of fish and seaweed, the subtle lapping of the water grating my nerves. Gabriel grasped my elbow as I stepped onto the slippery jetty, then lifted me into the barge that would carry us away.

We huddled together on the bench as the oarsmen rowed, the drumbeat that measured the strokes seeming to keep a funereal rhythm, carrying us ever nearer to the prison where so many others had disappeared. Sir Thomas More and Catherine Howard. Anne Boleyn, my grandmother if what Eppie claimed was true. Elizabeth had made this terrible journey as well in those dangerous days before I encountered her in the Tower Lieutenant's garden. I had offered her a key that day, my intention to set her free. Now she condemned me to those formidable walls and the endless waiting, the torture of picturing most horrible fates.

Heedless of the guards, Gabriel cradled me in his arms, pressed kisses to my temple. "As long as you carry our child you will be safe from the worst of Her Majesty's wrath."

"You mean, they will not execute a pregnant woman," I said. "But once the child is born—Gabriel, if we die, what will become of our babe?"

"We must both believe it will not come to that, Nell." He whispered encouragement, but we both knew he was a most accomplished liar. Soon, the water gate loomed, its bars giant claws dug into the water.

"Courage, Nell," he urged me. "Remember Elizabeth survived an ordeal in this place. We will, too."

But as I stumbled onto the landing and wound my way into the stone fortress, I could not imagine how.

At the foot of the Bell Tower, the Lieutenant met us, his greeting far different than that of Sir John Bridges, the kind man who had been Father's friend. "Sir Gabriel will be lodged in the Beauchamp Tower," he said in a crisp baritone, "while Mistress de Lacey's cell is in the Bell Tower." The guards moved to pull us apart.

"No!" I cried out, grasping Gabriel's arm tight. I saw pain crumple his face.

"It is Walsingham's order," he said, low. "Separate us to break us. Courage, Nell. You are the bravest woman I have ever known."

"I am frightened here alone."

"You'll not be alone." Gabriel scooped up my astrolabe and caressed the golden disk. "Look at the stars from your window, Nell. And I will mark them from my own. When you see them, I will be there."

Chapter Twenty-Eight

November 1565

WEEKS CRAWLED PAST IN MY COLD CELL, THE TIME broken by interrogations. Hour upon hour, Walsingham flayed at my nerves, questioning me first in the tone of a much grieved father, then with blistering rage. But the times I found most dreadful were after he had my guard lock me back in my tiny room, to suffer my fears alone.

I was denied a maid to tend my needs. Prisoners of gentle birth were often accorded that small comfort, but the peril I posed to the Crown was different from most. The most fearsome power I possessed was my voice. Neither Walsingham nor the queen dared risk giving me the chance to tell some servant the tale of my birth. They would not even let my mother see me, though she raced to London, someone having sent her word of my arrest. Had Mary Grey written or had Elizabeth summoned her? Proud Lady Calverley would make a fine hostage in this war of wills the queen and I waged.

Did Mother know she was to have a grandchild? Was she glad I married a man descended from the poet who was kind to her so long ago? I wondered. At least guards gave me the baskets of food that she sent. I prayed she might think to send similar gifts to Gabriel as well. The silence picked at my mind with pointed scissors, trying to unravel my sanity. My imagination did far worse. It transformed every shadow into an agent of the queen, stealing in to silence me forever. That would be the simplest solution, would it not? My death would buy the queen safety. Still, I doubted Elizabeth Tudor would stoop to clandestine murder, no matter how much Walsingham might wish her to. More likely, she would justify my death the way her father had so many. By trying me on manufactured evidence, convincing herself it was real.

Elizabeth could guarantee my silence once I was brought before the crowds. Traitors were hung, drawn, and quartered or burned alive at the queen's pleasure. The swift death from beheading was a mercy she could revoke. I kneaded the scar edging my hand, remembering how Anne Boleyn had asked her husband to bring a swordsman from Calais to be her executioner. Headsmen wielding axes were often clumsy.

I knew Elizabeth was not the bloodthirsty monster her father was. And yet, she held her crown by a thread. France and Spain both lusted to return England to the papal fold, Mary Stuart the center of their plots. Half of Elizabeth's own subjects condemned her for a heretic. Others believed her a bastard produced by their king's unholy alliance with a witch. The malcontents needed only a trifling ember to set the whole country ablaze. I was their burning brand.

My faint hope was that the queen would shrink from condemning her own daughter, *if* her daughter I was. It must be easier to suffocate a babe you never met than behead a young woman you had laughed with, fought with, come to hold in affection. But Elizabeth had made difficult choices before. One thing was certain: I would never leave this prison alive. I could not be certain which punishment would be the most grim: a quick brutal death or growing old without ever breathing free country air again.

And what of Gabriel during those hellish weeks? I could only imagine what he suffered. What small leash curbed Walsingham's ruthlessness because I was a woman would not hold the spymaster back when he confronted a man. I lived in terror that the queen might make good her threat and strike off Gabriel's hand. I twisted my wedding ring about my finger, read its engraving. Let reason rule. But this fortress, this cell, this peril was not a child of reason, but of fear. I could feel Walsingham tightening his noose. In time all pity for a girl who reminded him of his daughters would be vanquished. Once he realized his "gentler" persuasions would avail him nothing, he would move in for the kill.

I had marked fifty days on the stone wall and counted stars until my eyes ached, when I awakened to the sound of a key rasping in my cell door. I knew the ordeal I feared had come. What other reason could there be to disturb me in the middle of the night? I shoved myself to a sitting position in my bed and wrapped my arms around the growing bulge that was my babe, afraid I might lose this precious burden in the ordeal to come. But the child kicked in my womb like a lion cub, determined to cling to life.

My cell door opened, silhouetting two grim-faced guards against the cresset torch: Adam Renfrew, unmoved by the suffering he saw, and Josiah Barnaby, who reminded me of Jem from Calverley. "You must come with us, Mistress," Renfrew ordered.

"Give me a moment to dress properly," I managed, voice shaking.

Renfrew scowled. "You are to throw a cloak about you and be done."

Barnaby shifted nervously and I could see his toe poking out from a hole in his boot. "It is Sir Francis Walsingham's orders, Mistress."

"Where are we going?"

Even Renfrew would not meet my eyes. "You will find out soon enough."

I wedged my feet into shoes, then clutched my cloak about my body, praying for courage as the guards led me into the bowels of the White Tower. I smelled hot fire, acrid sweat, and something far more subtle. A hopeless agony, as if those who had suffered the horrors this chamber was famous for had smeared the walls with their screams.

Here the gentlewoman Anne Askew had suffered her ordeal, an

atrocity so repugnant the torture master had refused to work the rack. Wriothesley and Bishop Gardiner had applied the device themselves, so savagely Anne had to be carried to the stake in a chair. But Henry had been ruler during that abomination. A king so twisted in his soul that he had murdered two wives, cruelly hounded another into her grave, and signed the warrant for his sixth wife's arrest. Elizabeth was a far different monarch. She would not order the torture of a pregnant gentlewoman. *Why not?* A chilling voice whispered. *They can do whatever they wish here. If they broke you on the rack, who would know?*

My knees almost buckled as we neared our destination. As I entered the door I saw Walsingham, his simple black robes set in relief against the implements of torture. When he shifted to one side he revealed something more hellish still. Gabriel, his cheeks hollow, his hair filthy. Had they tormented him already? My gaze sought the end of his sleeves, fearful, but his hands were still safe. He clenched them into fists of helplessness and rage. "Nell," he breathed. His gaze locked on my belly and for a heartbeat desperation carved his face. I wanted to fling my arms around him one precious moment, but Renfrew caught my elbow in his vise-tight grip.

"Forgive me for denying you time for a reunion." Walsingham sounded almost sincere. "But I am a man of business and my patience is at an end. Sir Gabriel, Mistress Wyatt, we have a precarious situation here. One that troubles Her Majesty greatly as it drags on. I do not tolerate anything that robs her of her peace."

"Our peace has been somewhat beleaguered as well," Gabriel said.

"That was the point of imprisoning you here." Admiration for Gabriel's courage flickered in the spymaster's eyes. "I am certain we all agree it is best not to draw this out any longer. I am determined to put an end to this. *Tonight.*" My throat constricted at his resolve. "To that end, may I present Master Silas? His aid has become a regrettable necessity on occasion."

Another man stepped from the shadows, his shoulders massive, his arms thick as the bears at the baiting Elizabeth so loved. A heavy jerkin covered his barrel chest, the leather stained with the blood of sufferers who had come before.

"Master Silas is very talented at his craft," Walsingham said. "His secrets passed down through generations of his family."

The torture master's lips spread in a smile, pleased as if he were a schoolboy praised for excellence in his Latin exercise. "I do my best to serve the queen."

"You do, when I can see no other way to protect Her Majesty." Walsingham adjusted his sleeve. "Some might enjoy this spectacle, but I always hope the prisoner will be wise. It is my fondest prayer I will not have to watch them suffer." I sensed he meant it. Yet, he would do what he must, even if the brutality repulsed him.

The torture master crossed to where a fire blazed, plucked a white-hot object from the flames. When he turned, he held a crescent-shaped blade, a wooden handle mounted above the cutting surface. I had seen similar implements in the Calverley flesh kitchens for cleaving bones. I could only imagine what other uses the tool might have. I glanced at Gabriel, his face unreadable. "All is ready to do the queen's will," the torture master said, testing the blade edge against his broad thumb. I smelled the faint scent of burned flesh as he returned the instrument to the fire.

Walsingham sighed. "You do my will tonight more than the queen's. Her Majesty has given me leave to do what I must, but she finds such proceedings unpleasant. However, Sir Gabriel and Mistress Wyatt have left us no other choice."

"I appreciate Her Majesty's predicament, Sir Francis," Gabriel said. "And your own." How could Gabriel speak thus? His nerves ice cool while mine raged mad fire?

"I have always valued your powers of discernment," Walsingham said.

"And I, your Christian principles, despite the unpleasant work you do. Sir Francis, you do not make war on pregnant women. Let us keep this ugliness between men. Send my wife away."

I started to protest, but he shook his head slightly.

"You care for the lady, then?" Walsingham picked at Gabriel's brittle calm.

"I do." Gabriel feigned detachment. "She is, after all, my property now. You know how determined I am to keep what is mine in good repair." He was testing Walsingham. I could almost feel Gabriel, edging his way along the rim of a precipice, trying to find solid ground where he could turn, then fight.

The spymaster's gaze bored into Gabriel's, two minds equal in guile locked in a test of will. "Dare I hope your wife feels a warmer attachment to you?"

"I cannot imagine why she would." Gabriel's jaw clenched and I saw his gaze flick to the knife. His voice dropped low with unexpected earnestness. "I have done her a harm, Walsingham. And I am sorry for it."

"Gabriel," I choked out. "All is forgiven."

"She is most merciful to you, Wyatt." Regret shadowed Walsingham's homely face. "You do not deserve such a wife."

"Well I know it."

Walsingham paced to where writing implements were laid out. He examined a freshly mended quill. "Do you know what I sometimes envy in you, Sir Gabriel?"

"I am shocked a Puritan like you can find anything at all."

"You are not burdened by inconvenient scruples." How many times had I heard others speak of the Gypsy's Angel just so? "Better to surrender honor and live than cling to some foolhardy sense of nobility and die. Is that not your creed?"

Gabriel shrugged. "I had never found anything worth dying for."

Walsingham paused to consider. "Of course, when one examines the prospect rationally, dying might be a gift of sorts. A grand gesture, then peace."

"I thought you Calvinists believed in hell. Eternal damnation is hardly an inviting prospect."

"What would hell be like for a man of your sort? An athlete who values his physical prowess above all? Perhaps justice demands a hell fitted to be your very own." Walsingham rolled the quill between deft fingers. "I wonder, Sir Gabriel, what would it be like if I maimed you for life? Cleaved off your hand?"

I could see Gabriel's shoulders tense, but he sneered. "It would be a damned nuisance, since I have an unfortunate impulse to want to skewer people who annoy me."

"No!" I cried. "Sir Francis, you cannot take his hand."

"Quiet, woman!" Gabriel snapped. He turned to Walsingham. "Forgive my wife's outburst. Too much education, you understand. It is rather like allowing a dog to eat from the table, amusing at first, but in the end one must teach them their place."

I winced, his words echoing jibes from more close-minded men.

"Do you hear what he thinks of you? Sir Gabriel, it would be a pity to take your hand," Walsingham said. "All you have to do to prevent it is to tell the truth. It is simple enough to do. A few sentences only." His lip curled with irony. "Perhaps you can write them down as poetry."

Gabriel laughed, a ragged sound. "Now that would be a sin sure to send me to the devil. Jesus himself would not be magnanimous enough to forgive my butchery of the English language."

"This is not a jest!" Temper flared in Walsingham's eyes. "Before you and your lady leave this room you will be light of something—either your secret or your hand."

"It is quite simple then. As you say." Gabriel's gaze went to the chopping block that stood in the room's center. He examined it with almost negligible grace. "I suppose you have other inducements to offer? Bribes beyond just the saving of my hand?"

"All your father's lands will be restored to you. Your wife's inheritance will be yours, as will the baronetcy. It is such a trifle Her Majesty asks in return. Merely tell whatever treasonous lies this woman has whispered in your marriage bed."

"Am I to have no loyalty at all to my wife?"

"You have changed your loyalties before," Walsingham reasoned. "When Jane Grey lost the throne you pledged fealty to

Queen Mary rather than die honorably beside your father. And when you were released from prison you came to despise your own mother. Abandoning a traitorous wife is a petty thing in comparison."

"I suppose that is true."

Walsingham's features sharpened. "You are a courtier, Sir Gabriel. A consummate realist. Surely you value your hand as much as you did your head. Perhaps more. Do you wish to go through life burdened with a grotesque stump the ladies will recoil from? For you will have to find your pleasures with those ladies again. Before this is done you will be rid of your wife."

Gabriel's eyes turned black, impenetrable as marble.

"I understand her loss might grieve you. But Calverley is only the first reward the queen will offer for such loyalty. There is no telling how high you might reach."

"And my wife?"

"We can hardly allow a woman who might spread explosive rumors to live." It was true, then, what I had suspected all along. I would die here or rot in prison. And our child? Once it was born would it suffer the fate the two little princes did during the reign of their uncle, King Richard? Would our babe melt into the Tower's golden stone? Or be suffocated as I was meant to be?

I remembered Mary's attempt to soothe me when she spoke of Old Grisel ridding my womb of the child. *You and Gabriel are young . . . you will have other children.* Her wisdom was painful but true. Gabriel could have other children, even if this babe was lost. Lost as I was lost. Beyond all hope. He had to know what was so clear to me: Sacrificing himself would not save me *or* the child I carried. But he *could* save himself. In that moment I thanked God the Gypsy's Angel was no idealistic hero to fling himself to death in a futile cause.

Gabriel reached out his poet's fingers and stroked the contours of the wooden block, its top hollowed slightly by the blows that had been struck there over countless years. I imagined living flesh severed atop that grisly surface. The shock of agony, the spurt of blood. Did they allow the prisoner to bleed to death? Or need they bother? Here in the Tower's filth and damp and darkness, the wound would fester and do death's work. I clutched my belly, waiting for the horrific crack that was to come, not of the mallet that would drive the blade home, but rather the crack of Gabriel's will. Gabriel letting his reason rule— telling Walsingham everything the queen wanted to hear.

My babe kicked, to tell me how desperately it yearned for life. I feared it might wrench itself loose from my womb, come forth in a rush of blood, too weak to survive. Would that not be better than pitifully struggling as a pillow was pressed down on its tiny face? There was no way Sir Francis Walsingham could afford to let my child live once he had Gabriel's confession to add to Eppie's own. I started, suddenly aware of the weight of Gabriel's stare. He caught my gaze, held it for long minutes in his own.

"Tell me what you know, Sir Angel," Walsingham urged almost gently. "You cannot save Mistress Nell, even if you wanted to."

Tell him. I mouthed silent words. *Save yourself.*

Gabriel's hand knotted, its sinews tanned and strong. "I am sorry, Nell," he said, his voice rough with regret. "Know that much is true."

"I do," I said, forgiving him all with my eyes.

Walsingham was far too wise to gloat. "There is no point prolonging the misery."

"That is true enough." Gabriel looked at me with some emotion I could not name. *Do it.* My heart hammered. *Just tell him and it will be done.* "Let us finish this, Walsingham," he said, his jaw setting hard. I gasped as Gabriel took a step closer to the block. I realized what he meant to do.

"Gabriel, no!" I broke free of my guard's grasp, flung myself between Gabriel and the torture master. "You cannot do this!"

"It is done." Gabriel put me away from him with a tenderness that cut me to the core. My guards hauled me back, the chamber hellish with sweat and fear and pain. My knees buckled as Gabriel flattened his hand—his beautiful hand—upon the block.

I cried out to Walsingham, begged him to show mercy. The

spymaster merely compressed his lips and nodded to the torture master.

The floor bucked beneath my feet as Silas pulled the blade from the flame. Black dots swirled before my eyes. But that did not save me from the image that burned into my mind forever: the torture master placing his white-hot blade almost delicately on Gabriel's wrist.

He picked up his mallet and struck.

Chapter Twenty-Nine

The Same Day

WERE I TO LIVE A THOUSAND YEARS I WOULD NEVER forget the gout of blood, the stench of seared flesh, the agony as Gabriel staggered back, clutching his maimed wrist. He did not make a sound as he waged a valiant war to stay on his feet as the torture master slapped a searing cloth over the wound to seal it. I wrenched away from my guards and did my best to break his fall, but he crashed to the blood-slick floor, face gray as any corpse. I tore a strip of linen from my shift, struggled to tighten it about the stump, shrieking at Walsingham to fetch a surgeon.

Much later, back in my room, I shuddered at the absurdity. Why should Walsingham care if Gabriel perished? He believed Gabriel chose his own fate. The spymaster faced his own grim task—telling the queen he had failed to secure Gabriel's confession. For Walsingham had been dead certain my husband would betray me. But was I not just as guilty of thinking that? The knowledge tormented me as I paced the cell like a demented soul.

Walsingham ordered my guard to return me to the Bell Tower. I clung to Gabriel, fought them with all my strength. It took both men to wrench me away. They dragged me through the fortress, Josiah begging me to have a care lest I lose my babe. But I would lose that fragile life in any case. They locked me in my cell, though I pounded on the door until my fists bled. In time, I slid down the iron-bound panel to the cold damp floor. Dark engulfed me at last.

❦

I AWAKENED GOD knows how much later, my muscles cramped from the stones, my mind recounting the horror again and again with nightmare clarity. My hands were rusty with dried blood—Gabriel's and my own. I begged my jailor for any news. Did my husband yet live? Was he gripped with fever? No emotion softened Renfrew's violence-hardened features, but Barnaby's showed pity. I sensed his reluctance to face me whenever he had to bring me food.

"You must take a little bread, Mistress," Barnaby urged. "Or perhaps some meat broth. For the babe's sake, if not your own."

"Tell me how my husband fares."

"Not well, I fear." Barnaby fiddled with a piece of the manchet bread my mother sent me. He glanced over his shoulder as if to make sure Renfrew was nowhere near. "I heard from another guard that Sir Gabriel raves with fever. He may well die."

I feared as much already. Why, then, did my heart drop? I clutched at Barnaby's sleeve, blocking his path to the door. "Take me to him. Just for a moment."

"Mistress, you must let me go." He tried to disentangle his sleeve from my fingers, but without Renfrew to press him, Barnaby would not use force against a pregnant woman. His gentleness betrayed a tender side. I seized on that small hope.

"Do you not have a mother? A sister? A wife?" I asked him. "A woman who would suffer anything to tend you out of love? Can you return home and look them in the eye if you deny that tiny mercy to me?"

He flinched, looking terribly young. "I pity you, Mistress. By God, I do. And when I look at you I see my Sarah. She, too, is big with child. But I dare not help you. I would lose my position. Then how would I feed my own babes?"

"My mother has great wealth. If I ask it she will give you a hundred crowns."

"Your mother is not here. I cannot risk all for payment I may never get." He made a move to leave. I would not budge from his path.

"Wait! Wait. I have this ring the queen herself gave me." I pulled off the circle of gold Elizabeth had used to entrap my mother into betraying I had had a sixth finger on my right hand.

"I'll not take something so easily traced back to Her Majesty! Might as well thrust my head into a noose!"

"I have one other thing of value. Something wholly my own. I can give it to you now, with my word more will come." I unfastened the chain about my neck and held it out to him. My astrolabe glinted against my battered palm. "I beg you, sir. Barter the chain to the apothecary to buy the herbs I need to drive back my husband's fever. Keep the gold pendant, a payment toward all I will owe you."

"Mistress, I—"

I drew off my wedding ring as well. "I would give you more if I had it," I said, frantically searching my room for anything else he might want. "My cloak—it is warm. You can take it to your Sarah."

Barnaby stumbled back a step, as if pushed by the force of my desperation. "I'll not leave a pregnant woman to freeze! What kind of man do you think I am?"

"A decent one, though necessity demands you do ugly things. I only pray your good conscience will allow you to help me." My voice cracked. "What harm can it do?" Barnaby's throat worked. He paced away from me, and I knew his decision hung in the balance. I prayed his love for this Sarah would compel him to take my side.

"What supplies do you need?" he asked.

My tears streamed free as I told him.

❧ ❦ ❧

BE READY, MY coconspirator warned two days later as he smuggled precious herbs in with a basket of food my mother sent me. I took my contraband, distilling the precious Saracen's root as if each drop of its juice was gold, sprinkling other herbs into the brew as well, praying I would get the mixture right.

Why did I not listen to my mother when she told me such housewifely lessons were more important than Copernicus's theories? That it did not matter if the earth was center of the universe as the church claimed, or if we spun around the sun. Someday a person would be the center of my world—a husband, a child—whenever I grew up enough to love them. My hands trembled as I stored my mixture in a horn container, hoping Renfrew would not find it before my opportunity came.

The Tower lights had nearly all winked out when Barnaby opened my cell door, his face dotted with sweat, eyes busy with worry as we stole through the fortress. "Your husband is worse," he warned. "They take wagers in the guard room how soon he will die."

"He will not die," I said, so fiercely Barnaby hushed me. "I will not let him."

But I had not been able to rub warmth back into my father's skin. Death had taken him all the same. And he had been tucked in a clean bed, in a warm room, surrounded by the best care my mother could give.

At last, Barnaby opened Gabriel's cell. My stomach lurched at the stench of sweat, the sound of feverish groans. Torchlight fell across Gabriel's face and I fought not to cry out. Suffering gouged hollows under his eyes, flayed away flesh until he looked like a skull covered in parchment. I rushed to him, pressed my hand to his brow. "He's burning up."

My voice—Gabriel heard it even through the haze of fever. He tried to grasp my hand in both his own. I flinched, as his stump thudded against my arm, wrenching a cry of pain from his lips. Still, he held on with his good hand, so tight his nails dug into my flesh. His eyes fluttered open, the green depths haunted. "Nell."

I forced a smile. "I am come to make you well."

"This must be hell then, seeing you when you cannot be real."

A tear tracked through the grime on his face. "It is no more than a devil like me deserves."

"I am here. Touch me and you will see." I pressed his hand to my cheek, kissed his palm. Did my babe sense its father's despair or was it mere chance it kicked in my womb? Seizing that flutter of life, I dragged Gabriel's hand to my belly. Pressed it hard against the place where the child had moved. "Feel me, Gabriel," I urged. "Feel *us*." The child thrust at its prison as if it would fight for its father if it could.

Gabriel's eyes widened. I could see him battle to speak. "Real. You are real."

"I am going to make you well." I took the horn bottle from where I had hidden it in my bodice. I tugged the stopper free. "Drink this." I lifted his head from the pillow, pressed the bottle's rim to his lips. He coughed as the bitter mixture struck his tongue, but he was too weak to pull away. "Your son needs his father," I told him. "You must fight."

"No."

His surrender chilled my heart. "Gabriel, please."

"Not son." He struggled to form the words. "Want a daughter."

A sob tore from my throat. In a world hungry for sons at any price, Gabriel wished for a girl?

"Then live!" I gave him a little shake. "A girl needs a father to love her."

"Grace," Gabriel whispered. "Name her Grace." His eyes rolled back, his hand fell limp to his side. My heart ached with the fear Gabriel would never live to see her. I tucked his good arm beneath his blanket, put a poultice on his wound. I begged him to fight until the last star faded and Barnaby forced me to leave. Renfrew stood right outside my cell door.

Josiah Barnaby never returned.

No one dared give me news of Gabriel again.

❧❧❧

EIGHTY LINES ON the cell wall marked the days I had been imprisoned by the time my new guards escorted me to Traitor's Gate, where a barge was moored. I shivered, remembering the journey that brought me to this hellish place, how Gabriel and I watched the currents swirl, treacherous as the court I had come to hate. The queen's scholars and adventurers and exotic curiosities held no fascination anymore. At last I understood what my mother tried to tell me: Beneath the surface all is rotted at the core.

I possessed more precious things. My mother's courage, my husband's passion, my father's questing mind. Let the queen do what she would. I would not quail before her. I was Gabriel Wyatt's wife, Thomasin de Lacey's daughter. I was the mother of a child soon to be born.

The barge moored at the servant's wharf and I was led through hallways where few servants even strayed. I remembered the sensation when I first arrived at Whitehall, then again at Greenwich, as if I might never find my way out of the labyrinthine corridors again. How strange that Gabriel had always managed to find me. I would have given every shilling I possessed if he would pop around some corner. But Gabriel might be dead for all I knew, his devilish wit silenced, his reckless eyes closed forever. Was that what the queen was going to tell me? Did she hope to wrench a confession from me by telling me my husband was forever beyond my help?

At last, we entered the small, dark closet where Walsingham's scribe had recorded my words what seemed an eternity ago. A single candle cast its watery glow across the people gathered there. Robert Dudley pacing in agitation. Walsingham with his grim face. Would the queen enter as well? The thought of facing the woman who gave the order to take Gabriel's hand poured iron into my spine. Stiff with hatred, I thought of Anne Boleyn, whose sixth finger might have been like my own. It is said she was still haughty when she heard the sentence of death.

Time ticked by, the clocks Elizabeth adored seeming to roar loud as the bells church sextons ring. I steeled my nerves against them, vowing that Elizabeth Tudor would never see me cringe. In spite of my resolve, I froze when I heard footsteps nearing. I wrapped my arms around my unborn child to shield my babe from the news to come. I must not crumble for the child's sake. Even if they told me its father was dead. I turned toward the door, expecting to see the queen. But all my will could not hold back my cry. Dark hair, burning green eyes. Gabriel. Alive.

Joy surged in me. A moment later I bit my lip, grieving over the suffering carved in his dark angel's face. I remembered the day of the tournament, his armor gleaming, his athlete's body powerful. The Tower had whittled away his flesh until he seemed a different man. But it was his sleeve that broke my heart. His right cuff hung empty.

I started toward him, but my guard caught me. The spymaster's inscrutable gaze flicked to Gabriel's wrist. "Let her go to him."

I rushed to Gabriel, held him, reassured myself that he was alive. Gabriel wrapped his arms around me, my belly big between us. I could feel he still feared for me, and for our child. Walsingham frowned. "I still think it is a shame that your husband would tell us nothing, Mistress Wyatt."

"I am the one shamed because I doubted him."

A breathless page burst in, announced: "Her Majesty the queen."

But Elizabeth brushed him aside, ordering him to leave. He shut the door behind him with a thud.

I stared at her as if I had never seen her, as if she were Mab the fairy queen, brittle as glass and as unreal. Her skirts rustled, taffeta shot with gold, her perfume filling the air, its scent worlds away from prisons and dried blood. I hated her, even before I saw our death sentence in her hand—the scrap of cloth I so rashly hid in my writing box.

"Where did you get this?" she demanded, thrusting it beneath my nose.

"Eppie gave it to me."

Two flames darkened the queen's cheeks. Her lips tightened, bloodless. "That witch! Is it some sort of charm, then? Part of a wicked spell?"

For a heartbeat I froze, then imagined what Gabriel might say, his mind so quick. "It is nothing but a remembrance of my nurse's love. This scrap is all that was left from the gown she made my favorite poppet when I was a child. I know you can understand my cherishing it, Your Majesty, loving Lady Ashley as you did."

I hoped to remind her of the hours we had spent together during Kat's illness, stir in the queen's memory how she had trusted me with the fate of a person she loved most in the world. Yet I feared I might have gone too far, comparing simple Eppie to the governess Elizabeth loved. The queen stared as if measuring my resolve. Gabriel had already shown her his.

"So you keep your silence, even now?" Elizabeth marveled. "After all you have endured. Everything I might yet do? It seems I can still be surprised after all." She turned to Gabriel. "I did not mean to let them take your hand, though it was my right under law. My advisers convinced me to sign the sentence. By morning I regretted it. I rescinded the order, but it was too late."

Walsingham must have rushed to the Tower as soon as she signed the order, determined to carry it out before she could change her mind. It was a small thing, knowing the queen had tried to save Gabriel once her anger was past. Small, but precious.

The queen paced to the window, running her fingers over the smooth diamond pendants known as the Three Brothers. I thought of how often I had made the same nervous gesture with my astrolabe, trying to sort out the tangle my world had become. Suddenly the queen turned, fixing Walsingham with a regal eye. "Leave us."

"Majesty?"

"I would speak alone with Mistress Wyatt."

"Your Grace, I would not advise—"

"That is very wise, since I do not recall asking for your opinion, Sir Francis."

"Your Grace," Gabriel said. "I would not leave my wife."

"So it would seem. You, Lord Robert, and Sir Francis may pace outside the door and complain about the vagaries of women while my maid and I engage in one final scientific debate."

What could the three men do? They bowed, then retreated through the door. The panel closed, leaving Elizabeth and me alone.

My heart hammered with fear that this might be some device concocted earlier between the queen and Sir Francis, one last attempt to trick me into disclosing what I knew. Worse still, what if Walsingham was signaling the guard? Having them lead Gabriel away? I could not help but peer over my shoulder at the door, my fears naked on my face.

"You are in love with the very man I warned you against, are you not, Mistress?"

"I did not mean to be. It . . . happened, Majesty. I could not prevent it."

"An excuse I have heard before. Even spoken myself when I was young like you."

My surprise registered in my eyes. The queen smiled self-deprecatingly. "You are amazed I admit my folly? Why? My youthful indiscretions have all been written down, part of records generations in the future will see. I could order them destroyed, and yet . . . would that not make me seem guiltier than I am?"

I dropped my gaze to the hem of her skirt. I remembered the tales of Thomas Seymour holding the princess down, slashing her gown to ribbons.

"I did not mean to wound my stepmother's heart, not after she had been so generous in giving hers to me. No one sets out to do evil. Always there is an excuse. Justice, religion. Mine was not knowing who I really was, a Tudor princess, heir to the throne, or Lady Elizabeth, who was of no importance to anyone save my nurse."

"My mother said Katherine Parr loved you. Even after."

"She did. She had a mother's heart. It grieves me still that she did not live to watch her own daughter grow. Yet, it seems some are destined to be cheated of their deepest desires. Now you are a wife, perhaps soon a mother. I am destined to be neither. So I told Lord Robert when I was eight years old."

"I am certain in time Cecil will find a husband to suit you."

"Let my council delude itself as long as they choose. Their labors will be in vain. If I take a husband, he will be as God instructs—my lord and master. I would no longer be sole ruler of England. Were I to lavish my attention on one child of my body I would cheat a country full of unruly children I must lead. No, I am best as I am. Wed to England, and perhaps to the legacy my parents left me. The grim truth that marriage makes prisoners of us all."

"I believe you are wrong. Marriage can be like the lands adventurers are discovering. A lifetime can be spent mapping boundaries, unearthing its wealth."

Elizabeth shook her head. "Spoken like a true scientist. It is unfortunate Dr. Dee is to lose two of his most brilliant disciples. But he will find others." Was she saying we would die? I held my breath until she continued, "As for what you have suffered these past months—time blunts ugliness, scrubs it from your memory like the stains Kat scolded me over when Robin and I played in the mud as children. Perhaps all will fade."

Was she saying she would allow us to live? Hope warred with truth. "I cannot forget. I will remember every time I see Gabriel's cuff hanging empty."

"There are more terrible things to have severed. The gifts God offers to women. The passion of a man in the marriage bed. The feel of life growing inside you. Hope you will grow old together. It is not easy to surrender such comforts, Elinor." Elizabeth's voice dropped low. "It is not easy to surrender you."

She hesitated and I tried to decipher what she meant to say. After a moment she squared her shoulders. "Of all the maids of honor who have ever served me, you have been the closest match to my mind and the deepest in my affections. Perhaps it is because we are scholars. Wise enough to know sometimes there *are* no right answers. It is better to let questions remain." She fingered the scrap of bed curtain, tracing a silvery moon.

"My father used to say that we will never run out of wonders to explore. But we must not get tangled in what needs to be left behind."

"Did he?"

I was straying into dangerous territory, yet instinct urged me to reach out this one last time, challenge the intellect I had traveled so far to know. "You see, there was a man named Copernicus who believed the earth is not the center of all things."

"There are many who would condemn such an idea."

"But I believe he was right. My mother tried to teach that truth to me. The center of my world is right here." I laid my hands upon my swollen belly.

Elizabeth peered at the place where my child grew. "I would envy you, Elinor Wyatt, if I dared. I must inhabit a far wider world. Alone. Summon the gentlemen waiting outside the door. No doubt they are chafing and angry as we women so often are. There are some pleasures, you see, even in being a queen."

❧❧❧

I DID AS she bade me. Lord Robert, Walsingham, and my Gabriel came in, lines of temper and uncertainty etching their faces. Gabriel crossed to me, eyes full of questions as he slipped his arm around my waist.

After a moment, Elizabeth faced us. "I have made my decision. Sir Gabriel and Lady Elinor Wyatt, I command you to leave this court."

"You mean to set us free?" Gabriel gasped, stunned as I was.

"Your Majesty," Walsingham faltered, "are you certain?"

"It is done!" She turned, throwing something into the fire: the cloth, I think. It flared, burned to ash, consuming the last link between us. Elizabeth paced toward me, peered at me with unreadable eyes. She grasped a lock of my hair between her white fingers. A mother's touch? Or a warning?

"I will miss your mind, Elinor. One as like to mine as the color of your hair. But I must never see you or your husband again."

I swallowed hard. "You will not, Majesty. There is nothing for me here."

Elizabeth gave a wry smile, weighed down with a weariness I did not envy. "Thomasin once said exactly the same thing, you know. Yet you came anyway, Elinor. Perhaps, if your child is a girl, she will be drawn to my court as well."

"I would lock her away first," I said so grimly the queen's mouth softened. I glimpsed a hint of old pain.

"Young girls are reckless to a fault," Elizabeth said. "Like a horse yet to be bridled. The world will beckon, their hearts will race. They will not be wise. I remember . . ." Her voice trailed off. After a moment, she seemed to shake herself. "You must have better angels than most mortals, to escape the perils you faced. To survive our follies, Elinor. Sometimes that is miracle enough."

Her eyes shifted to Robert Dudley. I saw the man cast me a look stricken with despair and wonder. He turned to the queen with a love that chased back the years. And I guessed at why he did not tell the queen when he knew I was with child. Did he sense something in me? Perhaps the pale reflection of the young princess he once loved? Did the earl feel a confused loyalty to a child in his imagination, one he wished might be his daughter?

I never knew what words they spoke after Walsingham ushered us out of the room.

Am I Robert Dudley's child conceived when Elizabeth was banished from court by Queen Mary? My mother was ever vague about the year of my birth. Did I spring from Thomas Seymour's lust? Or am I neither? Just part of the elaborate imaginings of an old woman who loved me enough to believe I was a princess? Only the queen will ever know for certain. But it did not matter anymore, my past. Gabriel and I had a future.

❦

SOME WOULD CALL it madness for a woman so far gone with child to brave traveling even in such an unusually mild winter. But we dashed a missive off by messenger to my mother, then hastened toward Calverley as if the devil were behind us, neither believing we could truly be free. Gabriel's barge carried us up the river I had traveled down as a child. I bade farewell to the beautiful gardens, the great houses, London Bridge. I buried my face against Gabriel's doublet as we neared the bridge's arch, remembering my childish fascination with the grisly warnings mounted there—traitors' heads for all to see. "It might have been you," I said, remembering father's tale of how Sir Thomas More's brave daughter had gone to the bridge at night to steal her father's severed head, give him a decent burial, lay him to rest. I knew were matters different, I would have done the same thing. Gabriel kissed my forehead as if to drive such thoughts away.

"You are safe now, sweeting," he murmured, his warm breath on my skin. "Safe."

"But why? I still do not understand."

He drew back so he could see my face. "Because the queen—"

"It is not the queen that confuses me. It is you." I grasped his arm, drew his stump to my lips. "Why did you not tell Walsingham what he wanted to know? I would never have blamed you."

"I did it for the same reason I was fool enough to ask for your favor at the tournament that day. Because I love you."

"Love me?" My heart turned over in amazement.

"I realized it some time ago. You were playing with Mary Grey's spaniel in the garden, her puppies frolicking all around. That was when I wrote that abominable poem."

"Why did you never tell me?"

"You would not have believed me." He grimaced. "I would not have believed myself. But, Nell"—he caressed my cheek, tender—"this love I feel for you—it is the truest thing I ever felt."

Chapter Thirty

January 1566

CALVERLEY MANOR

MY DAUGHTER WAITED TO BE BORN UNTIL WE ARrived at the home where my mother was waiting. How she had reached Calverley before us I would never know, but she welcomed me into a chamber she prepared especially for my confinement, a testament of her love for me.

Father's chair was placed close by the hearth. The soothing lavender scent Eppie had always loved whispered on the air from bundles of the dried herb mother tucked about the room. A table tucked in a corner was covered in tiny clothes my mother had labored over during my imprisonment, softly stitched treasures for her grandchild to wear. My own efforts in the week that followed were far less perfect, yet it touched me when my mother took up a tiny, plain shift I had finished and smiled.

"Look how soft this is, and how sweet," she said without a breath of the criticism that once built walls between us. "This must be the first thing that touches your babe's skin to welcome her into the world."

Yet no garment, however lovingly fashioned, could have conveyed the welcome of my mother's hands. Black-and-blue from my clutching them during my travail, full of awe as they caught that fragile new life as I pushed it from my womb.

"She is perfect," mother breathed, and I remembered Eppie say-ing mother had once said the same words about me.

I thought nothing could touch me more deeply, not even the tears that shone in Gabriel's eyes when he first gathered our child in his arms.

But birthing is a woman's business, like healing wounds, mend-ing tears, as mother once told me, in clothes and in lives. And Thomasin de Lacey had one last thing to teach me.

Three weeks after Grace was born I waked from a nap, drowsy, my breasts heavy with milk. Grace was not in her cradle.

"Lady Calverley took her from the room so you could sleep," Moll told me, my loyal maid grateful to be back at Calverley, where Jem's gaze followed her, admiring the polish our time in London had given the once gullible girl. "I saw her ladyship walking toward the privy chambers."

Yet Mother was not in her own room. I wandered deeper into the private part of the manor, into Father's bedchamber, and then I saw it, the door to the library standing open, the room within aglow.

Silently I stole closer, seeing the light flickering from a fire upon the hearth, driving back the shadows. I had not entered Father's li-brary since the day the queen's missive had arrived, summoning me to court. The room that had once been my haven was now a hard reminder of my folly and the ugliness between me and my mother I longed to forget.

Surprise filled me, then tenderness as I heard the cadence of my mother's voice and observed the scene within. My mother sat in a sunny alcove, those ever-busy hands still upon an open book, Grace cradled in her arms as she read.

Grace gurgled and looked my way, no doubt scenting her next meal.

Mother looked up, flushed.

"It is time for me to feed her," I explained.

"You should have sent Moll to find us. It is too soon for you to be walking about. You must get your strength back."

"I feel stronger than I have ever been. What are you reading?"

"*Le Morte d' Arthur.* I thought it a bit early to attempt Copernicus."

I chuckled. "A bit."

"When I returned from court last January I thought I would go mad with fear for you. I began cleaning to distract myself and could not stop. The servants thought my mind had unhinged, I think. But in the process I found the one thing that kept me sane. I was sorting through Father's things and found journals he kept from the time you were small. Lists of books and the lessons he taught you. As I pored through them I came to know you better than I ever had before. I am grieved that I missed sharing all that with you. When Grace came, I vowed I would do things differently.

"And there is something else you must know. Grace has taken a liking to something else rather unusual." Mother pulled back the corner of the quilt, displaying what lay beneath, clutched in my daughter's tiny hands.

"Father's astrolabe."

"The sunlight made it shine upon the shelf, so I thought I would just let her touch it. Once she got hold of it she would not let it go. She has a most formidable will for such a tiny maid. But then, she is her mother's daughter."

"As I am," I said, holding tight to my mother's hand.

April 1603

ODAY A MESSENGER ARRIVED WITH A PACKAGE FROM London. A brooch in the shape of a key with a motto picked out in diamonds: I choose freedom over all. The key, a final bequest from the queen, the symbol of my effort to free Elizabeth Tudor when I was but five years old.

Accompanying the gift: A letter from one of the ladies I befriended. She told of the queen's last hours, the secret her attendants discovered upon her death on March twenty-fourth: A compartment hidden in a ring she always wore. When the stone folded back, it revealed a tiny portrait—Anne Boleyn, the mother the queen almost never mentioned.

I think of the poetry Sir Walter Raleigh wrote, comparing Elizabeth Tudor to Diana, the virgin goddess, the huntress, and remember the crescent moon, her symbol, so like the ones embroidered on the bit of bed curtain Eppie gave me. *Was there ever so apt a heraldic device for a queen who spent much of her life the hunted one?*

Grateful, I consider what the queen's death means for me and those I love. We are safe: Gabriel, who braved so much to secure our future. My precious wandering princess, my own Grace grown now into a woman, a mother herself. I am safe as well. My story dies with me if I choose it to be so. How simple it would be to pretend such a fantastical tale never happened. It would be as simple as flinging a bit of bed curtain into the flame. But I am too much Lord John de Lacey's daughter to cast away such a wondrous history. I will spend my mornings writing all that I remember, then hide this sheaf of papers in the space behind the loosened stone at Calverley. The place I hid my treasures as a child, including the letter from the new crowned queen, offering me a future. One even she did not suspect would lead us both into such danger.

> *My Grace, whenever you may find this, I ask this solemn promise: You never forget that we weathered the storm captured in these pages not by the strength of men, brave as your father was. Women made certain you came to be. Hepzibah Jones, your grandmother Thomasin de Lacey, and me. And perhaps her. The greatest queen England may ever know, the woman who ruled all but her heart.*
> *Remember this, your legacy, as you face the world and its many dangers. We women, whether linked by blood or just by circumstance, whatever names history chooses to call us—Jones or de Lacey, Wyatt, Boleyn, or Tudor. We are survivors, all.*

I lay down my pen and cradled my astrolabe in my hand, the treasure Gabriel had traced to my Tower guard and restored to me a second time. The light pooling around the tiny cogs shone, watery gold. I smiled, remembering another such glow, the wide-eyed delight that once shone in my Grace's eyes.

"Look in Grandfather's magical mirror, Mother! What is that glow?"

"It is magic, my darling," I told her. "And it is shining from you."

AFTERWORD

EVERY SO OFTEN WHEN AN AUTHOR STUMBLES ACROSS AN OB-
scure piece of research it can inspire an entire novel. So it was when
I read the tale of a midwife who alleged she delivered a baby to "a
very fair lady" she claimed was Elizabeth Tudor. Midwives were
sometimes blindfolded and taken to undisclosed locations to deliver
unwanted babies. Tragically, these children were sometimes murdered by servants or parents to prevent the shame of a bastard birth
or the burden of another mouth to feed. Midwives protected themselves from accusations related to such deaths by surreptitiously
snipping a bit of bed curtain from the bed where the child was delivered. While the midwife who said she had delivered Elizabeth's
child could not produce this "proof," I chose for fictional purposes
to use the scrap as the last bit of evidence in the queen's eyes.

As to whether Elizabeth Tudor had a baby, it is doubtful. She may
have miscarried. (Some think it might have damaged her so she
could never have borne another child even if she had married.) To
ease the flow of my story, I took the liberty of lengthening Elizabeth's
stay at Katherine Parr's Chelsea an extra three months. For this, I ask
your indulgence. But the premise of the Virgin Queen bearing a
child is one that lovers of Tudor history still debate. It is historically
documented that a man claiming to be the son of Elizabeth and

Robert Dudley surfaced in Italy, though his identity cannot be proven. Yet, I could not resist the chance to give Elizabeth Tudor a daughter, since my own has given me such joy, demanded of me such strength, and taught me far more about life and love than I ever hoped to learn.

ACKNOWLEDGMENTS

SOMETIMES A JOURNEY DOES NOT TAKE THE SHORTEST OR SIMplest route between two points, but you find things all the more beautiful because they were unexpected. *The Virgin Queen's Daughter* was such a journey for me. It was the culmination of a lifetime of dreams nurtured by my grandmother, Elinor Swanson, a children's librarian who provided me with biographies and books on history and told me I could write a book, too. My greatest wish is that she had lived long enough to read it. I offer this novel with love to my parents, who bought me books even though it meant I would be holed up in my bedroom all weekend. (They did occasionally make me come downstairs to watch *Bonanza* with the rest of the family.) I never would have survived this past year without my critique partner of twenty-six years, Susan Carroll, a gifted writer and cherished friend who has been to Mordor and back with me and shares my passion for obscure bits of history that whisper the secrets of people long dead.

It is a trait she shares with my daughter, Kate, and son-in-law Kevin Bautch. You inspire me. You make me laugh. (Yes, I am the luckiest mom in the world.) How can I thank you enough for giving me a quiet writer's retreat in Colorado when I most needed it, and showing me the best places to hide away with my laptop in the music library at UNC Greeley? "Running away from home" would have been impossible if my husband Dave had not volunteered to stay home and take care of the dogs. Never once did he say "You need to get a regular job" during this period of transition. Thank you for your patience. And to my furry muses: three Cavalier King Charles Spaniels named Sir Tristan, Sailor, and Huck, who greet me with the same enthusiasm whether I've been gone two weeks or two minutes.

I am blessed with strong, smart, and caring women who bring such gifts to my life: Maureen, who has more energy than anyone I've ever known; the Scoobies—who cried in all the right places; the Monday Night Movie ladies, Gina, Stephanie, Sheila, Sue, and Trudy. Thanks for dragging me away from the computer when I get to be a hermit. To the ladies at The Yarn Shoppe in Davenport, Iowa: Laurel, Judy, Joanne, Courtney, and Susan, who offer a wonderful haven where I can sit around their table and knit when my imaginary people are being uncooperative. To the librarians at the Moline Public Library, my second home: Your enthusiasm and knowledge humble me, and the fact that there is now a coffee shop downstairs means you are absolutely perfect in spite of the fines I get when I'm on deadline and blank on returning research books. To the Divas, who have been there since the beginning, especially Karyn Witmer-Gow, who soothed my pre-book jitters and introduced me to a gracious lady who offered me direction. Karen Harper, I can never thank you enough for your generosity to a fellow writer you barely knew.

A huge thank-you to the women in New York who steadied me when my confidence was shaky and my dreams for this book were as yet unclear: everyone at Jane Rotrosen Agency, especially Andrea Cirillo, whose faith in me never falters, and my editor at Crown, Allison McCabe. Thank you for imagining what *The Virgin Queen's Daughter* could be when it grew up.

Any mistakes in *The Virgin Queen's Daughter* are my own. I've never worked harder or had more fun in my life.

ABOUT THE AUTHOR

ELLA MARCH CHASE lives in East Moline, Illinois.
Visit her online at EllaMarchChase.com

THE *Virgin* Queen's Daughter

1. When *The Virgin Queen's Daughter* begins, Nell is imprisoned in the Tower of London. How does this set the tone of the book? Compare Nell's perception of the fortress as a child with her feelings about it upon her return. Contrast Elizabeth's experience as a prisoner to Nell's.

2. Parents during the Renaissance widely believed the warning of Juan Luis de Vives, a prominent educator of the time, who said: "The daughter especially shall be handled without cherishing for cherishing marreth sons, but it utterly destroyeth daughters." Which of Nell's parents were "right" in the way they educated Nell? From which parent does Nell learn the most valuable lessons in the end? How does Nell's perception of her parents change during her time at court?

3. Nell's father shows little discretion with her even from a very young age. Given the times, what do you think of his behavior? Why does Nell's mother disapprove of Nell knowing so much?

4. Nell seems completely blindsided by the stories she learns of her mother's time in court. Why do you think her mother never shared these stories—especially if she was so adamant about Nell staying away? How do the stories about Lady Thomasin's time at court change your perception of Nell's father?

5. Throughout the novel characters tell lies and keep secrets to "protect" themselves and people they love. Consider the lies both Gabriel's mother and Nell's mother tell their children. Do you think their decisions are justified? If not, what would you suggest they do under those circumstances? How might the story change if Nell's mother told the truth about why she did not want Nell to go to court?

6. In what ways does Elizabeth's court live up to Nell's expectations? How does it disappoint her? Was Nell's description of court as you pictured it to be? If not, what did you expect to be different? Did you share Nell's fascination with court, or Lady Thomasin's repulsion? Why? Given Nell's disconnect with her mother, do you see her attraction to court as genuine, or as a form of rebellion?

7. When Elizabeth sends Nell to Dr. John Dee's home at Mortlake, Nell is delighted to reacquaint herself with her father's brilliant friend, while Dr. Dee remembers the inquisitive child who wanted to "break open his scrying ball to let all the little people out." Dee invites Nell into his "sanctum sanctorum," a place where he kept his most controversial manuscripts. It is here we encounter the dangerous intersection between science and superstition during the Renaissance—where fear and grim punishments awaited those who dared to challenge the teachings of the Church. In a world changing so fast, it was difficult to reconcile science and religion. Can you draw some comparisons between our time and Nell's? How was Nell a feminist of her time? Does Nell remind you of anyone you know in your personal life, in politics, or in recent history? Dr. Dee talks of "destiny's children." What incidents in Nell's life made her one of these? What events in Elizabeth's life made her one?

8. At Mortlake, Gabriel and Nell argue about the precepts of Sir Thomas More's *Utopia*. What are the differences in their beliefs? How do their visions change as their relationship grows? Recalling

Nell's conversation with her father about Sir Thomas More's controversial life outside of his fictionalized *Utopia*, do you think this could have been Sir John de Lacey's subtle way of warning Nell against the world she would face as an adult? Does Nell's conversation with Gabriel bear any similarities to her conversation with her father? What attributes do Gabriel and Sir John de Lacey share?

9. The author wove the tale of Nell's birth from an account recorded during Elizabeth's reign of a midwife who claimed to deliver a baby to a "very fair young lady" she believed was the princess. Explore Nell's reaction to Eppie's story. When do you think she actually begins to believe it might be true? When Thomasin tells her part of the tale, including the origin of the scar on Nell's hand, how does this change Nell's perception of her mother? Why do you think Nell doesn't destroy the piece of bed curtain Eppie gives her?

10. Explore Elizabeth's moral dilemmas in the book as a fourteen-year-old and as a queen. What effect does Seymour's seduction have on Elizabeth? What about her betrayal of the stepmother who is the only mother she's ever known? Do you believe that such emotional trauma could wipe away the memory of childbirth from the mind of a frightened fourteen-year-old?

11. Discuss Gabriel's transformation from the consummate courtier to a man willing to sacrifice his hand to save Nell and the baby. How do you feel about his decision to continue seeing his mistress even after he and Nell are married? How does his decision to ask for Nell's favor at the tournament demonstrate the change in him? Is Nell justified when she believes he will betray her secret when Walsingham threatens to cut off his hand?

12. Elizabeth warns Nell that "curiosity can bring any world tumbling down." Later she says, "Wise enough to know sometimes there are no right answers. Better to let the questions remain." How

would Nell's life be different if she abided by this? How would her mother's life have been different? What did you think about their uneasy truce?

13. Both Nell and Elizabeth face difficult choices that place their hearts and intellects in conflict. To what lengths should a queen go to protect her throne? Is it acceptable to take one innocent life in order to assure the peace of a country? If Elizabeth had had Nell executed, what would have been the emotional cost for the queen? If the tale of Nell's birth had been revealed in the ensuing years, what would have been the consequences? What do you think truly meant more to Elizabeth—love or power? Do you see her aversion to marriage and love as a weakness or a strength?

14. In the account Nell is writing for her own daughter at the end of the book, she says: "*Never forget that we weathered the storm captured in these pages not by the strength of men, brave as your father was. Women made certain you came to be. Hepzibah Jones, your grandmother Thomasin de Lacey, and me. And perhaps her. The greatest queen England may ever know, the woman who ruled all but her heart. Remember this, your legacy as you face the world and its many dangers. We women, whether linked by blood or just by circumstance, whatever names history chooses to call us—Jones or de Lacey, Wyatt, Boleyn, or Tudor. We are survivors, all.*" Compare and contrast the relationships between the mothers and daughters featured in *The Virgin Queen's Daughter*: Anne Boleyn and Elizabeth; Katherine Parr and Elizabeth; Elizabeth and Nell; Thomasin and Nell. How did the mothers shape the women their daughters would become? Do you relate to the dynamic of any of these relationships?

15. Do you think Chase makes a believable case that Nell is Elizabeth's daughter? What are the most convincing arguments, both pro and con? Why was it so vital that Elizabeth be "the Virgin Queen"? In what ways does she still capture our imagination?